LORI
FOSTER
Scandalous

HQN™

Recycling programs
for this product may
not exist in your area.

ISBN-13: 978-0-373-77382-4
ISBN-10:   0-373-77382-X

SCANDALOUS

Copyright © 2009 by Harlequin Books S.A.

The publisher acknowledges the copyright holder of the
individual works as follows:

SCANDALIZED!
Copyright © 1997 by Lori Foster

SEX APPEAL
Copyright © 2001 by Lori Foster

CONTENTS

SCANDALIZED!

CHAPTER ONE

SHE WAS THE PERFECT WOMAN to have his baby.

Tony Austin continued to stare, analyzing her features, considering the construction of her body. He'd already done so, of course, but now he was more thorough. She wasn't beautiful, but that was okay, because beauty wasn't essential to his plan. And she *was* striking, even arresting in her presence, her confidence and poise.

Though he tried to stop himself, his gaze was repeatedly drawn to her, and finally Olivia Anderson caught him looking. The small, curious smile she sent him took his breath away, but he shook his head, deciding his reaction was excitement for his plan and nothing else.

That was all it could be.

As always, she looked elegant. She wore a simple black dress and black heels, but that had little to do with his heightened interest. He had made a decision, and she was deeply involved in that decision whether she knew it yet or not. He rubbed his hands together, feeling his anticipation build.

He'd been acquainted with her for three years now as a business associate, and he knew she'd only attended his party as a means of furthering that association. Nothing in their relationship was of a personal nature—and he intended to keep it that way.

Just two days ago, she'd presented him with a proposal to expand her business that would add one more of her novelty lingerie shops to another Austin Crown hotel. He hadn't given her an answer yet, but he would. Tonight. And then he'd have a question of his own to present.

For the first time in a very long time, he felt nervous on the verge of making a business proposition. Then Olivia started toward him with her determined, long-legged, graceful stride and all he could think of was what a beautiful baby they could create together.

He welcomed her with a smile.

HE'S GOING TO GIVE IT TO ME.

Olivia tingled with anticipation. Tony had been watching her, almost studying her, all evening. And there could only be one possible reason for that. The sense of impending victory thrilled her.

His gaze held hers as she neared. There was that slight tilting of his mouth—an unaffected sensual look that she knew got all the single women and even the not-so-single women excited. But Olivia would only get excited if he gave her the news she wanted.

Her business was her life, and she didn't allow herself the time or the desire for anything else. She was certain he didn't, either. At least, not with her.

She was well aware of Tony's reputation with other women, and it was the women building that reputation. They claimed he was a spectacular lover, though how many had firsthand knowledge she couldn't guess. He appeared very circumspect to her. He never spoke of his relationships. In fact, he seemed oblivious to the talk.

She tried to be oblivious as well; her only interest in

him was business related. But she had to admit there were occasions when she couldn't quite stop her mind from wandering…

She stood mere inches from him and at five-eleven or so with her heels on she nearly looked him in the eye. They stood by the balcony doors, no one else within hearing distance, the ambience soft and intimate. Olivia dismissed her wayward thoughts and lifted her glass of soda to him in a mock salute. "Tony."

"Hello, Olivia." His voice was deeper than usual, his gaze more intent. "Are you enjoying yourself?"

He seemed almost watchful, and anticipatory, not wearing the cool persona he usually assumed in her company. She looked around at the newly decorated offices, pretending an interest she didn't feel. This party was to launch the renovation of his massive downtown hotel, which had been standing for decades. With its new upscale furnishings and classy decor, it was positioned to compete with other hotels where price was no obstacle. "Everything is lovely, Tony. Why wouldn't I enjoy myself?"

His lazy smile deepened, his gaze became probing. "I don't think you're much for parties. You seem preoccupied." He tilted his head slightly. "Anxious to get back to business matters?"

Olivia swallowed her immediate response and the last sip in her glass. She allowed her gaze to follow a passing couple, then said, "I was wondering if you'd come to a decision, yet. Of course, a party isn't exactly the place to discuss such things, but…" She looked back at him and caught him watching her closely. Again. "If you'd care to enlighten me?"

Tony chuckled and ignored her question. He excelled at

business games, but then, so did she. "Would you like something else to drink?"

"No, thank you," she replied.

"Had too much already?"

"Of soda? I think I can handle it. You however…" She circled his thick wrist with her fingers to bring his glass toward her and then she sniffed. But she didn't detect the fumes of alcohol. She frowned.

"I don't drink, either. Too many of my associates do, and I think someone has to stay sober to oversee things."

Olivia didn't want to show him her surprise, but she found herself doing just that. "So you never indulge?"

"An occasional glass of wine with dinner. Very occasional."

"I'm a teetotaler."

"Personal reasons?"

Olivia hesitated. It was funny how you could know a person for years and never say or do anything outside the realm of related business, then suddenly be discussing very intimate, personal topics. She didn't really mind, though. She'd always believed the better you knew your business associates the easier it would be to deal with them. It was her fondest wish to do a great many deals with Tony Austin. She finally nodded and answered, "Very personal. I detest alcohol."

"Maybe someday you'll tell me why."

"Maybe."

Tony was silent a moment. He appeared to be studying her drop-pearl earrings until suddenly he asked, "Do you have a five-year goal for yourself, Olivia? Or some long-term destination that you're working toward?"

Again, Olivia felt that touch of excitement and tried to

quell it. He was showing an interest he'd never shown before, and that could only mean he approved her business management. Tony Austin was the epitome of business excellence. A person could learn everything she needed to know from him.

It was said Tony had doubled the Austin Crown hotel chain within three years of his father's death. Under Tony's guidance the hotels had grown from mediocre to posh and exclusive. Every upscale business convention around wanted to be on the receiving end of Crown's special treatment.

Tony Austin's employees loved him and praised his leadership. As a pioneer in the business world with one of the fastest growing hotel chains around, he was regularly featured in business magazines. Austin Crown hotels were located throughout the country and probably would soon be around the world.

Olivia watched now as he propped himself up against the wall, the breadth of his shoulders visible even beneath the elegant cut of his dark suit. He was a well-built man, she admitted to herself, in his early thirties, with more energy and determination than anyone she knew. Right now his brown hair, darker and richer than her own and with a spot more curl, had fallen forward over his brow, and his green eyes were intense on her features.

Olivia smiled. "Of course I have a plan. A very substantial plan. If you'd like, I could outline it for you."

To her surprise, Tony caught one of the servers milling through the crowd. "Miss Anderson and I will be in the inner office. Please bring us refreshments, nonalcoholic only, and see that we're not bothered unless it's absolutely necessary."

The server nodded, took their empty glasses and walked

away. Olivia felt her nerves tingle. *He's going to give it to me.* She hadn't expected this, hadn't expected Tony to want to discuss business tonight, but still…

Tony took her arm and began weaving through the crowd. Several people noticed, but she ignored them. Tony merely nodded to anyone who stared too long, but he was used to this. It was a fact he drew regular gossip from outsiders. After all, he was the local boy made good and there were always busybodies hoping to pick up a scrap of dirt. But they were in Willowbrook, Indiana, on Tony's home ground, and anyone who really knew him paid little heed to the rumors.

Olivia rehearsed her speech in her mind, preparing what she would say, how she would convince him to her way of thinking. She was busy wondering if she'd be able to shorten her five-year goal with his cooperation, when he tugged her into a dimly lit room that smelled of rich leather and Tony. Which, to her at least, was the scent of raw excitement. In this room she might get the break she'd been waiting for. All she had, all she would ever have, was her business. She'd given it everything she could, and it had given back all she had hoped for. Watching the business expand and grow was almost the same as having the life she really wanted. Almost.

TONY CLOSED THE DOOR and leaned against it. It was funny, but before tonight he had never really noticed how lovely Olivia Anderson could be when she was excited, when she smiled…. Of course, he'd made note of and approved each one of her individual features. But he'd never before put them all together, taken them as the whole, and understood just how tempting an appearance she made.

Tonight she had her soft dark brown hair pinned back in an elegant twist, though he knew it was nearly straight and fell to the tops of her shoulders. Olivia always looked elegant. She had more style and class than any woman he'd ever known. And it didn't matter that her eyes were dark brown, not green like his own. He liked her eyes. They showed her emotions clearly, showed the depth of her character and her passion. *Passion for her work, that is.*

He stepped away from the door and flipped on a single lamp that added a vague glow to the expansive room. It was cowardly of him, but he preferred to keep the lighting dim, to allow himself the cover of shadows while he presented her with his proposal. He said abruptly, "Have you ever been married, Olivia?"

She looked stunned by the question, but thankfully, not insulted. She shook her head. "No. Nor do I plan any such alliance in the near future."

"Alliance?" He found himself smiling again. She had the strangest way of looking at things, as if everything was a business venture.

Shrugging her shoulders, Olivia turned to find a chair, and sat down in one of a matching pair of chairs that sat adjacent to his massive desk. "My work is my life. I'm content that it stays that way."

Tony eased himself into the chair across from her, thoughtfully rubbing his chin. Though that was the answer he'd expected—anticipated—from her he was still a little disturbed. It wasn't right that a woman with her attributes, with her intelligence and personality, should spend her life alone.

"How old are you?"

She blinked, but she answered readily enough. "Twenty-six. Actually my five-year plan was only formulated last year. By the time I'm thirty, I hope to have created a very substantial business with at least three more shops."

He waved that away. "You don't leave yourself much room for a husband or children or any other personal pursuits."

Frowning now, she surveyed him with a wary eye. Tony knew he needed to retrench, to give her a bit more room. The thing was, he'd never been a patient man. When he wanted something, he wanted it now.

And he wanted a baby.

He reached out to take Olivia's hand, but she snatched it back, then looked embarrassed that she'd done so.

"I don't understand the need for such personal questions. I assumed you were satisfied with our business dealings…"

"More than satisfied. You run a very profitable business and your two existing shops have already benefited my hotels. I don't see any problem in expanding them."

Olivia let out a breath and gifted him with a beautiful smile. "Thank you. Obviously that's what I was hoping to hear. I'll admit, though, you threw me with all that personal stuff. I know it's important to understand your associates, to make certain they won't suddenly change their priorities and let their businesses flounder. If that was your worry, let me assure you—"

"I'd like to have a baby."

His timely, or not so timely, interruption, left Olivia with her mouth hanging open and her brows lifted high. It was a nice mouth, full and soft. He could see her tongue, pink and moist and… She also had beautiful skin, which of course would be a plus, along with her excellent health and unbelievable ingenuity.

She cleared her throat, and with a small, nervous laugh, said, "I believe that might be an anatomical impossibility."

"Not if I can find the right woman to carry the babe."

She fell back in her seat, her hands braced on the arms of the chair, her mouth once again open. Right then, Tony decided to stop noticing her enticing mouth.

He was saved from having to say anything by the knock on the door. Tony waited until the server left the room and softly closed the door behind him before meeting Olivia's eyes again. She still looked stunned.

"I can practically hear your brain working, Olivia, and I want to assure you, before anything else, that this has nothing to do with your business. The third shop is yours, regardless. I'll sign the papers Monday morning and have a courier deliver them to you."

Olivia's mouth opened twice before she managed to say, "Thank you."

He poured her a glass of soda and handed it to her. "However, I would like to discuss something else with you."

"I gathered as much."

He grinned at her dry tone. "As I said, I want a baby. I have excellent people who can see to the daily running of my business now, so I no longer need to put in such long hours. I can more than afford to raise a child with every privilege, but not so many that the child is spoiled or doesn't understand the value of work. I'll be very careful to make sure the babe is raised with good morals and strong convictions, and—"

Olivia leaned forward in her seat and touched his arm. Tony liked her touch, felt it all the way to his stomach, and immediately cursed himself for reacting in a way he'd forbidden. Olivia, thankfully, seemed unaware of his plight.

"I have no doubt you'd be an excellent father, Tony."

He felt warmed to his soul by her praise. "Thank you."

"You're welcome. But what does all this have to do with me?"

His gaze flickered from her hand on his arm, to her face. "Why...I want you to be the mother."

He didn't get quite the reaction he'd expected. She covered her mouth with one graceful hand, and after a long, stunned pause, a nearly hysterical laugh emerged. Tony stood, caught her forearms and lifted her from her chair. "Olivia! Are you all right?"

She shook her head, and another giggle escaped. "Didn't I just make myself clear? Didn't I just say that my business was my life? I can't get married, certainly not to—"

"Married? Good God, I don't want to marry you!" He immediately realized how horrid that sounded, and quickly explained, "I just need you to carry my baby. After you've delivered it, you're free to do as you please. I'll make certain you can relocate any place you choose, but of course, you would have to relocate. I don't want any interference with raising my child, and neither of us would want a scandal. I thought the northwest would serve your purposes."

"You just want me to..."

"Carry the baby." He was still holding her arms and felt the way she tensed, the way her body trembled. He forced himself to release her. "As you said, it's anatomically impossible for me to do so, not that I have any desire to suffer through such a thing. God in all his wisdom knew men weren't cut out for such a trial. And I don't want you to think I'm being...well, untoward. There are medical procedures that would guarantee the planting of my sperm. Everything would be..."

She staggered back as if he'd struck her.

"I'm really messing this up, aren't I?" He ran his hand

through his hair, then shrugged. "Believe it or not, this is the first time I've been uncertain of myself while presenting a business proposition. And that's exactly what this is, Olivia. A business deal." He waited, but when she remained silent, her eyes huge, he added, "Well? You could make this a little easier by saying...*something*."

"I would. If I had any idea what to say."

He nodded, then slowly drew a deep breath. "You need time to think it over. Why don't we sit back down and I'll go over all my reasons for choosing you, all the benefits that will be yours if you agree, how I intend to handle the legalities involved, and—"

"That's an awful lot of ground to cover, especially considering it's near midnight. I put in a full day already, and plan to visit the office tomorrow morning." Her voice still sounded shaky, but she did resume her seat. Tony let out a short sigh of relief. She wasn't crying sexual harassment, she wasn't storming out. No, Olivia, bless her, was a reasonable woman. It was one of the qualities that had drawn him to her.

"First of all, you please me very much, Olivia. Not as a wife or for any other personal relationship, but as a gene donor. Your intelligence sometimes staggers me, especially given what few advantages you had in the world. The way you've excelled—"

"Excuse me?"

Tony lifted his brows, silently asking for clarification to her interruption.

"How, exactly, would you know anything about my advantages or disadvantages?"

Uh-oh. He could tell by the mulish set to her chin that he'd pricked her temper. He quickly thought about lying, then just as quickly discarded the idea. As he'd said, she was very intelligent. "I had you investigated. Now, just hear me out, then you'll understand how necessary it was for me to do so." He waited, and when she simply watched him, he began reciting his findings. "I know your parents, of moderate, low middle-class income, died in a river accident during a flood when you were only sixteen. I know you carried a full course load in college and kept a job at the same time, that you gained everything you now own by your own wits, without a single smidgen of aid from family or friends. In fact, there was no real family, and as far as I could discern, no close friends."

He continued, seeing her hold herself silent and still. She managed to look both proud and violated, and he lowered his tone even more, feeling his heart kick against his ribs. "You've never been involved with a man for any length of time other than during business to further your goals, you live a modest, understated lifestyle, apparently with quite a substantial savings account, and you keep to yourself. The only social gatherings you attend are business related."

She was quiet a long moment, and he felt regret, then determination.

"You've been very thorough."

"I had to make certain you would suit, Olivia. Please, try to understand. I don't want a woman who, after conceiving, will decide she wants to keep the baby, me, or both. Everything I learned about you proves you have absolutely no interest in tying yourself down right now or anytime in the near future. It was completely necessary that I find evidence to prove you wouldn't want a baby or a husband. And you don't, do you?"

She turned her head away to stare at the far wall. "That's

right." After a shuddering breath, she glared at him again. "But I also have no interest in putting myself nine months behind. Carrying a child right now would sorely interrupt my schedule, not to mention what it would do to my reputation. I'd be gossiped about endlessly."

"Not so. Not if I promised to advance your five-year goal in one year. Not if I promised my backing to make certain you got a better start than you could ever have hoped to achieve, even in five years. Not if I have you relocated immediately, or provide for you to take an extended leave of absence."

"And you'd do all that?"

She was incredulous, but he didn't hesitate. "Of course. I'm very serious about this. I can afford to be generous, and I want the baby. Now. My birthday is November 14. Little more than a week away. By my following birthday, I want to be holding my own child. I'll be thirty-five then." He hesitated, a bit vulnerable in his feelings, but also knowing he needed to explain his desire fully to her.

"Thirty-five is getting up there. If I'm going to have a baby, it needs to be now. I'm still young enough to keep up with a toddler, but old enough to make wise decisions about the child's future. If I wait, even another year or two, I'll be close to forty before the child is born. I have to think long-term, of how my age will affect the child during his or her teenage years, when I'll be needed most."

She looked incredulous again, and her voice was strained when she asked, "You're worried about your... your biological clock?"

He felt disgruntled with the way she'd put it, but he nodded. "I suppose that's one way of looking at it."

"Why?"

"Why what?"

"Why do you want a child so badly? Why not just get a wife and do things the conventional way? And most of all, why me?"

Since she was still discussing it with him, Tony decided that was a good sign and took heart. He would win her over. After all, he had the advantage, being a man, and a more accomplished business dealer. He'd wrangled tougher deals than this when he'd first taken over the business.

But also true, he'd met few associates as tough as Olivia. It was one of the reasons he'd chosen her, one of the many things he admired about her.

He propped his elbows on his knees, leaned forward and forged on. "I want a child now because both my younger brother and sister have children. In fact, my brother only recently got his third child, a little boy, and it made me realize how much I was missing out on, how much I'll miss forever if I don't act soon. Don't get me wrong. I love being the doting uncle, getting to spoil the children and having them shout and jump around whenever I show up. It's good for the soul to be loved by a child, probably the biggest compliment a person can ever receive.

"But I have no real influence on the kids. And that's as it should be. I'm not their father, I'm only an uncle, good for bringing gifts and giving occasional unimportant advice. I want to be the one doing the raising, leaving a part of myself behind."

Olivia smiled. "You're feeling your mortality?"

"I suppose. But that's not all of it. Being business minded, forming a successful company and being respected by your colleagues, that's nothing compared to raising a child. My brother and sister chose not to get too involved in the business, but they're raising wonderful, loving, beautiful children. And that's a much greater accomplishment than mine. I want to do something that matters that much." He faced her, holding her gaze, then added, "And I want to be loved the way they are. Unconditionally, completely."

"But no wife?"

"The kind of relationship my brother and sister have with their spouses doesn't come easy, I'm finding." He was so relieved she hadn't mocked him that he smiled. It was proving much easier to talk to Olivia than he had thought. Without thinking about it, he'd bared his heart as he had never done with any other person. "It's almost like they're one with the other. They share everything, support each other, and they have fun together. Honest, guilt-free fun. They seem to know each other's thoughts sometimes, they're so in tune.

"It amazes me. At times, I'm even jealous. I think it would be unbelievable to have that kind of relationship, and after seeing it, I don't think I could settle for anything less. But I haven't found a woman who would suit, and to tell you the truth, I'm sick of looking. Most women can't tolerate the amount of time I dedicate to the business, unless they're businesswomen also. But then, most of them are so wrapped up in company policies, in proving themselves in the male-dominant corporate world, they don't have time for me, much less a child."

He saw her flinch, and realized she'd taken the criticism personally. "Olivia. I don't mean to condemn. I realize it's more difficult for women than men, that the same rules seldom apply. And I understand the need to get ahead. I was the same way until recently."

"Until your business no longer required quite so much attention."

"That's right." He wouldn't apologize for accomplishing his goals. He'd earned his time off. "You know, there's a downside to being successful. I always get the feeling women are sizing up my bank account instead of me."

Olivia gawked. "Don't you have any idea how attractive you are? How personable you are?" She waved a hand in the air. "How...*sensual* you are? Believe me, with or without your hotel chain, you'd have women chasing after you."

Settling back in his chair, he whispered, "Not you."

Olivia looked as if she wanted to bite off her tongue, but no way would Tony let her take the words back, nor would he fill the silence for her. He suddenly felt predatory, and she was his prey. He could feel the surge of energy her words had given him, supplying an interest he hadn't felt in too long. It was invigorating, though he did his best to ignore the feelings and concentrate on his goals. Her compliments weren't necessary to his plan—but they did fill him with male satisfaction.

He waited, his expectation extreme, to see what she would say next.

Her gaze never wavered. "Well, no. As I said, I have other goals in mind besides chasing down a man, regardless of his appeal."

Tony narrowed his eyes, watching her squirm as he pondered her words, then he smiled. "That's one of the reasons I chose you. Not once have you ever looked at me in a sexual way."

Olivia blinked again. "I don't think..."

"You know what I mean. I don't have to worry about you accepting my proposition with ulterior motives of trapping me, because you don't particularly want me." He waited, then asked, "Right?"

"Ah…right."

"But you are perfect to suit me. As I said, I admire your intelligence. With the two of us as parents, I know my son or daughter won't be lacking in that regard. You're also possessed of a great deal of savvy, something else to admire. You're healthy as a horse. I checked back as far as the last two years, and you haven't missed a single day of work. You have a kind and generous nature—everyone who knows you said so. And you're suitably built."

"Suitably built?"

She sounded as though she were strangling, and his gaze dropped to her legs. "Attractively built," he explained, allowing his gaze to linger for a moment. "Your legs are shapely, your shoulders squared, your back straight. You're large boned, not overly frail, but still very feminine. You're not prone to excess weight, but you are…sturdy. If I had a daughter, I wouldn't have to worry about her being too tiny, something I abhor in women. But she would make a very nice appearance. You always do."

Without his mind's permission, his gaze moved to her breasts, outlined so nicely by the black knit dress she wore. Tony heard her say, "I'm small busted."

He managed a shrug when at the moment he felt far from indifferent, then had to force himself to look up at her face. Her look was challenging, and he grinned at her small show of vanity. "Not at all. You're…fine. Besides, if I have a son, it certainly won't matter, and if I have a daughter, I won't have to worry about all the young men chasing after her before I'm prepared to deal with it."

She gave an uncertain smile at his wit, then looked away, as if considering all he'd said. He felt his stomach cramping in anxiety. And something more. It was so damn ridiculous, but the more he talked with her, the more he liked her. She hadn't reacted as most women would have, she hadn't reeled in shock or shouted in dismay. She hadn't looked particularly insulted, either. She did look a bit disoriented, though. And somewhat contemplative.

He didn't want to, but he said, "Why don't you think about it? Take the weekend, and get back to me on Monday. If you agree, we can contact the doctor I've spoken with and have everything taken care of well before my birthday."

She winced. "A clinical procedure, you said?"

"Yes." He hastened to reassure her. "But from what I understand, it's not bad. I deliver my sperm—"

One slim eyebrow quirked. "Deliver your sperm?"

"Yes." He knew his face was heating and felt like a fool. "How exactly is that accomplished?"

"Never mind." The order was ground out from between his teeth, and she chuckled. He'd never before seen her sense of humor; usually it was her determination to get ahead that she presented at a business meeting. He felt a touch of warmth at the sound of her laughter, then gave her an exasperated look and continued. "I deliver my sperm and they…well, I suppose it's much like visiting your gynecologist. Only instead of doing whatever it is they usually do, my sperm will be artificially planted—inseminated, it's called—and then we'll wait to see if it takes."

Olivia chewed her lips, then said slowly, "It sounds rather distasteful."

"I'll admit it isn't quite the way nature intended a woman to be impregnated, but it is certainly less personal, which is the main objective."

"Why?"

Her pointed look and bald question confused him. "Why what?"

"Why does it have to be so impersonal? Why can't you just…do it?"

"Do it?"

She made a sound of disgust. "Just impregnate the woman of your choice by nature's design."

He knew what she was asking, and felt an instant, unwanted tightening in his loins. Lust, damnable lust. He swallowed. "I want this to be as much of a business dealing as possible. Getting naked…" He felt himself harden and had to clear his throat. "Making love to a woman isn't at all a business proposition. It's very personal."

Olivia seemed relaxed now, arrogantly so, and somehow determined. Tony knew she was aware of his unease, and planned to take advantage of it—as any good business-woman would do. She nodded, a pseudo show of under-standing. Then she smiled. "I see."

He felt a twinge of anger at her for prodding him. "I should hope so."

"I believe I'll take your advice and think all this over. You said you don't want to hear from me until Monday?"

"I…" He had no idea what had come over her. She wasn't acting the way he'd expected, she wasn't even acting in a way he could have guessed or anticipated. He felt stymied. "You don't have to wait if you come to a decision before then."

"I think I probably will make up my mind before then. How about if I give you my decision tomorrow evening?"

He nodded, stiff-backed now, and forced a smile. He knew by her amused expression that she wasn't fooled, and that she was thoroughly enjoying his discomfort. "I'll give you my home number."

"No. I got the feeling you didn't want the fertile woman who would serve your needs to intrude on your life." He started to speak, but she forestalled him, her tone not nearly so sarcastic now. "Why don't I just give you my number instead—my privacy isn't nearly as threatened as your own. You can call me. Say, seven o'clock tomorrow?"

With her small chin raised, her straight nose in the air, she looked as proud and gutsy and almost as arrogant as he. She looked magnificent to him, and he merely nodded, distracted by thoughts of her feminine body rounded by his babe. They would make a beautiful, healthy child together. He reached out and touched her chin. "I wouldn't mind if the baby was a boy or a girl. I don't remember if I told you that."

She smiled, and seemed to relax again despite herself. "You didn't. But I had the impression it wouldn't matter." Then she went to his desk and picked up the gold pen from the marble holder and scrawled her home number across the desk pad.

"I had your number in my files."

"This way, you won't have to look it up."

He felt awkward now, but Olivia didn't seem to be suffering any such problems. She gave him a small salute.

"I'll be going home now. It's getting late, and I do have quite a bit to think over."

"I'll be a good father, Olivia." He hadn't meant to say that. He hadn't planned on trying to convince her what a good person he was. But he wanted the baby so badly, now, before he got any older, before he was left all alone in the world.

Again, she didn't mock him.

"I never doubted it." She looked almost sad, which didn't make any sense. "Tomorrow at seven, Tony." And then she was gone.

CHAPTER TWO

OLIVIA LAY IN BED that night, despising herself. She was a fraud and a manipulator and the worst kind of person for taking advantage of another. Tony had no idea the type of woman he was dealing with.

She'd known since she was sixteen that she would never have children. For her, it was physically impossible.

In the hospital, only hours before Olivia's mother had slipped away, she had explained about the condition that robbed her daughter of that particular function. Olivia wasn't a whole woman, could never lead a whole life. Having children was as beyond her as it was for Tony. And so she'd made her business her life. It was the only life she'd ever have.

Swallowing hard, Olivia felt the sting of tears as she recalled going to the hospital as a very young girl, her belly cramping painfully, the bleeding. It had been horrible, being examined by a male doctor. Beyond the pain, she'd felt violated and mortified. And then there were the days after when her mother and father had been so quiet, so withdrawn. She hated hospitals now, and she wouldn't go to the doctor unless it was absolutely necessary.

She thought she'd successfully put the past behind her, that she'd buried the wishes that couldn't come true. But now, with Tony's proposition, they all came flooding back. She wanted to be loved, to have children, to be desired by a special man who would accept her as a sensual woman.

She couldn't do anything about the first two wishes, but the third was a possibility.

It was rumored that Tony was an exceptional lover. She couldn't deny that the information had given her a few private fantasies of her own. After all, despite everything, she was still a woman, and on occasion, she'd seen him strictly as a man. But intimacy was something she'd neither expected nor wanted from Tony.

Until she'd heard his plan.

And now it was all she could think about. Tony obviously admired her, and that was something. It wasn't love, but it was a far cry from a totally detached sexual experience. She cared about Tony, thought he was a beautiful person and a very sexy man. And he wanted her as the mother of his child.

That was a precious gift all on its own, the highest of compliments.

Tony didn't have to know that she'd never be able to conceive a child, that she was infertile. She could insist on doing things the "natural" way, allow him to try his manly best for a couple of weeks, then confess it wasn't happening. He'd go on his way, none the wiser, find another woman, and have his baby by his designated time. She had not a single doubt of his eventual success. There were numerous women out there who would be more than willing to oblige him.

But he'd approached her, and she couldn't quite send him on his way. Not yet. Hearing him discuss his sperm in such a casual way, and talk of impregnating her as if he was referring to buying her coffee, had been somehow very arousing. Long dormant feelings had seemed to swell without her consent, and when she'd pictured him "supplying" his sperm, pictured the process necessary to such a deed, she'd felt a sexual heat at the image, along with an emotional tenderness that he wanted a child so badly. Together, the two feelings had conspired against her better sense.

She'd read every article she could ever find on him, and they were numerous. She'd tried to follow in his footsteps, as impossible as that seemed, because he was too dynamic, too overwhelming. And also, he loved his family, when she didn't even have a family to claim.

He was a good man, in every sense of the word. And she planned to corrupt him for her own purposes.

She was a fraud, but she wouldn't actually be hurting anyone. Other than herself.

IT HAD PROVED to be a long night and an even longer day. By seven o'clock, Olivia was so nervous her heart threatened to beat right out of her chest. When her phone rang, a good three minutes after seven, she jumped a foot. She forced herself to wait through four rings, feeling juvenile but determined not to look overanxious, and then she answered.

"Hello?"

"Olivia? It's Tony."

Just that, nothing more. She cleared her throat. "Hello." Her voice squeaked, but she didn't hang up. She could do this; she would grab the opportunity. But of course, she wouldn't accept anything from him, other than the additional shop he'd already agreed to. She would suffer no guilt for taking monetary advantage of him. She would only use his body, and only for a brief time.

"Hi." There was a long pause. "Have you made up your mind?"

She bit her lip, then took a deep breath. "I have. But I…I have a few stipulations I'd like to discuss."

She heard his indrawn breath. "Does that mean you'll do it?"

"Yes. But with a few—"

"I heard you. A few stipulations. Whatever it is, it's yours!"

His joy was impossible to ignore. The man was thrilled to be getting what he believed would eventually be his baby. Olivia swallowed her guilt and girded herself. "You probably ought to know what I want before you agree to it."

"I can afford whatever it is. I know you're not a greedy woman. You won't leave me bankrupt."

"I want to forget the doctor."

Deathly quiet. "Excuse me?"

Olivia knew she had thrown that out there awfully quick, but if she hadn't, she might never have said it at all. "I don't want to go through a doctor. I want…I want to do things naturally."

"Naturally?"

He sounded completely stupefied, and she nearly growled in frustration. "Yes, dammit! As in you and me, together, the way nature intended."

Not a single sound now. "Tony?"

"I'm here."

Olivia waited. Strangely enough, she could hear Tony trying to sort his thoughts as clearly as she could hear her own heart pounding.

Finally he said, "Would you mind telling me why?"

Olivia shook her head, realized how stupid that was and closed her eyes. "Of course not. I just…"

"No, wait. This isn't a conversation for the phone. Are you busy?"

"Now?"

"Yes, now. Believe me, I don't want to have to sleep on this without understanding."

"Of course not." Olivia looked around her apartment, hoping for inspiration, but found only the same quiet environment that always surrounded her. "I could meet you somewhere."

"No, I'll pick you up. I know where you live. It's—"

"It's in your records."

"Yes. I'll be there as soon as I can."

The phone clicked in her ear, and to Olivia it sounded like the beginning of a drumroll. Oh boy, too late to change her mind now. Then, because she had no idea how far away Tony was or how soon he would arrive, she rushed from the room to find something appropriate to wear.

When she reached her closet, she stopped, feeling ridiculous. What in the world would be considered proper dress for telling a man you'd agree to have his baby, but only if he'd pleasure you in the bargain?

Especially when you knew you were cheating him, and he wouldn't get a damn thing out of the deal, least of all, what he really wanted. A baby.

TONY STARED AT HER apartment door, started to knock, then lowered his hand. Dammit all, why couldn't women ever do anything the simple way? He'd offered Olivia a straightforward, up-front deal, and she'd had to go and muddy the waters by asking that he actually attend her. Not that it would be a hardship, but he didn't want to get involved. He'd made his plans and he didn't want to deviate from them.

Still, Olivia Anderson—business barracuda and proprietor of two sensual, sexy lingerie shops—wanted to make love with him.

Who would have ever thought she'd ask for such a thing? She was always an enigma, a mix of styles and personalities, but even so, this development had thrown him for a loop. He'd sometimes wondered, when he'd been in her shop and seen the very stimulating garments she carried, if *she* ever wore any of those little bits of nothing, if she spoiled her body with silks and lace. It hadn't seemed likely. But now…

She had him totally confused, and he didn't like it one bit. He also didn't want to have to start looking for a new mother. Time was running out. He wasn't getting any younger, and if he didn't act soon, he'd be past the age of thirty-five when he brought his baby home.

No. He'd chosen her, dammit, and he wouldn't give up without at least trying to reason with her.

He ran a hand through his hair, then knocked sharply on the door. Immediately three doors opened. Olivia and two neighbors stared at him, the latter with narrowed eyes and curious expressions. Just what he needed, an engrossed audience.

Olivia tried for a smile, but it wasn't her best effort. "Come on inside."

"No." He shook his head, glaring at the neighbors. An elderly couple now stood at one door, and a younger woman with curlers in her hair at the other; they glared right back at him. Tony turned his gaze back to Olivia. "Let's go for a drive instead."

Olivia hesitated, seemingly oblivious to the onlookers, then finally said, "All right. Just let me grab my jacket."

Tony cursed under his breath. This was exactly what he'd wanted to avoid. He didn't need anyone speculating on his relationship with Olivia, because he'd never intended to have a relationship with her. In his simple, uncomplicated, male-inspired plan, he would have given her the address of the doctor and then heard from her later to learn if she'd conceived. He certainly hadn't intended to stand in her doorway providing entertainment to the masses. Not that three people could be considered a mass, but with their eyes glued to him, he felt very uncomfortable.

Olivia finally produced herself. She stepped outside the door, turned to make certain it was locked, then dropped her keys into her pocket. "I'm ready."

Then, as if on cue, she turned to the neighbors and nodded to each one in turn. "Hello, Hilda, Leroy, Emma. This is Tony Austin. Hopefully I'll be opening another of my shops in his hotel chain. Isn't that marvelous?"

Everyone nodded, their suspicions visibly dissipating and en masse they began to sing Olivia's praises. Tony did his best to make an exit, but he had to spend several minutes nodding in agreement before he could leave.

As they walked out of the building onto the street, he said, "That's the last time for that."

"What?"

"Meeting at your apartment. It gives rise to too much speculation. If we're not careful, we'll have that scandal yet."

He opened the door to his car for Olivia, but she didn't get in. "Does that mean you intend to meet with me again? You will agree with my terms?"

Pushy woman. Why had he never realized before just how pushy she could be? Savvy was one thing, pushy was another. He summoned his most noncommittal tone. "We'll see." He practically tossed her into the passenger seat, before going around to his own side.

"There's really not a whole lot to see, Tony. I don't like the idea of the clinical approach, that's all. If you can't see your way clear to actually touch me, then there's nothing to talk about."

He clenched his hands on the steering wheel. He clenched his teeth. He even clenched his thighs, but still, her words affected him. Touch her? He'd like to touch her all right—now, this very minute, with his hands, his mouth, his entire body. But he wouldn't. Oh, no. Touching was bad. Touching would only lead to more touching, and then he'd be in over his head and...

"Tony?"

"How about doing me a favor, Olivia? How about keeping your thoughts to yourself for a few minutes until we get off the road and then we'll discuss your...terms."

"All right."

She sounded too damn agreeable and that rankled, but at least she kept her words behind her teeth for all of five minutes, giving him a blessed chance to gain control of his libido. Then she asked in a very tentative voice, "Have you considered the possibility that I won't conceive? After all, there's no guarantee that I'll prove to be...fertile ground for you to...plant your seed. How much time are you willing to devote to trying to get me pregnant?"

Fertile ground? Plant his seed? Tony's five minutes of calm were suddenly shot to hell. How was it such bland, ridiculous terms sounded sexier than the most erotic whispered words he'd ever heard? Perhaps it was because of the envisioned result. He'd never before considered a woman carrying his child, and that must be the reason every word out of her mouth aroused him to the point of pain.

He cleared his throat and kept his gaze steady on the darkened road. "The doctor mentioned that several attempts may be necessary before the insemination takes."

"But doing it naturally? Is there a projected time span on that?"

He felt strangled. "I never actually asked him that."

"Perhaps you should."

Out of sheer necessity, he pulled the car off the main street and onto a small dirt road that led to a dead end. When Tony was younger, he and his brother had come here to make out with girls. In those days there was a wide cornfield, but it had been replaced by a small park with a street lamp. Obviously things had changed, but the premise was the same. Isolation.

Despite the fact that he was sweating, he left the car running, for it was a cold night in early November. He killed the lights, though, giving himself some illusionary concealment. When he turned to face her, he already had his mouth open to start his argument, but he was brought up short by the picture she presented.

Moonlight poured over her, revealing the sheen of dark hair, the shape of her ears, her high arched brows. Her eyelashes left long feathery shadows on her cheeks and shielded her eyes from his gaze. Her hands were folded in her lap. She appeared somehow very unsure of herself... vulnerable. It wasn't a look he was used to, not from her. She lifted her gaze to his face, and once again he felt that deep frustration.

It wasn't that Olivia was beautiful. She was by far the most elegant woman he'd ever known, but she wasn't classically beautiful. He had dated more attractive women, made love to them, had long-standing affairs with them that had left him numb. But Olivia was the only woman whose personality, intelligence and disposition were attractive enough to entice him into asking her to carry his child. That was something. More than something, actually, when you figured it was usually looks that drew a man first, and the other, more important features of a woman that kept him drawn.

When he remained quiet, she said, "I know what I'm asking seems absurd. After all, you could have any woman you want, and after knowing you for so long, it's obvious you don't particularly want me. That's okay, because up until you mentioned your plan, I hadn't really thought about wanting you, either.

"But you see, I've made my career everything." Her hands twisted in her lap and her voice shook. "Just as you don't want any involvements now, neither do I. That's why the idea seems so perfect. I haven't taken the time or the effort to get to know very many men, and almost never on an intimate level. These days, only an idiot would indulge in casual sex. But starting a relationship isn't something I want, either. So I thought, maybe we could both get what we wanted."

Tony searched her face, feeling dumbfounded. Surely she wasn't suggesting what he thought she was. "I want a baby. What is it you want, Olivia?"

She turned her head away from him and looked out the window. Sounding so unlike herself, she whispered in a small voice, "I want a wild, hot, never-to-be-forgotten affair. For two weeks. If during that time I conceive, the baby will become yours, and we'll go on with the rest of your plans. If I don't conceive, I'll be on my way and you can find another woman who, hopefully, will prove more fertile. You won't owe me a thing. In fact, I'll consider myself well paid."

"*Well paid?* As in sex? You make yourself sound like a…"

"Like a woman who's desperate? I suppose I am." She finally met his gaze, her eyes huge and so very dark in the dim light. "I want to know what it's like to be with a man. But it has to be a man I trust, both with my safety and my health. I'm afraid you fit that bill."

The way she'd worded that had him frowning. "Olivia, you're not a virgin, are you?"

"No, but close." She held up two slim fingers.

"You've had sex with two different men?"

"No, I've had sex twice. With the same man, or boy rather. Neither time necessarily inspired an encore, but the second time I allowed myself to be convinced. I suppose I was hoping he'd improved from the week before, but he hadn't."

Tony found himself smiling. Olivia wanted to have sex with him, but she planned to keep a score card? "What did he do that was so wrong?"

"I'm not certain I know what was wrong, since I haven't yet experienced it *right,* but we were both practically fully clothed, cramped into the backseat of his car, and he grunted a lot. And by a lot, I mean for all of about three minutes. Continuously."

"Well…" Tony suppressed a laugh and tried to look serious. "I suppose I can improve on that, anyway."

"I should certainly hope so."

Tony couldn't help but chuckle at her serious tone. "I can't recall ever having a woman come right out and ask me to perform to her satisfaction. You're downright scary, do you know that?"

"I don't mean to be. And I don't mean to belittle that guy. We were in college, and he was majoring in football. It was probably my fault for not being more discriminating my first and second time, but even then I was very involved in getting ahead. Choosing an ideal mate simply took more energy than I wanted to give. At the time, it hadn't occurred to me to tell him specifically what I did and didn't like, which probably would have made things better. But now, since you've presented yourself on the proverbial silver platter, I can hope the results will be much more to my liking. After all, you have a reputation for fulfilling such expectations."

Reputation? He didn't even want to get into that with her. If she'd been listening to gossip… Well, at least the gossip appeared to have been flattering. He gave a groan that was loud and rife with confusion. "I just don't know, Olivia. I mean, this could all backfire."

She was all business, not moved in the least by his dramatic display of frustration. "You're afraid I'll be privy to your awesome technique, decide I can't possibly live without it or you and want to stake a marital claim?"

Actually she was pretty close to the mark. Not that he believed his technique was really all that awesome. But he knew women too often associated sex with love. He'd have to make it clear to her…

"I understand how you feel, Tony. I was concerned also, only for opposite reasons. Right now, you only want a baby, but as you see the woman who will give you your child grow, as you see the changes in her body—from you and your baby—are you certain you won't transfer your affection for the child to the mother?"

He stared stupidly. "I hadn't planned to watch any changes."

"No? But I understood, from books I read long ago, that the changes were the most fascinating part. You won't want to feel your baby kick? You won't want to be in on any prenatal pictures taken? I saw a documentary on TV once that was incredible. The ultrasound showed every small movement the baby made. You could even count toes and fingers."

His head began to pound with the growing complications. "I think…I think I may have more to think about."

"I'm sorry. Now I've confused you."

"You haven't confused me. It's just that I hadn't even considered prenatal observation. All my thoughts had been directed solely on the baby after its birth. But of course I'd want to see and feel the changes." He studied her closely. "You wouldn't mind?"

"Mind what?"

"If I watched you closely? If I observed all the changes in your body while my baby grew and if I examined those changes, took part in them?"

She was silent again, her fingers worrying the edge of her coat. Then she shook her head and in a hushed tone, she replied, "No. I wouldn't mind. If that was what you wanted—and if I got pregnant."

"Olivia, there's no reason to doubt you will. You're a healthy young woman, in the prime of your childbearing years. I've already been checked, and the doctor assures me I should possess sufficient potency to see the job done."

Olivia drew a deep breath and then held out her hand. "So. Do we have a deal?"

He was so aroused, he knew his hand would shake like the skinny branches on the naked tree shadowing the park, but he took her small palm in his anyway. His voice was little more than a croak when he said, "A deal."

"When do we start?"

She may as well have said, *when do you want to see me naked and touch me and come inside me,* because the effect was the same. He had trouble drawing a breath as images too erotic to bear shot through his already muddled brain. It took all his masculine power to bring himself back in order. "I suppose you should find out when you're…" He gulped, then forged manfully onward. "When you're most fertile. Do you, ah, keep track of such things?"

"Of course. All women do, if they don't want to be taken by surprise. How about if I let you know, then we'll see what works for both of us?"

It irritated him no end that she could speak so calmly after practically ordering him to pleasure her, to make certain he loved her in a way she would never forget. His brain was busy concentrating on the myriad ways he'd see the job done; he could barely form coherent words, damn her. "That's fine."

"I'll look at my calendar, find out exactly when I'm most likely to conceive, and then I'll call you."

"And you will take my home number now, Olivia. I don't want to miss your call if I'm not in the office when…when you're ready."

Her smile now was confident and made his insides twist. "Whatever you say, Tony."

Tony merely gulped, wondering if she would say that when she was naked beneath him, her thighs open, her womb ready to receive him and his sperm, her body his. He kept silent, words well beyond him, and determined to see the job done as quickly as possible. It was the only way to save his sanity.

OLIVIA SPENT THE REST of the weekend boning up on fertility procedures. Though she didn't really have a regular cycle that could be timed and knew there was no chance she'd get pregnant, she thought it would still be easier to do things in the proper course, just so Tony wouldn't get suspicious. She had to be able to claim a day her period would be due, so Tony wouldn't think they'd been precipitous in their efforts.

When she decided to claim her best time would be that weekend, she suffered through a mixture of anticipation, guilt and plain old self-doubt. But she shook off her insecurities. Monday, after the new contract arrived, just as Tony had said it would, she used it as an excuse to get in touch with him.

She rushed the contract past her lawyer, insisting he give it top priority. If he thought her request unusual, he didn't say so. He returned it, with a few minor changes, the next day. Olivia forced herself to take another day to look it over, but she okay'd it without her usual relentless perusal, then picked up the phone to set up a business luncheon through Tony's secretary. It was only Wednesday morning, four days after she'd gotten Tony's agreement, and already it felt like forever since the deal had been made.

Just as she hoped, his secretary came back with the news that Tony could make time to see her at their usual restaurant. They'd met there before to discuss business, but today was different. Olivia left her office with the contract in her briefcase, along with a book on fertility and an anticipatory smile on her face.

TONY WAS ALREADY SEATED when she arrived. He'd chosen an isolated table at the back of the restaurant, away from prying eyes and ears. Olivia silently approved his choice, and forced herself to greet him in a normal, businesslike manner. Tony stood until she was seated, his eyes never leaving her, then waited while the waitress handed them menus. Very few things, including excitement, ever dampened her appetite so she ordered a lunch of rich soup and a salad.

Tony surveyed her a moment longer, then asked, "You have a problem with the agreement I sent you?"

Olivia waved away his concern. "We only made a few minor alterations."

"You always have alterations, Olivia, but I'd rarely call them minor."

She grinned. He was right, after all. She was a shark, but proud of it. "You can't expect me to blindly accept rules of your making, now can you, Tony? The revised contract will suit my purpose much better, as you'll see."

He gave her a small smile. "I don't doubt I'll approve it. I seldom win with you."

The way he said that, with a touch of pride, confused her. Could he have been telling the complete truth, not just trying to gain her acceptance of his plan? Did he truly admire her business skills? She felt warmed by the very idea, especially since most of her other male associates either seemed intimidated by her or resentful of her confidence.

She sent Tony a cheeky grin and said, "You win all too often, anyway. Losing on occasion is good for your character."

"But winning's more fun." Then he held up a hand. "In this case, though, you didn't have to bother your lawyer. I already told you I'd give you whatever you wanted."

"No."

"Beg your pardon?"

Olivia wanted to make her point perfectly clear. Her conscience was nagging her enough about manipulating him emotionally. She certainly couldn't do so professionally, too. "I want this latest agreement to stand on its own, Tony. It doesn't have anything to do with…the other. Look over the agreement, judge it the same way you would any other, then get back to me."

"And you'll relent if I don't approve of your changes?"

"Absolutely not." She gave him another grin. "But I fully expect to have to work for them if they're not to your liking."

He looked amused, his chin propped in his palm, his elbow on the table. Then his gaze dropped to his napkin and he said, "Do you have anything else to discuss with me, Olivia?"

It was more than obvious what he was asking. She set down her salad fork and then pushed her plate to the side. After hefting her briefcase into her lap, she pulled out a slim volume on fertility and flipped the book open to the page she had marked.

Tony merely stared, his slouched position not so slouched now.

"I've been reading up on our latest subject, and it seems this weekend will be my most promising time. According to this book, I should be ovulating on Saturday, give or take a day."

"So you're due in two weeks? Right at the end of the deadline you set?"

Her two week time limit. Get her pregnant by then, or the deal was off. She almost groaned at her own audacity.

"That's right. Two weeks exactly." Actually she'd pulled that ridiculous number out of the air, just as she'd done with the deadline. She wouldn't conceive, not with only one ovary. And her periods were irregular, often nonexistent, so there was no true time frame. You couldn't get pregnant if you didn't ovulate, which was a fact she'd been living with for a very long time.

It was pure coincidence that she'd set up her most fertile time to fall precisely within her deadline. She glanced up and wished she wore reading glasses, just to provide her with a bit of camouflage. But despite her embarrassment, she was determined to follow through. Tony had been more than a little reluctant to agree to her terms, and if this was to be her one big romantic rendezvous, she wanted his wholehearted involvement. She *needed* his wholehearted involvement. As with any deal, success required planning. And Olivia had formulated her plan well. By the time she was finished with him, Tony would be beyond ready; he'd be anxious.

She braced herself and said, "I think I can get a few days away. How about you?"

"A few days?"

"Well of course." Olivia frowned at him. "According to the book, an extended amount of time might be necessary. Listen to this. *The couple should have intercourse at least twice with an interval of six hours between.* You see? There's no reason to do it if we aren't going to do it with proper enthusiasm. Things like this can't be rushed."

"I, ah…"

"There's something else, too."

Tony raised his brows, not deigning and frankly not able to verbalize at this point.

Olivia forged on. "It also mentions you should do without sex until then to allow your sperm count to build to a higher level." She paused, taking a small sip of her tea, then pinning him with her gaze. She felt horribly deceptive, but determined just the same. This was to be *her* time, and hers alone. "You should be celibate until we're together. Will that be a problem?"

"Olivia…"

She hurried to explain, wanting him to understand the supposed reasoning behind her request. It wouldn't do for him to know her remarks were prompted by a possessive attitude, rather than a legitimate concern. "You don't want to deplete your sperm, Tony, now do you?"

"No."

"Good." Olivia didn't want to admit to the relief she felt, and she certainly didn't want Tony to witness it, so she busied herself by smoothing back another page. Tony looked down and his eyes narrowed at the number of lines she'd highlighted. Olivia quickly tried to close the book, but Tony's finger got in the way.

"What's this? Other interesting facts you've made note of?" His voice sounded deeper than usual, and a little hoarse.

Olivia was very careful not to look at him. "A few."

"They apply to us?" When she only nodded, he said, "Please, enlighten me."

"Perhaps it would be better to wait until later—"

"But I'm dying of curiosity."

His mocking tone brought her head up. "All right." She held the book before her and made a show of clearing her throat. She'd bluffed her way through more than one difficult situation without losing her poise. "It also says, *For further assurance of success the woman should lie still on her back for several minutes, preferably with the man still*

*inside her, with her legs bent at the knee to allow a pool of
sperm to remain near the cervix.*"

Tony had just taken a sip from his glass as Olivia began
her discourse. When he choked, spewing water across the
small table, Olivia leaned over and pounded on his back,
nearly unseating him. He caught her hand and stared at her,
his face turning ruddy, until she finally subsided and pulled
away.

Olivia felt satisfied with his reaction. If she could keep
him off guard, he wouldn't stand a chance of dissecting her
motivation and discovering her perfidy. "Surely you know
all this already? It was your idea after all."

"No." He vehemently shook his head. "My idea did not
include *staying still inside you for several minutes.*"

"You find the idea repellent?" She did her best to look
affronted, knowing his problem now didn't stem from
distaste, but rather from the intimate level of the conversation—and possibly his response to it. "You would prefer,
of course, that I lie on a sterile table while a damn white-
coated doctor probed me with a syringe?"

"Olivia…" He reached across the table and took her
hand again. "I don't think you have any idea how all of this
is affecting me. I'm only a man, you know, and I'm not accustomed to this sort of conversation."

His hand felt warm and dry and very large. Olivia closed
her eyes, then experienced another wave of guilt. She was
twitting him mercilessly for her own benefit, and he was
having difficulty surviving it. "I'm sorry. I shouldn't carry
on. The truth is," she added, hoping just a touch of honesty
would help smooth over the situation, "I'm a little uncomfortable, too. I'm trying to be as straightforward and open

about this as I can, so that we can look at it in a purely businesslike fashion."

"I know, and I understand." He hesitated, then released her fingers and leaned back in his chair. His gaze seemed hot, and very intense. "But I don't think it's going to work, Olivia."

CHAPTER THREE

HER HEART SKIPPED A BEAT and a swelling sensation of near panic threatened to suffocate her. Had she pushed him too far? "You want to call it off?"

"No!" He abandoned his casual pose and was again leaning toward her. "No, I just don't think I'm going to be able to look at this as anything *but* personal. I've thought about it a lot over the past few days and I don't believe it's at all possible to sleep with a woman—a woman I know and admire—and pretend that it isn't the least bit intimate. I do think we can get past that, though, if we both try."

"I'm not sure I understand." At least he wasn't canceling on her, and that was all that really mattered.

"I think we should look at this as something of an adventure. So long as we limit our socializing to the…ah…process, we should be able to keep things in perspective."

"I see. No friendly visits between appointments."

"Exactly. We'll meet when we have to in order to see things through, but the rest of the time our relationship, such as it is, will remain the same."

"Which is strictly business."

"Yes."

Olivia toyed with her fork. For some ridiculous reason

she felt insulted. Her tone was a touch acerbic when she remarked, "That serves my purposes just fine. I'll enjoy you while you employ all your manly skills to impregnate me." A mental image formed with her words, and she had to catch her breath. "As to the rest, if you'll recall, I don't have time for frivolous dating."

He curled his hand into a fist and searched her face, looking as if he wanted to say more, but then he shook his head, and said, "All right, we're agreed then. And this weekend is fine for me, also. Should we begin Friday evening?"

"I'll be at the Southend location that day, but I'll finish up about six."

"That's good for me." He reached out to straighten his knife and fork, and Olivia saw that his hand was shaking. She shook, too, in impatience. "I'll make arrangements for us somewhere private, then meet you there. That way, no one will see us together, which I think is important. We need to maintain our social distance."

It was the physical closeness that interested Olivia, not the social distance, so she nodded. "I'd just as soon no one suspected us of enhancing our relationship, too. I don't want to start any nasty gossip and end up in a scandal."

He chuckled. "At least you wouldn't have to worry about your folks catching wind of it. My entire family lives nearby, and they all think they need to straighten out my life. Anytime the mere hint of a scandal surfaces, I find them all at my door ready and willing to butt right in."

"And what we're conspiring to do goes beyond the 'hint' stage. It *defines* the word scandalous."

"Which means my family would have a field day."

Olivia was fascinated. She'd often wondered what kind

of upbringing Tony had, especially in light of the fact she had no family at all. He was such a good person, she supposed his family had to be pretty good, too. "So they have no idea what you're planning? I mean, with the baby and all?"

"Hell no. My family is old-fashioned. They definitely believe in doing things in the right order."

"Marriage first?"

"Yep." He grinned again, that ready grin that made all the ladies of his acquaintance smile in yearning. "They've been very diligent in trying to get me married off. Every damn one of them has produced at least three prospective brides. I can't make them understand that I'd prefer to do the choosing myself when I decide the time is right."

Olivia suddenly realized they'd already broken their new set of rules. Learning about Tony's family definitely went beyond business and was dangerous besides; the more she knew about him, the more fascinating he seemed. It had taken her no time at all to become accustomed to wanting him, to accepting him as a desirable man. Every day, every minute it seemed, her feelings for him grew. She began to wonder if those feelings hadn't been there all along, waiting to be noticed.

It was a very scary prospect. She couldn't afford, professionally or emotionally, to get overly involved with him. So she changed the subject, away from his family, and tried to dwell on something less intimate.

Their soup was delivered and throughout the rest of the lunch they discussed Olivia's new shop and Tony's proposed agreement. To his credit, Tony argued fiercely, but Olivia wore him down. The meal ended with Tony promising to have his lawyer okay everything and return the finalized papers to her very soon.

They stood on the curb outside the restaurant, the lunchtime crowd flowing around them, and Tony touched her arm. "Friday at six."

"I'll be ready."

He started to move toward his car, then halted and turned back to her. "I hope you know what you've gotten yourself into."

Olivia never wavered. As with all her decisions, she didn't allow room for regrets. She held his gaze and nodded.

"Good. Because I think we'll barely make it inside the door before I'll lose my control. You've pushed a lot on this deal, lady, more than any before. You've demanded that I give you pleasure, and that I spend a great deal of time doing it." He reached up and flicked a finger over her cheek, so very briefly. "Friday night, you're liable to find I have a few demands of my own."

Olivia watched him stride away, and then as a smile spread over her face, she whispered, "Oh, I do hope so, Tony, I really do."

DISGUSTED WITH HERSELF, Olivia knew she wasn't going to get any real work done. She'd spent Friday afternoon having her legs waxed and her nails manicured, then left the shop early to go home and shower and change. She'd meant to get back in time to do some inventory, but she'd lingered over choosing an outfit, trying to find something simple and attractive, while not wanting to display too obviously her wish to be appealing. By the time she returned to the shop, she had only a little time before Tony was due to pick her up.

After saying good-night to her store manager, she settled down to look over the most recent batch of applications for new jobs, thanks to Tony. She'd already decided to promote one woman to manager of the new store, but then she had to fill that woman's position. Olivia was fortunate in always having found excellent employees. She'd learned from Tony that you got what you paid for, and she'd always been generous with her benefits.

As soon as thoughts of Tony entered her mind, she started daydreaming again. She should have bought a new outfit for today, she thought, looking down at her simple beige wool skirt and matching tunic. The top had a row of pearl buttons that started just above her breasts and ended at the hem. As she imagined Tony undoing those buttons, one by one, she shivered.

She'd tossed aside her normal panty hose in favor of silky stockings with a pale rose satin garter, a big seller for the shops. She had even dabbed on perfume in very naughty places. Her pumps were midheeled and made her legs extra long and shapely. To balance the effect, she'd left her hair loose, parted in the middle, and it fell to rest against the top of her shoulders. She was so nervous, she'd long since chewed off any lipstick she might have applied, and decided against fussing with more.

She'd probably feel more confident, she thought, if she'd worn something daring, something sinful and sexy. Her selection of underclothes often gave her confidence, especially when no one knew she was wearing them.

She walked to a rack and picked up a teddy that fairly screamed enticement with rosette patterns of lace across the breasts and between the legs. She fingered the material, feeling it slide through her hands. She drew in a deep, shuddering breath imagining it sliding through Tony's hands.

When she heard the bell over the door chime, even though

the Closed sign was up, she jerked, then quickly spun around to face the door.

Tony walked in, his hands shoved deep into the pockets of his dress pants, and she could only stare. His gaze connected with hers, and he started forward with a steady, determined stride. He didn't stop at the counter, but came to the rack where she stood, her lips parted, the teddy still in her hand.

His eyes moved over her, lingering on the teddy, and he asked, "Are we alone here?"

She nodded. "I was just finishing up—"

He laid a finger against her lips. There was no smile on his mouth, no welcome in his eyes. He looked intent and determined and very hungry. He slid his hand into her hair and cupped her head, stepping closer until his pant legs brushed her skirt. And then he kissed her.

IT HAD BEEN WORTH THE WAIT.

He couldn't remember ever feeling so anxious for a woman. It was the teasing, he was certain, that had brought him low. Olivia, in her usual forceful, decisive way, had seduced him most thoroughly. Odd, but he hadn't ever thought of her business manner carrying over into something so personal. He knew so damn little about her personal life.

Such as whether or not she really ever wore a garment as sexy as the teddy in her hand.

That was something he could soon find out. Because it was obvious she used the same tack of gaining what she wanted whether it was business or pleasure. And she wanted him.

That thought had plagued him all week, and it had been

all he could do to maintain a touch of control over himself. What he needed, he thought, was a long, hot, intimate evening alone with her. And then he'd be able to get her out of his system and put her, and his purpose for being with her, in proper perspective. But damn, she tasted good.

He knew he should pull back, give her time to catch her breath, but she wasn't fighting him, wasn't behaving in a particularly shocked manner. She merely stood there and gave him free rein. He slanted his mouth over hers again, then lightly coasted his tongue over her bottom lip. She groaned.

Apart from the one hand he had in her hair and his mouth, Tony didn't touch her. Olivia's hands remained at her sides, almost as if she was afraid to move them. He leaned back and stared down at her face. Her dark brown eyes were half closed, the thick lashes seeming to weigh them down. Her lips were still parted, and her cheeks were flushed. He liked that.

"We're going back to my house."

She blinked twice, then cleared her throat. "I assumed you'd rent a place…"

"My home is very private. And I don't want to be running around town. Too many people know me. Besides, today is my birthday. Someone might decide to surprise me with a bottle of champagne or some such nonsense, and once we're alone, I don't want to be disturbed."

Her eyes widened. "Happy birthday. I didn't realize… You should be celebrating with someone special."

He started to tell her she was special, almost too special, but he bit back the words. "It's okay. More than okay." He bent to kiss her very quickly. She looked disappointed when he pulled away. "I can't think of a better way to spend the day. You're giving me the best gift imaginable."

No sooner did he say it, than he realized she might misunderstand. So he quickly clarified, "A baby, I mean."

"I knew what you meant."

But he was lying, to both her and himself. Right now, he wanted her so much, thoughts of conception were taking a backseat to good old-fashioned lust. He still wanted his baby, very much, but he found himself hoping it would take a couple of tries before they found success. He wanted—needed—to expend all his desire for her so he could concentrate on other, more important things.

Olivia looked slightly rattled, which was new for her. She reached behind herself to feel for a hanger, then slipped the teddy onto it and back on the rack. Tony looked around, taking in the ambience of the shop. He'd been in them all, of course, but still, she never ceased to amaze him with her organization and natural ability for merchandising.

She did a remarkable amount of business, and it was easy to see why.

Everything was displayed in a way that bespoke intimacy with a touch of class. Mannequins were shyly posed in every corner, their perfect forms draped in soft pastel shades of silk and satin, musky scents filled the air from the perfume rack and the shelves of sachets. Every inch of space was utilized to the best advantage, so nothing looked crowded or busy.

Olivia cleared her throat, drawing his attention. "I was thinking of ordering more of these," she said, indicating the teddys. "I knew they'd be a big seller, but this week we went through more than even I had anticipated. They're just so comfortable."

"And incredibly sexy?"

She nodded. That Olivia felt the need for small talk

proved her nervousness, and Tony didn't want her nervous. He also couldn't stop himself from asking the question of the day. "How do you know they're comfortable, Olivia? Do you wear these things?" He reached over and caught at the lace edging the leg of the teddy, then rubbed his thumb over it.

Straightening her spine, a gesture of defiance he was beginning to recognize, she nodded. "Of course I do. I've personally tried everything I sell."

Tony took another quick survey of the shop, and this time his gaze landed on a midnight black bra and panty set, the bra designed to merely cup the fullness of the breast, leaving the nipples exposed, and the panties with a very convenient open seam. He felt his stomach constrict, and knew he had to get her out of the shop before his libido exploded. "Are you ready to go?"

Appearing as flustered as he felt, she nodded and reached behind the counter for her coat. Tony helped her slip it on, then took her arm to guide her out. She was trembling, and he wanted to reassure her somehow, but as she locked up the shop, he saw that her nipples were peaked against the soft wool of her tunic, and any coherent conversation escaped him. He wanted to touch her breasts, to see if they felt as soft as they looked. He wanted to taste her, all of her, and he wanted to give her the pleasure she'd requested.

At first, it had seemed like a tall order, and a bit intimidating. No woman had ever come right out and told him to give her the level of satisfaction she expected. It was enough to shrivel many a man. But he wasn't a man to cower under pressure, and the more he'd thought of it—and ways to see the job done—the more excited he'd become by the prospect. Going head-to-head with Olivia during business always exhilarated him. Doing so in bed would be even better. He felt challenged for the first time in a long time, and what red-blooded male could resist a challenge?

Besides, he decided, as they drove from the parking garage, if he didn't get it right the first time, he'd have plenty of time to keep trying. That thought brought a grin.

"What?"

He glanced at Olivia and realized she was watching him. She looked wary now, and a little self-conscious. "Hey, you're not having second thoughts, are you?"

"No, but I'll admit that grin of yours is a little unnerving."

He heard the slight tremor in her tone and reached over to take her hand from her lap. "I'm just…"

"Eager?"

"That's a very appropriate word." He grinned again. "What about you?"

She drew a quavering breath, then whispered, "Yes."

Tony had to put both hands on the wheel. Never had one simple word affected him so strongly. He wanted to speed, to race to his house, but the streets were congested with holiday shoppers. With Thanksgiving less than two weeks away, it seemed as if everyone had a reason to be out on a Friday evening. Curse them all.

"How far do we have to go?"

"It's about a twenty-minute drive." Twenty minutes that would seem like two hours. "Are you hungry?"

"No."

"Are you sure? I could stop at a drive-through."

She glared at him. "No. I am not hungry."

He liked the idea that she was as anxious to get under way as he. They stopped at a traffic light and he said, "Well, then how about scooting over here and giving me another kiss? It's the truth, I desperately need something to tide me over."

Her chest rose and fell in several deep breaths, then she scooted. Tony caught her mouth, pressing her back against the seat and this time skipping the teasing. He slid his tongue into her mouth and stroked her deeply. Olivia's hands came up to rest on his shoulders, and then curled to pull him closer.

The light changed, and at a snail's pace, traffic moved.

They continued to kiss and cuddle and touch at every opportunity, and Tony knew they were making each other just a bit crazy. But he didn't call a halt to the touching, and finally, after excruciating frustration, he pulled into his long driveway. It had taken twenty-five minutes, and every minute had been a form of inventive foreplay. Olivia had her eyes closed and appeared to be concentrating on breathing. Her coat laid open, her knees pressed tightly together, and her hands, where they rested on the seat on either side of her, shook.

Tony said very softly, "We're here."

She slowly sat forward and surveyed his home through bleary eyes. She was quiet for long seconds, then whispered, "Oh, Tony. It's beautiful."

He was pleased with her praise. "I had it built a few years ago. I made certain as many trees were left as possible."

"It almost seems a part of the landscape."

That had been his intention. Built of stone and wood and slate, the house blended in with the background, sprawling wide with only one level, and surrounded by oaks and pines and dogwoods. "Now, with the trees bare, you can see the house better. But in the spring and summer, it's nearly hidden."

He hit the remote to open the garage door, then drove inside. The four-car garage held only one other car, and was very quiet.

When he opened Olivia's door for her and she stepped out, he couldn't help but kiss her again. And this time, since they were assured of privacy, he gave his eager hands the freedom to roam. His palms coasted over her back, feeling her warmth even through the thickness of her coat, then scooped low to cuddle her soft rounded buttocks.

Olivia sucked in a deep breath and moaned when he brought her flush with his body. He knew she could feel his erection, knew she was reacting to it, and with every rapid pulse beat of his body, he thought: this is Olivia, the cool businesswoman, the shark, and she's pressing against me, trembling and wanting more. It was wonderful and strange and so exciting he almost couldn't bear it. He felt his body harden even more, felt himself expanding, growing. He felt ready to burst.

He back-stepped her toward the door leading into his house. Now that he was this close, he certainly didn't want to make love to her in the garage. But when he lifted his head, his eyes were immediately drawn to her heaving breasts, and he saw again her stiff little nipples. Her coat was open down the front, and he pushed it farther aside, then gently cupped her breasts, shaping them, weighing them in his palms. She was soft and warm and her nipples were pressed achingly against the fabric. She tilted her head back against the garage wall and made a small sound of pleasure and need.

Before he could give his mind time to approve his actions, he unbuttoned three small pearl buttons, and peeled aside the soft wool material. Her bra was lace and satin, a pale coffee color, but so sheer he could see the entire outline of her. It nearly sent him over the edge. He brushed his thumb over her nipple, gently, teasing, and watched her tremble. He lost control.

He growled low in his throat, pulled the bra down so it was cupped beneath her pale breast, pushing her up, seeming to offer her to his mouth, and then he brushed his thumb over her again. She panted as he toyed with her, building the suspense, the excitement.

"Tony."

It was her small, pleading voice that brought him around. He couldn't wait much longer to taste her, but neither should he be rushing things. He kept his eyes on her beautiful body, on the breast he'd bared, then wrapped his arm around her waist to guide her inside. He reached for the doorknob and turned it, then jerked when he heard a screamed, *"Surprise!"*

He looked up and saw his entire family, balloons in the background, streamers floating around. It took everyone a second to realize the misfortune of the entire scene, and then little by little, expressions changed. He saw his mother gasp, his grandfather chuckle. His brother was now wearing a wide grin.

His own face must have looked stunned, and he couldn't find the wherewithal to move. Both he and Olivia seemed frozen to the spot. Then he saw his six-year-old nephew turn his gaze to Olivia, and watched as his sister-in-law rushed over and slapped both hands over her son's eyes. Tony came reluctantly to his senses. He slammed the door shut, then tried to get his mind to function in some semblance of order so he could figure out what to do.

"Oh my God."

He glanced down at Olivia, her hands covering her face, her shoulders shaking. She said again, "Oh my God." Her breast was still uncovered, and more than anything, he wanted to taste that small pink nipple. He wished his family elsewhere, but when he heard the sudden roar of hysterical laughter inside, he knew not a single damn one of them would budge. Meddling bunch of irritants.

"Oh my God."

Tony frowned, his gaze still on that taunting nipple. He was beginning to feel like Pavlov's dog. "Are you praying or cursing?"

She peeked at him from between her fingers, her expression as evil as any he'd ever seen. Through gritted teeth, she said, "You promised me privacy, Tony. There must be fifty people in there."

"No. If everyone's present, and I suspect by the low roar that they are, there's ten, maybe twelve total. It only seems like more because a portion of them are kids. Noisy kids." She dropped her hands and glared at him. She seemed totally oblivious to the fact that her body was bared. Tony, still retaining a death grip on the doorknob in case anyone tried to open it, reached over to cup her with his free hand. She jerked.

"Tony."

How her voice could change from cold and angry to soft and pleading so quickly, he didn't know. "One small taste, Olivia, okay? Then I can sort the rest of this out."

She didn't appear to understand, which was probably the only reason she didn't protest.

Tony shook his head, then bent down and slowly drew his tongue around her nipple. She gasped, and he gently sucked her into his mouth, holding her captive with his teeth. Her flesh was hot and sweet and her nipple was so taut it pained him. He licked his tongue over her, flicking, teasing, making her nipple strain even more. When she moaned, he suckled, holding her close to his body.

Olivia's hands settled in his hair just as a discreet knock sounded on the door. "You might as well come in, Tony. I sent the kids into the kitchen for some punch."

Tony cursed, dropped his forehead to Olivia's chest, then felt himself rudely pushed aside as she frantically tried to right her bra and button herself up. "Calm down, Olivia, it's all right."

From the other side of the door, he heard his brother say, "Yeah, Olivia. It's all right. We're glad you're here for the party."

Tony growled. "Go away, John!"

"All right. But I'll be back in two minutes if you don't present yourself. Both of you."

Now that she was decently covered, Olivia sent her gaze searching around the garage, and Tony realized she was hoping to find a means of escape. "Forget it. They won't let me leave, therefore, you're stuck, too."

"But you don't want this," she wailed, her hands twisting together at her waist. "This is your family, Tony, part of your private life, and I don't want to intrude. We both agreed I wouldn't intrude."

Tony sighed, knowing she was right, but also accepting the inevitable. "I'll find some way to throw my family off the scent. Just play it cool. As far as they need to know, we're business associates and nothing more."

Olivia's look told him how stupid she thought that idea was. "Play it cool? After what they saw us doing?" She shook her head. "No. I'm not going in there."

"Olivia…"

"They *saw* us!"

He shrugged. "It's none of their damn business. If anyone gets impertinent with you, tell them to bug off. Or better still, just tell me, and I'll handle them."

She didn't look at all convinced, and Tony touched her face. "I've seen you at work, lady. You can easily handle a few curious relatives. You're a shark, remember? Now pull yourself together."

She drew a deep breath and gave an uncertain nod. Tony dropped his gaze to her mouth, then had to swallow a curse. His fingertips slid over her lower lip. "Do you have any idea how frustrated I am right now? How badly I'm hurting?"

Olivia seemed to regain some of her aplomb. "No more than I am, I assume. After all, this was my idea. You, as I recall, were very reluctant to agree."

"I was an idiot." He turned to the door again. "I suppose I can suffer through a few hours. How long can a family birthday party last anyway?"

OLIVIA TRIED FOR A serene smile as Tony's family lined up to meet her. Tony waited until he had everyone's attention, then said with astounding sincerity, "Everyone, this is Olivia Anderson. She's a business associate. She owns the lingerie shops Sugar and Spice in the hotels, and today we were working on finalizing the placement of one more."

Olivia held her breath, but no one called him on the obvious cover-up. Then Tony began pointing out people, too many of them for Olivia to keep straight, though she was usually very good with names and faces. The men seemed inclined to leave her be, their interest caught by a football game someone had turned on. Other than a wave in her direction when Tony introduced her, and a few ribald comments to Tony and the kind of *business* he conducted, they stayed on or near the family-room couch and the large-screen television.

The women, however, hovered. They were anxious to talk to her, and Tony, with little more than an apologetic glance, abandoned her when the men called him to watch a play. Sue, Tony's mother, invited her to join the women and children in the kitchen.

To Olivia's surprise, no one was the least bit unpleasant, despite what had happened. "I'm sorry if we've upset your plans," Sue said. "Tony, of course, didn't know we'd planned a party. And we didn't know Tony had made other arrangements."

Tony's sister, Kate, and sister-in-law, Lisa, both chuckled. Kate said, "If you could have seen his face! Well, we certainly did surprise him."

Olivia couldn't help but smile. Both women were very adept at keeping busy in the kitchen, and dodging the kids who ran in and out. "It was rather awkward."

Lisa laughed. "For us, too. Of course, John is just like Tony, and never lets a chance go by to goad his brother."

"And they both goad me. Endlessly!" Kate shook her head. "But now I have enough ammunition to twit Tony for a good month."

Olivia decided, even though their comments weren't malicious, it was time to change the subject. She didn't want to have to explain her business with Tony. "Could I help you do something?"

Sue was arranging ham slices on a platter, Kate was putting glasses and napkins on a tray, and Lisa was trying to balance a tiny infant in one arm and dish up potato salad with the other. She turned with a relieved smile when Olivia made her offer.

"If you wouldn't mind holding the baby, that would be a big help."

Olivia balked. "I, uh, how about I help with the food instead? I've never held an infant before."

"Piece of cake, believe me. And he's such a good baby, he won't give you any problems."

Before Olivia could form another denial, the baby was nestled in her arms. His mother had wrapped him in a soft blue blanket, and other than one tiny hand and a small, pink face, the child was completely covered. Olivia cuddled him carefully when he squirmed, settling himself with a small sigh that parted his pursed lips and made Olivia smile.

She felt a pain in her chest that had nothing to do with physical ailments and everything to do with a breaking heart.

One by one, the women left the kitchen to carry the trays into the dining room, and Olivia welcomed the privacy. She couldn't recall ever holding such a small baby before, and her curiosity was extreme. She carefully pushed the blanket back from the baby's head, then rubbed her cheek against his crown. So soft, she thought, wondering at the silky cap of hair. And the scents. Never had she smelled anything so sweet, so touching, as a baby. She wanted to breathe his scent all day. She had her nose close to him, gently nuzzling him, when Tony walked in.

"What are you doing?"

Olivia jerked at the alarm in his tone. She didn't have time to answer him, though, not that she would have told him she was smelling the baby. Lisa came back in then and thanked her. "I'll put him in his crib now that the other kids are all sitting down to eat. I worry when they're all running around that they'll wake him up. You know how kids are."

Olivia didn't know, but she could see Tony hadn't liked her holding the baby. Lisa left the room, and Tony whispered, "Do you think it's a good idea for you to do that?"

Olivia knew exactly what he meant. He was concerned she'd start wanting a baby herself if she held one. She could have told him it was too late for that worry, that it didn't matter. She could want forever and never get what she wished. At least, she couldn't get a baby. Now passion, it seemed Tony was ready to give her that in huge doses. What she'd felt during the ride and in his garage... It was almost everything she'd ever wanted with a man. Everything but the real emotion. Everything but love.

It angered her that he was pushing her and worrying about something that would never be, but she held in her words of resentment and instead, she shrugged. "Would you have rather I'd refused? What excuse would I give?"

He tunneled his fingers through his hair, then looked toward the dining room. "Come on. They're waiting for me to eat."

"This is going to be impossible, isn't it, Tony?"

"No. Everything's fine."

He didn't sound at all convincing, and Olivia had to wonder if John or Kate had already been teasing him. When they entered the dining room, Olivia looked around. She hadn't had the chance to actually see the inside of Tony's house, but now that she could look, she wasn't at all surprised. Everything, every dish, every piece of furniture, the wallpaper, all showed excellent taste, but without the blatant stamp of wealth. Tony never flaunted his financial success, and other than the size of the sprawling house, it showed only a sense of comfort and functional ease.

The house was very open. Each room seemed to flow into the next, and there were windows everywhere. The furniture was all highly polished mahogany. As little Maggie, who Olivia guessed to be around three, walked to her seat with one hand on the buffet, she left small smudge marks in her wake. Tony only scooped her up and tossed her in the air. The little girl giggled, wrapped her pudgy arms around Tony's neck and planted a very wet kiss on the side of his nose. He pretended to chew on her belly, then sat her in her booster seat and took his own chair next to Olivia. The rest of the children yelled for his attention.

The pain in her chest intensified.

She so desperately wanted this one sumptuous, sensuous affair. The whole purpose was to help her fill a void, because her life was destined to be a lonely one, without children and without a man who loved her. But she was getting more than she bargained for. She hadn't wanted to be shown all she was missing, to find more voids, to have firsthand knowledge of what could never be hers.

As she watched Tony laugh and play with the children, she knew it was too late for her. Perhaps this would yet turn out to be the wild fling she'd anticipated, but it would also leave her lonelier than ever before.

Dinner was a wonderful, riotous affair with children laughing, grown-ups talking and food being continuously resupplied. The kids quickly realized Olivia was a new face and, therefore, easy to entertain. Despite her growing melancholy, she laughed at their antics, listened to their stories, and when one child came over and tugged on her skirt, she didn't even flinch over the stain left behind. The child wanted to be lifted, and Olivia obliged. But the small hand was still holding her skirt, and when the child went up, so did her hem.

She hurried to right herself, pushing her skirt back down. But it was obvious everyone had seen the top of her stocking and the paler strip of flesh on her upper thigh. John grinned, Lisa gave him a playful smack to keep him from speaking, and Sue quickly began talking about Christmas shopping.

Olivia glanced at Tony and saw he had his eyes closed, looking close to prayer. Despite his brother's chuckles, it took him a few moments to collect his control. And then he sent Olivia a smile that made promises and threats at the same time.

After that, Tony did his best to deflect the kids from her. Olivia understood his reasoning, but no one else did. And all in all, everyone accepted her. They attempted to make her a part of their family, and for the short while it could last, Olivia loved it. Every few minutes, someone stood to check on the sleeping infant, whose crib they could see in the family room through the archway. The men took more turns than the women did, and Olivia saw that Tony, more than anyone, was interested in peeking in on the little one.

Olivia was being smothered by the sense of familial camaraderie. As welcoming as they all were, she felt like an interloper. And when she spied the pile of gaily wrapped birthday presents in the corner, she knew she couldn't stay.

She excused herself, asking directions to the powder room, then quickly located a phone. It happened to be in Tony's bedroom, or so she assumed judging from the open closet door and the lingering scent of his cologne…and his body. Again, she found herself breathing deeply, then shook her head and forced her mind to clear. She perched on the side of the bed to call for a cab.

She was still sitting there minutes later when Tony found her.

CHAPTER FOUR

TONY SLIPPED INTO THE room and quietly closed the door. Olivia looked up and their gazes touched, hers wide, his narrowed. He crossed his arms over his chest and kept his voice very low. "Hiding?"

"What do you think?"

"No. I don't think you'd hide. So what are you doing?"

Olivia came to her feet, feeling like a fool, like a sneaky fool. But she refused to be intimidated. "I called a cab. I think it's past time I went home."

Tony didn't say anything at first, just leaned back against the door. Then he closed his eyes and groaned. "You're going to make me wait another day, aren't you, Olivia?"

Her heartbeat jumped at the husky way he said that, and at the restrained hunger she heard in his tone. "This…this isn't the right time, Tony. You know that. Right now, I feel equal parts ridiculous and embarrassed."

His gaze pinned her, hot and intent. "I could make you forget your hesitation real fast, honey."

I'll just bet you could. It wasn't easy, but Olivia shook her head. "If I leave now, they might not suspect anything—"

"Olivia, they saw me kissing your breast. I think they're already a bit suspicious."

She felt the blood pound in her veins, but kept her gaze steady. "You weren't kissing my breast."

"I wanted to be."

Olivia curled her hands into fists and tried to calm her breathing. "They might decide that was just a temporary loss of control if I leave now. If I stay until they're all gone, they'll assume we're spending the night together, and that's what we wanted to avoid." She gentled her tone and asked, "No speculation, no gossip. No scandals. Remember?"

"Yeah, but—"

A knock sounded at the door, and John's jovial voice called out, "Everything okay in there?"

Tony closed his eyes, a look of annoyance etched in his features. "I'm going to kill him."

Olivia thought she might help.

"We'll be out in just a second, John. And if you dare knock on the damn door again, I'm going to knock on you."

"Hey! I just wanted to tell you they're ready to cut the cake."

"So you told me. Now disappear, will you?"

Olivia rubbed her forehead, knowing she'd fumbled again, that she'd only made matters worse. Good grief, Tony's brother was fetching them from the bedroom. "How that man produced such a beautiful, sweet baby, I don't know."

To her surprise, Tony laughed. "John's all right. Believe me, if he understood the situation, he wouldn't be hassling me."

"No?"

Tony slowly shook his head, then went to her and pulled her against his chest. "No. He'd be sympathetic as hell." He tilted her head back and growled, "I want you, Olivia."

Her stomach curled at his words. "Tomorrow?"

Tony placed damp kisses across her cheek, her throat. He touched the corner of her mouth with his tongue. "Early? You're not going to make me wait until evening, are you?"

Olivia thought she might agree to anything with him stroking her back and kissing her so softly. "Where?"

"Hell, I don't know. But I'll think of something before morning, okay? I'll pick you up. About ten o'clock?"

"That'll be fine." She forced herself to forget how sensual and romantic everything seemed with Tony, and to concentrate on their purpose. She had to keep in mind that this was temporary, that Tony didn't really want her, not for keeps. He only wanted to use her, just as she would use him. "I don't want you to worry, Tony. We still have time. I'm supposed to be very fertile for the next couple of days."

She'd barely finished with the words before he was giving her a real kiss, his tongue moving against her own, his teeth nipping. It was a kiss meant to last her through the night. Unfortunately she could still feel the heat in her cheeks when she was forced to walk back into the dining room. She was grateful that the lights had been turned out, and the candles on the cake were lit. She saw John standing by the light switch and knew he was responsible for the darkness. John gave Tony a wink, and Olivia decided he might not be so bad after all.

Kate's two girls, Angie and Allison, ages four and five, fought over who could sing the loudest during the requisite "Happy Birthday," and John's son, six-year-old Luke, wanted to cut and serve the cake. Though Olivia explained that she had to leave, they all insisted she eat a piece of cake first and enjoy a scoop of ice cream. Olivia couldn't remember the last time she'd had, or attended, a birthday party. It might have been fun today if she'd actually been a part of it, rather than a reluctant intruder.

She didn't want anyone to know she'd called a cab. She thought it might seem less awkward if everyone thought she was driving herself home, so she had her coat on and her purse in her hand when she saw the cab's lights coming down the long driveway. To her surprise, the kids all wanted to give her hugs goodbye, the parents all uttered enthusiastic wishes to see her again soon, and to her chagrin, Tony's mother invited her to Thanksgiving dinner. Olivia muttered a lame, "Thank you, but I'll have to see," along with something about a busy schedule, and then she rushed out the door, wanting only to escape the onslaught of emotions. Tony caught her on the last step of the porch.

"I'm sorry, Olivia. I know this wasn't easy for you." He glanced at the cab and cursed. "I should be driving you home."

"I don't mind the cab, Tony, and you can't very well leave your own birthday party."

He reached for his wallet, and she narrowed her eyes. "What do you think you're doing?"

"At least let me pay for the cab—"

"Absolutely not and I won't hear another word on it." She used her most inflexible tone, the one that got contracts altered and had suppliers promising early deliveries. "I'm not your responsibility."

His sigh was long and filled with irritation. "Will you do me a favor then, and at least call me when you get home?"

Olivia stared. She was used to taking care of herself and his request seemed more than absurd. "Why?"

"So I know you made it home okay."

"Tony, you can't start feeling responsible for me. That's breaking one of the rules, isn't it? I'm a big girl, and I know how to manage on my own. So don't worry."

"Call me."

He was insistent, using his own invaluable, corporate tone, and she could tell by his stubborn stance he wasn't going to relent. She didn't think it was a good idea, but she gave in anyway. "Okay. But only this once."

"Thanks." He was grinning hugely.

"You're not a gracious winner, Tony."

"I haven't won yet. Hell, I've still got a whole room full of relatives who are going to burst with rapid-fire questions as soon as I step back inside. Now that you're gone and therefore can't be offended, they'll revert to their normal unrestrained selves."

She knew he was teasing, knew he was very close to his family, and for that reason she suffered not a single twinge of guilt for leaving him to his fate. She stepped into the cab, and Tony came to lean inside, ignoring the cabdriver and giving her a quick kiss.

"Tomorrow, Olivia. Then I'll win."

He was taunting her, but she only grinned. It was in her nature to give as good as she got, so when he started to pull away, she caught his neck and drew him back for another kiss, this one much longer and hotter than the first. And while he was trying to catch his breath, she whispered, "We'll both win."

Tony chuckled. But as he stepped away from the cab, they both looked up. And there at the front door, huddled together as if for a kindergarten class picture, stood all of Tony's family. And even with only the moon for light, Olivia could see the wide grins on all their faces.

TONY GLANCED AT THE CLOCK, but it was only seven in the morning, and he had no real reason to get up, not when he wouldn't be seeing Olivia until ten. So he lingered in bed, thinking about her, about all that had happened the night before. Her vulnerability around his family stirred feelings he didn't want to acknowledge—especially when concentrating on the lust she engendered was so much more satisfying.

Not one single minute had passed during the night when he could completely put Olivia and her allure from his mind. It was ridiculous, but he wanted her more now than he'd ever wanted any woman. Of course, she was so different from any other woman he knew. She made demands, but she also gave freely of herself. She was a veritable shark whenever they did business, but she ran her business fairly, and with a generous hand toward her workers. It was a belief he subscribed to: Treat your employees honestly, and you get honesty and loyalty in return.

They actually had a lot in common.

And yet there was a multitude of reasons why he couldn't get overly involved with her. The very things he admired about her made her most unsuitable for an emotional relationship. He wanted a baby, pure and simple, someone to love him, and someone he could love without restrictions or qualifications. The baby would be his, only his, and Tony planned to smother the child with all the love he had inside him.

Olivia wanted a thriving business. She'd admitted she had no desire, no time for a family. She'd agreed to have his baby as part of a business deal, and while her agreement thrilled him, it also reemphasized the fact that business was still her main objective in life, while a baby was now his. He'd have to do his best to remember that.

The house was chilly when he finally rose and went to put on coffee. Naked except for a pair of snug cotton boxers, he felt the gooseflesh rise on his arms, but he ignored it. He needed a little cooling off if he was to deal with Olivia in a rational way.

He went into the bathroom and splashed water over his beard-rough face, then brushed his teeth while he waited for the coffee. Today, he thought, staring at his own contemplative expression in the mirror, he would get this business with Olivia back on an even keel. No more mingling with family, no more seeing her with a baby cuddled in her arms and an expression on her face that tore at his guts. He would view her with a detached eye and a reminder in his brain that she was a means to an end. They'd made an agreement, and it could be nothing more.

Not if he expected to escape this ordeal completely intact, with his heart whole and his mind sane.

He'd just poured his first cup of coffee when the doorbell rang. Padding barefoot into the living room, he leaned down to peer through the peephole and saw Olivia standing on his doorstep. A quick glance at the clock showed it to be only seven forty-five, and his first thought was that she was here to cancel, that something had come up and she had to go out of town; it wasn't uncommon in her business. Every muscle in his body protested.

He jerked the door open, forgetting for the moment that he wasn't even close to being dressed. Olivia took a long moment to stare at his chest, then down the length of his body before she lifted her gaze to his face.

"You're rather hairy, aren't you?"

"I'll shave."

Her lips quirked in a quick grin. "Your chest?"

If it would keep her from canceling. He only shrugged.

Tentatively she reached out and touched him, laying her palm flat where his heart beat in unsteady cadence. She stroked him, feeling him, tangling her fingers in his body hair. With a breathless whisper, she said, "I like it."

Tony didn't answer. He wasn't certain he could answer. And then she looked up at him, her eyes huge and bright. "I couldn't wait."

He felt the bottom drop out of his stomach. His hand shook as he set the cup of coffee on the entry table, then reached for her and pulled her inside. He needed to make certain he'd understood. "Olivia?"

She started to chatter. "I know you said ten, but we're both off today, right? And I'm really not used to this, being aroused and yet having to wait. It's terribly difficult. I couldn't sleep last night…"

"Me, either."

He couldn't believe she was here, looking shy and determined and he wanted her as much as he'd ever wanted anything in his life. Everything he'd just been telling himself about keeping his emotional distance vanished. He couldn't quite pry his hands from her shoulders, couldn't force himself to take an emotional step back. He felt her softness beneath the coat, the way she straightened her shoulders to face him. Ah, that small show of bravado, so like her, so endearing. So damn sexy.

The brisk morning air coming through the open door did little to impress him. As he felt himself harden, his pulse quicken, Olivia pushed the door shut behind her, then set an overnight bag on the floor. His gaze dropped to it, and she rushed to explain. "I… Well, I felt a little risqué this morning. And it stands to reason your house should be safe now. I mean, lightning doesn't strike twice in the same spot, right?"

He had no answer for that, not when he could see the heated need in her eyes, the way her lips trembled.

She swallowed hard. "I don't want you to think I'm intruding for the whole night, but I needed to bring something to wear for later… If we're going to spend the whole day together."

Before he could reassure her, she shook her head and started again, her tone anxious. "I'm making a mess of this. Remember, the book said we should wait a few hours then try again, and I thought…"

"Shh." He could barely restrain himself from lifting her and carrying her to his room. She had this strange mix of timidity and boldness that made him crazy with wanting. "Let me shower real quick and…"

"No." She shook her head and her dark hair fell over her shoulders, looking soft and silky. "I've waited long enough, Tony. I don't want to wait a single second more."

She was staring down at his body, her gaze resting on his blatant erection clearly defined within his soft cotton boxers. Another quarter inch, one more soft sound from her, and the boxers wouldn't cover him at all. He wanted her to touch him, he wanted… Feeling desperate, he said, "I have to at least shave, honey. I don't want to scratch you."

For a reply, she began unbuttoning her coat, and as each button slid free, his heartbeat accelerated. First he saw soft pale flesh; her throat, her upper chest, the gentle swells of her breasts. But as the coat began to part, he realized she wasn't dressed at all, that she was covered only by the teddy he'd admired the day before in her shop.

He'd had to know, he thought frantically, staring at her body, more perfect than any mannequin. She had a gentle grace that was made to wear such feminine items. He'd questioned whether she really wore the articles she carried, and now she'd proven to him that she did—with perfection. And suddenly it was too much.

Gripping the lapels of the coat in his fists, he shoved it over her shoulders and let it fall free to land unnoticed on the floor, abruptly ending her slow unveiling. Drawn by the sight of her, cheeks flushed, eyes anxious, he scooped her into his arms. He felt her slender thighs against his forearm, her soft breasts against his chest, her lips touching his throat, and he groaned. The bedroom was definitely too far away and he took three long steps to the living-room couch and landed there with her tucked close to his side. His mouth was on hers before she could protest, if that had been her intent. And his hands began exploring every soft swell and heated hollow. He moved too fast, he knew it, but he couldn't seem to stop himself.

She shuddered when his palm smoothed over her silky bottom, sliding between her buttocks, exploring her from behind. He dipped between her thighs to frantically finger the three small silver snaps there. They easily popped free at his prodding, and then his fingers were touching her warmth, gliding over softly swelled flesh, over crisp feminine curls. He stroked, feeling her wetness, her growing heat. The feel of her made him wonder why he didn't explode. He could hear her rapid breathing in his ears, feel her fingertips clenching tight on his shoulders.

He groaned, moving his mouth from hers, wanting to

taste her skin, to breathe in her scent. She was soft every-where, from her loose hair that brushed over his cheeks, to her arms that held him tight, to her slender thighs that will-ingly parted as he continued to cautiously explore her, exciting her, readying her.

Finding a puckered nipple beneath the sheer material of the teddy, he dampened it with his tongue, then looked at his handiwork. She showed pink and erect through the material. He suckled, flicking with his tongue, and Olivia arched her back, her panting, urgent breaths driving him on. He nipped and she gasped. With his big hand still between her thighs, he slid one long finger over her, again and again, finding her most sensitive flesh and plying it in much the same way he did her nipple, then pressing deep inside her, stroking. She made a high, keening sound. She was tight and wet and so hot Tony couldn't stand it another moment; he knew she was ready.

With frenzied motions, he shoved his shorts down and situated himself between her thighs. For one moment, their gazes met, and her look, that unique look of vulnerability and need and demand, pushed him over the edge. He covered her mouth with his own, thrusting his tongue past her lips just as his erection pressed inside her body.

There was a small amount of resistance as her body slowly loosened to accept his length, his size. And then with one even, rough thrust he slid deep, and even that, something beyond her control, appealed to him, made him that much more anxious to reach his final goal. He began moving, driving into her and then pulling away, hearing her panting breaths and feeling the way she tried to counter his moves, though the couch didn't allow her much freedom. He felt things he'd never felt before, as if he were a preda-tory animal, dominant, determined to stake a primal claim.

Pinning her beneath him so she couldn't move, he slid one hand beneath her hips and lifted, forcing her to take all of him, giving her no way to resist him at all. He briefly worried when she groaned raggedly, but then she squeezed him tight, her muscles clamping around him like a hot fist, and she was slick and wet and she wanted him—wanted him enough to demand that he make love to her. His explosive climax obliterated all other thought.

He knew he shouted like a wild man, knew Olivia watched him with a fascinated type of awe. He threw his head back, sensations continuing to wash over him, draining him, filling him, making his muscles quiver until finally, after long seconds, he collapsed onto her, gasping for breath.

Her arms gently, hesitantly slipped around his neck and her fingers smoothed through his hair. And when he felt the light brushing of her lips over his temple, a touch so unbelievably sweet and innocent, he came to the realization that he'd just used her very badly, that he'd totally ignored all her stipulations of the deal they'd made. He'd forgotten all about the damn deal. Hell, he hadn't given her pleasure.

He hadn't given her anything except a man's lust.

OLIVIA FELT TONY TENSE, knew what was going through his mind, and tightened her arms. He relented enough that he stayed very close to her, but lifted his head. She felt ridiculously shy about meeting his gaze, but she forced herself to do just that, if for no other reason than to reassure him. She couldn't quite prevent the small smile curling her lips.

He blew out a disgusted breath. "I'm sorry."

Placing two fingers against his mouth, she meant only to silence him. But then he kissed her fingers, and her heart flipped and she ended up lifting her own head enough to kiss him in return. "Don't ruin this for me by making unnecessary apologies, Tony. Please."

She said the words against his mouth, and before she'd even finished, his tongue was stroking hers, his narrow, muscular pelvis pushing close again. She tingled all over, a renewed rush of warmth making her stomach curl.

"I already ruined things, honey. And you deserve much more than an apology."

That was the second time he'd called her "honey" and she loved it. There had never been a relationship in her life since her parents' death that warranted an endearment. She hadn't realized that she'd even been missing it. But hearing Tony say it now, hearing the gentleness in his tone, the affection, she decided she liked it very much.

Since he seemed determined to talk about it, Olivia asked, "Why exactly are you apologizing?"

"Because I lost my head. I gave you nothing."

"Not true." Oh how she loved feeling his hard, lean body pressed against hers, the contrast of his firm muscles and his hair-roughened legs and his warmth. She tightened her arms and rubbed her nose against his chest, loving his morning musky scent. He always smelled so good, so sexy. So like himself. It made her dizzy and weak to breathe his delicious scent. "I've never made anyone lose their head before, Tony. I think it's a rather nice feeling."

He gave a strangled laugh, then tangled his hands in her hair to make her look at him. "I'll take the blame, especially given the fact I've never made love to a woman without a condom before. Feeling you, Olivia, all of you, was a heady experience."

She felt stunned by his admission. "Never?"

"Nope. I've always been the cautious sort, even when I was just a kid. But you're to blame just a bit, too, showing up here in that getup." He ran one large palm down her side, rubbing the material that was now bunched at her waist. His voice dropped to a low rumble when he whispered, "I almost died when you opened your coat, and I knew I wouldn't be able to draw another breath without getting inside you first."

And he thought he hadn't given her anything? With her heart racing and her throat tight with emotion, she kissed him again, getting quickly used to the feel of his mouth on hers. When he lifted his head this time, she was very aware of his renewed erection and the way his arms were taut with muscles as he restrained himself, holding his chest away from her.

Tony watched her so closely, it was hard to speak, but she forced the words out, for some strange reason, wanting to tell him her thoughts. "I was half afraid you'd laugh, that I'd look ridiculous. Though I love wearing sexy things, no one sees me as a sexy woman."

"You're sexier than any woman has a right to be."

"Tony…" The things he said made her light-headed.

"It'll be our little secret, okay?" He began tracing the small red marks left behind from his morning whiskers. That long finger moved over her throat, her breasts. He stopped at her nipples and lightly pinched, holding her between his finger and thumb. He watched her face as he tugged gently, plucking, rolling her flesh until she groaned. Olivia wanted nothing more than to make love with him again.

But Tony was suddenly lifting himself away. "I have to shower and shave," he said in deep, husky tones. "Despite what you say, I don't like leaving burns on your skin."

"No." She tried to protest, to hold him near, but he only stood up then lifted her again. The way he cradled her close to his heart was something else she could get used to.

"You can shower with me, Miss Anderson, then I'll see about attending you the right way."

"I loved the way you did things."

"You didn't come."

A flash of heat washed over her mostly naked body. He had such a blatant way of discussing things that excited her despite her embarrassment. "I... I enjoyed myself." She sounded defensive and added, "But I'm supposed to stay still for a while."

"I can promise you'll enjoy yourself more when I do things properly."

He seemed determined to fulfill her demands, when she now felt horrible for having made them. She didn't want this to be only about base satisfaction, a series of touches meant to excite, with no emotion involved. It was the emotion that she'd been craving for so long, that felt so good now. But there was no way she could say that to Tony, not after she'd told him she wanted to be privy to his excellent technique.

An idea came to mind, and as he stood her inside the shower stall, she said, "Aren't we supposed to wait two hours before doing this again? To give you time to...to replenish yourself?"

Tony stepped in behind her and began working the teddy up over her shoulders. When he finally tossed it outside the shower and stood looking at her completely bare, Olivia knew he'd have his way. He took a long time scrutinizing her, and that gave her a chance to look her fill also. He was such a gorgeous man, so solid, his body dark, his muscles tight.

She wondered if he enjoyed the sight of her near as much as she did him, but then he met her gaze and there was such heat in his green eyes, and more emotion than she could ever wish for, she forgot her own questions.

Tony inched closer to her until their bodies were touching from the waist down. His hard erection pressed into her belly, stealing her breath. His hands came up to cup her breasts. "You don't have to watch the clock, honey. I promise you, it'll take me at least that long to get my fill of looking at you and touching you."

Her heart thumped heavily and she could barely talk. "Tony?"

"It's called foreplay, Olivia. I intend to make up for the orgasm you missed—and then some. We've got all the time in the world."

Thirty minutes later, their still damp bodies tangled in the covers on his bed, Olivia knew she'd never survive two hours worth of this. Tony was gently lathing one nipple while his fingers were busy drifting over her hip and belly, pausing every so often for an excruciating moment between her thighs to torment and tease her until she groaned and begged. He used her own wetness as a lubricant, sometimes pressing his fingers deep, stretching her, other times circling her opening, sliding over ultrasensitive flesh.

He laughed at her soft demands, his fingers gently plucking, rolling. "Easy, sweetheart. I promise, you'll appreciate being patient."

"No. No more, Tony. I can't stand it." There was a touch of tears in her voice, but she was too new to this, too unskilled to rationalize an ending that she'd never before experienced. Tony kissed her softly on her parted lips, then whispered, "Trust me now, okay?"

When she felt Tony's cheek, now smooth from his shave, glide over her abdomen, the only thought she had was of finding relief. Every nerve ending in her body felt taut, tingling. There was no room for modesty, for shyness.

His hands curved around her knees and she willingly allowed him to part her thighs wide, leaving her totally exposed to his gaze. She felt his warm, gentle breath, the damp touch of his tongue. And then his mouth closed around her, hot and wet, and his teeth carefully nibbled.

No, she'd never survive this. She arched upward, again begging, feeling the sensations so keenly she screamed. He tightened his hold on her buttocks, holding her steady, forcing her to submit to his torment.

And then it happened and she was only aware of unbelievable pleasure. Tony encouraged her, controlled her, and when the sensations finally began to ebb, he eased, soothing her until she calmed.

When she opened her eyes—a move requiring considerable effort—Tony was beside her again, his hand idly cupping her breast and a look of profound interest on his face. She blinked at him, not understanding that look, and he said without a single qualm, "You've never had an orgasm before, have you?"

Her only recourse seemed to be to close her eyes again. But Tony laughed and kissed her nose. "Don't hide from me, Olivia. Talk to me."

"We're not supposed to be talking."

"No? Well, don't worry. We'll get on to making love again soon. But answer me first."

Disgruntled by his personal question and his persistence, she said, "It never seemed particularly important before. Besides, I told you my two attempts at this failed."

"Your two attempts with a partner." His voice gentled. "That doesn't mean you couldn't have—"

Her eyes rounded when she realized where this questioning was going, and it seemed imperative to divert his attention. "Aren't you supposed to be…uh, excited right about now?"

His smile proved she hadn't fooled him one bit. But to answer her question, he lifted her limp hand, kissed the palm, then carried it to his erection, curling her fingers around him. For one brief instant, he held himself still, his eyes closing as her fingers flexed. Then he gave a wry grin. "I'm plenty excited. But I'm also enjoying you most thoroughly."

"You're embarrassing me, is what you're doing." She said it with a severe frown, but he only chuckled.

"Why? Because I'm feeling like the most accomplished lover around? You screamed, Olivia." He cupped her cheek and turned her face toward him. "Look at me, honey."

There was that endearment again. She opened her eyes and stared at him. The tenderness in his gaze nearly undid her.

"I'm glad I could give you something you'd never had before. It makes this all seem very…special."

"Tony." She rolled toward him, wanting him again, right now, unwilling to wait another instant.

And then the doorbell rang, and she knew she might not have any choice.

Tony seemed inclined to ignore it at first, but the insistent pounding that came next had him cursing and rising from the bed. As he pulled on jeans, he surveyed her sprawled form, then cursed again. "Don't move. I'll be right back."

Olivia waited until he'd stomped out of the room before

scrambling off the bed and wrapping the sheet around herself. She went to the door and opened it to peek, then crept down the hall enough to see who had come calling so early. Tony's brother, John, stood in the entryway, the baby in his arms, and a very worried expression on his face.

Though they spoke in hushed tones, Olivia was able to hear every word.

"I know this is the worst possible time, Tony..."

"You have no idea."

"Yes I do. I saw the car. I assume Olivia is here?"

Tony crossed his arms over his bare chest and said, "What do you want, John?"

"I'm sorry, I really am. And I swear I wouldn't be here if there was anyone else. But Mom and Kate went on a shopping spree this morning and won't be back for hours, and I have to take Lisa to the hospital. You know she wasn't feeling great yesterday is why we left early. And she's always so busy with the three kids, she stays exhausted. But she started running a high fever early last night, coughing and having a hard time breathing, and she's gotten sicker by the hour. I've never seen her like this." There was an edge of desperation in John's tone when he added, "I can't watch my three hellions in a hospital and be with her, too."

Tony immediately straightened, then took the baby from his arms. "Is Lisa going to be okay?"

John looked almost sick himself. "I don't know what's wrong with her, hopefully just the flu, but..."

"Don't give it another thought. Of course I'll take the kids. Where are the other two?"

"Waiting in the car with their mother. I didn't want to leave Lisa alone, and I wasn't certain if you were home." He leaned out the door and waved his hand to get the kids to come in. "I really appreciate this, Tony. I know you probably wish we'd all go…"

"Don't be stupid, John. Just take care of Lisa and keep me informed, okay?"

As John stepped out to gather up a packed diaper bag and some essentials for the other kids, Tony rushed around the corner into the hallway and almost ran into Olivia. He had the overnight bag she'd brought in his left hand while he held the baby in the crook of his right arm. He didn't question her snooping, only led the way into the bedroom. "You heard?"

Olivia could sense the worry in his tone and expression, and was reminded once again how close he was to his family. "Yes. What can I do to help?"

He shook his head. "I'm sorry, babe. Here, can you get dressed real quick?" He no sooner handed her the bag than he was rushing to the living room again to relieve John of the children and send him on his way. Olivia closed the door and sighed. It seemed Tony was going to throw her out, which made sense considering he didn't want her around his family. But it still hurt. While they'd been making love, she'd entirely forgotten everything else in the world, including their twice-damned deal and all the reasons she couldn't feel what she was presently feeling.

Despite all her reasons for needing to stay detached from him, she wanted to stay and help; she wanted to stay, period. Very much.

Her body was still tingling, her heart still racing from Tony's sensual torment, but she managed to get her slacks and sweater on before he reopened the door. The baby was still nestled in his bare muscled arm, but that didn't stop him from coming toward her, then pulling her close with his free arm. "Damn, I can't believe my luck."

"Things do seem to be conspiring against us."

He brushed a kiss over her lips, then surprised her by asking, "Can you stay?"

Olivia blinked, not certain what to say.

"I know our plans have changed, hell, we might even have the kids all night. But… I don't feel right about all this. It worries me, Lisa coming down sick like that."

Olivia cupped his cheek, touched by his concern, and warmed by the way he'd included her. "You don't want to be alone?"

His jaw tightened and his eyes searched her face. He seemed reluctant to admit it even to himself, but then he nodded. "I guess that's about it."

"We're friends, Tony. Despite any other agreements, I'd like to believe that. And friends help friends. You don't have to worry that I'll read more into this than exists."

He stubbornly ignored her references to their situation, and asked, "Does that mean you'll stay, Olivia? Please?"

At that moment, she would have done anything for him, but of course, she couldn't tell him that. She looked up at him and smiled. "Yes, I'll stay. For as long as you need me."

CHAPTER FIVE

A LOOK OF RELIEF washed over Tony's features, then he hugged her close again. "I believe the coffee is still in the pot. It might be a little strong now, but I could sure use a cup. And the kids are probably hungry. Kids are always hungry, right? So what do you say? You up to breakfast?"

At just that moment, two faces peeked around the door frame, and they were both very solemn. Olivia's heart swelled with emotion for these two small people who were obviously concerned about their mother. She forgot Tony for the moment, forgot that she didn't know anything about kids, and went down on her knees to meet the children at their level.

"Hello. Remember me?"

Six-year-old Luke stared at her with serious eyes, all the energy of yesterday conspicuously missing. "Sure we remember. It was just last night. You was kissing Uncle Tony in his garage."

Olivia felt her face turn pink, but she smiled. "Actually it was the other way around. Your uncle was kissing me."

Maggie, who at three seemed very small and delicate, popped her thumb from her mouth to say with great wisdom, "Uncle Tony likes kissin'. He kisses me lots, too."

And just that easily, Olivia found a rapport. She reached

out and tugged Maggie closer, and the little girl came willingly, wrapping one arm around Olivia's neck while holding tight to a tattered blanket with the other. Olivia perched the little girl on her knee. "Are you two hungry? I think your uncle was planning on making breakfast for us."

Maggie nodded, but Luke turned away. Tony stopped him with only a word. "Your mom will be fine, Luke, I promise."

"Dad looked awful scared."

Tony caught Olivia's arm and helped her to stand, then began steering them all toward the kitchen. "Not scared. Upset. There's a big difference. Your dad can't stand to see any of you sick or feeling bad. The fact that your mom is sick makes him feel almost as bad as she does. He wants to take care of all of you, just as your mom does. But he needs time alone with her now, so he can make certain the doctors don't flirt with her too much. He can't watch her if he's busy watching you two."

Luke didn't look as if he understood Tony's humor. "Mom is awful pretty."

"Yes, she is. And so you guys get to stay here with me."

"For how long?"

Tony stopped to stare at Luke, pretending a great affront. "Good grief, boy, you'll have Olivia thinking you don't like me."

Maggie twisted loose from Olivia's hold to say in a very firm voice, "We do so like Unca' Tony. We like him lots." And Olivia couldn't help but smile.

The chatter continued all the while Tony cooked, and with each second, Olivia became more enamored of Tony's familial commitments. The kids, despite their concern, were happy and comfortable to be with him. There was so much love in the air, she could fill her lungs with it. And Tony proved to be as adept at holding a child while cooking as any mother. Olivia wondered if he did so because he enjoyed holding the baby so much, or because he didn't want Olivia to hold him.

Unfortunately, as the day wore on, the latter proved to be true. Not once, even at the most hectic times, did Tony request her assistance with the baby. Not long after they'd finished breakfast John called to say Lisa had pneumonia and they'd be keeping her overnight. She was worn down from all the daily running she did, not to mention having given birth not that long before. And since she was staying at the hospital, John wanted to leave the kids with Tony so he could be free to stay with her.

Tony agreed, and surprisingly, once the kids were assured their mother would be fine and probably home the next day, they seemed thrilled by the idea of staying. Tony promised to bring in a tent that they could set up in front of the fireplace. Maggie asked, "Will Livvy get to sleep with us, too?"

It seemed Tony was caught speechless for a moment, then he said, "If she wants to. And it's Olivia, sweetheart, not Livvy."

"I don't mind, Tony. Actually it's a familiar nickname."

"You look kinda funny, Olivia." Luke watched her closely, and Olivia was amazed by the child's perception.

"I'm fine, Luke, honest." But hearing little Maggie call her by the same name her own mother and father had always used dredged up long forgotten feelings and left her shaken. And Tony seemed to notice. He held her hand and gave it a squeeze, then went to call his mother and sister to let them know what was going on. He hadn't wanted to tell them Lisa was sick until he knew for certain she'd be all right. Olivia gathered by the one-sided conversation that his mother offered to come and take the children, but Tony only thanked her. He said they had already made plans, and she could have them in the morning, but not before their "campout."

Finally, right after an early dinner, Luke and Maggie got bundled up from head to toe and went out back to play. Being children, they seemed impervious to the cold, but Tony insisted that it could only be for a short spell.

Even though the yard was isolated, with no other neighbors in sight, Tony still admonished both children to stay very close by. They could use the tire swing in the tree or play in the small playhouse he and John had built the preceding summer for just such visits. The infant, Shawn, lay sleeping on a blanket on the floor and Tony and Olivia were left relatively alone.

Tony dropped down beside her on the couch, then grinned. "Man, am I worn-out. Kids, in the plural, can really keep you hopping, can't they?"

She knew he had loved every single minute, that he wasn't really complaining. It had been there on his face, the way he smiled, the way he held the baby and teased Maggie and spoke to Luke.

She licked her lips nervously and slanted him a cautious look. "I would have been glad to help you out a little, you know." She said it tentatively, hoping to broach the topic without setting off any alarm bells.

But all he did was pat her thigh in a now familiar way. "You help a lot just by being here. Pneumonia. Can you imagine that? Lisa always seems so healthy. But John said the doctor told him it could bring you low in just a few hours."

"Will she have to stay in the hospital long?"

"No. She'll probably get to come home tomorrow. And Mom and Kate are already making plans to take turns helping her out until she's completely well again. John is swearing he's going to hire someone to come and clean for her from now on, but he said Lisa told him to forget it. She's funny about her house, likes to do things a certain way, you know?"

His statement didn't really require an answer, and Olivia couldn't have given him one anyway. "Your whole family really sticks together, don't they?"

He seemed surprised by her question. "Of course we do."

"I mean, even though Lisa isn't really part of your family…"

"She's married to John. She's the mother of my niece and nephews. She's part of the family."

And that was that, Olivia supposed. It would be so nice to belong to such a family. She said without thinking, "When Maggie called me Livvy… It, well, it reminded me of when I was a child. That was what my mother and father always called me. But I'd forgotten until she said it."

Tony wrapped one large hand around the back of her neck and tugged her closer. His lips touched her temple, and she could feel their movement against her skin as he spoke. "I figured it must have been something like that. I'm sorry, Olivia. You looked so damn sad."

"No. Not sad really." She tried her best to look cavalier over the subject, even so far as giving him a smile. "It's been so long, I've forgotten what it's like to miss them. I guess I'm used to being alone."

It was a horrible lie, because who could actually get accustomed to spending her life alone? There was never anyone to share the triumphs, which made them seem almost hollow, and when the struggles to get ahead occasionally became too much, she had only herself to lean on.

Tony was staring at her in his intent, probing way and Olivia had the horrible suspicion he was reading her thoughts, knowing exactly what it was she concealed, and how empty she often felt.

He looked down at her hands, which were tightly pressed together in her lap, then covered them with one of his own. "Is that why you've isolated yourself?"

"I haven't."

His gaze snapped back to her face, as if struck that she would deny such an obvious thing. "Of course you have. You keep to yourself, don't date, don't form long-standing friendships. You put everything you have into the lingerie shops. It's almost like you're afraid of getting involved."

"I am not afraid." She didn't know what else she could say. She felt defensive, as if she had to explain her choice of lifestyle, but that was impossible. She would never be able to give Tony the truth.

"It's not natural for a woman like you to still be single, to not want some kind of commitment."

Despite herself, she stiffened. "A woman like me? What exactly is that supposed to mean?"

Tony closed his eyes and made a sound of frustration. "I'm sorry. I didn't mean that the way it sounded. It's just that…I never thought of you as you are. You always seemed pleasant enough, but so businesslike and…well, detached. And here you are, a very warm, caring woman, wearing sexy lingerie that makes me go a little crazy and looking so damn sweet and vulnerable at the most surprising times."

"Tony…" She didn't like being labeled vulnerable any more than she liked feeling defensive.

"I don't understand you, Olivia, and I want to. I really do."

But why?"

He quirked a smile. "Don't sound so panicked. I promise, I'm not asking for orange blossoms and golden rings. I just… I guess I like you more than I thought I would."

"Sex has a way of making a man feel like that. Believe me, it will pass."

He reached out to wrap a lock of her hair around his finger, then gently pulled until her face was closer to his. His tone was low, his expression heated. "Honey, you don't know enough about men and sex to make that assumption." He laid his palm warmly on her thigh, gently squeezing. "And I'd say that nasty little comment deserves some form of retribution, wouldn't you?"

Olivia tried to pull away, but she couldn't get very far. She wasn't afraid of Tony, but she didn't trust the look in his eyes. He was pushing, and there was too much she could never tell him.

"I didn't mean it to sound nasty, exactly." She was beginning to feel cornered, and that made her so very nervous. Then she went on the attack, hoping to force him to back off. "Dammit, Tony, we agreed not to get personal, right? And this discussion is getting very personal. You want a baby from me, not my life history. Why don't we talk about sex instead?" Trying to be subtle, she leaned into him, allowing her breasts to brush against his chest.

He allowed her closeness, but his expression didn't change. "Since I do want a baby from you, and you don't appear to be the woman I first thought you to be, I think your family history is very relevant." He continued to maintain his gentle hold on her hair as his hand left her thigh and curved around her waist.

She drew in a sharp breath when his fingers slipped upward to tease against the outer curves of her breast. She tried to squirm, to get his hand exactly where she wanted it, but he only grinned and continued to tease.

It was enough to set off her temper, and without thinking she jerked upright again. But Tony only pulled her back, using her hair as a leash.

Olivia gritted her teeth. "I'm not going to sit and let you practice your intimidation tactics. This isn't a boardroom."

"No, and it's not the bedroom, either. So stop trying to distract me with sex—believe me, we'll get back to that as soon as possible. Just tell me a little about your folks." He was still speaking in that soft, determined tone, and she could feel his stubbornness. The man had it in buckets.

It was apparent he wasn't going to give up, so she did. She just wasn't practiced enough to play this kind of game with a man. "Never say I don't know when to restructure my plans."

"And your plans were to run the show?"

"Something like that. But it's not important now."

Tony laughed softly, then turned her head toward him so he could kiss her mouth. His quick, soft peck turned into a lingering kiss, and he gave a low curse when he finally managed to pull himself away. "You're a fast learner, but I'm afraid I'm too curious to let you get away with it. Go ahead now. Tell me about your parents."

Her sigh was long, indicating her reluctance. "They were poor, not overly educated, and they worked harder than anybody I know." Speaking of them brought a tightness to her chest that always wanted to linger. She tried clearing her throat, but the discomfort remained. "Our furniture was usually tattered, but it was always clean. My mother kept an immaculate house."

"You were close with them?"

She simply couldn't remember—and it pained her. There were too many other memories in the way of the good times. "We didn't have much daily time to do things together. Whenever possible, my mother would make me a special cake, and my dad always kissed me good-night, no matter how late he got in. But they weren't always happy, which I suppose makes sense seeing how poor we were."

She drew a deep breath, the tightness now nearly choking her, and before she knew she would say the words, they tumbled out. "My parents loved me, they really did, and they tried to do the best for me that they could, but…sometimes they made mistakes."

Easing closer, Tony twined his fingers through her hair and began massaging her scalp. His nearness touched her, made some of the hurt from the memories fade.

He leaned down and placed a kiss on the bridge of her nose. "All parents make mistakes, honey. It's a built-in factor that you can't be a perfect parent."

Olivia only nodded, since she had no idea how other parents did things. But he had questions, and she wanted to give him his answers quickly, to get the telling over with so she could forget it all again. "I was an only child and we lived on the riverbank in a tiny little nothing town called Hattsburg, Mississippi. My mother worked at the local market, my father at the one factory in town. Sometimes…sometimes he drank too much. It was the way he escaped, my mom used to say."

Tony leaned into her, giving her silent comfort. She drew a deep breath and rushed through the rest of the story. "They died on the river, using a boat that couldn't have passed safety standards on its best day, but was especially hazardous in bad weather. The river had swelled from spring rains, and the boat capsized. My father was drunk and didn't use good judgment, the deputy said. He was knocked out when he went overboard and died before they reached the hospital. My mother had tried to save him, but the water was still frigid, and she suffered exposure and multiple injuries. And grief. She died in the hospital not too many days after my father."

She drew a deep breath, knowing the unwanted feelings would crowd her if she let them. She shook her head at herself, denying the feelings, the hurt. "I don't really miss them anymore, because I can hardly remember ever having a family. You're really pretty lucky, you know."

He was silent over that, and Olivia wondered if she'd said too much, if he was again having second thoughts about allowing her around his family. But then he tipped her chin up and without a word began nibbling lightly on her lips. She exchanged one set of concerns for another. "Tony... Don't tease me anymore. I swear, I don't think I can take it and there's no way we can do anything about it now."

"No, we can't. But I just like touching you. Don't deny me that." He slipped his tongue into her mouth, holding her head steady with his hand still on the back of her neck.

"When..." She gasped as his head lifted and his hand covered her breast, then she started over. "When will we be able to try again?"

"My mother will pick the kids up in the morning. Do you have to be at work early?"

His fingers found her nipple, encouraging her to give the right answer. After a breathless moan, she said, "I can take the morning off."

"Good. I have to go in for a while in the afternoon, but I want you to go with me. There's something I want to show you."

Olivia would have questioned that, but he suddenly tunneled both hands into her hair and leaned her into the padded back of the couch, his mouth ravenous, moving over her face, her throat.

"God, I think I've been wanting you forever."

Olivia thrilled at the words. It was such a pleasant alternative, going from the distressing memories of her childhood to the newfound feelings of adult desire, her mind simply accepted the change with no lingering remorse. Then a small, outraged voice intruded, and she practically leapt off the couch.

"Sheeesh! You guys are gross."

Luke stood there, his hands on his narrow hips, his skinny legs braced wide apart and a look of total disgust on his face.

With a sigh that turned into a laugh, Tony asked, "What do you want, squirt?"

"I wanted you to come out and toss with me. Maggie can't catch nothin'."

Tony considered it a moment, but his gaze kept going to the baby. She could tell the idea of a game of catch was enticing for him, and yet he was going to refuse. Olivia rolled her eyes. "Go on, Tony. If the baby starts fussing, I'll come get you."

Cupping her cheek, Tony drifted his thumb over her lips and whispered, "I don't want to leave you alone."

Again, Luke complained. "You two are worse than Mom and Dad!"

Olivia couldn't help but laugh. "Will you go on, before Luke gets sick? He's starting to turn a funny shade of green."

That had Luke laughing and looking for a mirror so he could see for himself.

Olivia pushed at Tony's solid shoulders. "Go on. I'll be fine. I'll just watch a little television."

"You're sure?"

"I'm positive. Now go."

It was a cool November day, and Tony pulled on his down jacket before stepping out the back door. Olivia went to the window to watch. The kids laughed and tackled Tony as he tried to throw the ball, and they all three went down in a pile. Tony began tickling Luke, while at the same time he managed to toss Maggie in the air. Olivia felt something damp on her cheek, and when she went to brush it away, she realized it was a tear.

Why the sight of Tony's gorgeous, healthy body in play with two kids should make her cry, she didn't know. It wasn't as if he wouldn't eventually get the child he wanted—and obviously deserved. He'd make a remarkable father, and she envied him the opportunity to be a parent. But she wasn't actually hampering him, only slowing him down for a few weeks. And what was that when compared with a lifetime of having a child of your own?

She would have stood there watching them forever, but the baby started to fuss, and since Olivia assumed he couldn't be hungry, not after Tony had just given him a bottle before putting him down, she decided he might just want to be held.

She knew she did.

Being very careful, she lifted the baby in her arms, and

like a small turtle, he stretched his head up to look at her. She grinned at his pouting expression. It was almost as if he were disgruntled at waking to unfamiliar surroundings. She cuddled him close and patted his back and listened to his lusty little yawn.

Sitting in the large padded chair not far from where little Shawn had been sleeping, she settled them both there. It was easy to relax while inhaling his unique, sweet baby scent. And Shawn seemed to like her, resting against her in a posture of trust, with his little head against her breasts, his legs tucked up against her belly. By instinct alone, she hummed a melody she knew and gently swayed in the chair, lulling him. Before long, she was yawning as well, and thinking that if she could never have a baby of her own, at least now she'd know what it was like to hold one.

TONY CAME IN CARRYING Maggie and listening to Luke tell him all the things he wanted for Christmas. It was an impressive list, and he was thinking Luke might be just a bit spoiled, then decided he'd buy him the expensive remote-control car he wanted. Grinning, he knew John would have a fit, but it didn't matter. That's what uncles were for—to indulge their nephews.

He stopped cold when he walked into the family room and found Olivia curled up in a chair with Shawn sleeping in her arms. Immediately he hushed Luke and Maggie, not wanting Olivia to awaken. In fact, he could have stood there for hours just looking at her.

It was such a revelation, discovering her like this and having his heart suddenly acknowledge all the things it had been denying. It seemed as if all his strength had just been stripped away, leaving him raw and unsteady.

This was what he wanted.

He wanted to come in from playing with the kids—his kids—and find his woman resting with his baby in her arms. He wanted to coddle her, to love her. He wanted an entire family to look after, not just a single baby. He wanted to share all his love, and have it returned. He wanted it all.

With his heart thundering and his stomach tight, he set little Maggie down and pulled Luke close. Speaking in hushed tones, he told the children, "I want you to get the bag your dad brought and find your pajamas, then go into the bathroom and wash up."

"Carry me." Maggie reached up again, but Tony shook his head.

"Not this time, munchkin. Luke, can you help Maggie with her clothes?"

"Sure. She sometimes puts her stuff on backwards."

Maggie frowned. "I'm only a little girl, so it's okay. Mommy says so."

Tony grinned. "And your mom is right." He gave Maggie a quick squeeze. "You can leave your clothes in the bathroom and I'll pick them up in a bit. Get ready for bed and I'll get the tent set up, okay?"

Luke sidled close to get his own hug. "Can we have marshmallows and chocolate?"

"I think I have some cocoa left. We'll check when you've finished up. Put your toothbrushes in the bathroom, though, so we don't forget to brush before we go to bed."

"It's not bedtime yet."

Tony patted Luke's head, hearing the touch of anxiety there. "Nope. We still have to read a story, too. But when it is time, I promise to sleep close by you, okay?"

Trying not to look too relieved, Luke nodded. "Maggie'll like that."

"Carry me."

Again Maggie lifted her arms to Tony, and he almost gave in. Then he shook his head. "Go on, imp. Luke will give you a hand."

She didn't look happy about it, but she let Luke take her hand and lead her down the hall. Tony felt a swell of pride at what good kids they were. He hoped, when Olivia finally conceived, that he'd be half as good a parent as his brother, John, was.

That thought had his stomach roiling again, and he went back in to look at Olivia. She hadn't moved a single muscle. He'd never thought it before, but looking at her now, relaxed with a small, content smile on her face, she was a very beautiful woman. He swallowed the lump of emotion in his throat, then carefully crept toward her chair.

She was obviously exhausted, the past two days wearing on her. He knew he'd slept little, and she'd confessed to the same problem. What they were doing, what they planned, it was enough to rattle a person's thoughts.

Seeing her in sleep, though, with all her pride and stubbornness and the attitude she generally affected wiped away by total relaxation, proved to be a great insight. He'd always seen Olivia in one way, as if any woman could be one-dimensional. He should have known Olivia would be more complex than most.

Talking about her family had upset her, had left her struggling for words in a way he'd never witnessed before. Her pain had become his, and he'd found himself wanting only to distract her, to ease her. When he'd kissed her, it had been with the intent to console, but as always with

Olivia since starting this strange bit of business, one touch had left him wanting another, and for a brief moment, he'd actually forgotten Maggie and Luke outside.

It was a good thing Luke had walked in when he did, because Tony didn't want her thinking everything between them was about sex, or even about getting a baby. As she'd told him earlier, they were friends. Certainly they were closer friends now than he'd ever envisioned them being, but he liked it, and he sensed a need in her to be reassured. He planned to do just that.

Little Shawn wiggled, then snuggled into her breast, and without opening her eyes, Olivia gently patted his back and made soft *shushing* sounds. Tony reached out and laid his hand over hers, hoping to convey so much with that one small gesture.

Olivia's eyes snapped open, but she didn't move or jar the baby in any way. It took her a moment to reorient herself, then she smiled. "Hi."

That one whispered word had his chest squeezing again. "Hi."

"He wanted to be held."

Her voice, pitched low and husky from sleep, rubbed over him like a caress. "So I see."

"He sleeps a lot, doesn't he?"

"He's still considered a newborn. I suppose," he whispered, staring into her dark eyes and wanting so much to hold her, "we should get a book on babies, one that tells you what to expect so we'll be prepared when ours is born."

A look of such intense pain filled her eyes he reached for her without thinking. "What is it, Olivia? Are you okay?"

She swallowed twice, then took a deep breath. "I'm okay. It's just...Tony, will you be very disappointed if I don't conceive? I mean, what if we try the agreed two weeks, and it just doesn't happen?"

"We'll keep trying." He was positive. He didn't want any other woman to birth his child. He wanted this woman.

"I…I don't know if that's a good idea. We agreed—"

He bridged his arms around her hips and laid his head against her thighs. Her hand touched his nape, then she threaded her fingers through his hair. "Tony?"

"Shh. You're borrowing trouble. Let's just wait and see what happens." He continued to hold her like that until he heard the kids start out of the bathroom. With a sigh, he sat up. "I guess I'd better get started on that tent. Will you camp out with us tonight?"

She shook her head. "I shouldn't. I didn't bring any pajamas or my toothbrush or any—"

"I have a silly pair of Mickey Mouse pajamas Kate bought for me one year as a joke. You can use those. And I have an extra toothbrush."

"You do? Should I ask why?"

Grinning, he came to his feet. "I'd rather you didn't."

Olivia frowned at him, and he decided he liked her small show of jealousy, even if he knew she would deny suffering such an emotion.

Being careful not to wake him, he lifted Shawn and returned him to his blanket. "Come on. You can help me pitch a tent."

Her frown left, and to his relief, she joined in wholeheartedly. It took them a half hour to get the tent assembled. They shoved all the furniture back so the tent sat in the middle of the room. Olivia lit a fire in the fireplace while Tony searched through his kitchen for marshmallows and cocoa. Shawn woke up and began fussing, and though Olivia wanted to help, she was hopeless at changing a diaper. Tony laughed at her efforts, then showed her the proper way to do it. Her intent fascination through the routine process had him grinning long after the job was done.

He knew she wanted to give Shawn his bottle, but she held back, pretending a great interest in the silly, rather long-winded story Maggie was telling her about a cartoon character on her favorite preschool show. Tony watched her surreptitiously, and a plan began to form.

Maybe, because of all she'd been through as a child, Olivia only thought she didn't want a family. Maybe he could convince her otherwise. As soon as the idea hit, he felt a sick sort of trepidation. Like any man, the thought of rejection was repugnant to him. And he knew he was being overly emotional about the whole thing, but this particular situation was one to inspire romantic notions. Being alone with a woman, acting as a family to three children, left his need for his own family with a sharpened edge.

But his original plan was much more realistic, and much easier to plan around. He *knew* he could love a child, that he could be a good father. He had the example of his own father, not to mention his brother and brother-in-law to go by. But a wife...that was a chancy matter. Could he really count on Olivia to restructure her life to fit a family into her busy schedule?

He decided what he needed was more time—time to watch her with the children, to be with her. He'd take her to the office tomorrow and show her the expansion plans beginning with the new Northwestern Crown. He'd planned to do that anyway, to judge her reaction to the site for her new lingerie shop.

In the meantime...

He went over to her, not really giving her a choice, and put Shawn in her lap. She opened her dark eyes wide and stared at him, looking hopeful, and a bit unsure of herself. Then he handed her the bottle of formula, and watched as Shawn began to fuss, and Olivia looked from him to the baby and back again.

"I think he's hungry, honey. Would you mind?"

"You want me to feed him?"

"Just keep the bottle up so he doesn't suck air, and keep a napkin under his chin because he tends to make a mess of it."

Looking as if she'd just been handed the world, Olivia carefully situated bottle and baby, then managed to listen as Maggie picked up where she'd been interrupted.

His heart seemed to swell, watching Olivia struggle with the baby. And more and more, he found himself wondering if keeping only the baby wouldn't mean giving up the better half of the deal.

CHAPTER SIX

AFTER SEVERAL STORIES and whispered giggles, Maggie and Luke finally fell asleep. It was way past their usual bedtime, but it had proven very difficult to get the kids to settle down. The combination of worrying about their mother, being in different surroundings and their general excitement, had all conspired to keep them wide-awake.

Tony had arranged everyone in a row, with Luke first, then himself, then Maggie, then Olivia. He would have preferred to have her right next to him, but he didn't trust himself, and he wasn't into self-torture. Now, at nearly midnight, Tony turned his head to look at Olivia, and even in the dim interior of the tent, he could see that her eyes were open. He reached across Maggie, who was taking up more room than one little three-year-old girl should, and slid one finger down Olivia's arm. Her eyes slanted in his direction, and she smiled. "They're asleep?"

He answered in the same hushed tone. "I do believe so."

"I've never slept on the floor before."

He grinned, then tugged on the sleeve of the pajamas she wore until she gave him her hand. "A lot of new experiences today, huh?"

When she bit her lip, he suppressed a laugh and said, "I was talking about wearing Micky Mouse pajamas. And giving a baby a bottle. And camping out in the family room with a three-year-old snoring next to you."

Olivia flashed her own grin. "And here I thought you meant something entirely different."

"Are you enjoying yourself?"

Turning on her side to face him, she laced her fingers with his, and they allowed their arms to rest over Maggie. The little girl sighed in her sleep. "You know, I believe I am having fun. I'd always thought of you as a stuffy businessman, and here you are, an adventurer."

"Me, stuffy? You're the one who eats, drinks and sleeps business."

She gave him another cheeky grin. "I learned from you."

"Ah, so it's my fault you're so ruthless?" His grin belied any insult.

"I'm serious. I've always respected you very much. Everyone does. When I negotiated my first shop in your hotels, I'd already read everything I could find on you. And there was plenty. You're considered a golden boy, you know. You took a mediocre hotel chain and turned it around to one of the fastest growing, most recognizable names in the industry. You gave new meaning to the name Austin Crown."

It was unbelievable the amount of pride he felt hearing her sing his praises. Of course he'd heard it before, but it meant more coming from Olivia. And he decided he liked this, liked talking quietly in the dark, getting to know her better, letting her know him. He seldom volunteered information about himself, but now, it seemed the most natural thing in the world.

"When my father died, I knew I had to do something to distract myself. It wasn't an easy time, and he'd been a really fantastic father—the best. He'd taught me what I needed to know in the industry, but like John, he refused to neglect his family to devote the time necessary to make the business what it is today. Sometimes I wonder if he'd lived, exactly where I'd be right now."

She answered with absolute conviction. "You'd have had your own business. You're a very driven, success-oriented man. I'll bet you were an overachiever in school, too, weren't you?"

He laughed quietly, knowing she'd pegged him. "I suppose. And it's not that I regret the life I've led. But there could have been so much more." He knew she understood when she squeezed his hand.

"And there will be. Now. You'll have your own family, Tony, just wait. You've still got plenty of time to do anything you want to do. You're young and intelligent and very handsome, and—"

It disturbed him, having her talk about his life with her being no part of it. Though that had been his original plan, and could still work out to be the best solution, he instinctively balked at the thought of losing her. Interrupting her to halt the words, he teased, "Very handsome, hmm?"

"Quit fishing for compliments. You know what you look like. Why not be honest about it?"

The glow from the fireplace barely penetrated the thick canvas of the tent, leaving the outline of Olivia's body a mere shadow beneath her blanket. But her eyes, so wide and sweet, were as discernible as her slight smile. "That's one of the things I like about you, Olivia. You believe in honesty. You're outspoken and truthful to a fault. I don't have to guess at your motives."

He felt her sudden stillness, the way she seemed to withdraw emotionally. She didn't say anything, though the tension was thick, and then she was trying to pull away. "We better get some sleep. As I told you, I didn't rest much last night."

He didn't understand the way her mood had abruptly altered, but he decided he wouldn't allow her to pull completely away from him. Rather than question her when she seemed so anxious, he merely replied to her statement. Holding tight to her fingers, he whispered, "I'm sorry you're tired, but I'm glad I didn't suffer alone." She had nothing to say to that, so he added, "Good night, sweetheart. If you need anything during the night, let me know."

Pillowing her head on her arm, she closed her eyes and very deliberately shut him out.

But she didn't take her hand away. And then he heard her whisper, "Good night, Tony."

IT WAS VERY EARLY when Olivia felt a puff of moist breath against her cheek. She opened one eye and jerked in startled surprise before she recognized the faint outline of Maggie's face in the dim interior of the tent. "What is it?"

Maggie's nose touched her cheek and she realized the child was trying to see her clearly. "Livvy, I gotta pee."

"Oh." For a second, Olivia drew a blank. She glanced at Tony to see that Luke was practically lying on top of him, draped sideways over his chest. They'd put Shawn to sleep outside the tent, surrounded by the cushions off the couch so no one would accidentally get up in the night and step on him. Twice, she had heard him fuss, but both times Tony had quietly slipped from the tent to prepare the baby's bottle.

Olivia didn't want to wake him again for something so minor, but she honestly had no idea how to deal with

Maggie's request. "Do you, uh…know how to go to the potty by yourself?"

She could barely see the bobbing of Maggie's head. "But you come wif me."

"Oh." Olivia was beginning to feel like an idiot. Of course the little girl wouldn't want to go on her own. The house was dark and unfamiliar. "Okay. But let's be quiet so we don't wake anyone up."

They crawled out of the tent, and Maggie caught at the hem of the Mickey Mouse pajama top, then held her arms in the air. "Carry me."

Since Maggie wasn't really asking, but insisting, Olivia lifted her sturdy little body and groped her way down the hall. The fluorescent bathroom light was bright and made them both squint. Olivia watched Maggie struggle with her nightgown, then she asked, "Do you…um, need any help?"

Shaking her head, Maggie said, "Stay wif me."

"Right. I won't go anywhere."

Maggie grinned at her, and Olivia felt rather complimented that her company had been required for such a female outing. Hadn't she seen plenty of women visit the "ladies' room" in groups? It was practically a tradition, and Maggie had just given her a part of it. She leaned against the wall and waited, and when Maggie had finished and again said, "Carry me," Olivia didn't hesitate. In fact, she found she liked having the small warm body clinging to her, trusting her.

They entered the tent without making a sound, but no sooner had she settled Maggie than she heard Tony say, "You have all the natural instincts, Olivia."

This time, the reference to something that could never

be didn't bother her. In fact, she felt a reluctant grin and realized she felt good. Damn good. "Go to sleep, Tony."

"Yeah," Maggie said. "Go sleep, Tony." And within seconds, the tent was again filled with soft snoring.

TONY'S MOTHER SHOWED UP at eight-thirty with a bag of doughnuts and the news that Lisa was feeling much improved, except for a great deal of lingering exhaustion. The penicillin had done its magic and she was more than anxious to see her children again.

"I'm going to take them to the hospital to visit her this morning," Sue said, "and they're hopeful she can come home this afternoon, after the doctor makes his rounds and checks her over."

"Isn't that rushing it a bit?" Tony asked. They were sitting at the dining-room table while Maggie and Luke gobbled doughnuts in the kitchen. Sue held Shawn, and every so often she'd make faces at him and babble in baby talk or nibble on his ears or feet. Tony glanced at Olivia and saw she was fascinated by his mother's behavior. In his family, no one felt the least hesitation in playing with a child—and acting like a fool in the process.

"She seemed to be doing okay to me, but of course, I'm not a doctor." Sue smiled at Olivia. "You know how it is with mothers. They can't bear to be away from their kids. Why, if they try to keep her another day while she's complaining and begging to leave, she's liable to make herself sick with worry. She's afraid the kids are terrorizing Tony. Of course, she didn't know he had you here to help him."

The sound of suggestion in his mother's tone couldn't have been missed by a deaf man. Tony glanced at Olivia again, but she was only smiling. He felt…proud, dammit.

Proud of the way Olivia had greeted his mother, her natural grace and composure. Being caught in your lover's house by your lover's mother wasn't something Olivia was used to. But she'd handled the situation remarkably well.

Dressed in casual khaki slacks with a sharp pleat and a black pullover sweater, she didn't look like a woman who had spent the night on the floor. She'd been up and dressed when he opened his eyes, and that had annoyed him. Usually the idea of facing a woman in the morning was an unpleasant prospect, but with Olivia, he'd wanted to see her sleeping in his house. He'd wanted to make her coffee and awaken her with a kiss. Instead she was the one who had prepared the coffee, and all traces of peaceful rest had been washed from her big brown eyes before he'd even crawled from the tent. She was again the composed, elegant lady he'd come to know through business, and while he appreciated the picture she made, he wanted to see that softer, more accessible side of her more often.

Olivia laughed at his mother's comments, and Tony could only stare, wanting her again. Always wanting her. The woman didn't have to do more than walk toward him and he got hard.

"Tony did all the work, Sue. I'm afraid I haven't had much experience with children. But please, tell Lisa that the kids were adorable. I very much enjoyed myself."

It was at that moment Maggie appeared at Olivia's side. Her face and hands were sticky with doughnut glaze, and without missing a beat, Olivia picked up a napkin and began wiping off the worst of it. Maggie grinned and said, "Carry me, Livvy."

Olivia bent down to scoop Maggie into her lap. "And where are we going?"

"Potty."

Turning to Sue, she said, "Excuse me just a moment."

She'd done that so naturally, without any hesitation at all, Tony knew he was making progress. Toward what end, he wasn't certain, but he took great satisfaction from the progress just the same.

He didn't realize he was smiling as he watched her leave the room until his mother nudged him with her foot. "She's a natural."

He laughed. "I told her the same thing last night."

Sue made a big production of rearranging Shawn's blanket. "It's worked out nice that she was here yesterday when John came by."

"I could have managed on my own."

"You've never had all three kids overnight before."

"True. But we'd have muddled through. Actually Shawn was the easiest to look after. He still sleeps most of the day away." It was apparent his small talk hadn't distracted his mother one iota. She had that look about her that gave him pause and let him know she was set on a course.

"So…what was Olivia doing here?"

Never let it be said that his mother couldn't use subtlety when it was required. "Women have been in my house before."

"It's been a while, though. And Olivia, unless I miss my guess, isn't just another woman."

Their relationship was too complicated by far to explain to his mother. Especially since he didn't understand it himself. He decided to nip her curiosity and parental meddling in the bud, at least until he could sort out his own feelings. "Olivia is more into business than I am. She wants to get ahead, not stay at home."

"So? Plenty of women work these days and tend a family, too. And you're not exactly helpless. I think between the two of you…"

"Mom, you're way ahead of yourself. Olivia is very clear on the fact she doesn't want a husband or family. She told me that herself. She would be totally unsuitable as a wife, so stop trying to plot against me."

Sue glanced up at the doorway, then cleared her throat. Olivia stood there, her face pink with embarrassment and a stricken look in her eyes. Tony wanted to curse; he wanted to stand up and hold her close and swear he hadn't meant what he'd just said. But there was his mother to consider, and besides, he didn't know how much of what he'd said might be true.

Olivia took the problem out of his hands by forcing a smile, then retaking her seat. "I'm afraid he's right, Sue. I'm not marriage material. This is the closest I've ever come to playing house, and I'm not at all certain I was successful. Which is okay. I'm a businesswoman, with not a domestic bone in my body." She laughed, but Tony knew her laughs now, and this one wasn't genuine. "I'm not cut out for this sort of thing. But after watching Tony last night, I'm convinced he is. He should have a few children of his own."

His mother agreed, then made deliberate small talk, but the tension in the air refused to dissipate. Once again Olivia was invited for Thanksgiving dinner, but the invitation was left open. And when the children were done eating and had their teeth brushed, Sue bustled them toward the door.

Giving Tony a listen-to-your-mother look, she said, "Try to talk Olivia into coming for Thanksgiving." Then to Olivia, "It's very casual and relaxed. With all the kids, it couldn't be any other way. But now that I know the children don't bother you—"

Maggie spoke up and said, "We don't bother, Livvy. She likes us."

Olivia patted her head and smiled. "Of course I do."

So Luke added, "Then you'll come? Grandma makes lots of desserts."

That was obviously supposed to be enough inducement to tilt the scales. Tony laughed. "I'll see what I can do about persuading her, guys, okay?"

There was another round of hugs, and this time Olivia didn't look nearly so uncomfortable. And when he finally closed the door, Tony turned to her and gave his best wolfish grin. "Now, you."

"Me, what?"

"How did you get up so early today and put yourself together so well without making a sound?"

"Put myself together?"

"Yeah." He reached out to smooth his hand over her tidy hair. She'd pulled it back into a French braid that looked both casual and classic. She wore only the faintest touch of makeup—all that was needed with her dark lashes and brows and perfect complexion. "You sure don't look like a woman who camped on the floor of a tent last night."

"Oh." Olivia reached up and put her hands on his shoulders. With flat heels on, she stood just a few inches shorter than he. "I knew your mother was coming, and I thought it might be less awkward if I was up and about when she arrived."

"These are the clothes you had packed in that bag?"

"Yes. Not dressy, but suitable for just about anything."

Skimming his gaze down her body, he said, "You look

wonderful. As always." Then his attention was drawn to her breasts, and he asked with increased interest, "Are you wearing sexy underwear again?"

"No."

"No?" She surprised him. "Why not? I thought you liked wearing that stuff. I was looking forward to you making me crazy again."

She cleared her throat. "I hadn't planned to spend the night. So just as I didn't pack a toothbrush, I didn't pack additional underthings."

"You didn't… Then what are you wearing underneath?"

"Nothing."

He froze for a heartbeat, then groaned and leaned down toward her mouth. "Next time, wake me before you get up."

Again, she surprised him. She pulled away and wrapped her arms around her stomach. "I don't think there should be a next time. This…spending the night, playing with children, morning visits with your mother—they weren't part of the deal, Tony."

He wanted to touch her, but her stance clearly warned him away. When he bent to try to read her expression, she kept her head averted. "I thought you enjoyed yourself."

Waving a hand to indicate the entire morning and night before, she said, "I wasn't supposed to be enjoying—" she waved her hand again "—all that. I was supposed to be enjoying…well…"

Tony grinned. "Ah. I've neglected my end of the bargain, haven't I? And I did promise to make it up to you."

She jerked away when he reached for her, her brows lowered in a stern frown. "You did not disappoint me! I meant…"

Tony caught her despite her resistance, then gently eased

her into his body. With his lips barely touching hers, he said, "You don't even know what you're missing yet."

Again, she tried to protest, but he was done discussing issues he'd rather avoid, so he silenced her in the best way known to man.

And this time, she voiced not a single complaint.

OLIVIA MOANED AS THE sensations just kept building. Tony was poised over her, in her, and his eyes held hers, touching her as intimately as his body did.

He was right. She hadn't known what she was missing.

One large warm hand curved around her buttocks, then urged her into a rhythm. "Move with me, sweetheart. That's it." He groaned, his eyes briefly closing as he fought for control. She loved that, loved watching him struggle, loved knowing she had such an effect on him.

When he hooked his arms under her legs and lifted them high, leaving her totally open and vulnerable, she nearly panicked. He was so deep that her feelings of pleasure were mixed with fear. Tony bent to press a kiss to her lax mouth.

"Shh. It's all right." He thrust just a little harder, watching her face. "Tell me if I hurt you."

"Tony…"

"Deep, honey, the book said deep. Remember? This was your idea."

She recalled sitting in the restaurant and taunting him about methods devised to better ensure conception. But what she felt now had nothing to do with receiving his sperm and everything to do with pleasure so intense it was frightening.

She felt the pressure build, felt Tony's heat washing over her, his scent filling her lungs, and she squeezed her eyes shut as her climax hit.

"Open your eyes!"

Tony's demand barely penetrated, but she managed to get her lids to lift, and then she connected with him in a way that went beyond the activities of their bodies. His eyes were bright, his face flushed, and as she watched he groaned, his jaw tight, his gaze locked to hers, and she knew he was experiencing his own explosive orgasm. She felt it with him, and her own again, and then he lowered himself, in slow degrees, to rest completely over her.

It seemed too much to bear, the emotional side to love-making, and she wondered that other people didn't find it too overwhelming. Tears came to her eyes, her breath starting to shudder, but thankfully, Tony was unaware, as he still struggled for his own breath. When he started to move away, she tightened her hold.

He wrapped his arms more firmly around her and pressed his face beside hers. "You're something else, you know that?"

She wondered if that was true. Was it always this way, or did they do something special? It certainly seemed special to her.

"What is it, honey?" Tony lifted away and smoothed her hair from her face. He noticed a tear and kissed it from her cheek, then smiled. "I can hear you thinking."

"That's impossible."

"Nope. I really can. You're worrying about something, aren't you?"

She noticed he wasn't apologizing this time for not doing it right. In fact, he looked downright smug, so she assumed this was how it was supposed to be. But... "It gets more intense every time."

"And that worries you?"

Shrugging her bare shoulders, she looked away from his astute gaze and mumbled, "Is it supposed to be like that?"

She could hear the smile in his tone. "Between us, yes."

"But not with other people?"

"Olivia." She knew she amused him and she frowned. He smoothed his thumb over her brow, making her relax again.

"Sex is different with everyone. It's certainly never been like this for me before, but it's nothing to worry about. Some people can be very cavalier about intimacy, but you're just not that way."

"Are you?"

He hesitated, then kissed her again. "I don't know. To me, sex is natural and not something to be ashamed of. But it was never just casual, either. I had to care for a woman. I didn't indulge in one-night stands. But…it was never quite like this. Not the way it is with you."

This time, Olivia couldn't look away. "Doesn't that bother you?"

His laugh made her jump, coming so unexpectedly. "No. It probably should, but…damn, I like it."

He forestalled all her other questions by rising from the bed, then looking down at her body. Rather than feeling embarrassment, she felt proud that he took pleasure in the sight of her. Then he reached down and smacked his open palm against her hip. "Come on, woman. Duty calls. I need to go into the office."

She stretched, not really wanting to leave his bed but knowing he was right. "I have to make a few calls, also."

"Will you come to my office with me?"

"Ah, the mysterious thing you have to show me. What is it, Tony?"

"You'll see when we get there."

Olivia rose and headed for the bathroom, amazed at how quickly she was getting used to being naked in front of a man. "I'll have to meet you there. I need to go home and shower properly and change, and check in at the office. I've got to hire a new manager now, you know."

She closed the bathroom door and reached for a washrag. When she saw the reflection of her own expression in the mirror—her smile, her look of contentment—she paused. She was such a fraud, and no doubt Tony would hate her if he ever knew.

She was about to contemplate the possibility of quitting the game before she got in too deep, and then Tony tapped on the door and said, "Come on, honey. Let's get going. If I get to the office soon, I can get my business done and make it an early day. Maybe we can do dinner tonight."

Of course, dinner was not part of the deal, either, but she desperately wanted to give in to him. And she knew by the way her heart jumped at the endearment, she was already in too deep to dig herself out.

She was falling in love with Tony.

CHAPTER SEVEN

THE CLICK OF HER HEELS echoed across the faux marble foyer as she headed for the hallway leading to Tony's office. Out of all the Crowns, this was her favorite. Probably because it was in her own hometown; possibly because it was where Tony spent most of his time. This was the office he ran the business from.

She'd been here numerous times, for professional discussions, to meet associates, but never as Tony Austin's lover. Because of that, she'd dressed her best, choosing her most professional outfit. Not by look or by deed did she intend to start the scandalmongers talking. It would be difficult to deal with him in an impassive way, to pretend she hadn't lain naked with him just that morning—that he hadn't done those sinfully wicked, wonderfully arousing things to her.

That she hadn't done some of them back to him.

As she rounded the corner, she met familiar faces and nodded a polite greeting.

"Ms. Anderson," she heard from one woman, and, "How're you doing today, Ms. Anderson?" from a young man.

"Hello, Cathi, George. I'm well, thank you." She kept

her responses brief, as was her norm. Tony was correct when he said she avoided even the simplest relationships. Interacting in a social sphere wasn't easy for her. She had to work much harder at such relationships than she did when in her business mode. Understanding social etiquette was so much more complicated than working a deal.

She hadn't been here since the night of the party, and she didn't pay much attention to the remodeling at the time. But now she did. The carpeting was so soft, the colors so soothing and gracious, she couldn't help but admire them. She would have chosen something similar herself. It was just one more way they were alike, she and Tony.

She opened the glass door and walked to Martha's desk, then waited while Martha finished up a phone call.

Be businesslike, Olivia reminded herself, not wanting to take a chance on giving herself away. She was ridiculously nervous, as if she feared Martha would look at her and notice something different, see some sign of her new intimacy with Tony. Of course the woman wouldn't know; it was impossible. But already the situation was far more complicated than she'd ever thought it could be, and she couldn't help but fidget as she waited, staring around the office as if she'd never seen it before.

Finally Martha hung up the phone. "Ms. Anderson. How nice to see you again."

"Hello, Martha. I need to speak with Mr. Austin. Is he busy now?"

"He left instructions to notify him right away if you dropped in. Just let me buzz him."

Drat the man, Olivia thought. Couldn't he even remember his own deception? Tony had a long-standing rule: everyone needed an appointment to see him at the office except family and very close friends. Telling Martha such a thing, as if it didn't matter in the least if Olivia interrupted his day, was as good as announcing their sexual relationship.

And then she remembered just how often she'd dropped by to discuss some contract dispute or other, and decided it didn't matter. She had never followed Tony's rules before, not when there was something she wanted.

Of course, usually what she wanted was a better deal, not Tony himself.

The office door opened and Tony stepped out, followed closely by his brother-in-law, Brian. She'd almost forgotten that Brian worked in the family business, but seeing him now, dressed in a dark suit and carrying a briefcase, jogged her memory. Two other men exited the office as well, and they all smiled at her. Olivia felt horribly conspicuous. Each of these men managed one of the Crowns; she remembered meeting them at Tony's party the night he'd propositioned her to have his baby.

Trying to work up her best professional expression proved almost impossible, especially given the fact that Tony stood there grinning in an intimate, very telling way. Surely the other men would notice, and then their secret would be revealed.

She was wondering how to react, what exactly to say, when Brian stepped forward and took her hand. "Olivia. It's nice to see you again. I hear you spent the weekend helping Tony babysit. Kate was so pleased. She judges everyone's character by how they treat our children, you know, and she claimed right up front you were a natural."

Olivia drew an appalled blank. Why did everyone keep saying she was a natural? She was hopelessly lost around kids and she knew it. And then it hit her.

Brian had just announced to the entire office that she'd spent the weekend with Tony. She almost groaned and couldn't quite bring herself to look away from Brian and judge the reactions of the other men. Watching Brian, she had the suspicious feeling he'd just done her and Tony in on purpose.

The silence dragged on, and she forced a polite nod. "It was my pleasure," she said, and then flinched at the squeak in her voice.

Brian laughed. "There, you see? Who would consider entertaining three kids overnight a pleasure? Other than Tony, of course. He's a man meant to spawn a dozen, I swear."

Tony laughed. "A dozen? No, thank you. Three was a handful."

Olivia couldn't believe Tony just stood there, joking and laughing and letting the conversation deteriorate in such a way. Did he want everyone to know their business? What had happened to avoiding a scandal?

Brian still held her hand, and with a small tug, he regained her attention. "I keep telling Tony I get a turn now. With our two girls, he'd spend all his time playing house and attending tea parties." Brian cocked an eyebrow. "I don't suppose I can get you and Tony next weekend, can I? The girls would love it, and Kate and I could use the time alone."

Tony shook his head, still grinning, and pretended to stagger with Brian's suggestion. "Give us a month to recuperate, then we'll think about it."

A month? Olivia wouldn't even be seeing him in a

month. Two weeks, and that was it. In fact, it was less than two weeks now, since they'd already started on the count-down, as it were.

The thought left her blank-brained for a moment more, and saddened with the reminder that this wouldn't last, that it was so very temporary. When she finally gained enough wit to assess her surroundings, she saw that Tony was dismissing the other two men and saying his goodbyes to Brian. She glanced at Martha, but that busy lady was bent over her computer, typing away. Then she felt Tony's hand on her arm.

In the gentlest tone she'd ever heard from him, he said, "Come on. We'll talk in my office."

Unlike the outer office, this one had solid walls, not glass, and guaranteed privacy, and so she went willingly, needing a moment to gather herself. Tony led her to a padded leather chair and urged her into the seat, then knelt down before her.

"Are you all right?"

She wanted to say that she was fine, but she didn't feel fine. She felt downright wretched. "This is awful."

"What is?"

She gaped at him, refusing to believe he could be so obtuse. "The gossip is probably all over the hotel by now! Everyone will know."

"You're making too much of it, honey. So people will think we're dating? It's not a big deal."

"Not a big deal? You wanted to keep our association private, remember?"

"Our *relationship* is private. No one will know we're trying to conceive a child. And as far as the other, you're attractive, we work together. Why shouldn't people assume we'd share a date or two?"

Olivia bit her lip, his logic irrefutable. "I suppose you could be right."

"I know I am. And as long as my family already knows all about us, you might as well give in and come to Thanksgiving dinner. I'll never hear the end of it if you refuse."

She honestly didn't think she could survive another family get-together. "I really don't…"

Leaning close, Tony framed her face then placed a soft kiss on her lips. "I know it's hard on you, but I'll be there. And after a while, being with a big family won't bother you so much. You might even enjoy yourself. Besides, the kids are looking forward to seeing you again. And I know you enjoyed them."

"I did." Her answer emerged as a whisper. She was tempted, but also a little afraid. She was losing complete control of the situation, and that hadn't happened to her in years, not since she'd been a child. "I don't want everyone thinking we're seriously involved."

"They'll think whatever they choose whether you're there or not. At least this way, some of their curiosity will die."

"Do you really think so?"

"Sure. Right now they assume I've been trying to keep you a secret. This way, they'll think we're only dating."

Convincing her proved to be much too easy, and Olivia admitted to herself that she actually wanted to go. "I guess you're right. And when the two weeks are over and we stop seeing each other, everyone will just believe we've broken up."

Abruptly Tony came to his feet and stalked toward his

desk. He stood there with his face turned away, one hand braced on the edge of the desk and his other hand pressed deep into his pants pocket. He was the perfect study of a man in deep thought, and Olivia wished she could decipher his mood.

Without looking at her, he asked, "How did you come up with this two-week time limit?"

On shaky ground now, she took a second to weigh her answer. "It seemed a reasonable amount of time. If I was going to conceive, it would probably happen by then."

"So you thought we'd just stop seeing each other, and if and when you turned up pregnant, you'd give me a quick call to break the news to me?"

It sounded very cold, having him spell it out that way. Of course, she knew she wouldn't conceive. "You agreed with that plan, Tony."

"Yeah, well now I don't like it." He glanced over his shoulder at her, then turned away again. "I think I have a better plan."

"And that is?" The mixed feelings of excitement and trepidation settled in her stomach.

"Let's continue to work at conception until we have positive news. If it takes three weeks, or four, what's the big deal? And this way, I'll be able to monitor every second of the pregnancy. You did agree to that, remember."

At that particular moment in time, Olivia wished with all her heart that she wasn't sterile. Spending more time with Tony, allowing him to be such a huge part of her life, would be next to perfection. But since she knew that couldn't happen, she was left floundering for an answer he could accept.

None came to mind, and she stared at his broad back,

seeing the rigid set to his shoulders, until finally he asked, "Olivia?"

"There's no guarantee that it'll happen in four weeks, either, Tony. We have to have some time limit. That's only reasonable."

He turned to face her, his expression stern. "Then give me a month."

That was his corporate I'm-the-boss tone, demanding and expecting to be obeyed. She laughed because that tone had never once intimidated her. Teasing him now, she said, "You feel you can come up with sufficient potency in a month, do you?"

He grinned, too, as if her mood had lightened his own. Then his eyes narrowed. "Come here, honey. I have something to show you."

There was a determined set to his jaw, a look of challenge, and Olivia's curiosity carried her quickly to the desk. Spread out over the mahogany surface was a variety of photographs depicting a very posh hotel. "This is a new purchase?"

"Yes." Tony moved the pictures around so she could see them all clearly. "What do you think?"

Olivia studied the photos. There was an immense, elegant banquet room done in burgundy and forest green and gold. One picture showed a pool that seemed to be outdoors, surrounded as it was with foliage and trees and what appeared to be a waterfall, but in fact it was centered within a large glass enclosure. Some of the photos showed ornate chandeliers hanging from many ceilings, and everything seemed to be accented in gold.

"It's beautiful."

"The building itself is actually ancient, and we've kept

most of the historic qualities, which will be a draw on their own. But inside, it's been renovated a great deal. It'll be supported by a very upscale clientele, and it's where I thought you might relocate—if you choose—after the baby's born."

Her eyes widened and she took an automatic step back. Her stomach began to churn with a sick kind of dread. "I see."

Tony's jaw tightened and he ran a hand through his hair. "Actually the shop space is yours whether you conceive or not."

It took her only a second, and then she shook her head. "No. Our deal…"

"To hell with the deal!" He drew a deep breath and shook his head. "I'm sorry. I feel lousy about this. You see, I'd already considered offering you the space before I talked with you about the baby. But I kept it to myself because I thought it might be an incentive for you to accept my proposition. But now…well, you deserve the space. You're a good choice for the Crown. Our guests always love your shops, so I know you'll do well."

Olivia felt her head swimming. She tried to think, but it seemed impossible. This had been a horrendous morning all the way around. "I don't know. It's such a drastic move…"

"It's a move up. A large expansion for your business. The sales potential here will be incredible." He waited a heartbeat, then added, "Of course, the added shop will keep you busy. Having locations so far apart will be time-consuming, leaving little time for anything but work. But that shouldn't be a problem for you."

She glanced up at the way he said that. His gaze bore

into her, hot and intent, waiting. But she didn't know what it was he waited for. Then he insisted, "That's what you want, right?"

"I… Yes. I want to grow." Despite everything, she felt a flutter of excitement. The new hotel was exactly the kind of place she eventually wanted to occupy. *Eventually.*

But she knew why Tony was offering it to her. He wanted her to be so busy she wouldn't be able to interfere in his and the baby's life. That hurt. She lifted her chin and gave him a level look. "It's a fantastic opportunity, Tony. But I don't want to get in over my head. The Northwest is so far away…"

"Seattle, to be exact."

He was watching her closely again, his arms crossed over his chest, and she had the feeling he was assessing her in some way. "Seattle." She stepped away, walking around his office to buy herself some time. It was actually an ideal situation, because she'd need to be away from Tony. She had no doubt that once the two weeks was over—and she would somehow have to keep it at two weeks—she would have a terrible time facing him, seeing him and pretending nothing had ever happened between them. The added work would help keep her mind off Tony, off what they had shared. But Seattle!

"I hadn't really considered this in great detail. After all, I've had other things on my mind." She flashed him a quick, nervous smile, which he thankfully returned.

"You can have some time to think about it if you want."

Time. Everything always came down to more time. Or the lack of it. "Yes, thank you." The relief she felt was plainly obvious in her tone.

He put his hand to his jaw, studying her a moment, then went to his office door and turned the lock. It caught with a soft *snick*. When he started toward her again, she could see the intent in his green eyes and she backed up until her bottom hit the desk.

He stopped before her, watching her, waiting. Then, lifting his hands to her shoulders, he gently turned her away from him until she faced the desk. Slipping her purse from her shoulder and setting it on the floor, he said, "Brace your hands flat on my desk."

She obeyed him without thought, her pulse beginning to race. "Tony?"

"I said I wanted to show you two things, honey, remember?"

"I remember." The trembling in her voice should have embarrassed her, but she was too concerned with the way his hands were busy lifting her skirt to pay much attention to anything else. "Tony, I don't think…"

"Shh. There's this quaint custom called a 'nooner.' I think you'll like it."

His fingers slid along the back of her thighs, higher, until they touched the lace edging on her panties. "But, what if Martha knocks?"

"Martha went to lunch," he said, his tone now husky and deep as he squeezed and petted her bottom. "I don't have any appointments, and at the moment, I'm feeling particularly *potent*." He lightly bit her ear to punctuate that statement.

"Um. I see." His palm slid around to her belly, then dipped into her panties, and she automatically parted her legs. "We can't very well waste your potency, now can we?"

He chuckled, his open mouth pressed to the back of her

neck, warm and damp and hungry. And with her heart rapping sharply against her ribs and the sound of his zipper hissing in the quiet of the room, she decided every quaint custom should get its due. And right now, she liked this one very much.

THANKSGIVING DAY ROLLED around quickly, but Olivia no longer felt any apprehension at joining Tony's family. Over the past two weeks, she'd come to know them all very well. They'd somehow managed to run into her repeatedly, one or the other of them having shown up at her shop whenever she was there ordering, or interviewing new managers for the new location.

It had started with his sister, Kate, who dropped in with the supposed intention of buying lingerie. She did leave with a couple of purchases, but most of her time there was spent chatting with Olivia, getting to know her better and sharing little details of her life.

Kate came again later that week with Lisa, and laughed as she described Brian's reaction to the lingerie Kate had bought.

"I guess I must have let things get a little stale, because when he saw me in that satin teddy with all the cleavage, he nearly fell off the bed."

Lisa joined in the laughter and ordered herself the same teddy in a different color, but Olivia blushed to have such an intimate scene discussed in her presence. In fact, she was blushing most of the time that Lisa and Kate stayed to visit, trying on numerous things and including her in all their "girl talk," as they called it. They didn't pry, didn't ask her anything personal about Tony, but they certainly talked about him.

If there was anything she'd wanted to know, they had the answer, and seemed to relish telling her.

"Tony's played patriarch since our father's death," Kate said, her voice becoming a little more solemn. "He's set himself up in a difficult role, and I for one think he deserves a little fun."

Olivia wondered if she fell under the heading of "fun." Kate and Lisa seemed to think so, given the way they included her.

"It hurt Tony even more than it did the rest of us," Kate continued. "He was the oldest and, even though Dad was always fair, there was a special bond between the two of them. John never had any real interest in the hotels, at least not to the extent Tony did, so it just happened that Tony and Dad spent more time together."

"When he died," Lisa added, "John was so concerned for Tony. But Tony being Tony, he hid whatever grief he felt and dived headfirst into turning the business around. I think he did it as much to keep himself busy as to watch the company grow."

"And he almost cut women out completely. Before that, he'd seemed determined to find a wife. He wanted to be married like the rest of us, and he gave different women a fair chance, though even I'll admit he really hooked up with some impossible choices. Tony is such an idiomatic man, arrogant, but kind. And always in charge. It would take a strong woman to satisfy him."

Lisa laughed, then nudged Kate in the shoulder. "He used to claim he was looking for the perfect woman."

Kate grinned. "And we'd tell him we were already taken."

All three women laughed, and Olivia began to feel some

sort of kinship with them. Without thinking, she said, "Well, unfortunately, I'm as far from perfect as he could possibly get."

Kate shook her head. "The idea of perfection exists only in the perspective of the person who's looking—and what that person is looking for. Besides, love has a way of finding perfection in the most unlikely places."

"And anyway," Lisa said, choosing another pair of "barely there" panties, "you and Tony are having fun, he's dating again and the kids all love you. For right now, that's more than enough, don't you think?"

Olivia avoided the context of the question, and said only, "I'm glad the kids approve of me."

"They adore you," Kate insisted. "And the way those kids worship their uncle Tony, that's a big requirement for any relationship he might have."

Of course, Olivia hadn't told them that her relationship with Tony had a set purpose and a time limit. He'd said to take it one day at a time, and she was doing just that, enjoying herself and storing away the memories so she would never be truly alone again. But her two weeks were rapidly coming to an end, and it wouldn't be fair of her to continue in the deception.

A FEW DAYS LATER at a different Sugar and Spice location, she was going over some backstock with one of her managers when Brian and John showed up. They looked around the shop with undiluted interest. John appeared to be enthralled, but Brian, unbelievably, had a dark flush to his lean cheeks. Olivia hid her smile.

"So," John called out, striding toward her with his cocky

walk and self-assured grin. "There's the lady who's managed to single-handedly put a honeymoon into the daily workweek."

Olivia felt her own cheeks heat, and slanted a look at Brian. But he had paused by a rack of a sheer lace camisoles and seemed to be engrossed in examining them.

"Hello, John."

He pulled her close and gave her a big kiss on the cheek. "I do love this place of yours, Livvy, I really do."

He'd affected Maggie's pet name for her, as had all the children. She felt flustered by such an effusive welcome, and tried to gather herself. "I'm glad you approve. Do you have business in the hotel today?"

"Nope. Brian and I are Christmas shopping. Since the ladies have been hanging out here so much, we figured you'd know which things they've shown an interest in."

"Well, yes." There were several items the women had liked, but had hesitated to purchase because they were a bit pricey. She hesitated herself, uncertain of how much they wanted to spend.

Brian took care of that worry for her. "Whatever she wants, I'll buy it."

John laughed at that firm statement. "Poor Brian. Kate has really got you tied up now, doesn't she?"

"You don't see me complaining, do you?"

John gave a mock frown. "I don't know if I like hearing this about my little sister."

"Your sister's not so little anymore, and whatever tendencies ran through the Austin men, she inherited her fair share."

John cast Olivia a look. "Now, Brian, you'll go and spook Livvy if you say things like that."

Olivia had no idea what they were talking about, but she was beginning to get used to the way the men razzed each other. She shrugged and said, "Not at all."

"There, you see? Anyone who knows Tony at all already knows he's a driven man. Just stands to reason that drive would cover every part of his life."

Understanding hit her, and she tightened her lips to hide her smile. Yes, Tony was a "driven" man, always excelling at whatever he did—including lovemaking. She certainly had no complaints there.

Feeling a little risqué herself, she asked, "So it's a family trait, is it?"

John laughed. "Indeed it is. So you see, you with your nifty little shops fit right in. And like all the Austins, Tony goes after what he wants—and doesn't give up until he gets it." She didn't have time to reply to that since he quickly rubbed his hands together and asked, "Now. What does Lisa want? I can hardly wait."

Brian snorted. "Are you sure this shouldn't be *your* Christmas gift?"

Both men paused as if they'd just had the same thought, then reached out to shake hands. "I'll pick what I want, and you pick what you want. At least this year, you won't give me an ugly tie."

"That was a silk tie, you idiot, and very expensive."

"It didn't match anything I own."

The men continued to argue as they each chose what the other would give them for a holiday gift. John picked out a satin Victorian-style corset, then grinned. "I'm going to be a very happy boy on Christmas morning."

Brian held up the gift John would give to him, a snow-white, stretch-lace teddy with attached garters. "Me, too."

The men were so outrageous that Olivia ended up laughing with them and feeling entirely at her ease. Before their shopping spree was over, they'd purchased numerous gifts for their wives, several for themselves, and instructed Olivia to point their wives in the direction of the more risqué items if they mentioned wondering what to get for their husbands. Olivia promised to do just that.

Her manager and the additional clerk had their hands full gift wrapping all the purchases.

They were such an open, loving family, the men so dedicated to their wives, all of them functioning with such unity. And they kept including her. Despite her intentions to stay detached, she found herself feeling a part of things, and actually looking forward to visiting with them again.

This would be the first Thanksgiving she hadn't spent alone since her parents had died, and she was suffering a mix of melancholy and excitement.

TONY ARRIVED RIGHT AT three to collect her. She'd dressed up a little more than usual, wanting to make the most of the day, and when she let him in, he gave a low whistle. "Honey, you'd make the perfect dessert tonight."

With his gaze ranging over her body, she knew the dress had been worth the extra expense. Made of soft black cashmere, it fit her body perfectly, the off-the-shoulder design making it just a bit daring. The hem ended a good two inches above her knees, and she wore heels, which put her on eye level with Tony.

He caught her hand and pulled her close, then bent to press a kiss to her collarbone. "Tony…"

He lifted one hand and palmed her breast, but paused when she sucked in a deep breath. "Did I hurt you?"

She shook her head, unable to catch her breath with him gently kneading her. She felt especially sensitive tonight, her breasts almost painfully tight.

"Your nipples are already hard and I've barely touched you." Tony groaned softly. "What I wouldn't give for an extra hour right now." Reluctantly he released her.

When she turned away to get her coat, he cursed, then mumbled, "If we weren't expected…"

"But we are." She grinned, though she felt every bit as urgent as he did. Even if she had a lifetime, rather than just a few more days, she'd never get enough of having him want her. She shook herself, refusing to think of the self-appointed time limit now. She didn't want anything to spoil this day.

A light snow had started that morning and now, as they stepped outside, Olivia saw that everything was coated in pristine white. The naked tree branches shimmered with it, and it clung to everything, including Tony's dark hair. After he opened the car door for her, she reached up and brushed his cheeks, her fingertips lingering.

"Olivia." Tony leaned down and gave her a melting kiss that should have thawed the snow. He lifted his head, searched her face, then bent to her mouth again. Olivia forgot the weather, forgot that they might be late, and wondered if they could go back inside again. Then they heard a tapping sound, like knuckles rapping on glass, and they looked up.

At the front door to the apartment building, her neighbors stood watching, huge grins on their faces. When Olivia laughed, they all waved.

"Like Snow White, they're seeing you off with the prince?"

"Hmm. You consider yourself a prince, do you?"

Tony waited for her to get in, then went around to the driver's side. After he'd started the car, he turned to her. "I only meant they're awfully protective of you."

Olivia had to agree on that. "And it's so strange, considering that I've kept to myself. I'm friendly, and I don't go out of my way to avoid them, but neither have I ever sought them out."

"You don't have to. There's just something about you, a genuine feeling, that makes people trust you. And today, with the world what it is, trust is everything."

She looked away. "It's sometimes foolish to trust anyone."

"I trust you."

Oh, why did he have to do this now? "Tony, don't. I don't want to talk about important issues or discuss anything heavy. I just…I want to have fun today."

Glancing at her, he reached for her hand. "And you have fun with my family?"

"I really do. They're all crazy and happy and so accepting, it's impossible not to have fun around them."

She could tell he wanted to say more, but he held his peace. "Okay. But tomorrow we have to talk."

Not really wanting to, but seeing no way around it, she nodded. They would have to talk. Time was running out, and Tony deserved to be set free.

They spent the rest of the drive in silence, holding hands and watching the snow fall.

When they reached his mother's place, Tony walked her to the front door, his arm around her shoulders. The house was decorated with bright Christmas lights, and a hearty wreath hung on the door. Tony tipped up her chin and kissed her. "Smile, sweetheart. Today is just for eating and visiting and, later, making love. Agreed?"

"Of course." She laughed as he pretended to be surprised by her quick agreement.

"Have I spoiled you, Olivia?"

"Shamefully."

"So you'd planned on seducing me later?"

"I had every intention of doing so, yes."

His hand slipped under her coat and lightly caressed her waist. "Does this mean you're wearing something sexy and scandalous and guaranteed to drive me nuts under this dress?"

With wide-eyed innocence, she said, "Of course not."

He frowned, and just as the door started to open, she whispered, "I'm not wearing anything at all."

CHAPTER EIGHT

OLIVIA FELT THE FIRST cramps right after dinner, but she ignored them. She was used to such pain, knew it was only her body reminding her that she wasn't what a woman should be. Since she'd had her first period when she was eleven, she'd suffered the cramps. Not normal period cramps, because there was nothing normal about her body's functions.

Sometimes the pains were pretty bad, other times only annoying, but she always managed to function despite their existence, ignoring them until they went away. Except when she'd been a child, and that was when her parents had taken her to the hospital.

She couldn't remember what actual medical term had been given to her condition, but it had to do with her ovaries and the fact they didn't function properly. She'd had surgery to remove a horribly painful mass, and lost one of her ovaries in the process. Since then she was so irregular, she sometimes went several months without menstruating.

Her mother had explained that she likely wouldn't have any children, and Olivia understood why. You couldn't very well conceive with only one ovary, especially if you didn't ovulate. She wasn't totally ignorant about her bodily functions.

There were times when she would have gone to the doctor, just to make certain her pain was normal, for her. But being examined by a man when she was still so innocent and shy had made her dread the thought of even a routine visit.

Now, as John made a jest and everyone laughed, Olivia was about to smile when she felt another cramp and winced instead. Tony leaned toward her. "Are you all right?"

He'd kept his voice low, thankfully. She didn't want to disrupt everyone's good time. "I'm fine. I think I just ate a little too much."

He grinned. "Me, too. I had one too many desserts." He leaned closer still, his lips touching her ear. "You'll have to help me work off some calories later. Got any ideas?"

At the moment, all she wanted was a pain pill. She patted his arm and got up from the table. "I'll think on it. Excuse me, please." Picking up her purse, she was aware of Tony's frowning gaze following her.

When she reached the powder room, she fished out two over-the-counter pain tablets and swallowed them, then leaned against the sink. The pain was a little more acute this time than it normally was. She wondered if the fact that she'd become sexually active had any bearing on it.

She waited a few minutes more, then left the room, only to find Tony standing there waiting for her. He searched her face with his gaze. "What is it, Olivia? What's wrong?"

What was one more lie? She tried surreptitiously to hug her stomach. "I'm feeling a little under the weather, Tony. Maybe I'm catching a cold."

Reaching out, he felt her forehead and then nodded. "You feel a little warm. Why don't we go ahead and leave?"

"No." She didn't want this day to end, not when there were so few days left. "I'm all right."

"You don't look all right, honey. You look like you're in pain."

"It's nothing, I promise."

She sounded a touch too desperate, which made Tony study her a little more thoroughly. "All right. But I want you to sit down and take it easy."

"The women are all helping to clean up the kitchen."

"No, they're not. The men have decided to do it. Now go rest somewhere, okay? And promise me, if you start to feel any worse, you'll let me know."

"I will," she lied, determined to stay for the duration of the family get-together.

But an hour later, the cramps were getting to be too much to ignore, and she couldn't put off leaving any longer. She glanced at Tony and he immediately stood, as if he'd only been waiting for a signal from her. It amazed her that he seemed to read her so easily, that he knew her thoughts and her feelings.

He did a wonderful job of excusing their early departure. Olivia knew, judging by the grin on John's face and the wink Kate sent to her, that everyone thought they were leaving so they could be alone.

When they got into his car, Olivia found that Tony had a similar idea. "I'll take you to my house. I can look after you if you *are* getting sick."

Appalled by such an idea, Olivia shook her head and tried to think of a viable reason to refuse his generous offer. Tending her when she was sick had never been part of the deal. "I'd rather go home, Tony. I'll be more comfortable there."

He glanced at her, then nodded. "All right. I'll grab a few things from my house and stay with you."

Until now she'd managed to avoid having him spend the night or any length of time in her apartment. Generally she met him at the door, and within minutes they would leave. She wanted her home to feel the same once their time together was over, and she knew that would be impossible if he slept in her bed or ate in her kitchen or showered in her bathroom. She would be reminded of him everywhere she looked, and she couldn't let that happen.

She reached over and touched his arm. "Tony, I'm sorry. I really am. But I'd rather be alone. Whenever I've been sick—"

"But you're never sick! You haven't missed a day of work in years."

True. But the cramps had never been this bad before. She bit her lip and looked out her side window. "I'll be more comfortable by myself."

There was an awful silence and she knew she'd hurt him when that had never been her intent. She felt choked by remorse, but there was no way out, no way to make up for all she'd done, all the lies she'd told.

Finally Tony said very quietly, "I'll take you home. But I want your promise you'll call me if you need anything."

"Of course."

They both knew she was lying.

OLIVIA FINALLY ACCEPTED that something was seriously wrong. The pain had nagged her off and on since she'd come home, and she'd started to bleed. Not heavily, but still, it was an unusual occurrence with her periods so horribly irregular. Then suddenly, at midnight, the pain seemed to explode. She didn't think she could drive herself to the hospital, but as much as she hated to admit it, she needed to go.

This pain no longer seemed familiar; it was nothing like what she was used to dealing with, so sharp she could barely breathe. She had a vague recollection of similar pain when she'd been a child, but it was too hard, feeling as she did, to remember if the two situations were at all the same.

She couldn't disrupt Tony, not after he'd called to check on her and she'd more or less told him not to bother. She'd been curt, as much from the pain as from the struggle to keep from giving in and telling him she needed him. She'd used him enough as it was, and now she didn't know who to turn to.

When she decided she couldn't wait a moment longer, she pulled a coat on over her pajamas. Bent over, holding her middle, she went into the hallway and knocked on Hilda's door. As usual, one knock had every door on that floor opening, and soon all her neighbors were there, fussing over her, fretting. Very quickly, Hilda reappeared fully clothed, car keys in her hand.

Held between Hilda and kindly old Leroy, Olivia made her way outside. Hilda spoke to those who followed. "I'll call and let everyone know when we've made it to the hospital. If I don't call within a half hour, send a car after us. That snow is really starting to pile up."

Olivia curled into the backseat, and then felt the tears start. It wasn't the pain, but the simple truth that she had good friends and hadn't realized it. Even while avoiding relationships, she'd still managed to form a few. She was only lying to herself when she claimed to be all alone. She was so touched by the sudden revelation, she couldn't halt the tears.

"It's all right, Olivia. Don't worry. I'll have you there in no time." The woman drove like a snail, but Olivia knew Hilda hated the snow. "When we get there, do you want me to call that boyfriend of yours?"

Olivia smiled, hearing Tony referred to as a boyfriend. There was nothing boyish about him, and he was now so much more than a friend. "No. Don't bother him, Hilda. I'll call him myself, later."

"He'd want to be with you, you know."

And then he'd find out what a fraud she was. "No. Please. I don't want to worry him."

Hilda didn't answer.

When they arrived at the hospital, Hilda ran inside, demanding attention, as Olivia struggled to get out of the car. Before she'd even set both feet on the ground, two nurses were there, assisting her into a wheelchair and rushing her in. The questions flew at her, one right after the other, but she was in so much pain she could barely answer. After that, she lost track of events as they ran an endless series of tests.

When a doctor came in and asked her if she might possibly be pregnant, she told him no and briefly explained what she knew of her own medical history. He wrote notes, smiled at her, then went about ordering a pregnancy test. Olivia balked at the idea. She wasn't up to creeping into the bathroom and utilizing their little plastic cups, especially for something that seemed totally unnecessary. But she was too sick to argue. She did as the doctor asked, then crawled back onto the narrow metal bed.

A few minutes later, the doctor leaned against the side rail and gave her a wry look. "Well, Ms. Anderson, it seems you are indeed pregnant."

Olivia stared. "That's impossible."

"I assure you, it isn't." He smiled benignly and went on. "I'd like to do an ultrasound. It will tell us exactly what's going on, why you're having so much pain and bleeding."

Olivia felt numb. Pregnant? She couldn't be pregnant. "But I only have one ovary."

"One is all it takes. Granted, your chances were decreased, but still—it happens."

"But I almost never have periods!"

He patted her hand and stood. "Let's do the ultrasound and then go from there, okay? Try not to worry."

Worry? She was too dumbfounded to worry. And then it hit her and she almost shouted with pleasure. She was pregnant! She would have her own baby, Tony's baby. The pain seemed to lessen with the knowledge, but it was still a reminder that all was not well, and she began praying, wanting this baby so badly she would have promised anything to hold on to it.

It was quite a while before the doctor was standing beside her again. He was a nice enough man, she thought, surprised that she actually felt comfortable with him. In fact, she was anxious to speak with him, to hear how her baby was faring.

He spoke in specific terms for her, making the situation very clear. She wasn't far enough along for the ultrasound to show the baby, but the test confirmed that she had a large cyst on her one remaining ovary—and it had ruptured.

She immediately began to panic, remembering what had happened when she was so young, remembering the surgery, losing an ovary… The doctor pulled up a chair and took her hand.

"Your ovary did rupture, and until your placenta is large enough and produces enough progesterone to maintain the pregnancy, I'll need to give you progesterone and hope it works. Things could still go wrong, and you could lose the baby, but there's no reason to start borrowing trouble yet."

Olivia had never considered herself a weak person. She drew on her strength now, mustering her courage. "I don't need to borrow trouble. It seems I have enough as it is."

"I gather you want to keep the baby."

"Oh, very much! I just never dreamed..."

"When did you lose your other ovary?"

"I was twelve. Not long after I'd started my period. I understood I wouldn't be able to get pregnant. And since my cycle seemed so haywire..."

"It was a common misconception years ago that a woman couldn't conceive with only one ovary, but as you see it is definitely possible." He grinned at her, and she grinned back.

"Yes." Hugging her arms around herself, she asked, "What now?"

"I'd like to keep you here until we can run a few more tests, rule out the possibility of a tubal pregnancy, make certain everything is as it should be. Also, I'd like you to come back a couple of times for blood tests. We'll check the hormone level, which should double in two days if everything is okay. We'll run the test again, just to make sure everything checks out."

He wrote a few notes on her chart, then asked, "Do you have an obstetrician in mind?"

"No." She was in a daze, answering questions she'd never imagined hearing.

"I can recommend someone if you'd like. You should see him right away, then set up frequent appointments until you get past the first three months."

"And after the first three months?"

"Well, then, the risk is greatly reduced."

Olivia hung on to that thought long after the doctor had left. He'd given her codeine for the pain, and it was tolerable now, but she couldn't rest. Her hand remained on her belly, and she couldn't seem to stop crying.

With a little luck and a lot of care, she was going to have a baby.

And there was no way she'd ever give her baby up to anyone—not even Tony.

Olivia worried that thought over and over in her mind, but it always came down to the same thing. She'd have to tell Tony the truth now. She wouldn't keep the baby from him, but neither would she give it up. He had a right to know. She knew he would be a wonderful father, even if he didn't have the situation he wanted, even if he was enraged by her deception.

For one brief, insane moment, she wondered whether Tony would go so far as to offer to marry her, just to get the baby. It was possible, but she wouldn't let that happen. She wasn't the average woman with the average pregnancy. She was more like a miracle. What would it do to Tony if he married her and she lost the baby? Just the thought had her squeezing her abdomen in a protective embrace; still, it was a very real possibility.

No. Tony needed to find a healthy woman who could give him as many children as he wanted, not just a miracle baby with risks. She'd confess to him, and she would set him free.

It turned out to be the longest night of her life—and the most joyous. A baby, she just couldn't believe she was having a baby.

OLIVIA ARRIVED HOME the next afternoon to a ringing phone. She was feeling much better, more like herself, and she rushed to answer before the caller hung up.

Breathless, weak from her painful ordeal and a sleepless night, she gasped out, "Hello?"

"Where the hell have you been?"

Oh my. She straightened, staring at the receiver in her hand. Tony was in quite a temper. Olivia bit her lip and tried to think of what to say to him.

"Olivia?" There was an edge of near panic to his tone. "Dammit, I'm sorry." He gave a long sigh and she could hear his frustration, could almost see him running his hand through his dark hair. "I was worried, honey. Where were you?"

"I, uh, I had to go out for a little while."

"I've been calling since early this morning. I wanted to make certain you were feeling all right."

That left her blank. She thought they'd agreed he wouldn't call to check on her. "I'm feeling much better. Tony? Are you busy right now?"

"I'm at the office. Why? Do you need something? You *are* still sick, aren't you?"

He sounded so anxious, she rushed to reassure him. "No, I just…" Her voice dropped as she was overcome with dread, but it was better to get it over with. "We need to talk."

Silence greeted her, and she bit her lip. "Tony?"

"This sounds like a heavy-duty brush-off, Olivia. Is it?"

How could she answer that? How could she possibly explain? She heard him curse, then curse again. "I'll come on over now."

"What?" She didn't want him in her apartment; she wasn't ready to face him. Her night in the hospital had left her looking wan and feeling lifeless. She'd planned to shower and clean up and meet him somewhere. "Why don't we just do lunch?"

"To hell with that. If we need to talk, we'll talk now. Whatever it is you've got planned, I'd rather get it over with. I'll be there in half an hour." He hung up and Olivia sank back onto the couch.

Half an hour to prepare herself. It wasn't much time, but then, from the moment Tony had propositioned her, there hadn't been enough time. She didn't know if a lifetime would be enough.

TONY RAPPED SHARPLY on the door, feeling his frustration ready to explode. The other doors opened, but this time he didn't even look to see who was watching him. He'd almost gotten used to her nosy neighbors who appeared each and every time he came to pick her up. But he was in no mood to be polite right now.

He slammed his fist on the door. "Open up, Olivia."

It didn't matter to him that his behavior was somewhat juvenile. She was dumping him, he was sure of it. *Damn her.* How could she make a decision like this, when he hadn't even made up his own mind about things? He'd thought they were getting closer, thought they might have been able to work through all the difficulties. He'd considered the possibility of offering her a compromise....

But no. She was done giving him time... He raised his hand to bang on the door again, just as it swung in. There stood Olivia.

He opened his mouth, but in the next instant whatever acerbic comment he might have made was forgotten. She looked awful—pale and drawn and tired. Concern immediately replaced all his other emotions. He pushed his way in, forcing her back, closing the door on the curious gazes of her neighbors.

"Olivia?" He caught her shoulders in his hands. "Are you all right, honey?"

"I'm fine." She tried to inch away from him, and he felt his anger renewed. He knew he had to get control of himself. He'd never been concerned with that before. He rarely lost his temper, and never with a woman. He'd never had a relationship with a woman outside the family that had warranted that much emotion. With Olivia, though, he was off balance, bombarded with unique feelings and apprehensions.

He bent to meet her at eye level. "Tell me what's wrong."

She twined her fingers together. "This is very difficult for me. I'm still in shock myself. But... I wanted you to know as soon as possible."

This didn't sound like a rehearsed brush-off. He dropped his hands, but when she staggered slightly, he caught her arm and led her to her couch. "Here, sit down."

She did, and he sat right next to her. "Now just tell me whatever it is. Are you sick?"

"I... I was. Last night." He started to question her, but she said quickly, "And I'm okay now. I promise. It's just that..." Her eyes were huge and dark and filled with uncertainty. Then a small smile flitted over her lips, and she covered her mouth with one trembling hand and whispered, "I'm pregnant."

Tony blinked. Of all the things he'd expected, all the horrible words he imagined... Elation welled, burst. He gave a shout, watching as Olivia blinked back tears, then pulled her close for a hug, rocking her and trying to contain himself. "Don't cry, sweetheart, it'll be all right. I promise."

She was afraid, he understood that now. And he didn't

blame her. It was a scary thing to have a baby, but especially so for her, a woman who until recently had never had any dealings with children at all.

Though she was nearly as tall as he, and, as he'd pointed out to her in one of his less auspicious moments, very sturdy, she felt small and frail. He cradled her close, and then she started to cry in earnest. Could it be she didn't want their time to end? He tipped her chin up and watched as she hiccuped, then wiped her eyes with her fist.

He knew there was a ridiculously tender smile on his face, but he couldn't help himself. She was so sweet, so vulnerable. And then she said in a surprisingly steady tone, "You can't have it."

He tilted his head. "What?"

"You can't have my baby."

He searched her face as realization dawned. She couldn't possibly mean what it had sounded like. "We can discuss—"

"No." She came to her feet, one hand braced on the arm of the couch as if to steady herself. "I have to explain something to you, Tony. When I agreed to your plan, it was because I believed I couldn't have children. When I was very young, I lost an ovary due to a condition called PCO, polycystic ovaries. My periods have never been normal, or even close to regular, and so I didn't think I could conceive. I believed I could make love with you without any risk of pregnancy, otherwise I never would have agreed to give you the baby."

He was frozen with shock, what she was saying too unbelievable to accept. "Then why…?"

She laughed harshly, and again covered her mouth. "Look at yourself. You're a very desirable man. You'd never shown any interest in me before, and most of my reasoning was true. I wanted to know what lovemaking was all about, with a man I admired and could trust."

"You lied to me?"

She choked on a sob. "Yes."

Slowly, feeling as if his body wouldn't function properly, Tony came to his feet. She hadn't dressed today as she normally did. Today she was wearing a long casual caftan, and her feet were bare; her hair was brushed but unstyled. Every time he thought he'd figured her out, she changed.

And this change was killing him.

"You used me for sex."

Wrapping her arms around her middle, she nodded. "I'm so sorry."

"Sorry?" His voice had risen to a shout, and she flinched. It hit him then: she was pregnant. With his baby. He didn't want to upset her, not knowing what it might do to the baby, and he fought hard to regain some calm. "This is why you kept telling me you might not conceive."

"Yes."

"And why you insisted on the two-week time period."

Again, she said only, "Yes."

"But everything backfired on you. Because you are pregnant?"

"I am. It's definite." Her lips trembled when she drew in a deep breath. "I wouldn't have realized it on my own for some time yet, but then I got…sick, and the doctor did a test, an accurate test, and now I know I'm going to have a baby."

His jaw tightened. "Must have been one hell of a shock for you."

Instinctively she placed her hand on her belly. "It was."

And there was that small smile again, as if she was glad, but trying desperately to keep her happiness to herself.

"So," he asked, not really wanting to, but having to know, "how do I fit into all this? It is my baby, too."

She turned away and walked to an end table, straightening a lamp shade, flicking at a speck of dust. He looked around and realized he hated her apartment. It was so like the business persona she presented to the world—detached, immaculate, no softness or giving anywhere. The place could have been empty and not seemed any less cold.

"I want you to take part in everything, if you want to."

Barking a rough laugh, he caught her shoulder and turned her back to face him. "If I *want* to?" Her eyes opened wide and he almost shook her. "I was the one who *wanted* the baby, not you! You had the grand five-year-plan, remember?"

Hands curled into fists, she jerked away. "Only because I didn't think I could have a baby! But I can, and I want this one."

"What about work? How are you going to raise a baby by yourself?" He knew he was being unfair, asking her questions she couldn't possibly have found the answers to yet, but at the moment, it didn't matter. He wanted to hurt her just as she'd hurt him.

And judging by the stricken look on her face, he had.

He tilted his head back and closed his eyes, silently counting to ten. Then he faced her. "Olivia, be reasonable. Do you have any idea how difficult it is to be a single parent?"

"I suppose I'll find out, won't I?"

He almost laughed, she looked so much like herself, digging in, ready to do battle. He rubbed his chin and studied her. "I could take you to court, you know? I can provide for the baby in a way you never could. I can give him things, my time and attention…"

"What if it's a girl?"

"You don't remember me telling you it wouldn't matter? I thought I was clear on that."

Abruptly she dropped back onto the couch, her face in her hands. "Don't do this, Tony. Don't make things more difficult for me. Please!"

His chest hurt, seeing her look so defeated. All her bravado had just vanished in a heartbeat. He sat beside her and awkwardly tried to find the right words. "I *will* be a part of the baby's life, Olivia."

She jerked around to face him, her expression anxious and fierce. "Of course you will be! I wouldn't keep you from him. Or her, or…" She paused, and then grinned past her tears. "Oh, Tony, I'm having a baby!"

She was crying and laughing, and he couldn't help but hug her to him. She started babbling, her words almost indistinguishable mingled as they were with her sobs.

Keeping her face close to his chest, she said, "I never, ever thought this was possible. And I swear, I'll be a good mother. I didn't mean for this to happen, and I know it wasn't what you wanted. It wasn't even what I wanted. But I won't tie you down. I promise. You can see the baby whenever you want, be as close to it as you want. Your life doesn't have to change, just because I want to remain the baby's mother. I'll figure out some way to keep my business going and take care of the baby, too. And you'll be the father, so you can—"

"Watch the baby for you while you go on about your business?" They had agreed the baby would be his, but now she planned to keep the baby, and use him again to make it easier on herself? He leaned back, holding her away from him.

She swallowed in the face of his renewed anger. "That wasn't what I was going to say."

"No? But you're seeing yourself with only half a problem, right? After all, I can support you both while you go about your plans to expand the business. And whenever the baby is inconvenient, I'll be a built-in babysitter. How could I ever refuse, when I'd wanted this child so much?"

She seemed to go perfectly still, not breathing, not moving so much as an eyelash. Then a placid, business smile came to her mouth, and he didn't like it, didn't like the way she'd pulled herself together and back into that protective shell of hers. It was the way she always looked during a business meeting, the look that had led him to believe she had no sensitivities, no vulnerabilities. He knew now that it was a sham.

Her back was very straight, her chin lifted when she said, "You thought I'd start using you that way? Not at all. I need nothing from you. I've never needed anything from anyone. The baby and I will be just fine."

"Olivia…"

"I think you should go now."

"We're not through talking."

"Yes, we are. I've told you all I have to tell you. Whether or not you choose to take part in the baby's life is up to you now."

He glared at her, his jaw so tight it ached. "You know damn good and well I want this baby."

"Fine." She stood, managing to look somehow regal and serene despite her obvious fatigue and whatever illness had plagued her. "When he or she is born, I'll let you know."

Then she went to the door and opened it, waiting for him to leave.

And he did, only because he was so angry, he was afraid he'd upset her again if he stayed, and he couldn't believe that would be good for the baby. Feeling numb and sick to his stomach, he stomped out to his car and then sat there. Damn her, she'd thrown him for a loop this time.

He realized there was still so much he didn't know about her—and despite everything, he wanted to know. She'd actually had some sort of surgery when she was young that made her believe she couldn't get pregnant.

And she'd pretended otherwise just so she could make love with him.

It seemed absurd, especially now that she'd been trapped by her own ridiculous plan. But he wasn't giving up yet. Olivia always wanted to run things, in business and in private. It was part of her nature to take charge and make all the decisions. She was pushy and arrogant and in the general course of things, very fair-minded.

But not this time.

Damn, he knew he should have stuck to his original plan. He should never have gotten involved on a personal level with Olivia Anderson. He hadn't gotten the baby he wanted so badly; he hadn't gotten anything at all.

Nothing except a broken heart.

CHAPTER NINE

"SO WHEN ARE YOU going to marry her?"

Slowly, wishing he didn't have to deal with this right now, Tony laid his papers aside. "I'm not."

John placed both palms on his desk and leaned forward to glare at him. "And why the hell not? She's perfect for you."

Perfect? Nothing felt perfect. It had been two weeks since he'd seen Olivia. He'd tried dropping in on her shops a couple of times, hoping to appear casual about seeing her since his pride was still bruised. He would have conjured up a business excuse, but in truth, he'd half hoped that seeing him again would give her a change of heart, that she would want him again, even though she was pregnant. But she hadn't been there.

He'd called her apartment once or twice, but each time he'd gotten her answering machine. No doubt she was busy organizing things for the new shop she would open.

And that thought made him angry all over again.

He glanced up at John, then back to his desk full of files, trying subtly to give the hint that he was busy. "It's none of your business, John."

"You've been moping around long enough. Hell, Mom's worried about you, Kate's worried about you. Why don't you just accept the inevitable and admit you love her?"

"Because she lied to me, that's why!" He hadn't meant to shout, but he'd had no one to talk to, and he was ready to explode with the effort of trying to understand Olivia and his own feelings.

John straightened, looking startled by Tony's display of temper. "Lied to you about what?"

Wishing he'd kept his mouth shut now, Tony shook his head. "Why don't you mind your own business?"

Instead John propped a hip against the desk. "Was it a big lie, or just a little lie? Now don't glare at me. I'm trying to help."

"If you want to help, find me a woman as perfect as Lisa."

A look of stunned disbelief crossed John's face, then he burst into hysterical laughter. "Lisa? Perfect? You've got to be kidding."

"She's perfect for you. The two of you never fight. And I know damn well she'd never lie to you."

"We fight all the time, actually. I enjoy it. And it gives me a good excuse to make up to her." He winked, which confounded Tony. "As far as lying…Lisa would never lie to me. But I lied to her once, and it was a doozy."

Tony laid aside the file he'd just picked up and stared. "When was this?"

"Before we were married. Almost ruined things, and that's a fact. But Lisa, bless her heart, didn't give up on me. She got madder than hell, then she schemed, and before I knew it, I was apologizing and begging her to marry me. As it turned out, she wasn't so upset over what I'd lied about, as she was that I'd lied at all. Is that true with you and Livvy?"

Tony considered the question a moment. Was he mad that Olivia had used him for sex, or that she didn't appear to want him now? He figured he could forgive her anything if she loved him, but… He shook his head, not really coming up with an answer. "I don't suppose you'd care to tell me what you lied to Lisa about?"

"Actually…no." He grinned. "It's history, and now I'd never lie to her about anything any more than I'd ever hurt her."

"But you two fight?" Tony was intrigued by the idea; he'd always thought his brother had the perfect marriage.

"All the time. Hell, you know me, Tony. Did you really think anyone could live with me without losing their temper on occasion?"

"And Kate and Brian?"

"They've had their share of whoppers. Kate can be a real pain, you know that. And she claims Brian is far from perfect. If you love Olivia, it won't matter."

Tony narrowed his eyes, considering what John said, but the big difference was that Olivia didn't appear to love him. "I don't know."

John slammed a palm on the desk. "I don't get it! She's a sexy lady. Smart. Sweet. The kids love her. The women love her."

Tony ignored him, going back to his papers and pretending a great interest in them, even though his eyes wouldn't seem to focus on a single line.

John crossed his arms over his chest and glared. "She is sexy, you know. Very sexy."

The paper crumpled in Tony's fist. He slanted his gaze up at his younger brother and asked in a growl, "Just what do you think you're doing, noticing if she's sexy or not?"

"Do I look blind? Olivia is one of those intriguing cool-on-the-outside, burning-up-on-the-inside kind of ladies.

Every guy who looks at her knows it. It's just that usually a guy's too afraid to get close enough to her to see just how sexy she is. She can be damn formidable as I remember it. Of course, after you got her to soften up a bit, it's more noticeable."

"Oh, that's just dandy." She no longer wanted him, but he'd managed to show the world how appealing she was? He didn't need to hear that.

"You don't have to worry about me or Brian. You know we're both well satisfied in our own marital bargains, but…"

"Brian, too?"

"He's not blind, either, big brother."

Tony threw the papers aside and shoved his chair back, then took an aggressive step toward John. He felt ready to chew nails, but John only shook his head.

"Look at you. This is pathetic. Give up and tell her you love her and you want her back."

Tony narrowed his eyes and against his best intentions, blurted, "She dumped me, you ass. Not the other way around."

It was almost funny the look that flashed over John's face. Obviously this possibility hadn't occurred to him. He asked simply, "Why?"

Shaking his head and stalking around the office, Tony knew he'd already said too much. No way would he ever confide in anyone—even his brother—the extent of Olivia's perfidy. "Go away and leave me alone, John."

John didn't budge an inch. "I don't get it. She seemed crazy about you. I was sure of it."

Crazy about him? Tony stared, wondering if it could have been possible.

Then John demanded, "What did you do to her to make her dump you? Did you yell at her over this lying business?"

This time he did laugh, but there was nothing humorous in the sound. What had he done? Made love to her, as per her request, giving her pleasure, giving her his baby.

Then he'd accused her of using him for money. It had been his anger talking, but still, he shouldn't have made such a ridiculous claim. Sex, yes, but Olivia would never use anyone for money. God, she'd spent her life proving her independence, isolating herself, facing each day alone.

But now she'd have the baby. His baby.

He cursed again, aiming his disgust at John. But it was a wasted effort. John only dropped into a chair and looked thoughtful. "I think we need to figure this one out."

"I need to get back to my work." He said it through gritted teeth, wanting privacy to wallow in his misery, but John shook his head.

"I don't understand why, if you want her, you don't just woo her."

"Woo her? *Woo* her? What kind of word is that?"

"An appropriate kind. Olivia must need something you haven't given her yet. When I was dating Lisa, I always thought I was saying the right thing, and it always turned out to be the wrong thing."

Brian opened the door just then and walked in to hear John's statement. He grinned. "You have a knack for saying the wrong thing. So what else is new?"

John turned and without a single hesitation, explained the situation to Brian. Tony threw up his hands and dropped back into the chair behind his desk. He listened as the two men discussed his life as if he weren't even in the room. Damn interfering…at least his mother and sister didn't know.

No sooner did he have the thought, than Kate came storming in.

"What did you do to Olivia?"

Tony leaned back in his chair and closed his eyes.

Again, John began to explain. Tony tried to tune them out, but then Kate said, "Oh. When I talked to her, she only said that they weren't seeing each other anymore."

"You talked to her?" Tony asked, sounding anxious in spite of himself. "When?"

"Just this morning. She sounds awful. Not at all like herself."

"What do you mean? Is she still sick?" He was aware of their looks, how they all exchanged glances, but at the moment, he didn't care.

"I don't know anything about her being sick, Tony. I assumed she was heartbroken. But then, I thought you had broken things off. I mean, it was obvious she was crazy about you."

There it was again. Tony leaned forward and said, "Why does everyone keep saying that! The woman dumped me."

"What did you do to her?" asked Kate and Brian together.

Tony had had enough. He came to his feet in a rush and said to the room at large, "I'm going out for lunch."

John grabbed his arm before he could leave the room. "I've always thought you were an intelligent man, Tony. But right now, you're acting pretty dumb. Don't sit around here sulking. Go fix things with her."

"And how am I supposed to do that?"

John slapped his shoulder and grinned. "As I said, you're smart. You'll think of something."

IT TOOK TONY A FEW more days to come up with a solid plan. But once he did, he couldn't believe he hadn't thought of it sooner. It was perfect, probably the only ploy that would work with Olivia.

He would appeal to her business ethics.

He tracked her down at the downtown shop where she was busy stringing white twinkle lights in the front store window that faced the lobby. She stood on a small stool, a smile on her face, looking beautiful and healthy and not at all like a woman pining away for a man. He almost balked, but then she looked up and met his gaze and her smile vanished. Her dark eyes took on a wary look.

He approached her and took her hand, helping her to step down from the stool. "Hello, Olivia."

"Tony. What brings you downtown?"

"I was looking for you, actually."

That wary look intensified and she nervously brushed her hands together. "Oh?"

"We have some things to discuss, I think. Don't you?" He kept his tone gentle, not wanting to upset her before it was absolutely necessary.

"I...I suppose we do." She turned and called to her assistant. "Finish hanging these lights, will you, Alicia? I'll be in my office."

Without a word to him, she started toward the back of the shop. This location was smaller than the one they'd met in before, but he liked it. There were the red bows and garlands strung around the shop and Tony wondered if she decorated her own home at all. Doubtful. Her apartment was utilitarian to the point of being depressing.

This year, he hadn't decorated, either. It just hadn't seemed important.

She closed her office door after he'd stepped inside, then went to sit behind her desk. There was only one other chair in the room, a plain wooden chair, and Tony pulled it forward. "How have you been, Olivia? Kate mentioned that you seemed ill."

She looked frightened for a second, then she visibly relaxed. "Morning sickness, I'm afraid. Although it hits me at the oddest times, not just in the morning."

Perfect, Tony thought, knowing he couldn't have asked for a better opening. "Any other changes you're noticing?"

Looking anxious, she smiled and said, "You know, there are. Small things, but it's amazing how the baby is making itself known. Even though I'm not very far along yet."

"What kind of things?" He held her gaze, refusing to let her look away.

She flushed, then shook her head. "Nothing big. Just… little things."

"But I want to know." He added gently, "That was part of our deal, remember?"

Olivia stiffened at the reminder of their original bargain. "What are you talking about?"

It took all his control to look negligent, to hide his growing anticipation. If she guessed at his ulterior motives, she'd throw him out on his ear. He picked up a lacy slip lying on the desk and pretended to examine it. "You agreed to allow me to view all the changes—if you got pregnant. I realize now of course that you only made the deal because you thought it would never come to this. But I've given it a lot of thought. And I've decided you should be fair-minded about the whole thing."

Her face was pale now and her hands were clenched together. "I already told you how sorry I am about all that, Tony. But I'm keeping my baby."

"I'll want visitation."

"I offered it to you."

"And," he went on, as if she hadn't spoken, "I'll want to pay for half the baby's bills. As to that, I should pay for half your medical bills as well."

"No!" She was out of her seat in an instant and leaning over the desk to glare at him. "I told you, I want nothing from you."

"And I believe you. But it's my right to pay half."

"But it's my body, my baby!" Then she stumbled back, realizing what she'd said. Tony merely waited, and she drew several deep breaths. "Okay. It's your baby, too. And when it's born, if you want to take part of the pediatrician's expenses on yourself, that's fine. Why should we argue? But my bills are my own."

"I could take you to court, you know."

She gaped at him. "You'd sue me to get half my bills?"

He shrugged. "That, and to get you to honor the bargain we made."

Feeling behind herself for her chair, she dropped down and concentrated on taking several deep breaths. Her face was pale, her eyes huge. "You're going to take the baby from me?"

Tony felt like a monster. He stood up and went around the desk, then turned her chair toward him. Kneeling, he took her hands in his and held them tightly. "Do you honestly think I'd do that to you, Olivia?"

She shook her head and her hair tumbled over her shoulders. "No. But you said…"

"We made other deals, sweetheart." He kept his tone low and soothing. "Don't you remember?"

Her gaze became wary.

"I want to be a part of the pregnancy as well as the birth. You promised me I could observe all the little changes, watch you as the baby caused changes in your body. I want to do that, Olivia. I want to know every little thing that occurs."

"But…everything is different now."

"No. The only thing that's different is that you've admitted you lied to me, and you want to keep the baby. The rest of our agreement should stand." He squeezed her fingers again and stared into her stunned gaze. "It's the least you could do."

He could tell she was considering it, thinking about it. His gaze dropped to her breasts and he whispered, "I bought a book that detailed all the changes. One of the first things to happen is your breasts should get tender and swollen." He glanced up and was caught by her wide dark eyes. "I remember now, the last time we made love, you seemed especially sensitive."

Her chest heaved as she watched him, and then she nodded.

"Ah. So they are swollen?"

Licking her lips, she nodded again. "A little."

"And they're tender?"

"Yes." Her voice was a barely discernible whisper, husky and deep and shaky.

"I want to see."

"Tony…"

The way she groaned his name did things to him, things that shouldn't be happening right now, not while he was trying so hard to get the upper hand. He rubbed his thumb over her knuckles and whispered to her. "Shh. It'll be all right. I'm just curious. You know how much this has meant to me. Can't you give me at least this much?"

"But I thought you'd find another woman."

The thought of touching anyone other than Olivia was somehow repugnant. He didn't want another woman. Even if he went the rest of his life without a child that would be solely his, he wouldn't want anyone but her. The idea was staggering, but true.

"No. I don't think that's necessary." He released her hands and stood, needing to put some space between them before he embarrassed himself by making declarations that would be better left unsaid. At least for now. "We'll have this baby, and that's enough to deal with. Hell, this is far more complicated than I'd ever intended."

He had his back to her and didn't hear her rise, but then she was touching him, and he turned. She stood looking up at him, her expression earnest. "I'm so sorry, Tony. Honestly. I never meant for any of this to happen. It seemed like such a simple plan to me."

Touching her cheek, he smiled. "Nothing about you is simple, honey. You're the most complex woman I know."

She looked crushed. "I've really messed things up for you, haven't I?"

She'd made him happier than he'd ever imagined being, but he didn't tell her that. "Things aren't just as I'd planned them, but I *will* get my child. I'll just be sharing it with you." He shoved his hands into his pockets to keep from touching her again. "But it would help if you'd abide by the agreement as much as possible. You knew from the start how I felt about things."

She nodded miserably, and he almost apologized for heaping on the guilt, but she deserved it for her deception. And it was the only way he could think of to reach his goal.

"Then you'll agree? You'll let me observe the changes and take part in everything?"

She turned away and wrapped her arms around herself. "What exactly do you mean by 'taking part'?"

"I want to attend your doctor appointments. If there are any sonograms taken, I want to be there so I can see whatever you see. When the doctor listens for a heartbeat, I want to hear it, too."

Her shoulders slumped in relief. "That's no problem."

"I also want to know about every spell of morning sickness. I want to see your ankles if they swell." Without his intention, his voice went husky. "And feel if your breasts are tender."

She shuddered, and he wanted her right then, so badly he could hardly breathe. "I've seen you before, Olivia, so it won't be a breach of your privacy. I've touched you…" He had to stop to draw his own breath, his lungs feeling constricted, his stomach tight with need. "I know your body, how it looks and how it feels. It'll be easy for me to see every tiny change. Will you let me?"

She nodded very slowly, and his pulse quickened. But he wanted to be sure. "Olivia?"

"Yes." She faced him, her cheeks flushed, her eyes bright. "Yes. That's the least I can do."

He recognized the signs of arousal in her expression and it took a moment before he was able to speak. "I can come over tonight."

"I'd rather…"

"I know. You don't want me in your apartment." She looked surprised, and he gave her a wry smile. "I realized after I left there the last time, you've always avoided having me in your home. That was because you had no intention of having my baby, of course, and you wanted to keep your life separate from mine. You didn't want me invading your inner sanctum."

With a guilty flush, she nodded.

"But now you are having my baby, and I will be visiting there, if for nothing else than to pick up the child. So it doesn't really matter anymore, does it?"

"I suppose not."

She looked reluctant as hell, and he almost grinned. *I've got you now,* he thought, knowing he was moving in on her, and knowing she didn't like it. He said, "How about six o'clock?"

"I suppose I should be finished by then."

"Good." He didn't want to go, but he decided to leave before she changed her mind. "I'll see you then."

OLIVIA STRAIGHTENED HER hair again, then stepped away from the mirror. Tony was five minutes late, and she was a nervous wreck. She couldn't believe he was doing this, but she was so glad. She'd missed Tony horribly, the days stretching on endlessly. She'd wanted so many times to tell Tony of all the little changes she'd noticed. Not even work had filled the void—a situation she had never encountered before.

Until now.

When the knock sounded on the door, she jumped, then raced to answer it. She didn't want to have to deal with her neighbors today; they'd been hovering over her ever since that night at the hospital. While she appreciated their concern, she didn't want Tony to know about the risks involved with the pregnancy.

But when she opened the door, Tony stood there surrounded by familiar faces. He gave her an ironic grin, said goodbye to all her neighbors and stepped inside. As she was closing the door again, Hilda called out, "You take good care of her now, you hear? I don't want to be making any more trips to the hospital."

Though she could have wished it otherwise, Olivia knew Tony had heard every word. He stared at her, then started to open the door again—to question Hilda she was certain.

"Don't, Tony."

"What the hell was that about the hospital?"

She tried to think of some excuse to give him, but he grabbed her shoulders and gave her a slight shake. "No more lies, Olivia. Dammit, just once give me the truth."

She flinched at his tone, and at his right to doubt her. "I'm sorry. I just didn't want to worry you."

"Worry me about what? Is the baby okay?"

"The baby is fine." She rushed past him to the end table to pick up a recent sonogram picture. "This is the baby."

Tony looked at the odd black and white picture, frowned, then asked, "Where?"

Olivia laughed in delight because his reaction was so much like her own had been. "You can't really see the baby, it's so tiny. In fact, right now, it's only about half an inch long. But did you know, by about eight weeks, it will already be getting fingers and toes?"

Tony stared, then a huge smile broke out over his features. "Fingers and toes, huh?"

Olivia held up the picture and pointed out what she did know, showing Tony her womb and explaining the dark shadows as they'd been explained to her. "My doctor is very big on ultrasound, especially since I didn't believe I could conceive."

"Okay, start with that. What exactly happened to you? And how is it you got pregnant when you thought you couldn't?"

She was so thrilled to have someone to talk all this out with, she took Tony's hand to lead him to the couch before she could think better of it. She explained her specialized problem at length, and Tony asked a million questions.

"But what happened the other night? Why did you go to the hospital?"

Feeling her way carefully now, not wanting him to know of the risks involved, she said simply, "I had another cyst on my ovary. It was causing me some pain." And before he could question that, she added, "But that's a good thing, because otherwise I wouldn't have gone to the hospital, and I wouldn't have known I was pregnant. Heaven only knows how far along I would have gotten before I realized what was happening."

He searched her face, his concern obvious. "You're sure you're okay now?"

"I'm positive. They took very good care of me. I felt wretched for a few days, and if you check, you'll find I missed a few days of work. But now, other than the morning sickness, I feel great."

"You don't look pregnant."

He was staring down at her body, and she felt a flash of heat. Clearing her throat, she tried to distract herself from thinking things she had no business thinking. "According to the book I bought, I won't start picking up any real weight until after the first three months."

"But you said you've noticed signs?"

This was the tricky part. "My skin is different. I don't need to use as much moisturizer. My hair is different, too. I've had to switch shampoos to get it to lay right." She laughed. "I have unbelievable cravings, and I have to go to the bathroom more."

"And your breasts are swollen and tender."

"Well…yes." She had hoped to slip that in with all the rest, but he hadn't given her a chance.

He took her hand and pulled her to her feet. She stared up at him, feeling her heart pound, her temperature rise. In a low, tender voice he said, "I want to see, Olivia. Take your shirt off for me."

CHAPTER TEN

OLIVIA SWALLOWED HARD and closed her eyes. Not for the life of her could she unbutton the pale flannel blouse she wore. Then she felt Tony take her hand and her eyes flew open again.

"Let's go in the bedroom so you can lie down. It'll be easier for me to…examine you that way."

Examine her. Her heart was tripping, her stomach pulling tight, and yet she let him lead her to her bedroom—a place he'd never been before—without a single complaint. She knew, in her own heart, she wanted him to touch her, to look at her. But she didn't think she could admit such a thing. Not after how badly she'd blundered so far. It was a wonder Tony would even talk to her, much less want to touch her.

She sat on the edge of the bed when he gently pressed her down, and then his hands were on her shoulders, urging her back. She squeezed her eyes shut and she could hear her own breath.

His knuckles brushed against her as he slowly unbuttoned her top and parted the material. Her bra was new, sturdier than those she usually wore, and it had a front closure that Tony deftly flicked open. He brushed the cups aside and then she felt nothing but the cool air on her breasts.

"Olivia. Open your eyes."

She did, feeling foolish, and saw that he was just standing there, looking down at her, his gaze intent. She started to cover herself, but he caught her hands then sat beside her on the bed. "You are much fuller."

She could hear the amazement in his gravelly tone, and she said, "I'm going to breast-feed when the baby is born."

His gaze shot to her face. "Are you?"

"Yes. I've been reading a lot of books about it." Her own voice crackled and shook in nervousness and arousal, but she ignored it. Tony was interested in all this, and she did owe it to him to keep him apprised of everything.

He lifted a hand and with one finger followed the tracing of a light blue vein to the edge of her nipple. She sucked in a deep breath, but he seemed unaware of her predicament as he cupped her fully in his palm, weighing her. When his thumb touched her nipple she shuddered.

"You're a lot more sensitive, aren't you?" There was awe in his whispered question, and she could only nod her head.

"Olivia?" His hand rested low on her midriff now, and she watched as he unbuttoned her tan wool slacks and slid the zipper down. "I want to see all of you." He tugged her pants off, and when she saw how his hands shook she had to bite back a groan.

She lay there, legs slightly parted, her upper body framed by the shirt that still hung from her arms, while Tony's gaze, so hot and fierce, roamed all over her. When he bent to press his cheek to her belly, she couldn't stand it a second more. She curled up to wrap her arms around him, and the tears started.

"Shh. Sweetheart, don't cry."

He held her close, gently rocking, but the tears wouldn't stop. "What is it, Olivia? Did I hurt you?"

As if he ever would. She shook her head and squeezed him tighter.

"I need you, Livvy. I want to make love to you."

She didn't need any encouragement beyond that. She shifted so she could find his mouth, then kissed him hard, clasping his face between her hands and biting his lips.

He laughed, then groaned and in a heartbeat he was over her, kissing her everywhere, kicking off his shoes.... Olivia struggled with his shirt until finally he sat up and stripped off his own clothes. As he lowered himself on top of her again, he said, "Tell me if I hurt you."

"You won't. You couldn't. Please, Tony, I missed you so much."

His hand slid down her belly and started to stroke her, but she curled her fingers around his erection and he froze. "Damn, sweetheart, don't do that. I won't be able to..."

"I don't want you to. Just make love to me, Tony. Now."

His gaze locked on hers for a long moment, and then his fingers were parting her, preparing her. She was already wet and ready for him, and when he lifted his damp fingers to his mouth, she groaned, watching him lick the taste of her from his hand, seeing the heat in his eyes. She pulled him over her, kissing him wildly, opening her legs wide and he gently pushed inside her until she groaned and wrapped herself around him. It was excruciatingly sweet and slow and hot, and it was all she could do not to tell him she loved him. He held her face still and kissed her as she climaxed, letting her suck his tongue, then whispering to her in a voice so low she couldn't hear what he was saying. He pressed his face into her throat and gave a deep, hoarse groan, and she held him, stroking his back until his breathing had calmed.

TONY PUSHED HER DAMP hair away from her face, smoothed her eyebrows, and all the while, she could see him thinking. It was the awkward moment after, and she wanted to put it off, but there was no place to hide. Before he said it, she knew what was coming.

"Marry me."

Oh God, it hurt. She shook her head as fresh tears rolled down her cheeks, as much denying the words as denying him. "I can't."

"Why?"

She'd known he would ask. Tony didn't like being refused—for any reason. She looked at him squarely and went on the defensive. "Why do you want to marry me?"

He gave her a disgruntled frown and shoved himself away from her, sitting on the edge of the bed with his naked back to her. "We're having a baby, and I can't keep my hands off you. Don't you think marriage would be a good idea?"

The disappointment was crushing, but she kept her tone level, not letting him see how much his reply had hurt. "You planned all along for us to have a baby, but you didn't want to marry me. As I recall, you were appalled when I first misunderstood that to be your intention."

"That was when I thought the baby would be mine alone."

"I see." She scooted up in the bed and began refastening her clothing. Her bra left her stymied for a moment and required all her attention. As she buttoned her shirt, she watched him. "I've told you I'll share the baby with you. I would never deny you your child, or deny the child a father. And you'll make an excellent one. You can take on as big a role as you wish."

He started to say something fierce—she could tell by the frown on his face—but the knocking at her front door stopped him. His expression turned comical for a moment and then he cursed. "I don't believe this, I really don't. I'd have thought we'd be safe here, at your place."

He moved over on the bed as she jumped up and started pulling on her slacks. "At least we know it can't be my family this time."

Olivia shook her head, glad of the reprieve, regardless of who it was. "I can't imagine who would call on me."

Tony lounged back, gloriously naked and unconcerned by that fact. "That's right. You avoid all relationships, don't you?"

His sarcasm was especially sharp after the tender way he'd made love to her. She slanted him a look as she headed out of the room, then had to force herself to look away from the sight of his blatant masculinity.

"Do me a favor and stay put, okay?" She didn't wait for an answer, but pulled the bedroom door shut and went to see who was knocking. It had to be one of her neighbors, she thought, trying to smooth her hair and wipe her eyes dry at the same time. She was wrong. She opened the door to find a good portion of Tony's family standing in the hallway, exchanging pleasantries with her neighbors, who of course had opened their own doors to see who was visiting the building.

Kate was the first one to notice Olivia. Grabbing her and giving her a big hug, Kate explained, "We were out shopping and realized we hadn't invited you to Christmas dinner yet."

Lisa stepped forward with John and Brian in tow, and Olivia had no choice but to move out of the way so they could enter. "The kids would love to see you again. They've been asking after you."

John grinned. "And Tony would love to see you, too, I'm sure."

Lisa poked her husband in the ribs. "John. You promised you'd behave yourself."

"I am behaving. I'm not telling her what a sullen ass Tony's been lately, am I?"

Olivia felt her stomach start to churn. It was always this way. The nausea would hit her at the most inopportune moments, usually when she was on her way to work or while she was at one of the shops, with customers all around.

Now, with Tony's family surrounding her, had to be the worst timing of all. She cringed, then laid a hand to her stomach, praying her belly would settle itself.

Kate stepped forward and put her arm around Olivia, misunderstanding her distress. "We don't mean to upset you, Olivia. But we really would love to have you. And in all honesty, the kids do ask after you. I think they miss you."

Olivia was thinking it couldn't get any worse when Tony came on the scene. "No fair, sis," he said, "using the kids as bait."

Everyone turned to stare at her bedroom doorway, where Tony stood wearing only his slacks—and those not properly fastened. It was no wonder John and Brian began to grin and Kate and Lisa looked at her with wide eyes. The questions would start any minute, questions Olivia didn't know how to answer. All at once, her stomach turned over and she knew she was going to vomit.

She clapped a hand to her mouth and ran.

Behind her, she could hear Kate's gasp and John's muttered, "What the hell?"

But mostly what she heard was Tony saying in a bland tone, "She's all right. It's just morning sickness. Excuse me, will you?"

HE CAUGHT THE BATHROOM door before she could slam it in his face, then quietly locked it for her while she dropped to her knees in front of the toilet. He winced as she gagged, his sympathy extreme. When she sat back on her heels, he flushed the toilet, dampened a washcloth in cool water and handed it to her.

"Are you okay now?"

"Go away." She sounded weak and croaky and he sat down behind her and pulled her against his chest. Taking the washcloth from her hand, he wiped her face for her, then laid it aside.

"Aren't you supposed to take deep breaths or something?"

"That's during labor, you idiot."

Tony grinned at her acerbic tone, weak though it was. "Well, I haven't gotten around to reading all the books you've evidently gone through. Give me a little time, okay?"

She groaned again and he barely managed to get the toilet lid up for her. This time when she finished, she glared at him and demanded, "Go away and leave me alone."

"Don't be silly, Olivia. So you're sick? I've seen worse, I promise."

She staggered to her feet and went to the sink where she splashed water on her face. "Yeah. Worse is waiting in the other room, and you can be the one to explain."

"What's to explain? We're having a baby. They'd have found out sooner or later anyway."

"You know it's more than that and you could have spoken to them when I wasn't around!"

They could hear the rush of whispered voices from his family, and Tony shook his head. "There's no hope for it now." He opened the door and took her hand, but she held back. "Don't be a coward."

Olivia would have happily detoured into her bedroom and locked the door, but Tony didn't release her hand. He dragged her into the living room, where everyone had taken a seat, and said to the room at large, "We're having a baby."

Kate was the first to shoot from her seat, squealing in happiness. "Tony, this is so fantastic! When is the wedding?"

And without missing a beat, he said, "There won't be one."

Everyone stilled, their smiles frozen. And then the first volley of righteous umbrage hit. Of course he had to marry her. What could he be thinking of? Hadn't he enjoyed enough freedom of late? And babies deserved two parents. Kate even went so far as to put her arm around Olivia and remain protectively at her side while she glared daggers at him.

It was laughable, he thought. His family should know him better than this, but obviously they'd switched loyalties somewhere through this farce of a courtship. Then he shook his head. No, it was only that they thought they would save him from his own poor judgment. He wished them luck in their efforts.

And poor Olivia. He could see she was beginning to fret over the way they crucified him. Obviously they didn't realize it was Olivia who'd shied away from marriage, and if he told them the truth of the matter, it would really put her on the spot. He couldn't do it.

But Olivia could.

She looked around at all of them, dazed by their reactions. Brian was shaking his head and trying to be reasonable, Kate kept squeezing Olivia and patting her hand, and John was red in the face, telling Tony what a mistake he was making. Lisa, the only quiet one, stood twisting her hands together, the perfect picture of concern.

"Tony asked me to marry him!" She had to practically shout to be heard, and then the room went silent.

John was the first to react. "So what's the problem then?"

Olivia looked to Tony for help, but he just crossed his arms over his chest and waited. He was as curious as anyone to hear her explanation.

"It's not as simple as that."

"When has love ever been simple?"

Lisa again smacked John. "It's their business, John. Maybe we should just leave them alone."

"But Tony wants to marry her! And she obviously cares about him." He paused, then looked at Olivia. "You do, don't you?"

"I…yes."

"Just not enough to marry him?"

"It's complicated!"

John snorted. "How complicated can it be? You care about Tony. He's crazy about you. Hell, he's been so maudlin all week, I thought I'd have to shoot him to put him out of my misery," he joked.

Olivia's gaze shot to Tony's face, and he gave her a grim smile. "I have been a miserable bastard."

Tears welled in her eyes. "Oh, Tony."

She looked cornered, and he hated it. Enough was enough. He walked across the room and jerked the front door open. "Why don't you all get lost, all right? She's having a terrible time of it with this morning sickness stuff, and now she has all of you badgering her. Give us some time alone."

Lisa patted Olivia's arm. "The morning sickness will pass in a few weeks. And the rest of being pregnant is a breeze in comparison."

Kate gave her a firm hug. "I had it all day long, too. Try nibbling dry crackers as soon as your stomach acts up. And don't worry about the tears. Both Lisa and I cried all the time when we were carrying."

Brian squeezed her shoulder. "Hope you're feeling better soon, hon. Try to make it for Christmas. Celebrating will take your mind off…other things."

Then only John was standing there, and Tony watched as he gave Olivia a stern look. "Whatever you think your reasons are, discuss them with him. Sometimes you find out the problems that worry you don't even exist." Then he gave her an affectionate kiss on the cheek and left.

The door closed with a resounding click, and the room was uncomfortably silent after that. For a moment, Tony didn't look at her. He kept his gaze on the door while he organized his thoughts. "You seemed surprised that I wasn't happy this past week."

Her response was trembling and uncertain. "I thought you'd still be too angry to be unhappy. Or if you were unhappy, I…well, was it because you thought I wouldn't involve you with the baby?"

Tony did turn to her then, and he made no effort to hide his anger. "The baby? I fell in love with you long before I knew you were carrying my baby. Hell, I think I may have been half in love with you for a long, long time. You were my first choice when I decided I wanted a baby. And then it didn't take me long to realize you were my *only* choice."

Her eyes were huge, her mouth open in a small O. Tony shook his head, amused by her astonishment. How could she not have realized how much he cared for her?

"Olivia, we just made love, and it didn't have a damn thing to do with the baby."

"No?"

Stalking toward her, he smiled and said, "Nope. I get near you and I want you. I think about you and I want you. Hell, you throw up in a toilet and I want you."

"You do?"

He nodded, still coming closer. "And it's not just sex. I want to hold you, talk to you, listen to you laugh. God, I love watching you negotiate a deal."

She laughed at that and he finally reached her, but he didn't touch her. He lowered his voice and admitted, "It makes me hot as hell seeing you in your shark mode, being demanding and unrelenting. Of course, it was almost the same watching you give little Shawn his bottle. And when you defended me just now to my family—you do funny things to my insides, lady."

"You love me?"

"Hell, yes. Isn't that what I've been saying?"

"Oh, Tony." To his chagrin, she started to cry. When he reached for her, she stepped away. "There's so much you have to know."

He sat on the couch and propped his feet up. "Then don't you think it's time you told me?"

She nodded uncertainly, and he patted the couch beside him. When she started to sit there, he caught her and tugged her into his lap instead, holding her close and tucking her face into his shoulder. "All right. Now talk. And don't leave anything out."

She did. She told him about her trip to the hospital, that the pregnancy was still at risk, that there was a good chance she'd never get pregnant again. Even if she was able to carry this baby full-term, it might be their only child.

She didn't look at him as she spoke, choosing to keep her face hidden against him. Tony was relieved. It was damn difficult keeping his anger hidden, but he wanted her to finish the story, to make certain there were no more secrets between them. When she grew silent and he didn't immediately respond, she turned stiff in his arms.

"Tony?" He heard the uncertainty, the vulnerability, and his anger doubled. But he remained silent.

"You're angry?" she persisted.

"I'm furious." And he was.

She gave a small sob, but he didn't relent. "How could you do this, plan to go through all this alone, leave me in the dark? Didn't you think, somewhere along the line, I'd earned your trust? Have I ever given you any reason to believe I'm such a shallow ass that I'd let you go through this alone? Damn you, Olivia, are you ever going to open up to me?"

She had gone very still just after he started his tirade, and now she whispered, "I just did."

"What?" He was almost too angry to make sense of her words.

"I just opened up to you. And I do trust you. I swear. It's just that I love you so much, I didn't want you to be burdened with a wife who couldn't give you what you want."

"And if what I want most is you?"

She pushed away so she could see his face. Her dark eyes were liquid with tears, her cheeks blotchy, and he loved her so much, he wanted to cry with her. "Olivia, I love you."

She sniffed and threw herself against him, squeezing his neck so tightly he couldn't breathe. He choked out a laugh and said, "Marry me."

"But you want a baby, too."

"We're having a baby."

"But what if…"

"Shh." He laid his finger against her lips. "No what-ifs. I love you. You love me. If something happens, we'll have other children. And if you can't carry them, we'll adopt. It doesn't matter. What matters is that I need you with me."

Olivia laughed and squeezed him again. "I want you, too. And this baby. I'm being so careful, following all the doctor's orders, taking my progesterone twice a day…"

"You have to take pills?"

She slanted him a look. "Don't ask. Just understand that my body needs to absorb it now to help the baby. After the first trimester, the risks aren't nearly so high."

He loved holding her like this, seeing her so animated. "You've really studied up on this, haven't you?"

She ducked her head. "I've been so afraid."

He held her face, making her look at him. "From now on, you'll tell me. We'll get through it together."

Smiling, she said, "Yes."

"And you'll marry me."

It was his I'm-in-charge-now voice, and Olivia said, "Yes, sir."

He grinned. "You've just made my family very happy."

"And you?"

"I've just gotten everything I ever wanted. Of course I'm happy."

Two years later

"SHOULD WE TAKE the diaper bag on the plane with us?"

Tony laughed. "I wouldn't leave home without it." He walked into the bedroom where Olivia was packing. Her body once again slim and beautiful, though it wouldn't be that way for long. "How are you feeling?"

She turned and gave him and their thirteen month old son, Devon, a big smile. "Fine. Anxious."

"No morning sickness?"

"It's the strangest thing, but this time I feel wonderful."

"Lisa and Kate swore each pregnancy was different for them, as well."

Devon reached for his mother and Tony transferred him into her waiting arms. There was no hesitancy on her part now as she cuddled him close and kissed him and breathed his scent. Devon laughed and kicked his pudgy legs.

"Do you think he'll like flying? Maybe I should wait a little longer before making the Seattle trip."

"You've waited long enough. Besides, we'll only be there a week to look things over, and the woman you hired to manage the place is counting on seeing you. I have no doubt she's gone to great pains to impress you. And I did want to check in on the hotel anyway."

She laughed at him and shook her head. "You're worse than me. But running a business from across the country is easier than I'd thought it would be."

"With hotels, you have to adjust. Can't be everywhere at once."

"I know. And you taught me the secret long ago." She balanced Devon on her hip and went back to her packing. It sometimes amazed him the things she could now do one-handed. "As long as I hire good people, treat them well and expect the best from them, things, for the most part, run smoothly."

She bent to tuck a pair of shoes into the suitcase, and Tony couldn't stop himself from patting her rear. "Did I ever tell you how hot it makes me when you use that logical corporate tone?"

She cast him a look and said, "Why do you think I use it so often?"

"You always were a devious woman." He laughed when she playfully smacked him. Her earlier ploy was no longer a sensitive issue between them, especially since things had turned out so well. They had their baby, they had each other, and it was the best deal either of them had ever made.

SEX APPEAL

CHAPTER ONE

YOU'VE BEEN A BAD BOY. Go to my room.

Those particular words, boldly printed on a soft, white cotton sweatshirt and drawn tight across a rounded female chest, caught Brent Bramwell's eye. He'd been perusing the new strip of eclectic shops, seeing that everything was in order now that most of the spaces had been leased, when he'd caught the flash of movement in a display window.

Curiosity got the better of him, and despite the icy chill of the early November wind, he slowed his gait. All he could see of the body in the sweatshirt was the middle. Involved in hanging new blinds, the woman stood on a stool or step-ladder, her face hidden from view by the sagging blinds. The windowsill concealed her legs from her thighs down.

But what he saw in between—now *that* was enticing. Curvy hips, slim thighs, luscious breasts.

He approached slowly, ignoring the lash of frozen snow pelting his cheeks and tossing his hair. He read the words on the sweatshirt again and wondered what type of female would advertise such a suggestion. Close to the window now, only a few feet away, he stopped to stare as she stretched upward. The sweatshirt rose to give him a view of the smooth, pale skin of her midriff. He even glimpsed her navel, a shallow dent in a very cute belly.

He caught his breath and in that instant she stepped down, looking directly at him. Her huge light-brown eyes, heavily lashed and faintly curious, sparkled with humor.

He fell. *Hard.*

Literally. His feet slid out from under him on the icy walk and Brent found himself flat on his back staring at the gray, blustery sky, the wind temporarily knocked from his lungs.

He was still struggling to breathe when he heard the shop door open. The woman rushed outside, the cold air ruffling her dark curly hair, then she, too, did a slip-slide act as she attempted to maneuver on the ice. Doing a better job than Brent, she caught her balance and knelt beside him. As she reached for his head and cradled it between her warm palms, he stared at her—stared into the prettiest brown eyes he'd ever seen. They were deep and compelling.

Her voice anxious, her cheeks flushed, she asked, "Are you okay?"

Brent searched for something to say, but came up blank. He simply nodded, not sure he could speak. Embarrassment warred with discomfort. The sidewalk was hard, scattered with bits of salt and ice, and so cold his teeth began to chatter.

She frowned. "Let me help you up. Can you walk?"

He started to respond with a disgruntled "yes," then thought better of it. She was cute, not shy in the least, and he was interested. "I think so," he answered, then waited to see what she would do.

Without hesitation she slipped one arm beneath his shoulders and attempted to help lift him. Brent was a big man. Another man would have had a hard time supporting him, but she tried, he'd give her that. He felt her slim arms go around his waist, felt her shoulder wedge into his armpit as she pulled his arm over her shoulders. Her softly curved hips pressed into his thigh. Once they both stood, he towered over her.

Together, slipping around a bit, they started forward. He gave her only a little of his weight, just enough to keep her glued to his side. She led him into her shop. "I'm really sorry about that. They've been throwing salt down all afternoon, but with these temperatures, the ground just keeps freezing." She peeked up at him, mesmerizing him with those big brown eyes. "I hope you didn't hurt anything."

She was, without a doubt, adorable. Her dark, curly hair was cut in a tousled style and looked as fine as silk. Her cheeks were now very pink from the cold, but otherwise she was pale, her skin flawless. Brent leisurely looked her over as she led him to a seat behind the checkout counter.

She had on very snug, faded jeans and white leather sneakers. The sweatshirt was softened by age, adapting to her body, to her breasts. Now that he was sitting down he could examine her more thoroughly. He didn't miss the fact that her nipples were puckered from the cold.

"I'm fine," he told her as she peered at him anxiously. "I believe I only bruised my pride."

Her wide grin took his breath again. "Oh, I don't know. I imagine you may have a few other bruises as well if you take the time to look closely."

Surprised by her brazenness, Brent said, "It's possible, I suppose." Then he asked, "Who are you?"

Thrusting out her small hand, she said, "Shadow Callahan. Proprietor."

Brent took her hand and continued to hold it, noticing

how small and delicate it was. And warm, despite the cold. "Shadow? That's an unusual name."

"Yes, well, most everyone tells me I'm an unusual person."

"How so?"

Shadow glanced down at their clasped hands. Her grin widened. "Isn't this a rather long handshake? According to an article I recently read, when a man retains his grasp on your hand for more than three seconds it's an unqualified come-on." Her eyes twinkled at him. "Are you perchance coming on to me?"

Brent was totally taken aback. He released her hand, but he did so slowly, refusing to let her see his surprise. He said deliberately, "I believe I was contemplating exactly how 'bad' I would have to be to get sent to your room."

She disconcerted him again when she laughed. "I didn't expect to see anyone today. The shop is closed for the rest of the evening. Usually I only wear this around close friends."

"Close male friends?"

She shrugged, drawing his eyes to her breasts once again. "A friend is a friend, regardless of their sex."

"Ah. Not true. Men only befriend attractive women when they have ulterior motives in mind."

She crossed her arms and leaned back on the wall, completely at ease. "You speak from experience?"

He openly studied her. "Of course."

"You know," she drawled, still smiling, "you look like the devious type. Let me guess at your name. Hector? Lucius? You look like a Lucius, with a foul and evil mind."

"If that's so," Brent answered slowly, somewhat irritated by her bold manner, "why did you bring me inside? Wouldn't you consider it dangerous to let a large, devious man in when you're all alone?"

She gestured at the uncovered windows and the flow of human traffic on the walk just outside. "I think if anything too outrageous or risqué occurred, someone would surely notice."

He rubbed his chin. "I suppose you're right."

"Don't sound so disappointed, Hector. I really didn't have the time right now to be ravished, anyway."

"Will you continue to call me Hector if I don't introduce myself?"

"Of course. At least, for about two more minutes. Then I'll really have to insist you allow me to get back to my chores."

Brent stood and formally offered his hand. She took it. "You'll be disappointed to know I'm an angelic Brent. Not a Hector. Brent Bramwell to be exact."

With a slight smile, she looked him over from head to toe. "It fits. And you're wrong. I'm not the least disappointed to meet you, Brent. On the contrary, you're just what I've been looking for."

She appeared amused as Brent again held her hand too long. "I must have fallen harder than I thought. What did you say?"

"You heard me right," she assured him as she pulled her hand free. "Just look at you. Tall and handsome. Your coat is a little concealing, but I believe you're even well built. And not too old. About mid-thirties?"

"Thirty-four," he answered automatically, then asked, "What exactly am I being interviewed for?"

SHADOW LAUGHED, drawing up another stool for herself and gesturing for Brent to sit.

He really was very attractive. She'd noted that right off. His green eyes were intent and direct, his tawny brows heavy, now lowered in an annoyed frown. He had lean features, his nose straight and narrow, his cheekbones high, his jaw firm. And his mouth… He had a very sexy mouth, sculpted, his bottom lip slightly full, a small dimple in his left cheek. She sighed.

Best of all, at least to her way of thinking, he had a dry, droll kind of wit that amused her. There were very few things she liked more than laughing. She was finally at a point in her life where she could indulge to her heart's content in the sheer happiness of being alive. Her constant and unwithering optimism was one reason people always thought she was different, perhaps even a touch strange. And even that she found amusing.

Her perusal of his person had him looking ready to spit, so she decided to explain. "The specialty stores in the complex have decided to group together and have a contest—we're calling it 'Love and Laughter.' Each of us is responsible for finding ten men who fit the description of what single women are looking for—mainly attractiveness, a sense of humor and a romantic nature. Photos of the contestants will be on display in our shops, and any woman coming in can vote for her favorite, one vote per visit. Of course, we hope that'll mean more traffic to the stores."

Apparently she'd shocked him again, so she went on before he could collect himself and start objecting. "There's lots of incentive for guys to enter. Each shop is contributing. The grand prize—the contest winner takes a lady of his choosing on a paid vacation—will be supplied through the travel agent. Photography's being supplied by the photographer two doors down. There are other prizes, like free coffee and a Danish every day for a month, and a variety of discount coupons. A two-hundred-dollar gift certificate from me. All in all, it's a pretty impressive package."

Brent didn't say anything, simply stared at her with narrowed eyes. Shadow had a hunch she'd somehow offended him, or at the very least, irritated him. She asked curiously, "How tall are you?"

That brought him to his feet. "I think I'll be going now. It was, uh…uncommon meeting you."

Shadow scrambled after him, wondering exactly which part of what she'd said had been too much, when he abruptly halted. He gazed around her small shop in something akin to wonder, his eyes alighting here and there on particular items. "What the hell kind of business is this?"

Immediately affronted, Shadow propped her hands on her hips. "It's a novelty shop."

Brent took two long strides toward the door, stuck his head out and looked up at the sign overhead. "*Sex Appeal? What kind of a name is that?*"

"I'll have you know a friend of mine in advertising came up with that name, along with a nice advertising campaign. She also contributes some of the slogans I use on shirts and things." His eyes were so dark now they looked black rather than green. Shadow tilted her head. "Would you like a brochure?"

He turned to face her. "Why don't you just explain to me what type of business you're running here."

She frowned, feeling stubborn for just a moment, then shrugged. It really wasn't worth getting annoyed over. She ran a hand through her hair, glanced around and wondered where to start. "I sort of specialize in sexy items," she said finally. "Not your usual silk and satin negligees. I'm not that serious and I don't think love should be, either. What

I sell is *fun*. And comfortable. Sexy can be fun, and vice versa, if the right woman wears it. I think men have known that for a long time."

She saw that she held his interest, and expounded on her theories. "I took a poll once, and do you know most men thought women looked very sexy when they were rumpled? Can you imagine? I mean, women run around all the time trying to be perfect. Perfectly manicured, perfectly attired, smelling perfect with their hair styled perfectly. It's all nonsense."

He didn't look convinced.

"One man," she said, "who'd been married to his wife for ten years, told me it really turned him on to see her in her apron, cooking. Another told me his wife was sexiest when she first woke in the morning, all warm and drowsy. There was a young college guy who said the sexiest thing he'd ever seen on any woman was a pair of well-worn cutoffs. But a sense of humor was top of their lists."

"So what do you sell?" Brent asked, his curiosity snagged. "Aprons and cutoffs?"

Shadow scoffed at him. "Of course not. I sell shirts, like this one, that are just plain humorous. And underthings made of the softest cotton, which I can tell you is a lot more comfortable than silk." She didn't miss the way his eyes widened, possibly over her disclosure of the type of underwear she preferred. She crossed the room to lift a nightgown from the rack. "Take this gown, for example. It's soft and warm and comfortable." She slipped her hand inside. "But also pretty much transparent. See my fingers?"

He watched as she pressed her palm against the bodice of the gown. "Hmm."

"And all these tiny buttons down the front are a challenge. Can you just imagine standing there, waiting, watching while a woman—"

"You?"

"Any woman you want," she clarified, "undid all those little buttons?"

"She could just pull it off over her head."

Exasperated, Shadow said, "That wouldn't be any fun. You have to use your imagination a little."

"I'll try to keep that in mind."

She stared at him, the gown hanging from her hand. "All right. I can see you aren't the type to appreciate humor at just any old time." She returned the gown to the rack. "Would you still like to fill out an application for the contest? I need three more men to meet my quota."

"I'll have to think about it."

At least he wasn't turning her down outright. She took a little comfort in that. "Don't wait too long," she cautioned him. "We have to have all the entrants photographed before the end of November. The contest will run the first two weeks of December."

"Photographed? As in posed in some lewd and revealing way?"

"Of course not." She almost laughed at his appalled expression. What did he have to hide? she wondered. Hoping to reassure him, she said, "You don't have to expose yourself, but we are encouraging the rugged look. You know, jeans and boots. You can show your chest if you want, but that's all. The friends I talked into entering wore flannel shirts or sweaters. This is a classy operation. No sleazy shots allowed."

Brent pursed his mouth, his darkened gaze going over her once again. It disconcerted Shadow.

"What are you doing?" she asked.

"Thinking."

"Oh? About what?"

"Actually," he said, his smile very nice, "I was thinking we should have dinner and discuss all this in more detail." He looked at her ringless hand pointedly. "You're not spoken for, are you?"

"Only by about a half dozen guys. Nothing serious." Despite herself, Shadow was interested. He was a little aloof, a little uptight, but he was still a hunk and quick with the banter. "What about you?"

"Is that part of the criteria?" he asked. "That I have to be single to enter the contest?"

"No. That's part of the criteria if you want me to have dinner with you."

"Then I suppose I should admit I'm entirely single, new to town and therefore completely alone and unattached."

"All that?" She grinned, realizing that he was flirting with her. She liked it. "Truth is, I'm fairly new to this area, too, although I've already made several friends, so I can't claim to be entirely alone."

He glanced at his watch. "I'm late now for a meeting, but I can come by and pick you up in an hour."

Shadow tilted her head, studying him. "Why don't we hold off on dinner. After all, I don't really know you. Your name could be Hector, and you might have lied about the rest. But I'd be glad to have lunch with you tomorrow. Here? At the coffee shop?"

He hesitated so long, Shadow was afraid her reserve had chased him off, but she had to be cautious. She knew that.

She was ready to call the whole thing off herself, hoping to save face, when he said, "You have beautiful eyes. I've never seen that shade of brown before. Warm, like whiskey. Lunch will be fine. Around noon?"

He'd said it all in one long, drawled comment. Had he done that on purpose, mixing outrageous compliments and suggestions to take her off guard? "Noon would be fine. I'll meet you there."

"No. I'll come here and we'll walk up together." As he left, he picked up one of her brochures, and Shadow saw him make note of her name and business number printed in the upper corner. He left without another word, this time stepping very carefully onto the icy walk.

After he'd gone, Shadow put her hand over her heart. It drummed madly against her palm. Good grief, a man like that carried a lot of impact, and she'd barely gotten to know him. Still, she'd recognized right off that he liked to control all situations. He had been equally put off by, and intrigued with, her bold manner.

Lunch, she thought, should prove interesting.

AFTER A LONG NIGHT of pondering possibilities, Brent had decided he was pleased to be leasing business space to Shadow Callahan. Very pleased. "Micky, I need you to hunt up a file."

"Yes, Mr. Bramwell. Which one?"

Brent lounged back in his office chair, his eyes on the brochure laid open on his desk. "Ms. Shadow Callahan. She's leasing at the new buildings over in Southwatch."

"I'll have it in a minute."

"Thank you." Brent studied the brochure, advertising everything from board games to perfumed oils, specialty clothing to self-help books promising to put the fun back into your sex life. It was so outrageous as to be laughable.

And profitable. Brent could easily see such a novel idea catching on. The woman who had come up with the concept most assuredly intrigued him.

He couldn't remember ever meeting anyone so animated, or so lovely. Ms. Callahan, even dressed in old jeans and a sweatshirt, exuded blatant sensuality and confidence. Her appeal had nothing to do with clothing or store-bought fragrances. It was attitude, the way she moved and spoke, the way she smiled so easily. She was sexy as hell.

Brent was always very conscious of women and their motives; he had to be. Women gravitated toward him because of his bankbook and his connections, not his looks, certainly not his character. He could have been a troll with the nastiest disposition and still women would try for his attention. It'd been a long time since he'd felt the thrill of the chase. Hell, it had been a long time since there'd been any need for a chase.

But Shadow Callahan, with all her compliments and open appreciation, didn't know he had money. So why had she been so intent on controlling the situation? He'd recognized that intention immediately, because it was usually his objective, as well. And for a minute or two there he'd actually allowed her the upper hand, merely out of surprise.

Micky brought in the requested folder and Brent got down to business. He'd be seeing her again in just a few short hours, and he wanted to be prepared this time. Shadow—*what a name*—didn't yet know that he held her lease, and that was just fine by him. He'd take all the advantages he could get. But before he had any more verbal skirmishes with her, he'd find out all he could about her, and there was no way he'd let her take him by surprise again.

SHADOW DIDN'T GIVE BRENT a single thought that morning. She was far too busy with holiday shoppers who used her novel stock of items to take care of those hard-to-buy-for people on their lists. She enjoyed it—the rush, the interaction with customers, the excitement over a particular item that someone decided was "just perfect!" She didn't have time to waste thinking of Brent.

Yesterday evening, though, she'd thought of him plenty. He was interesting. More so than the men she'd met of late, who mostly bored her with their attentions. She wasn't certain what exactly appealed to her about Brent, but she'd figure it out. When she had the time.

He came in at quarter to twelve, his lean cheeks ruddy from the cold. Shadow sent him a quick smile, then turned back to the young women who were trying to decide between two different board games.

"This one's a little more expensive and it takes longer to play. But the concessions each player has to give were designed and written up by a well-known psychologist, and—" she bobbed her eyebrows "—guaranteed effective."

The women giggled, suitably impressed. Shadow went on, motioning to the other game. "This one's more good-natured fun. You make up your own concessions or rewards as you go along, depending on your partner." The choice was made and Shadow rang up the sale, wishing the women luck and reminding them to enjoy themselves.

Brent approached her, taking in her outfit with careful consideration. Shadow grinned at him. "Do you like it?"

She'd dressed like a snow bunny. Her thick cotton top fell to the middle of her thighs and she wore leggings tucked into soft leather boots. As she turned for him, holding her arms out to the side, Brent read the words written across her back: *Face It—Forty Never Looked This GOOD*.

He shook his head. "Very nice. But you're not forty."

"How would you know?" She was thirty-one, but she hadn't told him that. She smiled. "My driver's license is safely tucked away in my bag. Have you been peeking?"

All he said was, "I know you're not forty."

"Do you think I look good for forty?"

"Too good," he said meaningfully. "I thought women always claimed to be younger, not older."

"Now why would I do that? If I said I was twenty, people would think I looked terrible for such a young age. But for forty, I ain't so bad."

"Lady, I think you look damn fine regardless of your age."

He said it so sincerely her heart gave a quick thump of excitement. She hid that reaction well. "Let me get my coat, drag my assistant up from the back and then we can go."

When Shadow returned from the back room, she was followed by a woman whose arms were laden with printed bedsheets. As Shadow shrugged into her coat, she made introductions. "This is Kallie, my indispensable right hand and a very nice, if somewhat shy, lady. Kallie, this is Brent Bramwell. We'll be down at the coffee shop if you need me."

Kallie smiled. "Take your time. I can handle things."

"Of course you can. I never doubted it for a minute. When you finish stacking those, hang one up so everyone can see the print, okay? Maybe even near the window, where passersby will catch a glimpse of it."

Brent took her arm and led her out the door. "What do the sheets have printed on them that you want everyone to see?"

Even with their heavy coats and the frigid wind, Shadow could feel the warmth of Brent beside her. She dodged an icy patch and stepped closer still. "The, ah, proper placement of body parts."

Brent missed a beat, then laughed. "You're kidding."

"Nope." She crossed her heart. "It's kind of a visual instruction manual. I expect them to be big sellers."

"Have you bought any for yourself yet?"

The coffee shop was only two doors down, so they had already reached it before Brent asked his question. Shadow went in, breathing deeply of the wonderful aroma of fresh baked bread, pastries and flavored coffees. "I love it in here," she said, in lieu of giving him an answer. "There's nothing quite like the smell of yeast and warm bread to make you feel comforted."

"Oh, I don't know. I can think of a few scents I prefer."

Shadow slipped off her coat, took a seat at a small table, then waited until Brent had removed his own coat and taken the seat across from her. Propping her cheek against her fist on the table, she studied him. "I've annoyed you. That's why you're being so outrageous."

Brent cocked one eyebrow upward. "Outrageous? I thought I was making idle conversation."

Shadow watched him a moment longer, then sighed. "Okay. No, and I suppose that's true for many men, and probably many women as well."

"I beg your pardon?"

She laughed at his confusion. "I was answering your questions, since you claim they weren't outrageous. No, I don't own a set of the sheets, and I agree many men might name scents other than baking bread as appealing. But that's also true for women."

"But not you?"

She wagged her finger at him. "Me, I like baked bread. Very safe, you know. Ah, here's Eliza."

Shadow went through more introductions. Eliza, one of her friends, looked Brent over with a calculating eye.

"I'll have a salad," Shadow said, interrupting the intent scrutiny, "and a tuna sandwich on rye, with an apple tart for dessert."

Brent glanced at the menu briefly, then ordered the same.

"Do you want to try today's special coffee blend?"

Before Brent could answer, Shadow said, "Sure. Bring us a pot."

As Eliza walked away, Brent frowned. "What exactly is the day's special blend?"

"I have no idea. But her coffee is always wonderful. And I like to be adventurous." She stared at her water glass and added, "Don't you?"

Brent leaned back in his chair. His eyes glittered with intent, giving her just a shade of warning.

"I'll be busy most of this week getting settled in," he told her, "but if you're really so adventurous, why don't you agree to have dinner with me on Friday?"

It was only Monday. Shadow felt a little crestfallen that he didn't want to see her again until the end of the week. "I don't know. I'm not at all sure you're trustworthy. Gorgeous, but also a quick talker. I get the feeling you can be danger-ous, and I'm usually pretty good at reading people. I didn't used to be…." She shrugged. "But I am now."

"You sound cautious, not adventurous."

"There's a difference between being adventurous and being just plain stupid." Leaning forward in her chair, she stared at him and said, "I am never stupid."

She saw his mouth quirk the tiniest bit at her indignation, but his reply was mild enough. "You don't need to convince me. I've been going over your brochure. It's obvious you're an intelligent woman with a head for business."

He sounded as though he meant that, but Shadow wasn't sure. She didn't want to be drawn in too quickly. It was enough that she found him so attractive, so charming. To be complimentary and observant, too, would almost make him a saint, and she wasn't fool enough to believe that.

Eliza brought their food, and they both were quiet until she'd finished serving them. Their eyes met several times, but it wasn't until after Shadow filled her mouth with a large bite of salad that Brent asked, "So. If you don't want to go to dinner, what would you like to do? I'm settling into a new house this week, but I'm sure I could organize well enough to have you over if you just want to skip the preliminaries."

Shadow chewed thoughtfully, not hurrying, aware that Brent baited her for some reason, that he felt justified in being so scandalously blunt.

Dressed in a dark gray business suit with a finely striped shirt and silk tie, he was the epitome of male elegance. A very expensive diamond watch peeked out from under the cuff of his shirt, and his hands were large, with light brown hair sprinkled over his knuckles. Shadow picked up her napkin and dabbed at her mouth. She'd given herself plenty of time to think.

"What do you do for a living, Brent?"

His eyes narrowed slightly. "I'm in real estate. Now why don't you answer my question?"

She twirled the spoon in her rich, dark coffee. "You're wealthy?"

Brent sighed, leaned back in his chair and crossed his

arms. "Your train of thought is a little hard to follow. Or do you need to know how much money I make before you'll tell me exactly what you want from me?"

Shadow felt bone-deep regret, she really did. He had seemed so different from other men. She stood, opened her purse and dug out a few bills to cover the cost of her meal. She could feel Brent's silent attention, but it wasn't until she'd slipped on her coat that she said to him, "I don't want anything from you. Unless, that is, you want to fill out a contest entry form. I still need three more men for that." She pulled her purse strap over her shoulder and smiled down at him. "Thanks for sharing lunch with me. It's been…educational."

Disbelief crossed his features. She turned and headed for the door without a backward glance. A stunned silence hung behind her for only an instant, then she heard the sounds of Brent scrambling to his feet. She had almost made it to the entrance of her shop when he caught up with her.

His large hand encircled her upper arm, pulling her to a halt and turning her to face him. "Wait a minute."

"Have you decided to enter the contest?" She kept her smile polite.

"Forget the damn contest. I thought we were going to have lunch."

Her smile almost slipped. "That was before you made it so clear why you had asked me in the first place. If I'd known what you wanted up front, I would never have agreed to go."

The wind whipped Shadow's hair into her face and made her shiver. She lowered her head against the sting of the cold.

With a sound of disgust, Brent said, "Come on. It's too damn cold to talk out here."

The shop was warm and only mildly busy. Kallie looked up as they entered, then called to Shadow, "You have a delivery in the back."

"Thanks." She turned to Brent. "I don't think there's anything for us to say. It's a pity, really, because you seemed so amusing. But I'm not interested in a one-night stand." Her smile now hurt, but she kept it firmly in place, refusing to give him even an ounce of satisfaction. "Thanks anyway."

Brent rolled his eyes. "Oh, no you don't. Not this time. You may not have anything to say, but I do."

Two people looked up, their attention drawn by Brent's harassed tone. With resignation Shadow said, "Come on, we can talk in my office. But only for a minute." She frowned at him over her shoulder. "I have work to do."

Brent was irritated. If his stomping footsteps didn't get that across, his frown was very expressive. Shadow opened the door to the small office and flipped on a light switch as she entered. A large bouquet of yellow roses sat in the middle of her desk. She stopped in midstride, momentarily nonplussed.

Brent nearly plowed into her. "What...?"

Shadow marveled aloud, "Someone sent me flowers!" Picking up the card, she read quickly, then looked at Brent suspiciously. "Did you do this?"

He glanced at the card in her hands. "What would make you think that? Who signed the card?"

"No one. It says they're from a secret admirer."

"Well, since I'm here, and I've made my intentions well-known, there's not much of a secret to it, is there?" He sounded more annoyed by the second.

"But then who? The only men I know are friends."

"I told you—"

"Yeah, I know. Men have ulterior motives." She made a face at him. "I should have remembered that when I agreed to have lunch with you."

Brent all but growled. "Why did you think I wanted to get to know you? So we could be pals?" His voice dropped and he took a step closer. "You're a beautiful woman, Shadow. Maybe a little nutty, but I can handle that. And you're the one who started telling me how attractive you thought I was."

"Well, you are." She refused to back up from him, and instead faced him squarely. "A woman would have to be blind not to notice that. But that doesn't automatically mean I want to jump into bed with you. I do have some scruples and discretion, you know."

He seemed to consider her words, then explained gently, "You come across as something of a tease, Shadow." He caught her shoulder, holding her still. "No, don't get mad. If I've read you wrong, I'm sorry. But you can't blame me entirely for getting my signals crossed. It's not often I run across a woman who's as open and outspoken in her conversation."

Shadow stepped away from him, breaking contact. "I've been told before that I should censor my thoughts before I voice them. I try, but sometimes it's just too annoying, having to pick myself apart before I can say what I think."

His severe expression softened. "So you're attracted to me?"

"Yes, of course."

That got her a smile. "And you wouldn't mind getting to know me better?"

"I'd like to. But not if you're only biding your time until you can score."

"Oh, I think being with you would be interesting," he said with a crooked smile, "no matter what the outcome."

There was that disarming sincerity again. "Thank you."

"You're very welcome." He looked relieved, and determined. "So how about we try lunch again? Say, Wednesday?"

She knew she should refuse, but instead she asked, "Will you enter the contest? I still need you."

It was his expression that made her realize how her words had sounded. She *needed* him. He looked at her mouth as he asked, "How about if I let you know on Wednesday?"

It was like being kissed, the way he looked at her. Her heart pumped hard; her lungs constricted. There was no way she could refuse.

Shadow stuck out her hand. "It's a deal."

His palm was hot, his grip strong, and he carefully tugged her forward. Shadow froze as he bent down, but she didn't pull away. His lips were warm, firm, brushing over her cheek in the lightest of touches. She was as stunned by her reaction to that simple kiss as she was by his audacity.

Unwilling to give him the upper hand, even for a moment, she said, "That was nice." She drew a deep breath to steady her voice. "Maybe on Wednesday you can improve upon it just a bit."

Brent laughed. "I'll see what I can do. In the meantime…" He opened his coat to reach inside his pocket. Extracting a business card, he handed it to her, instructing, "If you change your mind about dinner, give me a call at the office. I'm usually there late."

He whistled as he left, and Shadow wondered if she'd eventually figure him out. One thing was certain, getting to know him would be fun, and wasn't that her business? Fun? It had been awhile—a long while—since she'd reacted to a man like this. But she had a feeling it had been just as long since Brent had enjoyed any real fun. She had a feeling they were both in for some surprises.

CHAPTER TWO

THE BITTER COLD was refreshing. Originally from California, Shadow didn't think she would ever be bored with Ohio weather. It changed with each month, and she relished waking every day to something other than continual sunshine. Not that it was cloudy today. She had to squint to tolerate the almost magical reflection of sunlight off snow and ice.

The wind whistled down the little sidewalk in front of her shop, whipping the scarf around her neck and nearly dislodging the colorful red bow in her hair. She supposed a dress hadn't been the best thing to wear while hanging Christmas lights, but she rarely planned her days completely. Usually, she just did what she felt like doing, when she felt like doing it.

Today she felt like being outdoors, decorating. And she felt like seeing Brent Bramwell.

She'd thought of him often the past few days. She knew she had him confused, but he didn't seem to mind overly. He had made that crack about her being a little nutty, but she was used to that. Everyone thought her nutty. She liked to think it was part of her charm.

Even throughout her school years she'd been different, always occupied with gaining independence and maturity so she wouldn't have to conform to anyone else's rules. Other girls had been interested in clothes and boys and music. She'd wanted only to garner enough knowledge to understand why people couldn't be more accepting, more open to change. Unfortunately, the more she learned the more she understood just how different she was, and how rigid society could be when faced with the different and unique. She'd also learned to accept what she didn't care to change.

The wind gave a particularly vicious swipe at her skirt, blowing it up and over the hem of her coat. Shadow squealed, frantically trying to push it back down and nearly toppling from her stepladder in the process. It was sheer bad luck, or maybe good, depending on your point of view, that Brent happened along just then.

BRENT COULDN'T BELIEVE his eyes when he saw Shadow balanced precariously atop a rickety stepladder on the slick walkway, her skirt billowing upward to give him an unhindered view of her nicely rounded backside in a pair of red tights. Her arms were stretched high over her head as she struggled to attach twinkle lights to the framing. When he saw her begin to flounder, tangling herself in the lights, he bolted forward.

However, the icy pavement wasn't accommodating to heroism, and he reached Shadow just in time to lose his footing, thereby knocking her from her perch. They both went down, Brent on the bottom, Shadow landing in a sitting position on his stomach.

Stunned, she twisted around to stare at him. His eyes were closed, but they opened immediately to peer up at her.

"Are you all right?" she asked breathlessly.

"This is becoming a habit." The lights she held were now

draped over his chest, and her bow had slid forward to hang over one eye. Brent laughed, which wasn't easy, considering Shadow sat on his diaphragm. She bounced slightly with his movements. "I think I would be better if you could remove yourself."

"Oh." She flushed, then quickly scrambled to her feet. It was an ignominious process and Brent, gaining several glances of her slim legs and lush backside in the tights, realized her bottom half was as enticing as her top half. Perhaps more so. He levered himself up to a sitting position, then came slowly to his feet. The seat of his pants was wet from the snow, and when he felt his head, he discovered a bump.

Shadow still wore a pretty blush, but she brazened it out, untangling the lights from her arms and leaving them draped over the stepladder. "Come on inside to my office and let me look at your head."

Déjà vu, Brent thought as she literally dragged him inside. "My head is fine, it's just my pants that are a mess."

Shadow peered around behind him. Luckily, he hadn't worn a suit today, opting instead for casual corduroy slacks, a thick fisherman sweater and a bomber jacket. She looked at his butt, made a tsking sound and hurried him through the door.

Kallie glanced up as they came in, called a friendly hello to Brent, then went back to her work. There were a couple of customers loitering, but they didn't seem to have noticed the comedy on the front walk. He supposed that was something to be grateful for.

Inside her office, Shadow closed the door and turned to Brent. She bit her lip, looked him over, then blurted, "You could maybe take them off and I could try to clean them."

Brent smiled. "First, thank me for not feeling compelled to make any sexual comments in response to your offer."

"Thank you."

He nodded. "The pants will dry. Don't worry about it. Did you hurt yourself?"

"No. You broke my fall." She cleared her throat. "Thanks again."

"What exactly were you doing out there, anyway? You should have a handyman do that sort of thing for you."

"I can take care of anything that needs to be done. I'm not helpless. Besides, I was enjoying myself. Well, at least before my skirt blew up. I, ah, don't suppose you missed that?"

He didn't bother to temper his grin. "No."

Flushing a bit more, she said, "At least my tights covered me completely." She began removing the bow that now hung around her neck, then riffled her fingers through her short curls, pushing them off her forehead. They sprang right back. "Won't you be uncomfortable eating lunch with a wet seat?"

"Maybe we could just have lunch here. That way no one would stare and wonder."

"Women would look regardless, you know."

"Thank you." Damn, she had him grinning a lot. "If we eat here, I can go home and change afterward. I'm not needed in the office today. I got everything cleared out of the way in the hope you could take some extra time off. I'd like to talk a little more."

Shadow looked thoughtful, swinging the bow from her fingers. "I suppose I could. Wednesday isn't one of our busier days. Kallie could probably handle everything. And I would like to spend more time with you."

She never ceased to amaze him. "Are you this open with every man you meet?"

"Why? Does it bother you?"

"No. It's just that I'm not used to women being so blunt. That is, unless they want…"

"What?"

He shook his head. "Never mind."

She waited a moment more, then shrugged. "I never was any good at being diffident."

Feigning disbelief, he said, "I don't believe that."

She returned his smile. "It's just the way I am, and I stopped trying to change myself long ago. But I like you, so I hope you're not so offended you won't want to see me again."

"It'll take some getting used to, but I'll manage." *What a fabrication,* he thought. Get used to her? She fascinated him. "Now, about lunch? Can we order something in?"

She accepted his change of topic with a smile. "I'll run down to Take a Break. Eliza will fix us up something. Do you have anything particular in mind?"

"Whatever you're getting is fine." Brent reached in his pocket to pull out his wallet. Shadow grabbed his hand.

"It'll be my treat." He started to object, and she added with a frown, "I insist."

Brent paused, then went for a compromise. "All right. But only if you agree to let me buy you dinner. Tonight."

"I still don't know you that well—"

"You can pick the restaurant. Surely there must be some-place local where you'd feel comfortable."

She frowned in thought for so long, he said, "I didn't ask you to solve the question of world peace, Shadow."

She finally nodded. "All right."

"Such a concession," he teased, noting her wariness. "What time do you get off tonight? I'll pick you up."

"No. I'll meet you at Reba's in the mall. About seven?"

"I have a feeling that knowing you will be a constant tug-of-war over control." He touched her cheek, felt how soft and warm she was, and shook his head. "If I say one thing are you always going to say another?"

Shadow stilled, her bow dangling from her fingertips. "I wasn't aware," she said slowly, "that you were angling for control."

Careful, Brent warned himself. She was brazen, but she was also noticeably skittish. "Right now," he said with a smile, "all I'm angling for is lunch."

She looked at him hard and evidently came to a few favorable conclusions. With a jaunty salute, she said, "Have a seat. I'll be right back."

Rather than sit, Brent wandered around her office after she'd gone. It was small, no more than ten feet square, with a large desk, two extra chairs and a filing cabinet. She had a window and door that opened to the back alley, and on the sill were several small planters. His business card rested in the center of her desk. There was also a greeting card of sorts, and without any guilt, Brent picked it up to investigate.

It was from her secret admirer.

That amused him, thinking it was probably some young, inexperienced kid hoping to gain her favor. The words inside, written in a bold, masculine scrawl, were brief, stating only that she was basically "wonderful" and that her young swain was "deeply affectionate."

Brent wondered if Shadow was as open with all men as she'd been with him. He didn't like to think so, but that would explain some young pup thinking himself in love with her. She was the type of woman to turn any man's head, but especially someone inexperienced and vulnerable.

Brent was sitting in one of the chairs, his coat beneath him to protect the seat's floral fabric, when Shadow returned. She had a pot of coffee, two mugs and a large white sack of foodstuffs. Brent sniffed, then smiled appreciatively. "It smells good, whatever it is."

"Ham and cheese stuffed croissants with pasta salad. I'm not certain what flavor the coffee is, but we'll find out soon enough."

Shadow served up all the food, poured Brent some coffee, then settled back in her own chair. He had only enough time for three bites before she pulled out an entry form for the contest. "We can fill this out while you eat."

Brent eyed the form with distaste. "I don't know, Shadow. I'm not much for contests."

"Nonsense. You know you're attractive, and you don't strike me as being particularly shy. I still need three more men, and quite frankly, I'm getting tired of soliciting them on my own."

He froze in midchew.

"Ah, I didn't mean that quite the way it sounded."

Brent took a gulp of coffee. It was, unbelievably, flavored with orange and some spice that burned his tongue. "Do you mean to tell me," he asked with incredulity, "that you *have* approached other men just as you did me?"

"Well, maybe not exactly the same." She winced a little. "You're the only man who was alone. Here, I'll show you." She opened a desk drawer and pulled out a file. Within seconds, she had seven photographs, contest entries attached, spread out on the desk.

Brent was curious, no doubt about that. He leaned forward to survey each picture.

"This is Guy Donovan," she said. "His wife, Annie, made him enter."

"Couldn't he have at least combed his hair?"

"Annie likes his hair that way." Shadow slid another photo toward him. "This is her brother Daniel."

"He looks serious."

"Oh, he is. He's a doctor. His wife, Lace, tried to get him to show his chest for the photo, but he can be stubborn."

"Who's this guy?" Brent asked, none too pleased with the photo of a dark man wearing a devil's smile.

Shadow laughed. "That's Max. He's a rascal, and he was all for taking off his shirt, but his wife, Maddie, refused. She threatened to get her own picture taken—the same way—if he dared do that. He's Annie's brother, too."

"You know these people well?" It seemed to Brent she was overly familiar with other women's husbands.

"I met them through Bea. She's the lady who creates a lot of the slogans for the clothes for me. When I was new here, Bea brought them all in to meet me. Now we're friends."

A bit relieved, Brent asked, "Was your secret admirer one of the men who entered, do you think?"

"Actually, I was wondering about that." She turned the remaining photos around. "The young man here is Chad Moreland. He's a pharmacist close by. Friendly but shy. These two older gentlemen are brothers, Dean and Frank Stiles. They own a vet clinic on the next block and they're so funny they make my sides ache. And this stud," she added, laughing, "is Ricardo. He does the landscaping for the strip mall. He's an outrageous flirt, too."

"Do you think he'd send you gifts?"

"Ricardo? Naw, he's right there in your face with his compliments."

Brent felt a slow simmer of annoyance. "You're saying he comes on to you?"

She lifted one shoulder. "He comes on to everyone female. Young and old. It's just his way."

Brent didn't like hearing that, even though it was really none of his business. "What about the others?"

"They're all just nice guys as far as I know. I can't see any of them doing this." She indicated the card on her desk. "Not only did I receive a card and candy, but for the last two nights I've gotten breather phone calls. You know the type—you say 'hello' and no one answers. I hate that. Though I know it's nothing, just a prank, it still makes me nervous."

Which proved she was no dummy, as far as Brent was concerned. "Maybe you should have your home number changed."

Shadow flushed, picking at the remaining bite of her croissant. "I thought about it," she admitted. "But I had hoped you might call me, and if I had my number changed, there was no way for you to look me up in the book."

Brent leaned back in his chair, still appalled by how easily she shared her private thoughts. It was downright distracting and he had to wonder if this wasn't just another well-thought-up female game. When elusiveness didn't work, bring out the blatant truth. "I gave you my card," he pointed out. "You didn't call me, either."

She groused at him defensively. "You already thought I was easy! I know the rules, even if I don't always follow them. Women don't call men."

"I wouldn't have minded." He kept his tone gentle, his

gaze glued to hers. He reached across the desk and caught her hand. "What did you want to talk to me about?"

"I don't know." She went strangely breathless when he touched her. "I feel…nice, around you. Very aware and alive. I like that. I kept thinking of you, and I just wanted to hear your voice. Don't get me wrong," she added when he frowned again. "I'm not husband hunting or trying to claim love at first sight. It's just that I haven't met a man I was really attracted to in a long time, and it has nothing to do with how handsome you are. It's more that you're different, just as I am." Then she groaned. "Oh boy, now I sound insulting. I mean, I know most people think I'm kind of weird. I wasn't suggesting you're weird, also."

"Shadow." Brent reached one long arm across the desk, gently laying his fingers over her soft lips, silencing her. "I don't think you're weird. Different, certainly, but in a refreshing way. I like you, too, all right?"

Since his fingers were still on her mouth, Shadow could only nod.

"Good. Now, why don't you call and have your number changed, then let me know what it is." He leaned away from her to pick up a pencil from her desk, then pulled a small piece of paper from his pocket. "My home phone number," he said, showing her the paper. "I've only just settled into the house, and the number is still new to me. I can't remember it myself yet."

After copying it down for Shadow, he handed it to her. She glanced at it and said, "You have the same exchange as me. Where did you move to?"

"Woodbine Haven. Are you familiar with it?" Brent already knew the answer to that. He was, in fact, only a few blocks from where Shadow lived. He'd been pleased when he read her file and realized how close they would be. He waited for her reaction.

She disappointed him when she said only, "I know where it is." For another moment she was silent, then, sounding disgruntled, she said, "You really are rich, aren't you?"

What could he tell her? Woodbine Haven was a section of older, grand houses renovated and advertised as a prestigious neighborhood. It was a private section, containing only about twenty houses, and each was huge, with much of the original architecture from over a century ago. Seeing Shadow's disappointment and not really understanding it, he asked, "Is that a problem?"

"No. Not really." Her soft lips twisted in a wry grimace. "But I've known wealthy men and they tend to assume women will do anything they want just because they have money. They're arrogant and condescending and egotistical."

"Probably," he said, his back going stiff with memories, "because most women *will* do anything for money. I can tell you firsthand how attractive women find the size of my wallet."

Her eyes twinkled with mischief. "Don't you have any other sizable assets that could distract them, instead?"

Exasperation crowded out the more unpleasant emotions. "Shadow…"

Laughing, she raised her hands. "I meant your new home, of course! Woodbine Haven is positively extravagant!"

Brent shook his head in mock reproach. "As soon as I can manage it," he warned softly, "you're going to view the rest of my assets, firsthand."

She attempted to hide her grin and failed miserably. "Well, in the meantime, how about filling out the entry form? *Please.*"

With a dramatic sigh, Brent agreed. "If you insist."

Shadow stood to clear away the remains of their lunch, and it was then Brent realized she hadn't removed her coat yet. It wasn't cold in the office, but he'd at first assumed she wore it to ward off the chill caused by her trip to the coffee shop. He asked her now, "Planning on going somewhere?"

Shadow gave him a puzzled look as she threw the trash in the can. "No."

"Then why don't you take your coat off?"

Heated color rushed to her cheeks, but she lifted her chin. "I don't want you to see my dress."

He sat back, prepared to be amused again. "Why not?"

"It…well…"

"Stammering, Shadow? This is different."

Her mouth tightened, then she said, "It seemed kind of cute this morning when I first dressed, but now I've decided it would be better if I kept it under wraps."

Predictably enough, Brent's gaze went to the coat concealing her dress. "Now you've intrigued me." He stood and moved closer to her. "Take it off."

It wasn't an order, more like a coaxing suggestion. Shadow shook her head. "You'll think I'm being suggestive again."

With infinite care, Brent reached out and began to undo the buttons of her soft, down-filled coat. When Shadow didn't object, holding her breath instead, he continued. She began to babble.

"It's silly, really. Just one of those joke items I'll be selling this holiday season. I wouldn't wear it anywhere but the shop, but I was in a holiday spirit this morning, and not really thinking about how it might look if someone separated me from the items I sell."

"Hush." Brent was busy giving his eyes free rein over her body. Damn, she was fine. More than fine. He had only to think of her and his muscles tensed, heated. He wanted her, and he'd have her. Soon. He parted the coat.

The dress ended well above her knees and was made of dark green knit, soft and clinging to the dips and swells of her upper body, but with a full skirt. The front, imprinted with a glitzy, decorated Christmas tree, caught and reflected the office lights off the many small sequins and buttons and beads. Brent knew it was the message printed above the fancy tree that Shadow was now feeling timid over.

Deliberately, he read it out loud. "'There's Something Special under my Tree for You.'"

Since her body was under the tree, branches reaching across her breasts, the base ending at the notch of her thighs, Brent could understand her shyness. That she looked unbelievably enticing in the dress would only add to her dilemma. Brent skimmed the coat completely off her shoulders and down her arms, then tossed it onto the chair he'd just vacated. His hands went to her shoulders, straight and broad for a woman, emphasizing the tiny span of her waist.

"I don't ever want you to be embarrassed with me, Shadow. Promise me."

Nearly speechless, Shadow whispered, "I promise."

He caught her face in his hands. His thumbs stroked over the softness of her cheeks and chin and jaw, his fingers delving into her dark, loosely curling hair. So incredibly soft, so warm. For an endless moment he stood there like that, enjoying the differences in their sizes, the light, feminine fragrance of her, the way she watched him, her thoughts now transparent without her speaking a word.

Then he released her and stepped away. "You'll have your phone number changed tomorrow?"

Shadow cleared her throat, then took several deep, open-mouthed breaths. Finally she said, "Yes. I think it might be best. I've already told Kallie not to accept any more packages for me, to send them back if more should come."

"It's probably nothing to worry about, but be careful. Don't go to the parking lot alone, and keep your door locked at home."

Her slim brows lifted. "I do that anyway," she answered, obviously annoyed. "I'm not careless."

Not careless, but she was independent. "Fine." The last thing Brent had meant to do was insult her. "Let's get that damned entry form filled out then, if you really think it's necessary."

Shadow didn't give him a chance to change his mind. She hustled back behind her desk, picked up the form and smiled at him. "I've already filled in your name. Now I need your exact address."

It took only a few moments to fill out the top portion of the form. When they got to the next section, Shadow didn't bother hiding her anticipation.

"You said you're not married?"

"Am I disqualified if I say yes?"

"Availability is not a requirement for entering," Shadow said stiffly, glaring at him.

Brent chuckled. "I didn't lie. I'm not married now, nor have I ever been."

Tilting her head, Shadow asked, "Engaged? Or otherwise involved?"

"That's on the form?"

"No. It just seemed prudent to ask."

Again he laughed. "I already told you I was here alone, remember?"

"But that was when we'd just met. I thought it might be good to verify it."

His low laugh rumbled. "No. No engagement, no involvement."

Nodding, she glanced at the form, then asked, "Ever been engaged?"

"Let me guess," he said, eyeing Shadow lazily. "That's not actually on the form, either."

She shook her head, unrepentant. "Curiosity."

Brent took his time deciding whether or not he wanted to answer. Finally he figured what the hell. She may as well know how he felt about marriage. "Up until a few months ago I was engaged, but it's over now. And that was enough for me."

"Oh." The papers were laid on the desk, forgotten. "I'm sorry. I didn't mean to dredge up bad memories for you."

"You didn't. I knew I was being married for my money. I expected that. But then she informed me she didn't want children because it would ruin all her fun."

Shadow winced.

"Since having kids was the main reason *I* had wanted to marry, I ended it. And I'm not sorry that it's over. Just the opposite."

"How does she feel about it?"

Brent shrugged. "She still makes a nuisance of herself on occasion. When she found out I was moving, she took it as a sign that I was too heartbroken to stay in the same area with her."

"But you're not heartbroken?" Shadow asked.

Briefly closing his eyes, Brent said, "No. I would have

made her a lousy husband, and vice versa. I'd still like to have children someday. But now I know what to look for in a wife."

"Such as?"

Apparently, as long as he was talking, Shadow was more than willing to listen. He took her by surprise when he reached across the desk to chuck her under the chin.

"For one thing, she can't be a businesswoman. Too independent. And she would have to be biddable. Someone content to be a wife and mother above all things."

Shadow smiled in understanding. "What you're looking for isn't all that unique, and one of the reasons I don't plan to marry, even though I'd love to have children, too. I even tried once—marriage, I mean. When I was only seventeen."

"Seventeen?" She'd been little more than a child. The idea was appalling.

Her eyes a little sad, she said, "I thought I wanted someone who would love me, who would put me first. Now, looking back, I think I just wanted to have sex. With my family upbringing, I couldn't do that without being married."

"What happened?" Brent was genuinely curious, which wasn't at all usual for him. A woman's personal history had never interested him before. But then, he'd never met anyone even remotely like Shadow.

"We were both young and stupid." She straightened the papers on her desk, fidgeting, then came to some hidden decision. She looked up to meet his gaze. "He also liked to smack me around. The first time it happened, I kept quiet because I hated to admit everyone was right, that I'd made a mistake. The second time, I left him, but then I let him convince me to give our marriage another try. That was a real mistake."

Brent stared at her, aware of a slow burn churning in his gut. Someone had dared to hit her? He didn't care that it was long ago, that it had less than nothing to do with him. He hadn't even known her and barely knew her now.

But none of that mattered. If she pointed the guy out today, right this second, he'd beat him into the ground. Brent drew a breath, barely getting hold of himself, and asked, "What did you do?"

"The third time he hit me I decided to get even, and when he turned his back on me that night, I surprised him with a baseball bat."

Brent sat back, amazed. "Good for you."

"I broke two of his ribs." She added with a shrug, "He never asked me to come back after that."

Through the tumultuous mix of anger and disbelief, Brent found a spot of laughter. It amazed him that she could always do that, could always amuse him, no matter what.

Her incredible eyes were still twinkling when he commented, "That was a long time ago. You haven't had the urge to give it another try?"

"Only once. When I was twenty-four, seven years after my first marriage. I almost tied that stupid knot again, but like you, I luckily found out beforehand what I was getting into. Right before, actually. Two days prior to the wedding, I discovered my fiancé going into debt on the inheritance I'd just received from my grandmother. When I walked away, he was in a killing rage, because he'd promised most of my money on investments and was seriously in debt without it. I wasn't surprised when he told me he'd only wanted me for my money, anyway. Not that I'm in your league, but Grandmother Harrison did leave me a pretty sum, enough for me to finally decide I could be independent, both personally and financially."

She tapped the pencil on the desk. "That was seven years ago. Now I'm coming to realize how much I'd like to have children of my own. Of course, in this day and age, you don't need to tie yourself into a loveless marriage to become a parent. One of my new friends Annie says I'm suffering my 'seven year itch' since my relationship fiascoes seem to come seven years apart." Shadow laughed. "I told her I wasn't, because I had no intention of getting married. But I am giving the parent thing some thought. As they say, my biological clock is ticking."

"You want to be a mother *now?*"

"Don't look so worried! You're not in danger of being an unwilling sperm donor. I would never get pregnant by a man without asking him first. And anyway, I'd probably do it through a clinic. You know, artificially inseminated, and all that."

Brent recovered enough to comment, "That doesn't sound like any fun."

"No, it doesn't. But then, the alternative isn't always that great, either."

Brent quirked a brow at that artless confession, then laughed when Shadow slapped her hand over her mouth. "Go on," he encouraged her, anxious to hear more.

"Forget I said that," she mumbled past her fingers. "I didn't mean to cast aspersions on the male species and their abilities."

Brent continued to smile. "I was taking it more as a challenge."

"Well, for Pete's sake, don't! I certainly didn't mean it as one."

"You make me laugh, Shadow. I like that. I like you. And as long as we're both in agreement that marriage is not a state to be devoutly sought, I think we can have some of your acclaimed *fun* together. Don't you?"

"I suppose," she agreed, but without as much enthusiasm as Brent had hoped for.

Nodding at her desk, he suggested, "Why don't we finish that contest form, then I'll help you hang the rest of your decorations."

"You don't have to do that," she assured him.

"I want to. Besides, I have nothing better to do with my time today."

"Oh. Well then, the next question is what three qualities do you look for most in a woman?"

"Attractiveness, honesty and sensuality."

Shadow stared. "That was mighty quick. You don't need time to think about it?"

Propping his elbow on the arm of his chair, he rested his chin in his palm. "Nope."

Shadow smacked her pencil down on her desk. "In that order, I suppose?"

"Certainly. If a woman isn't attractive, I wouldn't pursue her in the first place. If I got to know her, and she wasn't honest—a new criterion of mine—I wouldn't trust her, and therefore wouldn't want a relationship with her. If we started a relationship, and she was a cold fish, or a prude, there'd be no point in continuing." He shrugged.

Shadow shook her head in dismay, but then quipped, "At least you're honest about it."

"Which part are you objecting to, Shadow? It can't be the looks part, because you have to know how sexy you are."

"I'm…average. That's all."

He just smiled. "I find it hard to believe you could be a prude."

She scowled at him. "If you're trying to find out if I'm honest, the answer should be obvious. I wouldn't put out the effort necessary to lie. But what bothered me was that you didn't think a sense of humor was important. Or honor. Or generosity."

"They would have come in place after sensuality."

She rolled her eyes. "Next question—what would you consider the perfect romantic evening?"

"You mean there's only one?"

She clicked her teeth together. "You'll have to narrow it down to your favorite."

He shifted, propping his elbows on his knees, tapping his fingers together thoughtfully. When his eyes came to hold Shadow's gaze, hers darkened in reaction. He said quietly, his words deep and slow, "Being alone with a woman, the sounds of a storm outside, a warm fire. Naked, with all the time in the world ahead of us."

She looked taken aback by his deliberate and intimate use of "us." She shook her head when she realized she hadn't written his comments down, and hurried to do so, though her fingers shook slightly with the effort.

"Anything else?" Brent asked, enjoying her reaction.

"What…" Shadow cleared her throat, then tried again. "What do you like to do for fun?"

"Water ski, swim, jog." He grinned at her. "Make love."

Her pencil paused, then she quickly scribbled down his answer. "And what type of work do you do?" She was writing as she asked the final question, studiously avoiding his gaze, so she missed his expression of doubt and determination.

Beyond the bare bones, his work shouldn't interest her.

Glancing up, she said, "You gave me a business card, but it doesn't really say. Just your name and a number."

He had many businesses, and even more managers to see to those businesses. That was why he hadn't known about Shadow until boredom had forced him to come to Ohio, involving himself with his newest venture. He answered vaguely, hoping she wouldn't press. "I'm self-employed, running my own affairs. As I said earlier, I'm in real estate."

"Is it interesting?" Shadow asked as she wrote down the final information.

He looked at her bent head, the way her silky curls loosely framed her face. "More so each day."

She smiled at Brent as she folded the papers. "That's about it. All we need now is a picture. As I told you, Hot Shots here in the complex has offered to take the contestants' photos for free. We can go there now if you like, or sometime later in the week."

"If you have the time, we might as well get it over with."

THE PHOTOGRAPHER WAS very friendly—a little too friendly, Shadow thought. The woman fawned over Brent, insisting he do the shot without a shirt, and Brent, surprising Shadow, decided to oblige her. He stripped off his shirt without a hint of modesty—not that modesty was necessary. He looked incredible.

Though his hair was light brown, the hair on his chest was darker, not overly thick, but sexy. He was muscular, with broad sinewy shoulders and sculpted biceps. His abdomen was hard, lean, divided by a slender line of that dark body hair. It swirled around his navel, then disappeared into his trousers.

Shadow's heart began an erratic tattoo.

Just watching him, she flushed. Her eyes narrowed as the photographer moved Brent this way and that, taking far more shots than she had with the other contestants, her hands lingering on his bare skin. By the time they were done, Shadow wasn't feeling particularly charitable toward the woman and left without saying farewell.

Brent ignored her mood, going right to work on hanging up the remaining decorations. She insisted on helping, and took immense pleasure in each light they connected, each wreath they hung. The November weather was characteristically biting, and by the time they finished, Brent's cheekbones were red with the cold, Shadow's nose just as rosy. They went inside, laughing, and plugged in the electrical cord.

Twinkle lights wound around the outside frame of the door and the overhang, where a huge wreath was centered. Inside, each window sported a different colored light, with a smaller wreath. The results weren't uniform or elegant, but rather festive and fun. She liked it.

Shadow was taken off guard when Brent gave her a huge hug, enfolding her in his arms and lifting her off her feet.

"Thank you. I've enjoyed myself."

Aware of Kallie watching surreptitiously, and of the few customers who gave them their attention, Shadow forced herself to pull away. She didn't want to. She wanted to pull him down to the ground and have her way with him.

She sighed. "It was fun, wasn't it? Thank you for helping."

Brent, too, noticed their audience. He caught her cold hand, led her to her office and closed the door. In the next instant, she found herself pressed up against him.

"Brent?"

"I can't wait until tonight to kiss you, Shadow." He

stripped off his leather gloves and his hands came up to cup her face, his palms warm and firm. He searched her face, lingering on each small detail, and a small smile flirted with his mouth. "You're making me nuts, you know that?"

Shadow didn't have time to answer. Brent lowered his head and touched his lips to hers—not tentatively, as she would have expected a first kiss to be, but purposefully, his mouth moving over hers, his body pressing closer until she was held securely against his length.

She could hear his breathing, smell the spicy scent of his aftershave, feel the heat and hardness of his body. Tension pulsed beneath her skin, a reaction she'd never felt before, certainly not from a simple kiss. When his tongue came out to lick over her lips, she opened, and he immediately took advantage of her quiet submission.

He tasted wonderful, she thought, curling her hands over his shoulders. Without conscious thought she closed her lips on his tongue and gently sucked.

Brent went rigid, then groaned. His body crushed closer, his breath pelting her cheek, hot and fast.

"Damn." He drew away, his eyes searching her face in near wonder. "I knew from the minute I saw you you'd be like this." He pressed his forehead to hers. "I want you, Shadow."

The words leaped from her tongue. "I want you, too. I really do."

His eyes flared, then quickly narrowed when she added with regret, "But it's too soon. I…we can't just give in to lust, Brent. I hardly know you."

He released her to shove his hands in his pockets. His sigh was long and heartfelt. "How did I know you were going to say that?"

Shadow turned her back on him. This was when he

would start issuing ultimatums. She wanted to see him again, and she hadn't lied about wanting him. She did, more than she could remember wanting a man in a long, long time. But she also had deeply ingrained morals, and sleeping with a man she hardly knew went against everything she believed right and proper. Never mind that she felt she'd known him forever.

BRENT STARED AT SHADOW'S dejected stance. Withdrawn? Shadow? Not a chance. It had to be simply another part of the game she enjoyed playing. He said easily, "I better be going. I'll see you tonight at Reba's. And Shadow?"

She turned, her surprise evident.

"Don't be late."

"You still want to see me tonight?"

With a crooked grin, Brent moved toward her. Touching one finger to her soft mouth, he whispered, "Most definitely. But for my peace of mind, I think we should keep the kissing to a minimum." He laughed. "My libido just can't take all these sudden changes."

CHAPTER THREE

IT WAS TEN MINUTES after seven, and the parking lot was dark and icy cold. Shadow couldn't believe her luck, had in fact been cursing the lack of it for the past fifteen minutes.

Leaving her '66 Mustang convertible, a beauty she had always loved until now, Shadow slammed the door. It made a hollow, echoing sound across the deserted lot. The main parking area had plenty of spaces in it, but she preferred to leave her car in the back. It was less convenient to the entrance of the shops, but out of harm's way from heavy traffic and loose shopping carts.

Shadow shivered as she hurried across the pavement, holding her coat collar tight around her throat. Brent would think she'd stood him up, when that was the very last thing she'd do.

Kallie was already gone, the shop locked up. Wednesday was their only early evening, every other night of the week they were open till nine, except Sunday, when they worked only a half day. Rather than go to the bother of re-opening the shop, Shadow stepped into a phone booth and closed the door so the light would come on. With numb fingers she flipped through the phone book until she found the listing for Reba's. Her teeth were chattering by the time she managed to dial the number and get an answer.

It was no surprise that she had to wait several minutes before Brent could be located. The restaurant-bar was busy in the early evening. Shadow felt such relief when Brent finally came to the phone, she actually sank back against the icy glass wall of the phone booth.

"Shadow?"

"Oh, Brent, I—I—I'm so sorry."

There was a heavy silence, then with some urgency, he demanded, "Are you all right?"

"I—I'm fine. Just f-freezing. My stupid car won't start. I d-d-didn't want you to think I'd stood you up."

Another pause, and Brent asked, "Where are you?"

"I'm outside the sh-shop. I've already locked it up for the night…. Brent?"

"I'm trying to figure out how long it'll take me to get to you. I'm still new to the area, remember."

"You don't have to—"

"Yes I do." She heard the smile in his voice. "Get in your car and lock the doors. I'll be there as quick as I can."

"I could call a cab."

"I won't argue with you, Shadow. Do as I told you and I'll be there in about five minutes."

She stared at the phone, appalled by his peremptory gall. She was more than ready to tell him what she thought, despite the bitter cold, when the phone went dead.

She returned the receiver to its cradle. Five minutes? Only if he sped. More like ten, probably. Bracing herself for the blast of bone-chilling cold, Shadow left the dubious comfort of the phone booth and hurried back to her car. She immediately locked herself inside—which she would have done with or without his instruction.

It was only about four minutes later when she saw the

man approaching. But it wasn't Brent; she was certain of that. He wasn't nearly tall enough, didn't have Brent's long-legged, purposeful stride. The lighting at this section of the lot was dim, not quite reaching into the corner where she'd parked. Shadow stared, wide-eyed, as a face came into view.

The stocking cap pulled over his forehead and the scarf around his neck concealed his features until he stood directly in front of her window. He gave a broad smile and motioned for her to roll down the window.

With immense relief, Shadow recognized him.

"Hi," she called through the window.

He leaned against her door, propped his arms on the window frame and stared in at her. "You need some help?"

She shook her head. "No, everything's fine."

Again, he motioned for her to roll down the window.

The lie came easily to her lips. "I can't," she called loudly. "It's broken."

He frowned then, but said, "Open your door. I'll see if I can fix your car."

Again she lied. "There's nothing wrong with it. I'm just waiting for someone."

He seemed surprised by her answer. He straightened, stalked two steps away from the car, but quickly returned. There was a distinct scowl on his features now. "Open the door," he said again, and added, "I need to talk to you about the contest."

Shadow looked up in relief when headlights flashed across her windshield. Staring toward Brent, she said, "There's my friend now." She watched, awed by the midnight-black Jaguar XJS he drove, as he pulled up close. He parked directly in front of her, his headlights nearly blinding, and after he'd climbed from his car, she turned to open her door.

The other man was gone.

Brent looked past her. He frowned ferociously when Shadow stepped up beside him.

"A friend of yours?" he asked, his gaze still focused on the darkness beyond the lot.

"N-no." The cold immediately wrapped around her. "He was one of the contestants, actually. The pharmacist. I have no idea what he was doing here."

Brent noticed her shivers then, and quickly hustled her to his car. The motor was still running and the interior was filled with warmth. He pressed her into the passenger's seat, quickly asked her to explain what her car was doing, then gave her a firm kiss on her trembling lips. He closed the door, leaving to investigate her engine.

Shadow watched as he lifted the hood. He was very commanding, taking charge, ushering her about with a proprietary air. She couldn't decide if she should let him get away with it or not. On principle, she shouldn't. But cold as she was, she couldn't honestly say she resented his assistance.

Brent finished in only a minute. She saw him close her hood, make certain her doors were locked, then he moved his big body heavily into the seat beside her. He was silent a moment, gazing out the windshield. When he did turn to her, his expression was impassive.

"Where did the guy come from—the contestant—and what did he want?"

Something in his probing gaze drove away the last of her chills. "He just showed up," she admitted, "and asked if I needed any help. I told him I didn't, refused to open my window or my door, and told him I was waiting for someone. Why?"

"Your distributor cap is gone. Someone had to have taken it."

Incredulous, Shadow demanded, "Someone had the nerve to tamper with my car? With *my* car?"

Brent looked down at his clasped hands on the wheel. "I'd suggest we call the police, but I don't think there's anything they could do about it." Then he looked up again. "I just hate leaving your car here overnight. A classic like that, someone might feel tempted to make off with it."

Shadow considered that, then suggested, "I could have the security guys keep an eye on it for me. They're really nice, so I don't think they'll mind."

Brent slanted her a look. "Do you know everyone around here?"

"I'm friendly," she said with a shrug. "And when I first leased the shop, it needed a lot of decorating done to it. I spent some pretty late hours here. The security guys made a habit of checking up on me. Still do sometimes. I only recently put the finishing touches on everything, like the window blinds the day I, ah, met you." She flushed, remembering that day. She rushed on, saying, "They're nice men, but they flatly refused to enter the contest."

He made a sound somewhere between laughter and irritation. "Have you solicited every guy in the area?"

"Yeah, pretty much." She grinned at him. "I was about out of hope when I found you. Now I only need two more." He touched her cheek, the corner of her mouth. "Do you have a number for the security people?"

"Yes."

"Are you hungry, or would you rather I just take you home?"

"Well," she said, feeling suddenly shy, "I was thinking,

if you hadn't already eaten, we could pick up a pizza and take it to my place. I could call security from there."

Brent went very still beside her. "Your place?"

"It isn't an invitation for anything more than pizza. I...I'm trusting you."

Slowly nodding, Brent answered just as quietly. "I can handle that. Pizza sounds great." Then he reached across the seat to take her hand, and to Shadow's immense pleasure, he didn't release it until they had reached the pizza parlor and had to get out to order.

She wanted to be with Brent, but she didn't want to sit in a crowded restaurant and look at him across a table. She was willing to trust her instincts, and that meant trusting Brent, because she felt safe with him. Even stranger than that, she was relaxed in his company, comfortable with him as a man. There was no way she was going to let such an appealing aberration pass her by.

OPENING THE WINE was a mistake. Brent had purchased it, along with the large, loaded pizza, while she'd gone to the ladies' room to refresh herself. She'd been nervous over her decision to take him to her home, and had needed a few private moments to collect herself. When she'd returned, Brent had already paid and was waiting for her by the door.

He pointed out his house on the way and Shadow noted she would pass it each time she traveled to or from work. It was every bit as massive and impressive as she'd imagined it to be. Brent had, predictably, shrugged off her awe. What had surprised Shadow, though, was that he was just as impressed with her much smaller home. It, too, was very old, but not nearly as large or in as excellent shape. But she was working on that.

"Did you do all these renovations by yourself?"

She puffed up with pride. "For the most part. My father was a handyman. He taught me quite a bit about repairs and upkeep. But you can see I have a long way to go yet."

Sitting in the kitchen, a large airy room with solid oak cabinets and an ancient, rustic stove, Shadow pointed out the need for new wainscoting and chair rails. Wallpaper would be the last thing she purchased.

A fat, bright red candle burned on the round, pedestal-base oak table between them. Shadow watched, slightly light-headed, as Brent refilled her wineglass. The pale, golden shimmer of the candle shone through the crimson wine, illuminating it, fascinating her. She hadn't particularly liked the taste of it at first, but had been hesitant to admit that to Brent. He was more sophisticated than her and plainly assumed wine was necessary with pizza.

Now, however, after three full glasses, and the resulting lethargic unconcern, Shadow was beginning to wonder if she should tell him the sorry truth. She was, plainly put, a down-home girl and painfully unsophisticated.

Shoving the empty pizza box aside, Brent caught her limp hand and tugged her from her seat. "Show me the rest of your house."

Blinking at his handsome face, Shadow noticed things she hadn't noticed before: the way his light brown hair curled slightly over his forehead, despite the perfection of the cut, and his rugged beard shadow, now apparent at this hour of the evening. And the way his green eyes seemed so warm and mellow, so…caressing. Swaying toward him, Shadow whispered, "Kiss me again first."

Brent drew up short at her request, but only for a

moment. He lowered his head and touched his mouth discreetly to the corner of her parted lips.

Shadow sighed in disappointment. Her heart shuddered, her breathing quickened, but mostly in anticipation. His kiss was over with before she even finished reacting to it.

His smile was gentle now, the grip on her arm firm.

Turning her away with a small chuckle, Brent reminded her, "Your house? I would like to see the rest of it. You'd made me think it was small, but it's not. Not at all. How many rooms do you have?"

It was impossible to hide her disgruntled irritation with him and his avuncular kiss, but she tried. "There are five bedrooms, four upstairs. But I haven't done a thing up there yet. It's all locked up, and it'll probably stay that way until summer."

"I love your dining room and living room."

"Thank you." She sent him a sappy smile. "I refinished the floors myself. There was this musty old carpet hiding the hardwood floors. Some of the flooring had to be replaced along the outside wall, but other than that, it was in good shape, just needing a thorough polishing."

As SHADOW EXTOLLED the magnificence of her house, Brent made appropriate sounds of appreciation, but his attention was on her. She wasn't walking quite steadily, and she couldn't seem to take her eyes off him for more than a few moments.

Shadow grinned at him suddenly. "My room is the only one I have completely finished. Would you like to see it?"

He hesitated in answering, but only for a second. "Lead the way."

The living room and dining room were on the left side

of the house, a curved, polished wood stairway gracing the middle. The kitchen and a small guest bathroom were situated at the back, and to the right was a family room with a huge, full wall stone fireplace. Behind that, adjacent to the kitchen, was the room Shadow had claimed as her own.

Double doors opened into a spacious, high-ceilinged room, with an ornately etched cornice framing the walls. Patterned rugs in pastel shades of yellow, green and blue covered the floor. The down-filled comforter on her bed was plush and colored the palest yellow, with deep green floral throw pillows tossed near the high headboard.

The room abounded in plants, hanging from the corners, set on the sills of the three high, narrow windows and placed on every available surface. Vine printed wallpaper covered three of the walls, but behind her bed there was a thin, gauzy, pale yellow material, parted to hang on either side, framing her bed and giving it prominence in the room. All the furniture was antique, heavy and dark. It was a mix of feminine and masculine, beautifully done.

Brent wandered about the room, idly touching various picture frames, small jewelry cases and the abundance of womanly items: hair bows, earrings, perfume bottles. He came to a closed door, not the type to open to a closet, and turned to Shadow.

"You can go in. It's my bathroom, another room I'm real proud of. Maybe my favorite room in the house."

Shadow remained by the door where they'd first entered. To Brent's discerning eye, she appeared to be propping herself up against the wall.

She waited for his reaction to the bathroom, watching him closely. What wasn't to like? The antiquated tub sat on clawed feet, two narrow wooden Shaker tables beside it holding an array of bath oils, thick towels and a few lush plants. Directly over the tub she'd built a ledge, trimmed in brass and nearly covered with different-sized colored candles that gave off a blend of subtle fragrances. He thought the room downright decadent, but it also showed what a traditionalist she was.

Everything—sink, tub and ceramic tiles—was white. The wide window on the back wall, glazed and opaque, was covered with only a thin, pale sheer to allow sunlight, or moonlight, to shine into the room. Brent stared at the tub for a long time, imagining her in it, naked, with each and every candle glowing around her.

He turned just in time to see her tip up her glass, gulping the remainder of her wine, which she had carried with her. He watched her with a slight smile as he approached.

"These rooms are very much like you, Shadow. Bright and open. A little different, but pleasantly so. And very inviting." He took the wineglass from her hand and set it on her nightstand. "You've turned bathing into a hedonistic experience, sweetheart."

Her eyes widened at the endearment. She gave a slight groan and swayed toward him, her gaze on his mouth, which Brent couldn't keep from tilting up in an amused grin.

He caught her shoulders and held her away, his sigh long, but indulgent. "You don't drink very often, do you, Shadow?"

"Never." She nestled close to his chest and he allowed it, even stroked her soft hair. "You smell delicious," she said, rubbing her nose against the front of his shirt, then upward, against his throat.

Brent went rigid as his body reacted predictably to her innocent—intoxicated—seduction. It wasn't easy, and his hands even shook, but he caught her shoulders again and moved her back so her body could no longer lean into his.

"You're going to force me," he said with a growl, "to prove how noble I can be."

Ignoring his proffered nobility, Shadow ran her small, warm hands over his chest, down his ribs. His breath caught as she skimmed her fingers over his abdomen, but she stopped there. He was equally disappointed and relieved.

"Brent," she implored in a whisper, "kiss me."

She didn't wait for him to comply, but grasped the hair at the back of his neck and pulled his face down so she could reach his mouth. Brent was half laughing, half groaning at his predicament, until her soft breasts came up against his chest and her belly pressed into his erection.

He wasn't a damn saint, Brent told himself, giving up all at once and kissing her as he'd wanted to since he'd first spotted her in the window. He forced her mouth open, sank his tongue deep, tasting her, devouring her. She was an irresistible temptation and he was tired of resisting.

She groaned with appreciation. "You make me crazy, Brent," she said between kissing his throat, his ear, his mouth again. "I've never felt like this before."

"It's the wine," he rasped harshly, struggling between guilt and lust. But Shadow only shook her head.

Taking his words as an excuse, not the complaint they had actually been, she whispered, "It's not just a physical thing, you know? I mean, all those books that proclaim fireworks and explosions and..." Her hands curled into the front of his sweater, fisting in the material. She shook him slightly, or at least tried to, and said, "I'm feeling them, Brent!"

He almost laughed at her turbulent expression. He did untangle her fingers from his clothes and carefully pinned her arms to her sides. If he wasn't so damned aroused, the situation might actually have been funny. "Shadow, we have to stop now. I'm only here for the pizza, remember?" He smoothed her dark hair, continually drawn by the silkiness of it. "If you keep kissing me like that, I'm going to lose my head. And unfortunately, I have the feeling you'll never forgive me if I take advantage of you tonight."

"Oh, Brent, please," she said, "take advantage of me." Her look was earnest and filled with worry. "It might not ever be like this again."

Damn, how could one eccentric little woman twist him inside out? "Sweetheart, the feelings aren't going anywhere. When you're ready, you'll feel them again, I promise."

Abruptly moving away from him, she asked, horrified, "You don't want me?"

Brent ran a hand over his face. He should give her what she wanted, nobility be damned. But the truth was he didn't want to alienate her and possibly lose her so soon simply because he couldn't control himself. Even now she was swaying where she stood, the wine affecting her more than he would have thought possible. She trembled, her cheeks flushed, her eyes heavy. All in all, she made a very enticing picture standing there before him in the Christmas tree dress and red tights.

And she looked so damned forlorn, as if she really believed he didn't want her. If she took a closer look at his lap, she'd find the evidence she wanted. But he was a man, not a boy, and he had himself firmly in control. Always.

It was that thought that made up his mind. He could use this situation, as absurd as it seemed, to show Shadow a thing or two about his character. Come the morning, she would no longer doubt who was in control.

She whispered suddenly, "I'm in an agony of suspense, Brent. What are you thinking?"

"I'm thinking," he said gently, "that you're drunk."

She licked her lips. "It's true, I don't drink much. But it wouldn't have happened this way with any other man, I'm sure of that." She stared up him, her big brown eyes slumberous, heated. "There's just…something about you."

Feeling very pleased with her statement, Brent said, "I'm glad," and he hugged her close. She misunderstood his intent and cried out in relief, squeezing her arms around his neck in a near choke hold.

Carefully, Brent gauged his actions and her responses as he took her mouth again. She tasted sweet, and he wanted to kiss her all over. He'd prove himself trustworthy, a man in control, if it killed him.

She accepted the thrust of his tongue and gave him her own. He held her steady for his well-planned onslaught. When her body moved against his, he countered her movements, making her heartbeat race and her breathing hitch. His erection throbbed against her soft belly. He stroked her slender back, down her spine, until he could fill his hands with her firm backside. He lifted her a bit, caressing her, holding her against him.

Their mingled groans echoed loudly in the silent room. Slowly, Brent began backing her toward her bed. He wanted her—as much or more than she wanted him.

The bed was large and raised high off the floor so that the backs of her thighs bumped into the firm mattress. Brent didn't lower her right away, as she seemed anxious for him to do. Instead, he went to work on the zipper at the back of her dress, teasing her by lowering it slowly, letting the tips of his fingers graze her spine as he did so.

His mouth never left hers for long; he couldn't seem to stop kissing her, touching her. He knew his touted discipline was precarious at best.

He pushed her dress over her shoulders and down her arms, bunching it around her wrists. When Shadow went to pull it free, Brent stopped her, holding her hands and watching the small thrill in her eyes as she realized she was caught, her arms pinned to her sides. He had a feeling she'd never have allowed such a thing if she hadn't been tipsy. But the fact was she had drunk too much, and now she was at his mercy. He had plenty to spare, but he also intended to show her a thing or two.

Brent stared down at her, then carefully guided her to lie flat on the bed. His chest rose and fell with his deep breathing and his hands trembled with need. He visually explored her exposed skin, her throat, the soft swells of her full breasts above the red demi-bra she wore. Lowering himself, he half reclined on her, his hips between her legs, which still dangled over the side of the bed, his upper body supported by his bent arms. He dipped his head, letting her feel first the heat of his breath, then the moist touch of his tongue on her skin.

"You're a tease, Brent Bramwell," she whispered breathlessly.

Using his teeth, he lightly nibbled where her pulse fluttered at the base of her throat. "I fully intend," he whispered, "to get as much enjoyment out of this as I can under the circumstances. So don't think to rush me."

"What circumstances?" she asked him, but he easily distracted her. Her eyes closed languorously when he moved his attention to her ear. She squirmed a little as he licked, teased, and her breath sighed out brokenly.

He cupped her breast and her small nipple grew taut beneath the layer of silky material. Using his thumb, Brent flicked and rubbed, and she arched, trying to align their bodies, but he wouldn't allow it.

Slowly, he dragged the narrow straps of her bra down her upper arms. Damn, he wanted to see her, all of her. He tugged the bra down the rest of the way until it caught beneath her breasts. Her nipples were dark pink, puckered tight. He took only a moment to nuzzle his face into her softness before he closed his mouth over one sensitive peak.

Shadow jerked sharply. "Brent!"

"What?" He licked, tugged carefully with his teeth. "Tell me, sweetheart."

"It's…almost too much," she gasped.

"It's not enough." He switched to her other breast, drawing her deep. He used one hand to soothe the nipple he'd just abandoned, while the other grasped her leg high on her thigh, urging it up and over his hip.

The heat was nearly unbearable, pulsing beneath his skin, gathering between his legs. More than anything, he wanted to be inside her.

Shadow redoubled her efforts to get her arms free, but now her bra added to her restraints.

"Shh," he said, leaning back to look at her breasts.

"Brent, don't leave me."

"How are you feeling, sweetheart?"

She struggled for breath. "My head is whirling, but it's not the wine."

He felt grim, and determined. "Of course not."

"It's not! It's you and what you're doing to me, how you're kissing me."

"This?" he asked, and gave another sweet sucking kiss to her nipple, while flattening his palm on her small belly.

"Yes." Her legs moved restlessly beneath him.

He'd never known a woman to be so wild, so urgent and demanding. He didn't dare undress her; he knew he didn't have that much restraint.

Breathing hard, he shoved down her tights until he had free access to her body. It was nearly his undoing.

Hot. And wet and so damned soft he knew he had to hurry or he'd never make it. Her curls were dark here, too, glossy, and she gasped at his first touch, then went perfectly still.

He tested her with gentle touches that only caused her to demand more. She gave a hoarse groan, lifting her hips when he slid his middle finger deep inside her. She was so tight, so silky wet and ready for him. He could just imagine…

No, he'd better not. He could already feel the clench of her muscles, the tiny spasms. Damn, he'd barely touched her and she was as far gone as he. Her response was surprising, and arousing.

Concentrating on her every reaction, Brent began to caress her, carefully, calculating each move and her reaction to it, discovering what pleased her most. It wasn't long before he had what he wanted.

"Ahh, Brent." Her words were strangled, rasped out through parted lips.

"That's it, honey." He felt on the verge of his own climax, every muscle in his body taut and straining. "Open your eyes, Shadow, and look at me."

She did and he felt seared to his bones by the heat in her gaze. Keeping his eyes locked with hers, he squeezed another finger inside her, then used his thumb to stroke her where she needed his touch most. It was incredible, watching her as she climaxed. Her body tensed, trembled; her eyes were wild on his face, her hips straining against his fingers. It took all his control to keep from coming himself. He kissed her deeply, taking her cries into his own mouth, holding her close until the very last shudder had ended, until she went limp and drowsy.

His heart still galloped, but hers had settled into a slow, deep rhythm. Brent levered himself upward, taking in her sprawled form with triumph and possession. Shadow didn't move, not even when he sat up fully at her side.

She was sound asleep, partly from the wine, most likely, but he was taking a great deal of the credit after the screaming climax he'd just given her. Brent couldn't ever remember feeling quite so satisfied, especially given the fact that his erection still throbbed and his muscles were bunched and rigid.

He was a little chagrined when Shadow didn't stir even as he pulled her arms free from the confines of her clothing. She looked sexy, but also adorable, her soft, slightly swollen lips still parted, her thick lashes lying heavily against her flushed cheeks.

Both her legs hung limply over the side of the bed, one shoe still dangling from her toes. Brent smiled, a strange tenderness invading his chest, making him shake his head at the irony of the situation. It was the first time he'd ever undressed a woman who was dead to the world and unable to appreciate his efforts.

But seeing her, all of her—that was something. She had pale skin, so smooth, her belly soft, her thighs sleek. For a long time he merely looked at her, and did his best to ignore those emotions he couldn't put a name to.

No doubt about it, he had a long night ahead of him. But

he fully intended to be on hand when Shadow awoke in the morning. In fact, he wouldn't miss it for the world.

SHADOW HAD ALWAYS BEEN a sound sleeper. When she was a little girl, her father had teased her, saying he could drop her down the steps once she was asleep, and she wouldn't even flicker an eyelid. But she also woke with no remnants of lethargy to cloud her brain. She simply opened her eyes and was completely alert. She did that now, but once awake, she didn't move.

Something wasn't right, and it wasn't just that she was naked, an unusual sleeping state for her. She always bundled up in warm thermal pajamas to stay warm. She was warm now. Toasty even.

But she wasn't alone, a fact verified by the hairy leg thrown so casually over her own and the heavy, muscled arm possessively circling her chest, just beneath her breasts. Even in the very dim morning light, she recognized Brent.

Her stomach flip-flopped and she froze.

In a rush, she remembered quite a bit of last night: the wine, the kissing. The significant other things that had happened. But she didn't remember undressing and going to bed. It wasn't possible that she'd fallen asleep before Brent could satisfy himself, was it? Yet, that must be what had happened, since she had absolutely no recollection of making love.

Shadow was so deep into her thoughts it was a miracle that the tiny motion by the window caught her attention at all. But it did, and when she turned her head, she could have sworn she saw the murky outline of a face. She quite naturally screamed before she could stop herself.

Like an alley cat, Brent leaped from the bed, his hair on end, his eyes wild, his body in a defensive stance.

Forgetting the possibility of a Peeping Tom for one single moment, Shadow stared at Brent's naked body. Good grief, she'd gone to sleep and missed out on *that?*

"What?" Brent demanded, his eyes still wide, his head turning this way and that in his effort to locate the cause of her scream. "What the hell's the matter?"

"I'm sorry," Shadow replied, chagrined for a number of reasons while her gaze remained on his hard belly—and below. "I've never actually screamed before." She managed to drag her attention to his face, but it wasn't easy. "I think there was someone peeking in the window."

Brent's brows lowered in a furious frown. He stalked to the window, giving Shadow a back view that made her flush, and peered out. "All I see is an empty side yard and the brick wall of your neighbor's house."

She cleared her throat. He was gloriously naked, so speech wasn't exactly easy. "I'm pretty sure I saw—"

Without letting her finish, he went around the bed in a determined stomp and growled, "Stay here."

Shadow watched, incredulous, as Brent left the room. "Ohmigod." She grabbed the comforter around herself and stared after him. "Brent, you're naked!"

He never slowed, just waved her back, and she sank into the bed in disbelief. He was gone only a minute, but it was long enough. The second he strode back into the bedroom, she threw a pillow at him...and missed.

"Are you nuts?" she yelled, swinging another pillow at his head. "You don't try to confront an intruder buck naked! What would you have done if he'd jumped on you?"

Brent dodged the second pillow, then caught it in midair and tossed it back at Shadow before coming onto the bed with her. "There wasn't anyone out there," he informed her, and wrestled her down, ignoring her fit of anger. She fought him only halfheartedly. After all, they were both nude and there was a lot of skin touching. When he finally had her pinned to the mattress, he kissed her.

He smelled wonderful, she thought, musky and male. Early morning beard stubble abraded her skin, but she didn't mind. She was too busy feeling him, all of him. His skin was hot, even after his brief glimpse out the back door, and his arms felt like steel. He was so hard all over.

Brent ended the kiss, but came back for several more, pressing tiny, biting nibbles on her lips, her chin, her jaw. His voice was very deep and rough when he asked, "Are you completely sober this morning?"

Shadow frowned, not understanding, but Brent kept running his palms up and down her body and she couldn't really think straight. "I'm sober."

He kissed her again, his tongue invading leisurely to stroke over her own, then soothe gently over her bottom lip. "And do you still want me?"

"Oh, Brent. I'm so sorry." This, she thought, was the epitome of the awkward "morning after." "I can't imagine how I fell asleep last night. You must think I'm awful."

"Actually," he said, licking her throat and driving her crazy, "you were spectacular."

Shadow frowned again, and this time she didn't let Brent distract her. "What do you mean?"

"I mean you're beautiful when you come. Wild and natural. That was all I wanted last night, sweetheart." He smiled at her, his expression...smug. "I could have awakened you if I'd really wanted to. But I was content to wait until this morning."

"You mean to tell me," Shadow inquired with false calm,

"that you had no intention of making love to me last night, despite what you did…what I let you do…what happened?"

Grinning at the way she stammered, wrongly assuming she suffered belated shyness from having been so abandoned, Brent felt safe in teasing her. "I'm not a teenager, Shadow. I can control myself, and you, when necessary. But I have to admit, it wasn't easy getting to sleep last night with your warm, sweet body next to me."

He started to lean down to kiss her again, but Shadow stiffened her arms to hold him off. "You undressed me? After I was asleep?"

"All I did was pull off your tights and shove your dress the rest of the way down. You were already nearly there, if you remember."

Her shove sent him sprawling on the bed beside her. In a heartbeat she gained her feet, the comforter wrapped around her. "You big jerk! You…you *toyed* with me!"

Throwing one arm over his eyes in exasperation, Brent said, "I don't believe this."

"I don't either!" Shadow couldn't remember ever being so embarrassed in her life. "How could you?"

He dropped his arm to glare at her. Lifting himself up on one elbow, he said, "You were drunk, damn it! Should I have taken advantage of you?"

"That's like saying you haven't stolen the apple if you only take one bite of it! Since you did me, you should have done you, too."

"Did you? *Did you?* What the hell does that mean?"

Through clenched teeth, Shadow said, "You know what it means."

"You were half-drunk and crawling all over me. You'd said earlier that it was too damn soon to make love, so rather than take advantage of your condition, and not being a bastard who'd leave you unsatisfied, I took care of it."

Shadow stared at him. She'd been crawling all over him? It was even worse than she'd thought.

Brent shrugged. "I *assumed* you'd be grateful."

"Grateful," she all but sputtered.

"I sure as hell didn't think you'd get mad."

She tipped her chin stubbornly. "Why would you start something you had no intention of finishing? That's just not...male." Never in her life had she known a man to give without taking, not where sex was concerned.

Brent lost his temper. Rising from the bed in a quiet rage, he stalked toward her. His words were low and mean, his brows drawn into a fierce scowl. "I did finish it, or are you going to tell me you faked it?"

His insulting suggestion nearly made her hair stand on end. "As if I would."

Her quick agreement earned her a dubious double take. His mouth opened, closed. Finally, he said, "Exactly. So tell me, lady. What the hell are you complaining about?"

Men could be so dense. "You got nothing out of it."

Eyes blazing, he tweaked her chin and said, "I watched you come. I heard you yell and felt you tighten on my fingers. That's a lot. A hell of a lot, actually. I'd do it again in a heartbeat if you weren't being so damn unreasonable. So don't tell me what I did or didn't get out of our little interlude, because I have a feeling you don't know jack about men, and worse, you're judging me by some jerks from long ago. I don't like it."

Shadow watched him, openmouthed and for once speechless, as he turned and stalked away. Well, hell.

CHAPTER FOUR

HAVING HELPED HIMSELF to coffee, Brent was at the kitchen table when Shadow entered. Sunlight now poured through the windows, making the kitchen appear warm and cozy. She was fresh from her shower, properly dressed and still chagrined.

Brent glanced up. "Feeling better?"

Knowing there was no hope for it, she blurted, "I'm sorry."

One tawny brow arched up a good inch. "Oh? What for, exactly?" Brent waved her into a chair and stood to pour her a cup of coffee. His cordial good spirits put her further on edge. She had a very hard time figuring him out.

Swallowing a good dose of caffeine before answering, she admitted, "You were right. I really had no reason to complain. I'm just not used to waking up with naked men in my bed."

He grinned at that.

"And," she added, liking his grin even less than his good humor, "it's especially strange for a naked man to be in my bed and not want to…well, have sex."

Brent studied her over the rim of his coffee mug as he took his own cautious sip. "I already accepted that last night wasn't something you do on a regular basis. But let's get clear on this. I did want you very much. I still do, for that matter."

He sat at the table, at his leisure, a man without a care. Her disgruntlement amplified. "You show remarkable restraint."

"Should I throw you over my shoulder, Shadow? Drag you off to bed and do the caveman routine?"

Shadow stared into her coffee cup. He'd actually hurt her feelings, she admitted to herself. They'd slept together in celibate bliss and it made her feel less than appealing. "Of course not. But don't you think I'd know the difference between real desire and wine-induced lust?"

He didn't answer. *In for a penny,* she thought. She curled her fingers around the warm coffee mug and forged onward. "Had I been with anyone other than you, Brent, it wouldn't have happened. But I was with you, and I wanted you. You're…special. What you make me feel is special." She let out her breath and added, "That's why I'm upset."

Her admission both pleased and perplexed Brent. He'd had time to think while she dressed in fresh jeans and a pastel pink sweatshirt. It said H.S.A. State. Brent had no idea what that meant, and at the moment, he didn't care.

Waking to a scream had thrown him all off balance. He'd assumed Shadow had a bit of a hangover, which had caused her to mistake a shadow for a man, but he didn't say as much. He wasn't a complete idiot. And besides, she didn't act hungover. Other than that startling scream and her grumbling because they hadn't made love, she was the same as ever. Which meant she was as difficult as ever to understand.

He, however, felt forever changed. He wasn't used to such an amalgam of feelings where women were concerned, but Shadow affected him, no way around it. He had only to look at her with her fresh scrubbed face, her hair damp from her shower, and he wanted her, fiercely. Control?

Ha. His control was so thin it was laughable. His body had been semihard all morning and he didn't think the condition would go away anytime soon.

But it was, strangely enough, more than just lust, though the lust was strong enough to bring him low. He also wanted to talk to her, to hold her. Feeling her next to him throughout the night had been torturous, and oddly satisfying.

"The problem," Shadow said, interrupting his thoughts, "is that for the first time, despite the wine, I lost my senses. I've never done that. It's a bit disappointing that you... didn't, too. I'll admit I don't like it." She made a face. "It sort of leaves things unbalanced."

"You're mad because I didn't lose control?" He felt disbelief and a touch of annoyance. Every woman he'd ever known had valued his control, relied on it, counted on it. He also felt a surge of hunger so strong it shook him. She was so open about wanting him, how could he not return the favor?

"There it is." She looked as confused as he felt. "You leave me at a disadvantage, which is a place I've been too many times with men. I swore I wouldn't ever let that happen again."

Running his hand roughly through his already rumpled hair, Brent fell back in his chair, resigned. "So you don't want to see me again?" Not that it mattered. He had no intention of walking away just yet, and since he held her lease, he'd have plenty of reasons to see her if she did try to end things.

"I'm not sure." She took a deep breath, warning him that he wouldn't like what he was about to hear. And he was right.

"But I'm not going to sleep with you until I've had time to think about this, to figure it out."

Talk about a plan backfiring... With a humorless laugh,

Brent stood. "First you raise hell because I didn't take you, and now you're saying you may not even want me to. You're fickle, Shadow."

"I'm just trying to—"

"I know what you're trying to do, honey. You want to run the show, to call all the shots. Fine. But don't expect me to sit around waiting for you to make up your mind how to do it."

Her big brown eyes were direct, but also solemn. She wasn't going to give an inch. "If that's how you want it."

She had the upper hand and he hated it. In fact, he wouldn't tolerate it. He gulped down the last of his coffee and said matter-of-factly, "Go get your coat. We'll see what we can do about your car."

Uncertainty, and if he wasn't mistaken, hopefulness, settled over her. "My coat?"

"Yes. It's cold outside, and it snowed again last night." When a slow, impish smile lit her face, Brent felt his chest constrict. Unfulfilled lust, he decided, nothing more. "I'll take you by the auto parts store and we can pick up a distributor cap."

She scampered out of her chair. "I'll just be a minute."

When she turned to leave, Brent finally read the words on the back of her sweatshirt. His laugh took her by surprise.

"I think I'm the one who should be wearing that," he said.

"What?"

"Your shirt. H.S.A. State? I didn't understand what the initials stood for until now." He read aloud, still chuckling, "'The State of Heightened Sexual Arousal.' Very catchy."

Shadow's smile went crooked. "It's a very big seller."

"I can imagine." With Shadow in the vicinity, every male for miles probably knew that state.

All humor vanished when they stepped outside. Brent was the first to notice the footprints in the snow. They led around the house, leaving the walkway occasionally, where it was obvious someone had approached the house to peer inside the windows. When he'd looked out the door earlier, it had been too dark to notice them. But now he saw there was even one window where the ice had been scratched off, to give a clearer view.

"I told you I saw someone," Shadow reminded him, trudging behind him as he retraced each print. They made a marked path at the side of the house, then headed toward the street. Brent broke into a trot when he realized they led to his car, which he'd left parked on the curb in front.

His curses should have melted the snow. A single, long, deeply etched scratch ran from the front fender to the back. Shadow looked nearly sick, and Brent went rigid with rage.

"Oh, Brent. I'm so sorry."

"I'll get the bastard," he said through his teeth, "don't worry about that." His anger shifted to near fear when he realized the ramifications of the damage. "This is too much of a coincidence to ignore. Your secret admirer, probably the guy from last night, has crossed the line from annoying to dangerous. Phone calls are one thing, breaching someone's privacy and damaging their property is too damn much."

She caught her hands together. "You really think it's him? But that doesn't make any sense. It's just been a few calls, a few small gifts."

"And a missing distributor cap."

Her brown eyes were grim, a little scared. "You don't think those are unrelated incidents?"

Brent would have liked to reassure her, but he couldn't.

"You have the address and phone number of the guy who was in the parking lot last night?" he asked.

"Yes. When he entered the contest, he filled out all the papers you did."

"I think he's the one."

She looked around her quiet street, her cheeks pale, her mouth tight. "We should call the police."

"Damn right." He took her arm, his mind made up. "And from now on, until this is resolved, I'm keeping a very close eye on you—whether you want to see me or not."

SHADOW COULDN'T DECIDE which was worse, having someone harass her or having Brent constantly glaring over her shoulder. She wouldn't have minded the latter so much, except that was all he did.

He hadn't kissed her again, made no reference to their one night together and acted more like an overanxious parent than an interested male. Shadow was fed up with it.

Her secret admirer was still a secret. Despite Brent's assumption that Chad Moreland, the pharmacist who'd entered her contest, was the guilty man, it hadn't worked out that way.

Brent had ranted and raved at the police station when he was told Chad had a solid alibi for his whereabouts the day Brent's car had been vandalized. And sending flowers and cards wasn't a crime, even if they could prove he'd done so, which they couldn't. Chad denied any association with Shadow, other than participation in her contest. She was embarrassed to have accused him, and Brent was furious that he didn't have answers. He wasn't convinced Chad was innocent, but there was nothing the police could do.

What had further enraged Brent was the warning the

officer felt compelled to give him. Brent couldn't touch Chad and shouldn't threaten him. A restraining order was out of the question, unless they could provide proof of identification that Chad was the man who'd been at her house. They couldn't. The only thing Chad had done was offer Shadow assistance the night her car wouldn't start. He'd been on his way to a party, he'd said, and it had turned into an all-nighter. He even seemed hurt by Shadow's accusations. She didn't know what to think.

"Are you ready to go yet?" Brent asked from the office doorway.

Shadow looked up from her inventory check. Brent stood there, dressed in black jeans, a charcoal-gray pullover and a black leather jacket. It was an effort to draw her eyes away from him. Although it had been little more than a week since the fateful night that had sent everything awry, it felt like months to Shadow. She couldn't sleep for wanting to touch him again, to kiss him and have him kiss her back, to...

But she'd ended all that herself. If Brent was still interested, he was evidently waiting for her to start things back up. Damn, but she hated getting herself into these impossible situations.

"I'll be ready in just a moment," she answered with a sigh.

"Any calls today? Any gifts?"

Same old song, same old dance, she thought. "Not a thing." She closed her books and went to get her coat from the rack. "We probably overreacted."

"Don't sound so hopeful. I think it's more likely my presence has scared him off, but I'm not taking any chances."

She already knew that. Brent proved to be a most ardent protector. So far, he hadn't once behaved as she'd expected.

He took her arm as they started out the door and even that innocent touch had Shadow's pulse leaping. His hands were so large, so strong and always so warm. Turning her face up to his, she suggested, "Why don't we celebrate his disappearance? We could stop and eat somewhere. Or maybe—"

Brent interrupted her, his jaw tensing in a noticeable way. "I already have plans."

"Oh." Her heart sank. Their relationship, started with such intimacy, had dwindled to a friendship; Brent wanted her safe, but that's all he wanted. She should have been pleased with his concern, but instead dejection weighed her down.

Brent slanted her a look as he opened her car door and helped her inside. Leaning one arm against the roof, oblivious to the snow that had gathered there, he explained gently, "I usually go home to see my parents on Thanksgiving. But I canceled this year, so they're coming here for a short visit. They're arriving tonight."

Her heart sputtered back to life. *His parents.* That was definitely preferable to another woman!

"They won't stay long," he explained, "because they need to be back in Chicago before Thanksgiving. My grandparents and other relatives usually show up there for the holidays."

Shadow knew immediately why Brent had changed his plans. Guilt swamped her. "This is ridiculous, Brent. You shouldn't miss a family gathering just for me."

It was the first tender look he'd given her since the night he'd stayed at her house. He said gently, "I didn't feel up to going all the way to Chicago, anyway. And my parents were curious to see where I'm living, so they're actually looking forward to coming here."

He tried to make light of it, to make her feel better, but

it only made her feel worse. "Does that mean you'll be all alone on Thanksgiving?"

"Shadow…"

She didn't let him finish. "You could come home with me. My parents would love to meet you."

Brent stepped away from the car. "I don't think that'd be a good idea."

His immediate rejection felt like a slap, but she hid her hurt. The last thing she wanted was his pity. "If you change your mind, just let me know."

"I'll do that." Brent closed her door, then waited until she'd started her car before going to his own. As usual, he followed her to her house. There was no sign of Chad or anyone else hanging around.

Shadow unlocked the front door, reached inside to turn on the wall switches, then turned back to the street, waving to Brent. He returned her wave, but didn't pull away. He waited in his car, watching, until she finally closed and locked the door.

As she shrugged out of her coat, she pressed the button on her answering machine to receive her messages. Listening to her friend Annie extend an invitation for holiday shopping, Shadow almost missed the note on the floor.

She picked it up, and one quick look made her knees weak. Written in a childish scrawl, it said, "No other man can replace me. I'm patient, so I'll wait. For now. Yours, always."

He'd been in her house, was Shadow's first horrified thought. She ran from door to door, checking the locks and thankfully finding each secure. Her heart was still hammering when she realized the note could have easily been slipped through the mail slot, which was right over the telephone table. She took several deep breaths to calm herself and then a new thought came to mind.

If Brent found out, he'd never stop hovering. She was already disrupting his Thanksgiving holiday; how could she impose further? Why he felt it his duty to protect her in the first place, Shadow couldn't fathom. It was apparent he no longer wanted her sexually—even his superhuman control wasn't that strong. And they'd only known each other a little over a week, so he couldn't feel obligated out of long association.

He owed her nothing. But she knew instinctively that he'd become even more diligent if he found out about the note.

It was ironic, since she was the one who'd put him off, but with each new day, Shadow wanted him more. Brent was strong and stubborn and proud. And protective.

She admired him too much to keep him at her side when he didn't really want her, simply because he suffered some outdated notions of male obligation. The police weren't overly concerned, so she wouldn't be, either. She wasn't a helpless female. She'd been taking care of herself for a long time and she liked it that way. Any relationship she had would have to be reciprocal. Her sense of independence demanded that much.

Giving the note a scathing glare, she picked up the phone and called the police. The same officer who'd taken her earlier complaint stopped by. He was solicitous, but as she'd suspected, there wasn't much they could do, given that the note was anonymous and nonthreatening. He cautioned her to be extra careful—which she'd already planned on her own—and to call immediately if even the smallest thing overset her. Then he left.

Shadow suffered a sleepless night, more from fretting over Brent's apparent disinterest than the blasted note.

As usual, he arrived the next morning intent on seeing her to work. She'd tried complaining to him, but he'd insisted it wasn't out of his way, and she enjoyed being with him each day.

He came through the doorway, his green eyes were dark. He was watchful, his gaze piercing, as if he expected something from her, but Shadow had no idea what it was and she was too tired to try to figure it out.

Brent crossed his arms, studying her as she donned her coat. "I don't want you working alone at the shop. Keep Kallie with you when you're there."

For a man with limited interest in her, he was far too autocratic. "It's the holidays," she told him flatly. "She's off three days next week for Thanksgiving and an entire week right before Christmas. Besides that, you can't expect her to spend ten hours a day at the shop."

"Then hire someone else," he insisted. "Hell, if you can't afford it, I'll hire someone."

"You most certainly will not!"

"Shadow." He said her name in two distinct syllables, drawing it out in his exasperation.

"You're being unreasonable," she pointed out. "He hasn't threatened me physically. And maybe we were wrong about your car. Maybe it wasn't him."

"I have a gut feeling about this. It isn't over. I'm sure of it."

Shadow drew a deep breath to steady herself. Then, stiffening her spine, she met his gaze squarely. "It's not really a concern of yours, Brent. You're not responsible for me. I didn't mind at first, because I thought you…well, I thought things would be different between us. But now your folks are in town and here you are, babysitting me. I'm a big girl. I can take care of myself."

Brent shoved away from the door in a sudden burst of anger. He ran his fingers through his hair, then gripped a handful and gave a vicious tug. Shadow stared, amazed.

Stomping back to stand directly in front of her, Brent demanded, "Do you do it on purpose?"

"What?" Her eyes were wide, purely fascinated by his spate of ire. She peered up at him, waiting curiously for his answer.

"Drive me nuts! Make me crazy!" His hands came out to grip her shoulders and he gave her a gentle shake. "Make me want you."

That last had been said more softly, almost as if he hadn't wanted to say it at all. Everything inside Shadow melted. "Brent…you still do? You still want me?"

He stared at her, searching her face as if to reassure himself she could actually be asking such an asinine question, then he released her to give a ferocious growl, throwing his hands up and staring at the ceiling.

"Exactly when," he asked, "have I not been particularly clear about that? *You're* the one who said 'no go,' not me. Hell, I've just been patiently hanging around waiting for you to make up your mind!"

Shadow blinked, then propped her hands on her hips. "How was I supposed to know you were being patient, something I've never seen you be, when it seemed to me you just weren't interested any longer? You haven't once tried to kiss—"

"If I had," he growled, "do you really think I could have left it at that? After touching you, after watching you climax?" He touched her cheek, her jaw. His hand was shaking. "You said you had to have time to think. I've been giving you time."

"But I didn't know that!" she wailed. Then another thought struck her and she frowned suspiciously. "Is that the only reason you seem so concerned about me? You're only trying to—"

"Don't finish that thought." It was the quiet of his voice that filled his words with menace. "I've worried my ass off over you and if you dare to suggest I'd go to these lengths just for a lay…!" He pressed his face close to hers, bending so they were nose-to-nose. "I can have a woman any damn time I want one. It just so happens I want *you.*"

He moved away in disgust. "Hell, woman, you've turned me inside out. All I can do is think about you and…*oof.*"

Shadow threw herself into his arms, literally, giving him only a moment to brace himself for her weight. He stumbled, but immediately steadied himself and wrapped hard arms around her, squeezing her tight. The small telephone table toppled as they bumped into it. He ignored it. "Shadow."

"I have to warn you, Brent," she mumbled against his throat, not willing to loosen her hold on him. "I'm starting to really care about you. I mean, *really* care. I think about you all the time, too. And I miss you when you're not around, and—"

"Hush." His mouth settled on hers, insistent, hot. From one heartbeat to the next, his hands were everywhere, touching her breasts, sliding down her back to her bottom, pulling her hard against his body. Just as quickly, he set her away from him.

"Damn." His head was down, his hands on his lean hips. "My parents are at my house waiting for me."

Shadow managed to nod, but it was a difficult feat. "And...and I have to get to the shop."

Brent looked at her, saw the way she gazed back at him, and groaned. "We better get out of here now or we never will."

She nodded again, but she didn't move.

Brent cupped her cheek, his gaze probing. "My parents are leaving this evening. Come to dinner with us so I can introduce you."

He wanted her to meet his parents? Her heart thumped in excitement, but she said only, "I'd love to."

Brent stared down at her, then his gaze dropped to her shirt. It was pale blue, with two cuddly stuffed bears printed on the front, one over each breast. Below was written *Don't You Just Love my Teddies?* He said, "Uh, Shadow?"

"Hmm?"

"Before dinner? Do you think you could cover your teddies?"

A slow grin came to her lips. "Are you afraid I'll wear something that would embarrass you in front of your mama?"

"You? Of course not." His arms circled her waist. "You're always dressed in the height of fashion."

Shadow punched him lightly in the ribs. "Tell me where we'll be eating and I'll dress appropriately."

Brent pretended to give the matter serious thought, then said, "Wear something black. That should cover it and satisfy my mother."

"I'm not particularly concerned with satisfying your mother." She touched his bottom lip. "Will it satisfy you?"

He gave her a sinner's wicked smile. "I have no doubt you'll satisfy me, honey. That's why I've been going crazy."

Feeling her stomach tumble with the meaning of his

words, Shadow decided she'd better behave—for her own salvation. Otherwise, she just might drag him to the bedroom and take him forcibly, her work and his parents be damned. Since she couldn't be positive he would appreciate her effort, she bent to right the telephone table that had overturned.

Brent was at her side, helping. "I hope nothing broke."

"Just scattered a few things. Don't worry about it. It was worth any mess to see your fit of temper."

"I don't indulge in fits of temper. What you saw was my remarkable restraint in keeping my hands off you."

Shadow laughed, but the humor instantly died when Brent picked up the note. He glanced at her still face, then read.

His expression hardened with annoyance. "You weren't going to tell me about this?"

"Actually…no. I was planning on throwing it away."

"Throw it away? Some maniac writes you a threatening note and you don't intend to tell me?"

Shadow frowned. "It wasn't exactly threatening."

"I beg your pardon. The exact wording is, 'I see you all the time. Soon you'll see me, too.'"

Shadow blinked, then frowned. "Let me see that." After Brent handed her the note, she quickly skimmed it, then raised worried eyes to his face. "It's another one. He must have dropped it through the mail slot last night, after I'd gone to bed."

"You mean this is the second note?"

Nodding, Shadow said, "I already spoke to the police, so you can quit frowning at me."

That didn't appease him. "What exactly did the first note say?"

Shadow recited it as best she could remember. "He evidently slipped both notes through my mail slot. The other one was here when I got in yesterday."

"Then this one," he said, "was delivered during the night while you were asleep."

Shadow couldn't help it. She paled at the thought of a man creeping around her house during the night.

Brent took her arm and started out the front door, making certain it was locked behind them. He hustled her along to her car, barely letting her feet touch the ground. She could feel the tension in him, his annoyance. "I've had enough, Shadow. I'm going to have an alarm system installed today. No! Not a word out of you."

She stopped in the middle of the sidewalk. "You'll get more than a word from me if you don't stop being such a jerk."

"I'm a worried jerk, all right?" She didn't answer and he sighed. He reached out, caught her hand and pulled her alongside him. "I'm sorry. I'm not used to worrying."

"Then stop doing it."

"I also don't want you at the shop alone, or anywhere else alone, for that matter."

Shadow could only shake her head. "I'm a single woman, Brent. I *live* alone. Or are you planning to move in?" She could tell by the look on his face that he wasn't, that she had presented him with something of a quandary.

Collecting himself, Brent said easily, "Once the alarm is installed, you should be safe enough." He stopped beside her car and looked at her with a frown. "That is, if you're not afraid?"

Shadow withered him with a look of disdain. "I'm not afraid of the dark or bogeymen or rainstorms." Her lie sounded credible even to her own ears. She was afraid, but he didn't need to know it. "I think you're right about an alarm system, though."

"Of course I am." He looked relieved at her concurrence.

"However," she added sternly, "I'll be the one to have the alarm installed. I'm not penniless. And it is my house and my hide that'll be protected. So it's my responsibility."

Brent said only, "At least let me put in the order. I want to make certain you get an infallible system." When she started to object, he added, "You can't cut corners on this sort of thing. It should cover the perimeter of the house, and most especially the doors and all the windows...."

"I agree."

He smiled, satisfied. "I'll talk to the security people today." He gave her a brief, hard kiss, then took her keys to unlock her car, seeing her safely deposited inside. "I have an early meeting to get out of the way so I can spend the rest of the afternoon with my parents. I'll follow you to work, then come by later for you tonight. We'll go to dinner just as soon as you've had time to change. All right?"

"If I say yes, do I get another kiss?" His eyes darkened further and it fascinated Shadow. Seeing his gaze settle on her mouth, she tipped her face up to him, her lips slightly pursed. Brent swore softly, then cupped her cheeks, now cold from the frigid winter air, and took her mouth.

She wouldn't need her heater if he kept that up. She slumped in the seat when he drew away, patted her cheek, then locked her door and closed it. "Drive carefully," he called from the window, and left for his own car.

Shadow stared after him. She wasn't at all certain she approved of his bossiness, but she more than approved of his kisses. Maybe she could get him to compromise on the rest. And as for her not staying alone at the shop, she hadn't really agreed to that, but she also hadn't wanted to argue with him about it.

But then, on second thought, arguing with Brent was probably the second most exciting thing she'd ever done with him. All in all, he kept her senses stimulated. She couldn't wait to see him that night.

THEY HAD THEIR FIRST huge argument the minute they got back to her house. Shadow started down her front walk, and Brent knew he couldn't hesitate any longer. "Just a minute, Shadow."

She glanced at him with a smile. Well, her smile wouldn't last much longer, but hopefully she'd understand. He didn't, but then, around Shadow, he never seemed to understand himself. He crossed his arms over his chest, ignored the howling wind and said, "I have to tell you the code for the alarm system."

Her smile never slipped. "Alarm system?"

"The one I had installed today."

She caught her hair back from her face, gave him a quizzical look and said, as if speaking to a simpleton, "I haven't chosen an alarm system yet, therefore it's impossible that one has been installed."

He'd done what was right, damn it, and he'd just keep telling himself that. "I had it installed. All the downstairs doors and windows are covered. Security lights will be taken care of tomorrow morning." He drew a breath, eyed her still features and continued. "If anyone tries to break in, the lights will come on and the police will automatically be called."

She glanced over her shoulder at the house. "You did this?"

"I want you safe," he said reasonably.

When she faced him again, her expression was no longer still. "No, you want to take charge of my life," she accused, and he couldn't very well deny it. When he remained quiet, she threw up her arms and shouted, "Good grief, one stalker is enough."

She turned to stomp away, slipped on the ice and started to fall. Brent had already been reaching for her, and he grabbed for her waist, but wasn't quick enough. They both went down, him flat on his back, Shadow draped across him.

Her knee damn near got him in the groin when she immediately struggled to sit up. He held her tightly. "Why is it," he asked, leashing his temper with care, "that every damn time I'm near you, you bring me low."

She whipped around, fully atop him, and said not two inches away from his face, "You keep overstepping yourself, that's why! I won't have it, Brent."

Thinking quickly, he suggested, "You can pay me back. It's an excellent system and now it's done and you know it was necessary."

"It was my decision to make!"

He'd never known a woman like her. Every other woman of his acquaintance wanted to be taken care of, wanted him to spend his money—the more the better. They'd have been flattered with his concern, complimented by his thoughtfulness, but not Shadow. No, she looked ready to bang his head into the icy sidewalk.

Being a perverse bastard, he smiled. "I'm sorry."

Shadow drew back, watching him warily. "You don't look sorry. You're grinning like a sinner."

"That's because you're so cute. No," he said, catching her when she would have flung away from him again, "I'm not patronizing you. You are cute and I like you and I worry about you, whether you want me to—hell, whether *I* want me to—and so I did it and I'm sorry it upset you, but I'd do it again in order to keep you safe."

She stared at him a moment longer, then grumbled, "You're impossible. Let me up. I hurt my hip when I fell."

He was immediately concerned. His own posterior felt bruised, as well as frozen. Three times. Three times now he'd ended up on his back in front of her. He caught her beneath the arms and lifted them both together. Dusting snowflakes and ice crystals from her coat, he asked, "Do you need me to carry you?"

Her look nearly fried him, despite the temperature. "How do I get in?"

Brent chose to take her question as a good sign. As if she hadn't just been glaring at him, he put his arm around her shoulders and started her forward. "I'll show you."

He produced a new key for her—to go with the new lock—and then punched in the code on the keypad. "Always do it right away or the police will come knocking to see what's wrong."

Looking around her house as if it wasn't her own anymore, she asked, "How much do I owe you?"

Brent winced, divided the actual price in half and watched her face for signs of distress. He really had no idea of her finances, though she claimed to be comfortable enough.

She never blinked. She just went to her checkbook and made out a check. As she handed it to him, she said, "I'll forgive you this once. Just this once. On the condition you promise to never ever again—"

"I promise," he said, not even wanting her to finish that

statement. He had no idea what he might do in the future, so it was best to keep his promise vague.

She didn't look at all convinced, but said only, "I have to go shower. I'll be back down in fifteen minutes."

"We have time," he told her, hoping the shower would restore her good mood. He loved her smiles, her quick laughter, the way she found humor in everything.

When she emerged twenty minutes later, already wearing a black cloak, her dark curls decorated with a silk ribbon, Brent was relieved to see her smiling.

She flitted around her house, talking nonstop, apparently excited about the evening. As she pulled on a pair of black leather gloves, Brent gave a brief thought to his parents. His father was amiable enough, but his mother could be extremely rigid to the women Brent chose to date. Of course, Shadow was different, and since his mother wasn't stupid, he imagined she'd quickly realize that Shadow was open and honest. He only hoped she didn't hurt Shadow's feelings or in some way insult her.

Brent held her hand on the drive, listening to her light conversation on everything from the sales at the shop to how her backside was still slightly numb from her fall. He couldn't recall this much enjoyment from chitchatting with any other woman. But Shadow was so lively, always smiling, quick to forgive—thankfully—and just as quick to laugh. She enjoyed life, even the mundane ventures, and that made him enjoy them, too.

"You didn't bruise yourself, did you?"

Her eyes twinkled at him in the dim interior of his car. "I didn't look, actually, so I don't know." She added, peering at him through her lashes, "But I wouldn't be a bit surprised."

"Should I kiss it for you to make it all better?"

"That could work," she murmured with false sincerity, only to say, "but a massage would probably be more effective. If you really want to help, that is."

The thought of getting his hands on her soft, rounded bottom again played havoc with his libido. It had been too long since he'd really touched her and it seemed he'd been wanting her forever.

His eyes shone at her, intent and filled with subtle meaning. "Depend on it."

A valet parked the car, and after Shadow had taken Brent's arm, they started inside.

He watched her expression, curious as to how she would react to the grand and elegant establishment. It was new, and Brent thought it particularly ostentatious, but his father had chosen it. Usually his parents' company could be excessively boring, especially in "polite" society. They were nearly regimented in their manners and social behavior. He had looked upon Shadow's company as a salvation to the evening. But now he began to worry.

He didn't know if Shadow would be comfortable in the outlandishly expensive surroundings. Not for the world would Brent want to make her ill at ease. He adored her forthright and outspoken manner, and wanted to encourage it. He wanted Shadow to be herself, always, despite his parents' opinions or the quiet elegance of the dining room. He totally disregarded the fact that up until meeting Shadow, he himself had been very remote and reserved.

She didn't gaze around in wonder at the glittering chandeliers hanging overhead, and the uniformed checker who asked for her cloak only received a dimpled smile and a simple thank-you. All would be fine, Brent decided; he'd worried for nothing. Shadow could definitely take care of herself.

She took off her cloak—and he got his first good look at what she wore.

CHAPTER FIVE

THE LOUD BURST OF laughter was startling. Peering over her shoulder, her expression deliberately demure, Shadow asked, "Is something wrong?"

Brent grinned at her, then kissed her fingers. "You never disappoint me, sweetheart, do you know that?"

She bestowed a very pleased smile on him. "I do try to be accommodating."

Dismissing the curious and disapproving stares, Brent took Shadow's arm as they made their way to the table. She looked delectable. And she had followed his suggestion—at least as far as the black was concerned. "The suspenders add a certain sensuality to the outfit."

She didn't slow her pace. "Do you think so?"

"Umm. You look like a very sexy schoolgirl."

She slanted him a provocative look. "I keep telling you—sexy comes in many different forms."

"I think I like your form just fine." And her "form" was clearly defined in the narrow velvet slacks. They were high waisted, cinching tight just below her breasts, lying smooth over her belly. Wide suspenders went over her shoulders and then crisscrossed in the back. Her white silk blouse buttoned with pearls and her pointed collar closed about her throat with a thin, black silk tie, as expertly knotted as Brent's own.

The outfit emphasized the lush fullness of her breasts. The material of the blouse was so soft and clinging Brent could detect each swell and curve. He wondered if she could possibly be wearing a bra. He couldn't see the outlines of it, but neither could he see even a hint of her nipples, and God knows he looked.

He felt his body reacting to his thoughts, and brought his attention back to his waiting parents. They were wide-eyed as Brent and Shadow approached. Slowly, his father stood, while his mother only laid a hand to her throat, clearly shocked. Brent made the introductions, doing his best to hold in his laughter.

"How do you do, Mr. Bramwell?"

Brent watched, smiling, as Shadow thrust her hand out to his father, taking him off guard.

With only a moment's hesitation, his father took her proffered hand. "Martin, please. It's nice to meet you, er, Shadow, was it?"

"Yes, sir. Shadow Callahan." At his curious look, she expounded, "My parents had a whimsical way about them. I have two younger sisters, Storm and Windy, and a baby brother, Sunny—with a *u*."

Brent was amazed he'd never heard this story. "Did she name each of you according to the weather when you were born?"

Shadow sent him a crooked smile. "No. Actually, it was the weather when we were conceived, or so I'm told."

Shadow was seated across from Brent's mother, and when she gasped, Shadow looked up in concern. "Are you all right? Did you choke on your drink?"

Brent reached over to pat his mother's back, handing her

the water goblet. "Here, Mother. Sip this." Then he dismissed her, smiling gently at Shadow.

The waiter appeared, taking orders for their drinks. Martin said, "I'll have another Scotch. And a white wine for Debra." He turned to Brent. "Scotch?"

Nodding, Brent said, "That'll be fine." All eyes turned to Shadow.

"No alcohol for me, please. How about a soda?"

The waiter, without flicking an eyelash, walked away. But Debra frowned at her. "That was rather crudely put, young lady. Do you have difficulty maintaining a discreet consumption?"

Shadow smiled with tender remembrance, forewarning Brent of disaster. "Not at all. At least, I don't think so." Then she dropped her bomb. "But Brent got me a little drunk the other day, and took complete advantage of the situation. I don't intend to give him such an opportunity again."

This time it was Brent who choked, while his parents stared. Damn the little witch, she was probably getting even over the alarm system.

In a performance worthy of the stage, Shadow seemed to rethink her words. "Oh, I don't mean…that is, he was a complete gentleman. Too much so, in fact, which was actually the problem."

"Shadow…" he said in warning.

Of course she ignored him.

Patting his hand as if to placate him, she said, "You know, Brent has a terrible time controlling his temper. He's just too intense for things to ever go smoothly around him." She leaned forward slightly to confide, "It's one of the things I like most about him."

Martin blinked at her, then slowly grinned. "Is that so? I've always found my son to be in perfect control of every situation. He must always be the employer, not the employee."

"I know just what you mean. He tries to bulldoze me, too. The stories I could tell…" Brent turned his hand over and squeezed her fingers. "Well," she said, giving him a look, "maybe that's for another time. But I can hold my own. Not even Brent, gorgeous and appealing as he is, can run my life for me."

This time she looked directly at him, ignoring his parents. "I have things well in hand."

The drinks came, keeping Brent from saying anything in return. No sooner had the waiter taken the order for their meals and departed than Debra again tried to grab her own measure of control over the dinner conversation.

"Brent, Joan sends her love. She misses you fiercely."

Brent shook his head, casting a surreptitious look at Shadow. "She misses my money, Mother, not me."

"You're being uncharitable. Of course she expected you to show a certain amount of affection with gifts and such. That's the way of it." Debra shrugged delicately, expressing her unconcern.

Shadow asked, "Is this the past fiancée who is making a pest of herself?"

Brent nodded, watching Shadow for some sign of jealousy. There was none and it annoyed him. "She no doubt expected to see me over Thanksgiving," he told Shadow, egging her on just a bit.

Debra continued to address Shadow, undaunted. "Brent gave her a beautiful diamond bracelet just before they broke off. She still wears it, poor girl."

"He's generous to a fault," Shadow agreed, her expression impossible to read. "Just today, he tried to buy me this expensive security alarm system." She sighed dramatically. "But I persevere. Hopefully, he'll catch on soon that I'm not a charity case and I don't want his money." She grinned. "But I do enjoy arguing with him. He's so outrageous."

Martin laughed, while Debra looked very disapproving. Brent simply sat back and enjoyed himself. Never before had he seen anyone put his mother in her place, and Shadow did it with ease.

Dinner was certainly different, Brent decided. The food was excellent, of course, but the conversation surrounding the table was a volley of subtle insults from his mother, each of which Shadow deflected with quick wit and candid honesty. Brent realized with some surprise that his father was equally amused, and they shared an indulgent masculine chuckle.

Shadow ate with perfect manners, but unlike most women of Brent's acquaintance, she had a hearty appetite, and no fear of displaying it. He and his parents had chosen seafood, but Shadow had ordered steak and potatoes.

After she'd eaten every bite, she leaned back in her seat, patted her belly and sighed. "That was delicious. My stomach was growling all the way over here."

Debra was appalled. "You have a very bad habit of speaking thoughts that are better left private."

In a mock-mournful voice, Shadow answered, "I know. I have a lot of nasty habits. Most people do, however. What bad habits do you have?"

Debra frowned at her. "I have no idea."

Shadow's grin could be called nothing less than sly, but her tone was pleasant enough. "Would you like for me to help you distinguish a few of them?"

"Well! I never."

Brows raised, she said, "You should," then added when everyone grew quiet, "No really. I've always believed we should be aware of ourselves and our shortcomings, just as we should acknowledge our accomplishments and our more favorable characteristics. It's good to know yourself inside and out. That way, no one can take you by surprise with an insult, because you'll already be aware of it—" she tilted her head "—or else know it to be mere malice or spite that provoked them to lie."

Brent studied her, intrigued anew. She'd said that a lot of people thought her nutty, and he had issued that damn insult as well. He wondered now just how much guff she'd had to put up with from the conformists. His heart swelled with compassion. "All that?" he asked gently. "I had no idea." He reached over to take her hand, unmindful of the attention he received from his parents. "What would you say your own faults are?"

He didn't mean for her to be overly serious, to lay herself open to criticism from himself and his parents. He'd only hoped to tease her into another smile. But Shadow took his question to heart. "I'm too trusting. And not very percep- tive when it comes to innuendo or discreet insults." She grinned at Brent's mother. "Your insults were thankfully plain. But there have been others who thought it was fun to make a fool of me." She shrugged. "I guess I'm an easy mark."

"That's very hard to imagine," Brent murmured. "You're too smart for that."

"Smart," she agreed without modesty, "but I also have a very strange perception of people and their place around me. I find humor in almost everything, even when it doesn't exist. It made it rough getting through school, because everyone seemed to think I was slow or simple, even though I made high grades and was on the dean's list in college. Also, as your mama already noted, I'm entirely too candid."

Brent felt tenderness expand inside him. Squeezing her hand, he commented, "But you're certainly a snappy dresser."

Shadow laughed. "I like to think so."

There was a heavy pause at the table, then Debra tossed down her napkin. "Will you have any time off for Christmas?"

Shadow looked at her curiously. "I'll close Christmas Eve and Christmas Day."

Debra turned to Brent. "Get her to take some time off so you can bring her home for Christmas." She gave her attention to folding her napkin as she added, "Your grandparents would enjoy meeting her, I'm sure. And it would probably end Joan's pursuit if she saw you with Shadow."

Enthusiastic about the proposal, Martin said, "That's an excellent idea! We'd be pleased to have you join us, Shadow. Very pleased."

Amazed by his parents' acceptance, Brent heard Shadow say, "Thank you. I'll see what *I* can work out." Which Brent knew meant she didn't want or need his interference. He bit back a grin. Her independence was refreshing, even when it annoyed him.

Brent spent the entire drive to the airport pondering the amazing means Shadow had used to win over his mother: simple honesty. During their farewells, Debra actually told Brent how lucky he was to have found such a levelheaded female. Martin, winking at Shadow, said, "And she's very cute besides."

Brent thought Shadow to be a bit more than "cute," and plans for the coming night had him ending the send-off with noticeable haste. His parents smiled after him as he turned away, Shadow by his side.

"Brent, you're being unbelievably conspicuous."

Without slowing his pace to the car, Brent asked, "About what?"

"About wanting to sleep with me."

They were in the parking lot, the night air too brisk, but the wind thankfully calm for once. He stopped and turned to stare down at her. The glow of a full moon highlighted her soft black curls, her pale cheeks, her wide dark eyes. Brent felt nearly overwhelmed with a myriad of sensations and he didn't fully understand a one of them. Except for the need that was both recognizable and unique. Lust, but stronger than lust. He wanted her, right now, this instant. He wanted to be inside her, hearing her cries, feeling the clench of her body around his erection as he went deep, so deep she became a part of him.

Searching her face, he noted when her lips parted slightly, when her breathing sped up, and he bent to touch her mouth with his own, a light, brief touch.

"It's true," he said into her mouth, inhaling her scent and the cold crisp evening air. "I want you so much I hurt, sweetheart. More than I can recall ever wanting anything." She trembled and Brent cupped her cheeks gently with his gloved hands. "I'm also willing to wait if you're not ready. I want you to want me, too. I want you to want me as much."

"I do."

Her warm breath fogged in the darkness between them. Brent groaned and took her hand again, nearly running to his car.

They were almost to her house when Shadow suddenly

broke the silence, whispering, "Brent? It's been a long time for me."

He parked the car, then turned to Shadow, seeing the glimmer in her eyes, so huge and filled with anxiety and urgency. He said softly, "You think I'm going to drag you inside and straight to your bedroom? Maybe pounce on you?"

"I don't know."

Always so honest, he thought, and laughed softly. "I could probably manage ten minutes of conversation, if that'd help."

An impish grin, only slightly nervous, flashed across her face. "Are you going to be timing it?"

"Very discreetly. You won't notice me watching the clock, I promise."

"All right." She bit her lip, but asked, "Maybe we could warm up a bit with a few more of those kisses?"

"Oh, there'll be kisses." His muscles tensed with that statement. He'd driven to her home with an erection, with shaking hands, and part of that was due to thinking of all the places, all the ways, he intended to kiss her. "Plenty of kisses, Shadow. Don't worry about that."

Once inside the house, Brent reset the alarm code, then deliberately led Shadow to the family room. He needed time to collect himself and garner his patience. She didn't deserve to be rushed, and he wanted her too much to test himself. Shadow watched him with attentive wariness.

Attempting a casualness he didn't feel, Brent asked, "Would you mind if I lit the fire?"

She shook her head. "Everything is ready. There should be some matches on the mantel. I try to keep things set up so…"

"Shadow." He said her name softly, hoping to reassure her, to help her relax. "I'm not going to jump on you. I promise."

"And here I was so hopeful," she teased, more to herself than anything.

"That's better." Brent had a warm, blazing fire going in no time. Keeping his gaze off Shadow with an effort, he went around turning off the lamps she had just turned on. When he stopped before her, he said, "That's much nicer, don't you think?"

"Yes." And then she came to her feet. "Would you like something to drink?"

Brent smiled at her lazily. "Do you have any wine?"

"No!" She gave him a dirty look for that. "But I do have some eggnog, and some lemon snap cookies I bought from this little bakery that does them especially well. They always save an extra batch for me at the end of the day. I have a running account. I just grab them from the back room on my way home—"

Her rambling monologue stopped abruptly. She gulped.

"All right." Brent didn't want her tense. He wanted her hot, soft. He smiled, but it was a painful smile. "We'll drink the eggnog and eat the cookies. But don't forget, I'm watching the clock."

They went to the kitchen together. Shadow bustled around, filling their glasses and picking up a good half dozen cookies to put on a plate. Brent was proud of his show of indulgence. Waiting until they had reseated themselves on the sofa and Shadow had stuffed an entire cookie into her mouth, Brent asked, "How long has it been for you, Shadow?"

Still chewing, she raised her brows in question, so he clarified. "How long since you've been with a man?"

She didn't choke, she didn't gasp with indignation or look insulted. She shrugged slightly, then swallowed. "Awhile."

"How long is awhile?"

With a look that was almost apologetic, she said, "Seven years?"

"*Seven…*" Brent stared at her, thoroughly appalled, and Shadow downed another cookie. That made three for her. He himself hadn't touched the things. "Are you telling me you haven't had sex in seven years?"

Again she had to chew and swallow before she could say, "Don't sound so disbelieving. I told you I'd had terrible luck with men. After my husband, and before I was engaged the second time, I had a few semiserious relationships. They were total fiascoes. I ended up looking like a fool. So I swore off men."

Damn if his heart didn't expand. He could actually feel it, crowding his chest. "Then you saw me."

"Just one look, as the song goes." Her admission had the effect of gasoline on an already raging inferno.

Brent leaned toward her. He studied her soft mouth, now dusty with cookie crumbs, her narrow nose and her stubborn chin and her incredible eyes. "I haven't been able to put you from my mind since that first look."

Shadow blindly reached for another cookie.

"Are the cookies really that good?" Amusement warred with impatience.

Shadow looked at the cookie in her hand. "Uh…I have no idea. I don't think I've tasted a single one." She turned her gaze up to him, her honeyed eyes very sincere and warm. "I always eat when I'm nervous. I'm sorry. Really."

Brent very gently disengaged the cookie from her hand, placing it back on the plate. "Come here, honey. Let me just hold you for a bit."

She did. Then she whispered, "I know I'm acting like an idiot, but I want things to be right with you, Brent."

Because things for her usually went wrong, where men were concerned? He shook his head. "Hush."

This time it would be different, because he was different. He'd see to it that she enjoyed herself. A lot.

He'd slipped his suit coat off before he made the fire, and now she snuggled close, pressing her nose into his chest and breathing deeply.

Sifting his fingers through her hair, he dislodged her ribbon, then laid it on the coffee table with the cookies. With a crooked finger under her chin, he tilted her face up and kissed her.

She immediately softened against him, relaxed, and he realized he should have kissed her sooner. He licked her lips, teasing and tasting, sliding deep inside, stroking her with his tongue as he'd soon be stroking her body. His erection throbbed and he knew he was going too fast. He pulled back, lightly nipping her throat, her ear.

"I love it when you kiss me."

Her words were breathless, hot. Brent intended to show her all the other pleasurable places he would kiss her. *Control,* he reminded himself. This first time had to be just right. And knowing Shadow, the best way to control the situation would be to let her think *she* had the control.

At one time that thought might have been unacceptable; with Shadow, it made his lust more urgent than ever.

Slowly, Brent began to lean back on the sofa. Following his lead, Shadow ended up sprawled over his chest, her slight weight pressing into him. With each deep breath, her stiffened nipples caressed him. Her arms were tight, her legs restless. Brent couldn't stop the groan from deep in his throat.

Shadow didn't seem to notice his hands on her hips,

aligning her pelvis with his own. She didn't notice the way he slid one leg between hers, opening her to his touch, having her practically ride his thigh. She did pay attention, however, when he began unknotting her tie.

"Brent?"

He kissed her bottom lip, tugged gently on it with his teeth. "You could do the same for me."

"All right." Between their fumbling hands, they soon had their collars open. Brent had quite a few more buttons undone on Shadow's shirt than she had managed to undo on his. He stared at the smooth, creamy rise of her breasts beneath the shirt.

"You didn't wear a bra. I couldn't be sure at dinner."

"I wore a teddy."

Amused, he asked, "You wore a teddy? I thought you preferred fun stuff to the traditional. Teddies are pretty damn traditional."

"No." She curled a finger in the hair on his chest, not quite meeting his gaze. "I said other things can be equally as sexy. But a good teddy has its place."

Brent traced his fingertips along the opening of her shirt, touching satin and lace and warm soft skin. He undid a few more buttons, then pushed her suspenders and the shirt off her shoulders.

"You are so damn beautiful," he murmured, so close to the edge he didn't know if he could hang on much longer. This kiss was different, filled with hunger and possession. He worked the shirt from her body, leaving her back bare to his hands, her throat and upper chest available to his mouth. He nuzzled against her, his lips rooting over her satin-covered breasts until he found a nipple. It was a gentle bite, but Shadow jumped, then groaned when he began to suckle. Her back arched and her belly pressed down, inadvertently stroking his hard-on.

In a rasping voice, he said, "Let's get out of these clothes."

Shadow moved, dazed, to Brent's side. She lay there, eyes wide and soft, while he pulled away her shoes and unfastened her trousers. Slowly, teasing himself, he dragged them off her hips and down the length of her legs. He felt so urgent, so hungry, he couldn't take his gaze off her as he stood to jerk free of his own clothes. The teddy was mere decoration, in no way concealing her breasts with the rosy, puckered nipples, or the dark triangle of hair between her thighs.

His chest rose and fell with his uneven breathing.

And then she said, "I gather my ten minutes are up?"

SHADOW SAW BRENT GO STILL, but only for a moment. Beautifully naked except for a pair of charcoal-gray, snug-fitting boxers that barely contained his erection, he awed her. She wanted to touch him, to explore his sex with her hands, but he seemed on the ragged edge as he came to kneel before her. His large hands settled lightly on her thighs. "Don't be shy, sweetheart. Not with me."

"No. No, I'm not." He was so large and imposing, the width of his muscled chest blocking her view of the fire, which framed his body with a golden glow. "I want to see you," she admitted.

His smile was heart-meltingly sensual. The warmth of his palms penetrated the skimpy teddy, and Shadow closed her eyes in pleasure as he caressed her hips, down her thighs, over the arches of her feet. Keeping her eyes closed, she grinned.

"You're ticklish," he observed with rough-toned affection.

"A little." Her nipples drew tighter, and between her thighs she ached. She needed him.

Brent pressed his face into her belly and his arms went around her to hold her tight. It was an endearing embrace, filling Shadow with warmth. Moved by his tenderness, she tangled her fingers in his hair, holding him close.

Any concerns or trepidation she had been harboring evaporated. The things Brent made her feel were too complex to understand or control. Later she would try to figure them out, but for now, she only wanted to experience them fully.

"Tell me what you feel," he said as he stroked her breasts through the teddy. Her breath sighed out; her body trembled. He alternately watched her face and his hands on her body.

He grasped her hips and pulled her to the edge of the sofa, snug against his groin. There was only the insubstantial material of the teddy to shield her, and she was aware of every throbbing inch of his erection.

"You have large hands," she noted as his palms stroked her from breasts to thighs, covering nearly every inch of her body.

"Yes, thankfully. I can't decide where to kiss you first." He lowered the straps of the teddy, baring her breasts. "Tell me what you're feeling," he said again, then caught her nipples between his fingers, lightly pinching and tugging, rolling her sensitized flesh until Shadow found it impossible to remain still.

"Desperate," she said in a low murmur, "I feel tight and urgent and almost in pain. Brent, please…" She ended with a groan.

He leaned forward to lave her with his tongue. "I've waited forever for you, Shadow. You have to give me time to play."

She held him to her as he sucked strongly at her breast.

The tension in her built and drew tighter, stronger, until she moaned, feeling on the verge of climax. As if he knew, understood, his hand slid over her belly, then lower, between her thighs, where she was open and wanting.

His fingers were insistent, knowing. The material covering her grew damp as his middle fingertip found one ultrasensitive spot, pressing, plying.

She squeezed her eyes shut, dropped her head back on the sofa. Brent switched to her other breast, and even the warmth of the air caressing her bare nipple, now wet from his mouth, was a stimulant. As if he'd read her mind, he released her breast and blew gently on the straining peak, watching avidly as it puckered further, as Shadow cried out, her hips thrusting against his fingers.

Brent reached for the snaps at the seam of her teddy, no longer willing or able to wait and tease. With no warning at all, he pressed two fingers deep inside her. She cried out, shocked, alarmed by the slight discomfort, and so close to coming she couldn't seem to see straight. Everything blurred, spun. "Brent!"

He ignored her, his fingers sliding in and out in a tantalizing rhythm, unhindered by the tight clasp of her body. He simply forced his way in, then withdrew, again and again.

"Oh…oh…" She literally felt faint, her heart beating far too fast.

Brent lowered himself, his mouth urgently burning a trail from her breasts to her open legs. He bit the soft flesh on the inside of her right thigh, and then he was there, his mouth covering her, his rough tongue licking, sucking.

Shadow fell apart. She'd never experienced anything like it, mind numbing and burning, a pleasure so sharp she felt herself fracture. He held her there, pushing her, not letting the pleasure fade until she went limp and boneless. Her heart was still pounding too hard, a deafening tattoo in her ears. Her skin prickled, both with sweat and sensation.

As if from far away, she felt Brent's tender touch, the stroking of his knuckles across her cheek, the sweep of his hand over her hair. "Hey, sleepyhead." His voice was amused, concerned. "Have I put you out for the night?"

She struggled to open her eyes, but it was an effort. He smiled down at her, his green eyes tender, still hot with arousal. "Brent…" His name sounded slurred, nearly incoherent. She didn't understand what was wrong. "I'm so sorry, but I'm…" She couldn't quite fashion the right words to explain. Exhaustion pulled at her; she was more tired than she could ever remember being in her entire life. She gave up and closed her eyes again. "I am sorry."

She barely heard Brent's disbelieving laugh. Mumbling under his breath, he said, "I should market myself as a sleep aid."

It was beyond Shadow to reply, though she wanted to. She wanted to sit up and look at him and explore his splendid body and kiss him as he'd kissed her. She couldn't. It was all she could do to blink at him again, to bring his handsome face into focus.

There was a resigned sigh, a gust of breath that gently blew her hair, and then she felt Brent's strong arms slide beneath her. "To bed with you, sleepyhead. I suppose my turn will come in the morning."

She wanted to protest, to tell him that it wasn't fair he'd have to wait. Something was terribly wrong, but what? He laid her in the bed and she managed to whisper again, "I'm sorry."

He kissed her forehead. "You obviously work too damn hard."

But that wasn't it, she knew, yet she couldn't quite get the thoughts to form in her mind. All she could comprehend was her embarrassment and her disappointment.

"Brent…"

"Go on to sleep," he said, "and if you wake up refreshed, I'll be here."

Shadow forced her heavy eyes open to stare up at him. She whispered miserably, "I told you I had wretched luck with men. Now you see what I mean."

"Nonsense. You have me." To her blurry mind, he sounded agitated, but not angry. "I'd say you have excellent luck." He stood next to the bed, skimmed off his boxers, then stretched.

Shadow looked at him, seeing him through a gray haze. His erection drew her attention first and she groaned, but the sound was too weak, too faint for him to notice. His legs were long and strong, his stomach flat and lightly muscled, not nearly as hairy as his chest, and very appealing. Broad, straight shoulders and lean, sinewy arms… He was beautiful and Shadow was beginning to wonder if she'd ever get to fully enjoy his body.

"Don't look so glum, sweetheart. I'm almost certain I'll survive." He slid into bed beside her, pulling her close and settling her against his side. He pulled her left leg up and over his. "Is this okay?"

She couldn't get a single word out. Shadow nodded the tiniest bit against his chest.

Brent turned her face up slightly so he could see her eyes. "You look as though you're already asleep." Amazingly, he smiled. "Things will work out eventually. I promise."

He closed his eyes, easing into the mattress with familiarity. She breathed deeply, loving his scent, loving the way his presence soothed her, though why she was suddenly so afraid, she wasn't sure. She loved his strength, his pride. She loved him.

It was the last thought she had before she literally passed out.

CHAPTER SIX

"I *WAS* DRUGGED!"

The shout was shrill and piercing, filled with outrage. Brent wasn't quite quick enough to get his feet beneath him this time. He landed on the floor beside the bed, his naked body twisted in the blankets.

"What! *What?*"

Shadow hunched over on the mattress, her face in her hands. "Someone," she reiterated slowly, "drugged me."

"What the hell are you talking about?"

"Last night I couldn't keep my eyes open, couldn't think straight. I didn't want to go to bed, but I couldn't figure out how to tell you. This morning I understand, but last night I couldn't."

With a sigh, Brent ran his hand through his rumpled hair, then down his whiskered face. She had been exhausted, limp as a noodle when he'd carried her to bed. He shook his head. "How would someone do that?"

She looked at him and her expression was nearly blank with fear. "I don't know. It must have been in something I drank." She fretted her bottom lip with her teeth, twisted her hands in the sheet. "Maybe the eggnog. I'm the only one who drank it." Then her expression transformed, became so enraged, so mean, he blinked in surprise.

"Someone," she growled, thumping the mattress with a fist, "got in here and *drugged my eggnog.*"

Pulling himself up from the floor gave Brent a moment to hide his grin. Damn, but she could be a ferocious little thing. He smoothed the covers, then sat beside her. After taking her hand, he said, "The doors haven't been opened. If they had, the alarm would have sounded. You're just stressed out from not getting enough sleep."

"I got enough sleep!"

"Then you're stressed out because you haven't yet made love with me. Hell, I know I'm stressed over it." He did grin this time. "We should remedy that."

"I know what I'm talking about, Brent. I'm a hard sleeper, but I don't pass out like that."

Brent gazed at her steadily, but in truth, he was distracted by her warm body, clothed only in the transparent teddy and held so close to his naked one. He said softly, "You'd been nervous about being with me and you were tense." He kissed her temple and said, "It'd been a really long time for you, and I know you came." In a teasing, somewhat bragging voice, he added, "That wasn't a wimpy little orgasm you had, but a mind-blower."

He waited and finally she said, "It was incredible." She twisted to look up at him. "You were incredible. I'm so sorry I fell asleep."

He tangled his hand in her hair, fitting his palm to her skull when she dropped her cheek to his chest. She smelled good, Brent thought, rubbing his nose against her neck, kissing a path to her ear. "You had a melt-down," he suggested. "It's nothing to be embarrassed about, sweetheart. I understand. Hell, I'm even a little proud."

She laughed, just as he'd intended. "You feel like strutting, do you?"

"You wanna know what I feel like doing?" He was still aroused from last night, and even her scream hadn't taken care of it. He was here with her, she was awake now and he wanted her. He was beginning to think he'd always want her.

Unfortunately, just as he started to kiss her, she seemed to become self-conscious. Brent allowed her to draw slightly away, but kept his arms around her shoulders.

"Brent, I still feel a little vague, and I...I need to, ah..."

It was odd, but Shadow managed to keep him on the verge of laughter, whether deliberately or not. His patience astounded him, but he had all morning and he planned to make use of it. He could afford to be patient just a little longer.

He gave her a smacking kiss. "Why don't you take a shower and see if that'll clear away the cobwebs? If you want, I could start some breakfast."

She was frowning, still apparently convinced she'd been drugged. But she said only, "Toast and coffee would be wonderful."

"Shadow?"

"Hmm?"

"Don't take too long."

"I won't."

A few minutes later, Brent heard the shower start. He found his pants and stepped into them, but didn't bother with his shirt or shoes. If he had his way, he would only be taking them off again soon.

Twice now. *Twice* he had slept with Shadow and not made love to her. It had to be some kind of unbelievable record. But he wouldn't have missed either experience for the world. She was so much more than he'd first imagined.

Too headstrong for her own good, with a kind of twisted, zany wisdom few people ever acquired.

She was sweet and serious, intelligent and nutty, by far the most sensuous woman he had ever known…who dressed in the most outlandish outfits. She would never be boring, but she would keep him on his toes.

No way in hell would he ever let anyone hurt her.

He obligingly started the coffee and placed a few slices of bread in the toaster. He set the table with butter, jam, cream and sugar. Then, remembering something he'd been meaning to do, he called his office.

His secretary seemed surprised by his order. "Yes, that's what I said. Two men. I don't care where you find them, but they can't work for me. Find someone from the other offices in the building. It's for the Love and Laughter contest, or some such. Just tell them to go to the little stretch of businesses I'm leasing over by the complexes. There's a shop there called Sex Appeal. They can pick up an application there."

Brent laughed, then added, "I was actually entered, but being as I own the property, if I won, I'd have to be disqualified." He hesitated, then smiled. "Why, thank you. The owner obviously thought I was a worthy contender, too, but she doesn't realize she's leasing from me. Now, don't forget we'll need two men." He chuckled again as he said, "She has to fill her quota."

Brent paced a few steps, one hand in his pocket. "Right. Thanks, Micky. I think that will do it. Why don't you clock out early today? Cancel any appointments I had this morning and reschedule them for Monday. Thanks."

He was still smiling slightly over Micky's comments when he turned and found Shadow standing there, utterly still, looking more vulnerable than he'd ever thought possible. *How much had she heard?*

She wore a long, man-size football jersey and nothing else. Her hair was damp, a mass of dark ringlets. She looked fresh and dewy and warm. Brent felt his body clench. "Feeling better?" he asked.

"I'm fine."

There was something oddly distant in her words and the way she said them. "There's coffee in the kitchen and I can have the toast ready in just a few minutes."

"Don't bother." She stared right at him and said, "I want you to leave now."

His jaw locked. *Damn.* "I don't think so, Shadow."

"Why not? Because you didn't get what you came for? I trusted you. I thought you cared a little about me." With each word, she became more rigid. "Why did you lie to me?"

"I never—"

She turned her back on him and walked away. Brent saw red. "I can't believe," he said very quietly, "that you're going to take this attitude today. Not after everything that happened last night."

"Last night wouldn't have happened at all if I'd known you were lying to me! You own my damn building!"

"So?" He propped his hands on his hips and his brows lowered in a fierce scowl. "You had to lease it from someone."

Her nose went into the air. "If it's not a big deal, then why didn't you tell me?"

"Stop shouting and maybe I'll explain."

She gave him a mutinous look. "I have to get dressed."

The morning had quickly deteriorated, and so had his temper. "Why? It looked to me as if you were willing to pick up where we left off. I imagine you don't even have anything on under that jersey, do you?"

She flushed. "Go to hell."

"You have to know how crazy that would make me. So why change your mind now?"

"Because now I'm mad. Now I know you lied to me." Her eyes were dark, dilated. "Until I know why, I'll feel much better fully dressed."

The quiet, deliberate closing of her bedroom door enraged him. Damn her, how could she turn so cold so quickly? Especially when he wanted her so much. Maybe, he thought, remembering her reserve of the night before, she was just stringing him along.

Granted, she couldn't have faked her exhaustion; she'd been dead to the world, her body lax, her deep breathing occasionally turning to soft snores. He almost smiled. No, she'd been totally wiped out, of that he was certain.

But she played a constant game of advance and retreat, and it was possible he'd fallen into a trap. A unique trap, but still a trap. It wasn't a very uplifting thought.

Brent waited until Shadow came out of the bedroom, then went in to dress. He emerged five minutes later, more collected, determined on his course. He would not be manipulated.

"I'm going to the office. If you settle down and want to talk calmly, give me a call." He didn't pay the least bit of attention to her sullen frown. "Also, the security people will be here today to finish installing the system." He looked at her directly, his expression hard. "Don't give them any trouble."

"Oh, don't worry. If I decide I don't want them here, I'll tell them so very nicely. I do tend to be nice, Brent. Remember?"

In two long strides he stood before her, her chin caught in his hand. "Too nice. Don't even think of flirting with some other guy to make me jealous, Shadow. I already told you I don't like games and you've played one too many already."

This time her tone was uncharacteristically solemn, and almost accusing. "I don't play games."

"No? What would you call this little tug-of-war with 'let's make love' and 'let's don't make love'? Normal procedure?"

Shadow looked down, then turned her back completely on him. "I'd call it the worst of luck. Or maybe the best." She was quiet a moment, then added in a sad whisper, "Please go, now."

"Shadow…" Brent didn't know what to say. Why the hell had he let his temper get the best of him? Not that it mattered now. He couldn't continue to let her lead him in circles. Still watching her averted profile, he shrugged on his coat. "I'll give you a call tonight to make certain everything went okay with the security people."

She didn't move, and Brent was forced to take her shoulders and turn her. She could have been carved in stone, her face was so still, her eyes so dull. He didn't like it. In fact, he hated it. "Be careful, and let me know if anything happens."

"The same refrain, Brent. I'm a big girl and I'm not stupid."

"No, but apparently you're someone's obsession. That means you have to be on guard." He left before he said anything else to upset her, but in his mind he knew the truth. *He* was obsessed, and the sensation got worse every day.

IT HAD BEEN A WISE decision to come to work. Not only had she managed to sort through all the new orders, she had perked up immensely.

Melancholy was for the birds. So Brent had lied? So what? He was like other men, after all, and that certainly shouldn't come as a shock.

But it did. Shadow couldn't help but chastise herself for handling the situation badly. She hadn't given him a chance to explain—if there was indeed an explanation.

She'd gotten hurt, and in the process, she'd ruined a very special morning. A morning that had held the potential for being the most memorable morning she'd ever been given.

Why was her timing so lousy with Brent? She was considering the vagaries of romance—hers in particular—when the phone rang. Kallie was busy with customers so Shadow picked it up herself.

"I've missed you."

Oh, no. That most definitely was not Brent's voice on the line. Very carefully, Shadow said, "I thought I'd seen the last of you."

There was a friendly, almost cheerful chuckle. "You aren't very observant. I saw you just today."

She gripped the receiver tightly. "Where?"

"On your way to work."

She bit her lip, trying to remember any cars she'd passed, any people she'd seen on the way.

"You're wearing a shirt that has vultures on the front. And I like the tight jeans. You look really cute."

The day had been a disaster and she was still berating herself over her part in it. She had no tolerance or patience for this right now. "Look, I've about had it with you. I think you're childish and awfully annoying. Do us both a favor and leave me alone." She slammed the phone down so hard the items on her desk rattled.

So he hadn't given up, after all. She considered Brent's earlier instructions, to call if anything happened. Damned if she would.

She was capable. She *wanted* Brent, but she didn't *need* him.

The snow started coming down around three o'clock and by six everything was blanketed in white. They announced a traveler's advisory, so Shadow decided to close the shop early.

To be on the safe side, she notified the security guard and he happily gave her escort to her car. He even waited until she was well on her way before moving on. The salt trucks hadn't had a chance to cover all the roads yet so Shadow drove slowly and very cautiously. For the first time in a long time, she dreaded going home to an empty house. She blamed Brent for that, for showing her how nice it was having him around.

And the stupid phone call had unsettled her more than she liked. She realized whoever it was must have gotten close enough to the shop to see her, because anytime she'd been outside and visible, she'd been wearing her coat. How could he possibly have known about the vultures on her sweatshirt? It made her uneasy.

The temperature dropped rapidly. Forecasters predicted a low of ten degrees, and that wasn't taking into account the windchill factor. Shadow turned the heater up a notch and squeezed her arms close to her body. It was bitterly cold, no two ways about it.

Distracted, she watched the houses to her left as she passed Brent's place, trying to determine, out of sheer curiosity and nosiness, if he was home. She almost ran the red light, but the roads were pretty much deserted, so it really wouldn't have mattered. Still, habit had her hitting the brakes and going into a full slide.

Right off the road and into the ditch.

The car rocked to a halt against a snowbank and Shadow slammed her hand onto the steering wheel in a fit of anger. "My luck can't be this bad!"

She made an effort to rock the car out, but it was good and stuck, and probably would be until she hired a tow truck to drag her out.

Going over her options took all of about three seconds. Her house was still a good walking distance away, while Brent's was right there, once you trod the long drive to the front door. Pride had its place, but compared with freezing, it was less than nothing.

Snowflakes as big as cotton balls covered her head the minute she stepped from the car. The snow was already so deep her ankles disappeared in the frozen drifts. Tucking her hands into her pockets, Shadow lowered her face to protect it from the force of the gusting wind and headed for Brent's driveway.

The chattering of her teeth should have announced her arrival. When it obviously didn't, Shadow lifted one snow-covered foot and kicked the door soundly. No way was she going to remove her hands from the dubious warmth of her pockets simply to give a polite knock.

But she was worried. The house was dark, not a single light on that she could tell. Whatever would she do if Brent wasn't home? If she could be certain he didn't have an alarm system himself, she would gladly break in. But then it wasn't necessary. Brent opened the door a moment later, a dim flashlight in his hand. He looked as if he'd been deep in thought, his face a shadowy mask of fatigue. Or was that worry?

Grabbing her arm, Brent pulled her in the door, then slammed it shut. He began brushing snow from her head, her shoulders. "Where the hell have you been?"

Shadow blinked, trying to stop her shivers, but unable to. Brent cursed, then dragged her into his arms, squeezing her tight for just a moment before taking her hand and hurrying her through his house and into the family room.

It was immense, filled with posh leather furnishings and highly polished, heavy wood tables. An elaborate marble fireplace dominated an entire wall and in it was a huge, raging fire, the heat emanating in waves.

Brent dragged a wing chair near the blaze and gently pushed Shadow into it. Dropping to his knees before her, he began removing her wet shoes and socks.

"Are you nuts, Shadow? What the hell are you doing out in this storm? I thought you were staying home. I've been calling your house since the storm started."

Through chattering teeth, she said, "I was upset. I needed something to do other than sitting around the house moping. So I went in to work."

Brent held her frozen toes in his palms, trying to warm her. "You were upset?"

Nodding, Shadow answered truthfully. "I don't like being mad at you, Brent."

Brent looked at her for a long moment, then stood. "Take off those jeans. They're wet clear up to your knees. I'm going to get you a drink and a blanket."

Shadow did as he bade her, mostly because the wet pants were uncomfortably cold. She had her bare feet stretched out toward the fire, wiggling her toes to warm them, when Brent returned. He handed her a glass of whiskey, which she promptly set aside, then she watched, fascinated as he spread a large quilt before the fire and laid another at the bottom of it.

"Come on, sit here where you can feel the fire."

"Brent, why is it so dark in here?"

"The electricity is out on the whole street. A result of the storm. And unfortunately, the heating was all redone with the remodeling. I now have electric heat, which means the house is going to cool off considerably as the night goes on."

Shadow had no sooner stood than Brent began pulling off her coat. "This is wet, too. You'll feel better without it."

She blushed when Brent's gaze went to her shirt and stayed there a long moment. Finally, he smiled.

"I was thinking of you," she explained, "when I changed to go to work this morning."

Two vultures adorned the front of her shirt. Sitting on a barren branch, their expressions sullen, one said, "Patience, hell. I'm gonna kill somebody." Brent chuckled even as he lowered Shadow to the quilt, then tucked the extra blanket around her. "I hope it wasn't my death you were anticipating."

His soft, husky words sent a tingle down her spine. "No. My impatience for something else entirely." She smiled up into his green eyes, the reflection of the fire sending mysterious shadows to dance in them. "Brent, why didn't you tell me you owned my building?"

He leaned forward to place a gentle kiss on her forehead. "I knew that would disqualify me from your little contest and at first I wanted to use the contest as an excuse to get to know you better. And then I suppose I was...concerned that you might treat me differently if you knew you were leasing from me. Personal finances have a way of influencing how people treat each other."

Incredulous, Shadow demanded, "You thought I might cozy up to you just because you hold my lease?"

He gently tucked an errant curl behind her ear. Her hair was damp from her walk in the snow, her cheeks and nose still very cold. "I know now that you wouldn't."

"But you think I would deliberately lead you on, then pull back before making love to you?"

He sighed. "I was mad, Shadow. I didn't mean half of what I said, and I almost immediately regretted saying it." He flopped onto his back beside her and closed his eyes. He wore a T-shirt, even as cool as the house was, and Shadow could see the definition of his chest, his strength and power. The shirt stretched taut over his broad shoulders. "You're tearing me apart, honey. I've never felt so damn on edge before."

With her heartbeat racing and her body quickly warming, Shadow moved so she loomed over him. "I think I'm in love with you, Brent."

That got his eyes open in a hurry. Before he could speak, Shadow laid her fingers against his mouth. "Just listen. If I sometimes seem contrary, or like I'm giving off mixed signals, you should realize I'm a little confused, too. It's been an awfully long time since anyone made me feel the way you do. In fact, I don't think I've ever felt this way. And I've only just decided I might like it. So," she said, laying her heart on the line, "would you like to make love with me, Brent? Now?"

Brent's answer was a low groan and a sudden movement of his body that had Shadow flat on her back, the blankets shoved aside and the warmth of his hands and mouth touching her everywhere. He'd never been like this before, wild and frenzied. Usually he was so methodical and thorough in his lovemaking, but now he was ravenous. Shadow grinned at that thought, but it fit. Brent seemed intent on devouring her, quickly, before she could change her mind.

As if she would?

Certainly not, not when it was so wonderful. The cool air didn't faze her when her shirt was thrown aside, and she was instantly imbued with heat at the touch of his tongue on her nipple, the nip of his teeth.

He reared back and jerked his shirt over his head, tossing it away. With shaking, fumbling fingers, he worked the snap and zipper on his jeans. Shadow reached out, cupping her hand beneath his testicles, holding him gently, and his breath hissed out while his eyes squeezed shut.

"I've waited too long," he muttered through his teeth, then pushed her hand away and shoved his pants down. Shadow wanted to touch him, to measure him with her fingers and stroke him and explore him, but he didn't give her a chance.

He stripped her panties from her body, then positioned himself between her thighs. For a long moment he knelt there, frozen, looking at her, his hands on her thighs holding her open. His chest labored; his nostrils flared. "No matter what," he said, "this time we finish things. I don't give a damn if the house burns down."

"Yes." Shadow reached for him, but he caught her hands and held them near her chest. With his free hand, he stroked her, just riffling his fingers through her curls, teasing her.

He glanced at her face. "You like that?"

"Brent…" She liked it so much, she couldn't take it. "Make love to me."

"I am." His fingers went deep, easing inside her body, stretching her. He used his thumb to stroke her clitoris until her hips were lifting and she could do no more than gasp.

He released her hands so he could feel her breasts, and Shadow used the moment to clutch at him, to try to drag him down to her. "Here," he said, rubbing her left nipple between finger and thumb, "and here." His other thumb teased between her thighs. "These are the two most sensitive places on your body."

The rough pad of his thumb tormented her, rasping her delicate, swollen flesh while two of his long fingers stayed pressed deep inside her. He leaned down, slowly, adding to her tension, heightening her anticipation, and licked her nipple. "I love how soft and warm you feel in my mouth." His gaze heated, locked on to hers. "Here," he whispered, "and *here.*"

Her body arched, the orgasm taking her by surprise. Brent stayed close, watching her, breathing hard while whispering encouragement.

The pleasure finally ebbed and Brent came up and over her, holding himself away on stiffened arms. She saw that he was desperately trying to get himself under control.

She didn't want control. She wanted him wild and eager, as eager as she herself had been. She said, only half teasing, "Don't make me get rough with you, Brent. Enough is enough. I want you now. This minute."

The sound he made was part laugh, part groan, but there was no indecision in his actions. He snagged his slacks, retrieved his wallet and located a condom. He held it up for her to see. "I've been hopeful," he said, giving her a heated look as he rolled it on, letting Shadow watch in fascination.

Holding her knees apart, he lowered himself between her thighs, his gaze never leaving hers. Then slowly, with one long thrust, he pushed into her body.

Shadow was enthralled. Even though it was difficult accommodating his size, nothing had ever felt so right. Without even thinking, she wrapped her legs around his hips and held him tight. Brent tipped his head back, squeezed his eyes shut. The cords of his neck were drawn taut, his shoulders rigid. His chest heaved, but he held perfectly still and Shadow instinctively knew he was fighting to keep it from ending too soon.

"I've just made up my mind," she whispered. "I love you, Brent. I really do."

His arms collapsed, his face coming down beside hers, a loud groan sounding in her ear. And then he was thrusting heavily into her. The friction was exquisite, the unbelievable feelings rapidly building again. Shadow wrapped her arms around him and held on.

He pounded into her and a moment later she climaxed. Even through her own pleasure, Shadow heard the sounds of Brent exploding with her, his moans low and guttural and real. It pleased her and she told him again, louder this time, that she loved him.

It was sometime later when the uncomfortable coolness of the room forced them to move. Shadow was beginning to shiver now that her body was no longer heated, was instead languid and relaxed and nearly asleep. Brent raised himself to his elbows to look down at her. There was an unfathomable intensity in his gaze, but he kissed her gently on her parted lips, then rolled to the side.

Shadow immediately followed, curling against him for his warmth. He obligingly put his arm beneath her, tugging her close, then kicked and shuffled until he reached the blanket and could pull it over them both.

Shadow asked, "Are we going to sleep here?"

Brent didn't answer her at first, then he asked, "Do you

want to? It's too cold for you to try to go home. And this will be the warmest room in the house."

After yawning, Shadow explained, "I couldn't go home now, anyway. My car is in the ditch. That's why I ended up here in the first place."

Brent went curiously still, then repeated, "Your car is in a ditch?"

Nodding, Shadow said, "I was on my way home from work, tried to stop at a red light and slid right off the road."

"How far away?"

She didn't understand the suspicion in his tone, but was too tired to worry about it anyway. "Nearly in front of your house, actually."

Brent twisted around to face her. "Tomorrow, we're really going to find your car in a ditch?"

Shadow frowned at him. "Unless someone steals it tonight. But in this storm, I think that's unlikely."

Brent scowled in thought, but his hand idly, almost automatically stroked Shadow's hip. Staring down at the top of her breasts, he said, "You know, Shadow, you didn't need an excuse to come by. I want us to be at ease with each other. If you wanted to apologize, you could have just called and not gone out in this weather."

Eyes narrowing slightly, Shadow asked, "Apologize? I didn't apologize, Brent. And I wasn't looking for an excuse to come by." Enunciating carefully, as if he were dim-witted, Shadow explained, "I was on my way home from work. Granted, I was looking over at your house as I passed, which is probably why I didn't see the red light right off, but I didn't land my car—a car I love—in a ditch, just to have a reason to come by. In fact," she added as he started to speak, "I wouldn't have come here if I could have made it home in this storm."

"Shadow…" He faltered at her antagonistic look, but then blundered on. "Honey, I'm glad you're here. Really. But I'd rather you just admit—"

Shadow sat up to glare at him. The blanket fell over her lap and covered most of her legs, bent beneath her. He didn't say another word, his eyes glued to her exposed breasts and belly. He reached out to touch her, his eyes going all smoky again. Shadow didn't move, but she did say, "Please, Brent. Finish enlightening me on what I ought to admit."

He caught her arms and pulled her down to his chest. "Admit you love me. Again."

Startled, Shadow said, "That wasn't what you were going to say."

"No, but neither am I going to get into another argument with you. Unbelievable coincidences happen all the time, and besides that, at the moment, I don't care how it is you came to be here. I'm just glad you did."

Well, put like that, how could she stay mad? She'd convince him in the morning that she hadn't fabricated a reason to see him. Right now, he had his large hands spread over her backside, holding her close to his rapidly hardening body. Arguing with Brent was invigorating, but making love with him most definitely had it beat.

HE'D NEVER IMAGINED sleeping on a floor could be so relaxing. For the first time in weeks, he felt replete, all his tension—mostly sexual—melted away. He'd awakened several times during the night, but not because of the hard floor. Shadow's softness, her enticing scent, had interrupted his sleep. She was finally with him, beside him, in his house. He took incredible satisfaction in having her here and he couldn't keep himself from reaching for her again and again. He'd never enjoyed a sleepless night more. He'd never enjoyed a woman more.

Even now her hair tickled his chin and one small hand lay open over his heart. More than that, her silky thigh rested on his lap, making his erection twitch with her every breath. That same incredible need of the night before rushed through him, but he didn't move, content to simply lie back and enjoy her, having her near, feeling her warm breath brushing his skin.

When Shadow finally awoke, she did so loudly, a rough, heartfelt groan emerging as she stretched her body against his. With each muscle she moved, she moaned anew, and Brent suffered a twinge of pity for her. He had been rather relentless last night; but then, so had she.

Suddenly she went very still. Cautiously, slowly, she raised herself on one elbow. Brent pretended to be asleep. He could feel her peering down at him, knew her eyes were wide, her breath held. He was hard-pressed not to smile. When her hand touched him, gently inquisitive, he barely resisted the urge to cover her again. She explored him with a tentative curiosity that had his muscles tightening in anticipation.

Sitting up more fully, Shadow inadvertently pulled the covers from Brent's lower body. At least he thought it had been an accident. But when she made no move to rectify the situation, Brent had to assume her gaze was somewhere south of his abdomen. He could picture her, the intensity of her expression, and suddenly it wasn't enough. He peeked at her, and sure enough, she was studying his hard-on. Closely.

Leaning forward, her beautiful, heavy breasts very near his ribs, she scrutinized him. His hands were already above his head, a typical sleeping position for Brent. But now he locked his fingers together, fighting the urge to return her interest.

He heard a small chuckle and Shadow said, "Quit playing possum, Brent. I know you're awake."

Looking at her lazily, he smiled. "I didn't want to inhibit your…explorations."

He felt her fingers curl warmly around him, bolder now, but he kept his eyes on her face, watching her watch the movement of her hand. It was innocently erotic. It made him insane.

"You don't mind that I'm curious?"

"Not at all." His words sounded like a croak. Out of self-preservation, Brent closed his eyes again, but that only heightened his awareness of her fingers stroking him, her warm breath on his belly. He jumped when she began talking again.

"I liked what you did last night. Where you kissed me."

His entire being clenched with the memory of her sweet taste, her spicy scent. "I liked it, too."

"Would you…like it if I kissed you?"

His heart threatened to come through his chest. "Yes."

"I never have before, but then…I never knew you."

Undone by her words, her sincerity, he tensed. He felt her settle beside him, one hand still holding him, the other stretched over his belly. He had to touch her, even though he feared breaking the moment, and he reached down to tangle his right hand in her hair. "Shadow. If you feel uncomfortable, I wouldn't want…*oh, God.*"

He couldn't think straight—all his concentration centered on maintaining control and enjoying the soft, moist warmth of her mouth for as long as he could. She tasted him, not tentatively—licking, then gently taking the head of his penis in her mouth and sucking.

His hips arched from the floor and he cursed, struggling for some faint measure of control. Rather than pull away when she felt his response, she drew him deeper, her tongue curling around him as her hand curled, tighter, holding him still, consuming him. A ragged groan broke past his clenched teeth and she made a responding sound of pleasure.

It was too much. He tugged her away, not giving her time to complain about his sudden actions. He drew her up and under him.

His fingers slid over her, once, twice. He hadn't taken the proper time to prepare her, but she was ready for him, wet and swollen, hot. He knew she'd enjoyed what she'd done to him and that only added to his urgency. He thrust into her, hard, deep, and knew it was all over for him.

It was unbelievable, undeniable and a bit frightening. Brent couldn't stop kissing her. Even as he thrust that final time, his whole body straining with his release, he felt he couldn't get enough of her, his hands wanting to be filled with her breasts, his nostrils hungry for the scent of her, needing her taste in his mouth. It was the gentle movements of Shadow's hands on his shoulders that finally brought him some measure of reason.

Releasing his hold on her slightly, he gained enough coherence to ask, "Are you okay?"

He could feel her smile. "After all that? After having my body explode into a million pieces? I think my head may have shot off somewhere. Is it still on my shoulders?"

He leaned up to smile at her. They were both sweaty, and Shadow's hair was a damp tangle. Her eyes were puffy from sleep, her lips puffy from his kisses. She was by far the most beautiful woman he'd ever seen. "Are you telling me," he asked, touching her ear, her jaw, "that you enjoyed yourself?"

"*Enjoyed* is an inadequate word." Her eyes drifted over him lazily. "You're wonderful, Brent. It's rather obvious why I love you."

The first time she'd said it, she'd startled him. He hadn't remarked on it, taking it as one of those female things that got said at various moments. Now he wondered if it could be true. Either way, he liked the sound of it. He managed enough strength to raise one brow a good inch. "Oh? And why is it you love me?"

"Your body, of course. And your stamina. Do all men make love so voraciously?"

He closed his eyes on a wave of emotion. "You really must have had lousy taste in men." He sighed, looked at her and said, "I would think any man who touched you would be the same. They were obviously idiots."

She gave him a fat smile. "This is kind of neat, isn't it?"

"What?"

"Lying here, still a part of each other, making small talk. There's only one problem."

"You mean other than the fact we don't have any heat or electricity, and I'm starving and desperately in need of a hot shower, and we're most probably snowed in?"

"Yes. Other than all that."

Brent felt his eyes widen suddenly. "Oh, hell. I just realized the problem."

Shadow waited, her look one of keen interest.

"We didn't use anything."

"Use anything?"

"Protection. I don't suppose you're on the pill?"

She snorted at him. "Whatever for? I told you it had been seven years."

"I know, but…" But what? he wondered. Shadow wasn't

the average modern woman. She wasn't average in any way. "Damn, sweetheart, I'm sorry. I've never, absolutely *never* done anything so irresponsible. You took me by surprise, showing up here yesterday. I just lost control." He groaned. "I don't believe I just said that. I never lose control."

She looked skeptical at that, but kept quiet.

"And then you gave me that sweet story about accidentally going into a ditch…."

Her hands on his shoulders tightened, her fingers biting into his flesh. "What," she asked with quiet menace, "is so sweet about me landing in a ditch?"

Brent didn't want to get into any of that; she was here and he was glad, however it had happened. He said again, "I'm sorry."

She raised one hand to touch his cheek. "It doesn't matter. I told you, I love you. Besides, that's not the problem I was talking about." She hesitated, then asked, "Do you love me?"

Brent stared at her, his guts cramping. "Shadow…" He didn't know what to say. Love? Hell, he didn't know. The practical side of him told him it was impossible. They hadn't known each other long enough to be in love.

Shadow moved restlessly. "Never mind."

"Honey, don't." He felt panicked by the look in her dark eyes, and he hated it. "Don't shy away from me."

"I didn't mean to put you on the spot. I guess I was being too forward again."

"No." He said it urgently, wanting her to understand. "You're being you. And I care a great deal about you, Shadow. But…love? I…"

The shrill ringing of the phone kept Brent from stammering around further and making a complete ass of himself. He rolled to Shadow's side, then reached for the phone on the small table set next to the chair.

"Hello?"

"She's there, isn't she!" The voice was male, anxious and angry. "She spent the night with you, didn't she?"

"Who is this?" Brent demanded, drawing into a sitting position, his muscles rigid.

Low and mean, almost sulky, the voice dropped in pitch. "She doesn't need you! Besides, I found her first and she's mine. You remember that!" And the line went dead.

CHAPTER SEVEN

"What is it?"

Brent feigned a casual shrug, avoiding her eyes. "Nothing."

"Oh? Then why were you cursing a blue streak and why are you frowning and grinding your teeth?" As Shadow asked that, she stood, wrapping one blanket around herself. It was getting colder by the moment, and she needed to make a trip to Brent's bathroom. The thought of putting on her clothes, still rumpled on the floor from the night before and no doubt cold to boot, had her shivering in earnest.

Brent had kept the fire going all night, getting up between lovemaking to add more wood. It took Shadow a minute to untangle her bra from her shirt; Brent had pulled them both off together, without unfastening anything. Then she hooked it across the brass handles on the fireplace screen to warm it.

Brent stared. "I wasn't grinding my teeth or… Shadow, what the hell are you doing?"

She now had each item of her clothing hanging from some part of the fireplace. "I'm warming them," she explained. "Have you ever put your chest into a cold bra? It isn't very pleasant."

"I can imagine." He tried to figure some way to get her

out of the room for just a moment. He wanted to call the police. Actually, he wanted to get hold of the bastard hounding her and beat some sense into him. Since that option wasn't open to him, he would have to try the police. This was getting to be too damned much. Surely the police could do something.

Shadow saved him from finding a believable excuse for privacy when she asked where his bathroom could be found. Brent remembered with some satisfaction that they'd never made it beyond the family room. She hadn't seen the rest of his house.

The tour he gave her was necessarily short and quick. Shadow was shaking and her knees were locked together. Brent showed her into his bathroom, massive compared to her own, complete with an overhead skylight and Jacuzzi tub. He'd located a pair of his sweats for her to put on in lieu of her cold, wrinkled clothing, and showed her where to find a toothbrush and towels. There was probably enough hot water left in the water heater to supply a basic washing, so Brent assumed he'd have a few minutes to himself to make his call.

The cold was more of an inducement for speed than he had reckoned. He was in midconversation, with no way to terminate the call other than hanging up on the officer, when Shadow came back into the room, sat herself in front of the fire and began brushing the tangles from her hair.

There was nothing for it but to let her hear. He hadn't wanted to worry her. He wanted to protect her. Then he realized that, even though she listened, she didn't look particularly worried.

She even interjected at one point, "I got a call yesterday, also. He called the shop and described to me what

I was wearing. He must have gotten close and looked in the window, since I had my coat buttoned anytime I went outside."

The officer was forgotten, the phone hanging from Brent's hand. "You what? Why the hell didn't you tell me that sooner?"

She glanced up at him and shrugged. "The same reason you didn't tell me who called a few minutes ago, I suppose. I didn't want to worry you." She went back to brushing her hair. "By the way, my caller ID said 'unknown.'"

Brent was furious. He finished his conversation with the officer, accepting the assurance that someone would get back to them soon. But he knew there was nothing that could be done.

He stalked around the family room attempting to get a handle on his temper. He'd pulled on sweats, too, but he knew his hair was in bad need of a comb and there was dark stubble shadowing his face. Shadow watched him. He imagined he looked pretty scruffy at the moment, which could explain the intensity of her interest.

Finally, he went to stand before her, staring down at her in reproach. "I can't believe you didn't say anything about that bastard calling you. Did he threaten you?"

She laid the brush aside. "Nope. He repeated what I was wearing and said I was cute. I hung up on him."

Brent went down on his knees before her, his hands on her thighs. He said with as much stern sobriety as he could muster, "You had no business driving in to work alone yesterday."

"He called me at work, not before."

Brent ignored her interruption. "And beyond that, you had no business putting your car in a ditch and allowing yourself to be alone—at night—where he could have grabbed you."

"Brent." Her sigh was long and impatient. "We don't know that he plans to 'grab' me. So far he's only been an aggravation. And I don't know what choice I had about coming here once my car was stuck. I couldn't very well sit in the damn thing and freeze, waiting to see if anyone came by. And going to my house would have taken much longer."

She leaned past Brent to pull on her shoes. Brent realized he was grinding his teeth again, stopped abruptly, then gave her a look of strained patience.

"You should never have put yourself in that situation in the first place."

"I did not," she said, "ditch my car on purpose just to have an excuse to see you. That would be lame and pathetic and dishonest."

Running an agitated hand through his hair, Brent replied reasonably, "You said your car is right in front of my house? Isn't that one hell of a coincidence, Shadow?"

She watched him a moment longer, then stood. "You're making me very angry again, Brent."

"I just want complete honesty between us. That's all.... Now what do you think you're doing?"

"Going home." She shrugged into her coat. "You're totally unreasonable and I don't enjoy being accused of something I didn't do."

"Aw, damn it...wait a minute!" He stepped in front of her when she headed for the door. "You can't walk home in this weather."

"It's stopped snowing."

"But it must be a foot deep out there."

"That's an exaggeration. I'd say not more than half a foot." She poked him in the chest. "So get out of my way."

"No."

"No?"

Brent had never witnessed such an incredulous and outraged expression. He wanted to pull her into his arms and kiss the frown from her forehead. He said instead, "Be reasonable, sweetheart. There's no way I'm going to let you walk home alone in this weather. And don't forget about your secret admirer. He may be watching for you. It's stupid to even think of going out there."

"So now I'm stupid?"

He barely caught her arm as she started past again. Unable to help himself, he chuckled. "For such a small woman, you take incredibly long, stomping strides when you're angry." She tried to resist him, but he finally got her into the circle of his arms. "Give me a break, sweetheart. I'm only a man. And last night was enough to leave anyone fuddled. This morning I even forgot to wear a rubber. I've never forgotten myself like that before. Do you realize I could have gotten you pregnant?"

Shadow raised her chin. "I don't care. I told you, I want children before I get too old."

"Thirty-one is not old, Shadow. There's plenty of time yet to do things the right way."

"I disagree," she said mutinously, "because every time I'm around you, you manage to enrage me."

"But you love me?"

"Rather proves I'm not as intelligent as I claimed, doesn't it? Now, let me go. I'm leaving."

Brent readied himself for battle. His mouth was already open, loaded with convincing arguments, when the doorbell rang. His teeth clicked shut with a snap and he gripped her shoulders. "Stay right here. Don't move."

Shadow proceeded to ignore him, following him to the front door. "You might own a lot of businesses, and I guess you're used to being in charge. But you're not my boss, Brent. Nor will you ever be my boss. I wish you'd try to accept that."

Highly harassed, Brent opened the door.

It took him a moment to believe his eyes, and then he wanted to groan, or quite literally find a hole to sink into. He wasn't given a chance to do either. "Brent, sweetheart! Thank goodness you're home!" Joan flew through the door in a flurry of white fur. Her hat, coat, even her gloves were trimmed in white ermine. She was tall, slender, and at the moment wrapped firmly around him.

Doing his best to disengage himself and close the door at the same time, Brent looked to Shadow. "Ah, Shadow, this is Joan Howard."

"I'm not leaving," Shadow stated.

It was such an about-face, Brent grinned, and finally managed, thanks to the length of his arms, to set Joan a good distance away from his person.

Joan began explaining, a pitiful expression on her lovely face, "I had to spend the night in the most horrible little hotel. The roads were awful. They've only just now become passable. I would have called last night, but the storm disrupted the phone lines somehow, and it was impossible." She drew to a halt, a beautiful smile appearing. "Oh, Brent. It's so good to see you again."

Trying once more to lock herself in his arms, Joan seemed distressed by his quick maneuvering, which put him out of range. He said easily, reaching for Shadow, "I want you to meet my…"

His what? He turned to Shadow in a silent bid for assistance, but she only blinked slowly at him. Then, to his immense relief, she came to his side.

Sticking her hand out and smiling enigmatically, Shadow explained, "I'm Shadow Callahan. I spent the night."

Joan straightened, her nose a good two inches in the air as she stared down at Shadow's rumpled form. "Whatever for?"

"Whatever...?" Shadow laughed, turning to Brent to ask incredulously, "Is this the woman you were engaged to?"

"Uh...yeah."

"And she doesn't understand why I spent the night? Why, shame on you, Brent." Shadow smacked him playfully. "You weren't really putting your all into that engagement, now were you?"

Brent nearly choked. "I...we—"

Shadow waved him to silence. "Never mind." Turning back to Joan, she asked, "Won't you come in? It's dreadfully cold outside. Of course, it's not much warmer in here."

Joan walked, dumbfounded, at Shadow's side, her arm held securely. Shadow continued to chatter, obviously enjoying Brent's moment of distress. "Brent's electricity went out. We had to sleep on the floor in front of the fireplace. And even then it was chilly. Of course, Brent is always so warm... but you'd know that, wouldn't you?"

Joan stopped abruptly, digging in her expensive leather boot heels. She jerked away from Shadow, confronted Brent with her hands on her hips and demanded, "Whoever is this woman and why would you have her here?"

Brent took a lesson from Shadow's book and answered, "She's here because I want her here. I can't seem to keep my hands off her."

Joan actually reeled. "That's disgustingly crude!"

"Actually," Shadow confided, "it wasn't. It was wonderful."

Nostrils flaring delicately, Joan ignored Shadow, and said, "You'd better explain yourself, Brent."

Brent rapidly became irritated. "You're welcome to stay and warm yourself, Joan, but you should understand up front that I won't hear any insults or slurs on Shadow. If you can't behave politely, you may as well leave."

Joan huffed. "When did you plan to tell me about her?"

"I didn't. My relationship with Shadow is none of your business. But you probably would have met her over Christmas. She's coming to Chicago for a visit then."

"You must be joking! Your parents would have a fit."

Shadow laughed. Loudly. It was actually quite rude, but Brent only smiled fondly at her. She said, "Martin and Debra were the ones who invited me."

"You're lying."

Brent was shocked into silence. Immediately he swiveled his gaze to Shadow, leery of how she might retaliate to such a blatant insult. To his surprise, she laughed all the more.

"Joan, you really are funny."

She huffed again. Staring down her nose at Shadow, she breathed in her haughtiest tone, "I beg your pardon?"

"Oh, that's okay. No harm done. Desperate words from a desperate woman. I didn't take offense."

Brent had to fight to hold in his laughter. Joan looked confused by Shadow, and Shadow appeared smug, if a little sympathetic. He asked her quietly, "To the victor goes the spoils?"

Shadow slanted him a look. "If the victor wants them. Which at this moment she's not at all certain she does."

"Of course you do. You love me, remember?"

Joan shook her head as if to clear it, then remarked, "This is absurd."

By silent agreement, they ventured into the family room, the only warm room in the house. Joan drew up short at the sight of Shadow's bra and other clothing stretched about the fireplace. Brent cleared his throat, but Shadow grinned. She really was enjoying herself, he realized.

"I don't suppose you could scrounge up something for breakfast, could you, Brent? I'm starving," she exclaimed.

Brent eyed Shadow's relaxed pose in the chair, then glanced at Joan, sitting rigidly on the very edge of her seat. She looked provoked and ready to do serious damage to somebody. He decided Shadow could better defend herself than he could, and agreed to figure out breakfast.

But he rushed it, not willing to press his luck.

SHADOW GAVE JOAN a moment to acclimate herself to the situation. It was rather sad, she thought, that a woman would feel compelled to chase a man. Shadow hoped she would have more pride should such a circumstance ever occur to her. Any failed relationships she'd had she'd been more than thrilled to see the end of. But Brent? Well, she didn't think she would ever be truly content away from him. She loved him.

Brent had said Joan only wanted him for his money, but Shadow needed to know if that was true. She watched dispassionately as Joan seemed to gather herself, her haughtiness returning with a vengeance. She stood, removed her ermine coat and hat, then tossed them on the chair. Pacing the room, she eyed Shadow's clothes on the fireplace with distaste.

"As you can see," Shadow said easily, "my clothes were wet and cold last night when I arrived. I put them there to warm them so I could dress. But then Brent gave me some sweats to put on. They're really comfortable, even though they're too big. I had to roll the waistband up three times to make the pants fit. But I like the top being so large."

Joan gave her a look of great dislike. "Do you have to rattle on like that? I'm trying to think."

"About what?"

Joan ignored her question to ask one of her own. "How long have you known Brent?"

"Not long really. A couple of weeks."

"Good. He should be tiring of you soon, then. He did this all the time in Chicago. Had his little flings. I tolerated it, of course, but once we marry, it will stop."

Shadow felt her chin drop. Incredulous, she asked, "You didn't mind if he was unfaithful to you?"

Joan lifted one elegant shoulder. "It's the way he does things. He must always be in control, which means forever proving to me where my place is. He's always made up to me later by buying me something exquisite." She dangled her bracelet for Shadow to see. "This is a little something he gave me before he left Chicago."

Brent entered at that moment, saying, "Actually, it was about three months before I left. An apology, I believe it was, for breaking off with you."

Joan visibly jerked at his entrance, and Shadow knew that everything Joan had told her was a lie. Joan was watching Brent warily, her gaze occasionally flicking toward Shadow, waiting, probably, to find out if her lies would be revealed. Shadow said, "It's a beautiful bracelet. And it looks lovely on you."

It had likely cost a small fortune, Shadow thought, looking at the diamond-encrusted gold bracelet. It was fashioned like a tennis bracelet, but heavier, the diamonds so large the bracelet would have very little flexibility. It should have adorned a queen, not an everyday, average woman. Shadow couldn't imagine ever putting something so lavish and expensive on her own arm. It wouldn't go with her jeans.

She noticed Brent watching her and smiled. "What did you round up for food? After all our…exertions, I'm ready to faint from hunger."

Brent was silent for just a moment, then carried the tray toward her. "The electricity is still out, so all I have is fruit and juice, some cold bagels and jam. Will that do for now?"

Rolling her eyes in bliss, Shadow said, "Sounds delicious," then added politely, "Joan, would you like something? Brent must still be in a state of uncertainty. Otherwise, I'm sure he would have remembered his manners and made the offer himself."

Joan turned to Brent, a disbelieving frown marring her smooth brow. "I can't believe you tolerate this, tolerate her! She's unbelievably crass and outspoken."

Shadow saw Brent's eyes narrow in anger, and she quickly waved him to silence, concerned about what he might do. Around a mouthful of bagel, she explained, "He likes it that I'm outspoken. And unbelievably enough, he doesn't think me crass—at least not often."

Brent walked over and shoved the bagel back into Shadow's mouth. "Eat. I'll speak for myself if you don't mind."

He faced Joan. "If you came here thinking there was some way we could reconcile, I'm sorry. But I made it clear in Chicago that it was over. As you see, I'm very much involved with Shadow, and that's not going to change with your presence."

"She's a distraction, an oddity," Joan said finally, her tone filled with spite. "You'll tire of her soon enough. In the meantime, I think I'll stick around." She picked up her coat and headed for the door, sending a look of pure dislike toward Shadow, who merely waved, taking another drink of her juice.

Joan said from the doorway, "I'll keep in touch," then stormed out.

Shadow chided Brent, "You should have escorted her to the door to see her out."

"She's a malicious bitch. She can see herself out."

Shadow chuckled. "Aw, poor baby. You really let her get to you, didn't you?"

Brent stiffened. "It's not funny, Shadow. It was bad enough in Chicago, but now she's following me here?"

Shadow set her glass of juice on the tray and went to Brent, crawling, uninvited, into his lap. Despite his stiff posture, she wiggled around until she was comfortable, then gave him a hug. "I'm sorry. I suppose I should be more sympathetic."

"Yes, you should." He relaxed enough to loop his arms loosely around her. "She's a pain in the butt, and I won't tolerate her insulting you."

"Brent, I didn't pay any attention to that. It was just jealousy. If it weren't for you, someone like Joan wouldn't even have noticed me, much less made the effort to comment on my behavior or appearance. It's a beautiful day. Don't let her spoil it."

Brent rubbed his face in agitation. "A beautiful day? There's not a single color visible outside other than white, it's probably ten degrees, if that, we've had a maniac call to threaten you and another maniac show up to annoy me, and we have no electricity. This is a beautiful day?"

Shadow kissed his jaw. She slipped her hand beneath the rounded neckline of his sweatshirt. "You're not using the right perspective. You're seeing things all wrong."

His skin heated, from just her simple touch. He asked in a low voice, "How do you see today?"

"I'm sitting on the lap of the man I love. We're all alone, and I for one don't have anyplace urgent to go. The sun is shining so brightly the reflection on all that snow is almost blinding. We're warm and comfortable and dry. And alive. To me, it's truly a spectacular day."

There was a moment of thoughtful silence before Brent said, sounding much struck, "You're right. And I thank you for pointing it out to me." He nuzzled beneath her chin. "You really don't have to go to the shop?"

"Nope. Kallie works by herself today. I'll just call to check in later. And I'm considering hiring someone else as you suggested." She didn't add that she had decided to do that so she would have more time to spend with him. She had made enough declarations of her feelings without getting any in return.

Brent put his hand to her cheek, turning her to face him. "Will you spend the day with me? And the night? I rather liked the way you woke me this morning."

Shadow chuckled. "It was a little different from the way I woke you at my house, wasn't it?"

Brent nodded. "Morning screams are hell on my nervous system."

"I'll have to go home later to get a change of clothes and check my messages. Other than that, I'm all yours."

He stared at her mouth. "Hmm. I like the sound of that."

Shadow traced his huge grin with the tip of her finger. "Do you really want me to be all yours, Brent?"

Brent kissed her, a kiss filled with tenderness, but Shadow felt his hunger and need, too. He hadn't given her an answer, but she felt certain he cared for her, if just a little. He was smart to be cautious, especially with the way women had apparently feigned their affections, their real interest based on his financial standing.

It was beyond Shadow how any woman could be with Brent and not see the whole man—the strength, the intelligence, the innate compassion for other people. Thoughts of his money never entered her mind, except when he was trying to spend it on her, forcing her to object. But she understood his caution; Joan's visit had proved the necessity of that. That woman had plainly said she didn't mind sharing him with other women, as long as she was richly compensated. Shadow couldn't comprehend such a sentiment. If Brent went to another woman now, she'd want to scream, to maim and then cry, probably in that order. And she didn't think it was something she would ever be able to forgive him, for it would be such a break in trust. Just the thought made her shiver.

She snuggled closer to Brent, then laughed. "Your lap isn't quite as comfortable now as it was a minute ago. What happened?"

Brent said into her ear, his words gruff, "There's this incredibly soft, sexy woman sitting on me who keeps squirming around. She caused my libido to jump-start, and now it's in overdrive." He gently bit her earlobe, then licked the tender spot beneath her ear.

Shadow squirmed again. Her only comment to his outrageous teasing was, "Overdrive, huh? Oh good."

BRENT DIDN'T KNOW it was possible to have so much fun. Everything Shadow did, she did with pizzazz.

The electricity finally came back on that afternoon, and Shadow decided they should cook their own lunch. But she neglected to inform Brent she didn't know any more about cooking than he did, until it was too late. Making lasagna was a messy business. Shadow laughed her way through it, and even though the end result didn't look particularly appealing, it tasted perfect. Brent wasn't certain if that was due to the actual flavor of the dish or the fact that he shared it with Shadow.

She set up a picnic of sorts, using the same quilt they'd used the night before, spread before the fireplace, with lit candles all around and soft music in the background. She'd also insisted they eat naked. She said it greatly enhanced the flavor of the food. Later, she confessed hoping the sight of her nudity would distract Brent from what he ate, so he wouldn't actually notice what a poor job she'd done of it.

Later that day, after they had seen to having her car towed from the ditch, Shadow called in to Sex Appeal. Kallie had put a Help Wanted sign in the window, as per Shadow's instructions. Already there'd been several applications taken. It was while they were in his tub, enjoying a leisurely bath together, that Brent found out about her strange list of requirements for all applicants.

Shadow sat between his thighs, her back to his chest. Brent alternately rubbed his chin against the softness of her hair, breathed her scent and found various excuses to touch and stroke her. At the moment, he was washing her knee. "Why does the new assistant have to read a book in front of you?"

"Not just *any* book," Shadow clarified, "but a specific book that I've always found hilariously funny. If she reads it while I'm watching, and doesn't so much as crack a smile, or worse, if she actually frowns, I'll know she's not right for the job."

Brent ran a soapy hand over Shadow's shoulder. "What exactly is in this book?"

She leaned her head against his wet chest and looked at him upside down. "Slightly crude cartoons. Like the one with a couple lying under the covers in their bed, a multitude of, ah, sex toys scattered around them. The woman is looking at the poor guy, who has just emptied the entire box trying to spark her fancy, and she complains, 'I'm bored.'"

Brent smiled.

"There's also one where two businesswomen are talking over tea. One says, 'The only interesting man I've met lately was an obscene phone caller, and he refused to give me his name no matter how I begged.'"

Idly cupping her breasts in his palms, Brent asked, "So if this unwary reader fails to laugh the appropriate number of times, you won't hire her?"

"That's right. But there are other deciding factors. Does she look pleasant or stern? And how she reacts to me. I can't have someone working for me who thinks I'm a certifiable nut. Not if she thinks being a nut is a bad thing."

Brent laughed, hugging Shadow to his chest. "You're priceless, honey, you know that? I've had so much fun today. Real fun. I think it's a first for me. Thank you."

"You're very welcome." She twisted in his arms, seeking a kiss. When the water cooled, Brent reluctantly moved her aside, then stood, quickly wrapping a towel around his waist.

Shadow, too, stepped out of the large tub, concerned by his withdrawal.

"Brent…?"

After slicking his wet hair off his forehead, he faced her. With his hands on his hips, not seeing any other way of broaching this, he said, "Stay here with me until this is all over."

She caught her breath. "Until *this* is over?"

"Until whoever is making those calls is either caught or goes away."

She shook her head. "I can't do that."

Though he'd half expected her refusal, it still annoyed him. "Why not? It's not like we haven't been intimate. And in this day and age, no one thinks anything of two people living together."

"I agreed to spend one night here, Brent. Not to move in. Remember, I told you I come from an old-fashioned family. They'd be shocked if they found out I was living with a man."

"I want you safe, Shadow."

"I know," she replied gently. "And I appreciate your concern. But my house is safe, too. Judging by the cost of that dumb alarm system, it had better be secure."

Her attempt at humor went flat. "You think I'm only 'concerned' about you?" Brent gripped her bare shoulders, shaking her slightly. "I care about you, Shadow. Very much. It's a hell of a lot more than concern!"

She eyed him curiously, but said only, "What is it then, exactly?"

He released her with a muffled curse, turning away. Just as quickly he turned back. "Would you marry me if I asked?"

Her eyes rounded and her mouth opened twice before she managed to say, "If? You want to know before you actually ask?"

"Just answer the damn question," he growled.

She studied him in silence. "Why would you be asking?"

"What the hell do you mean, why?"

She tightened the towel around her waist, looking vulnerable. "You never said you love me. A proposal based on some noble sacrifice definitely wouldn't be acceptable."

Brent ground his teeth. "I'm not noble."

She nodded slowly. "Yes you are."

"I'm asking," he said succinctly, with flagging patience, "because I want you to marry me."

"But why?" She hugged herself tighter. "You're worried about me and you think marrying me is a way to keep me safe?"

There were a number of women who would have jumped at a proposal from him, and not one of them would have given him the third degree. They'd have said yes with alacrity and been thrilled. But not Shadow. No, she had to torture him a bit more by asking him questions he didn't have answers to.

Brent paced the floor, his hands fisted. Finally he turned to her again. "You could be pregnant," he reminded her.

She wasn't swayed. "So? I can take care of a baby. I may not have your wealth, but I can manage just fine. That would be a lousy reason to get married."

"You said you were old-fashioned," he accused with heat. "Children are a damn conventional reason to marry!"

"That's your only reason for asking? Suddenly, because I might be pregnant, you want to marry me?"

Brent floundered. Finally he took both her hands in his and led her to the bed. After she sat on the edge he started to speak again.

His eyes dropped to her exposed breasts, still damp from

the bath. "I could do this a lot easier if you covered yourself properly."

She put one hand over each breast. "Now talk."

His groan turned into a laugh. "That doesn't help, honey. Your hands are too small to do an adequate job." He reached to the top of his large mahogany bed and jerked the pillow from beneath the spread. "Here. Hide yourself from me."

She covered herself, then gave him an expectant look.

"I care about you, Shadow. You know that." He waited until she nodded, then continued. "And after this morning, you could be pregnant."

He frowned pensively, adding, "I enjoy your company, which isn't something I can honestly say about any other woman I'm not related to, and even the relatives are few. Most of all, I don't like worrying about you. You can accuse me of being chauvinistic later, but I feel responsible for you and protective. So please," he asked quietly, "will you marry me?"

Sadness filled her eyes, making his heart almost stop. Then she smiled and leaned over to kiss him. Brent, wanting an answer, not a distraction, tried to pry her loose. But she fell against him and they both toppled to the floor. He landed with a thump, then groaned, but only until Shadow held his face between her hands and started kissing him.

Brent chuckled and finally managed to pull himself free enough to talk. "Does this mean yes or no?"

Shadow shoved away her towel, then his. Her fingers spread across his chest, tangling in his body hair. She straddled his hips and said, "No."

He froze, frustrated, angry. But Shadow was naked, astride his hips, and he was hard, ready. She rubbed against him, her eyes closed, her head tipped back, and he thought he'd shout with the pleasure of it.

"Shadow." He caught her hips and held her tighter to him. "Where do you keep protection?"

She looked around the room until he said hoarsely, "In the nightstand." They'd talk later, he decided. He'd convince her then. Right now, he could barely breathe.

She curled her slender fingers around the base of his straining erection, stroked her thumb over the sensitive head, then did a tantalizing job of rolling on the condom. She held him steady and slowly lowered herself to slide down his length. He stiffened, his hips rising to meet her. She whispered breathlessly, all the while moving, "I'll never again marry a man who doesn't love me. For any reason."

Brent raised his hands to her breasts, urging her on, his fingers finding and toying with her nipples, plucking, tugging, rolling them gently. Shadow arched her back and her thighs tightened. At the moment of her release, she again shouted that she loved him, then collapsed against his chest. He came with his own deep groan of fulfillment.

Long after the waves of her climax had receded, Shadow was still kissing him, though gently now, tender little nips on his chin and throat. She said again, "I love you, Brent."

Brent sighed, his hands holding her close in near desperation for just a moment. "What am I going to do with you, Shadow?"

She propped her elbows on his chest and stared down at him. "Do with me? You mean more than you've already done? I didn't know there was more, but hey, I'm all for it."

He smiled, but it was only a halfhearted effort.

Shadow leaned back down and cuddled against him. "We can simply continue as we are. Having fun. Enjoying each other. Making the most of our time together."

"I don't like the sound of that," he warned, eyeing her closely. "As if our time is limited."

"Well…" She toyed with the lock of hair over his forehead, before meeting his gaze. "I don't plan to go anywhere. But I wouldn't want you to stay here if you were unhappy."

"How could I be unhappy with you around?"

Brent could tell by her remote shrug that he'd hurt her. He wanted to kick his own ass, but more than that, he wanted to see her smile again, to hear her laugh. Her laughter never failed to arouse him and her smiles made him feel like the luckiest man alive.

He could tell her he loved her, he thought, whether he was certain of his feelings or not. But Shadow was always honest with him and she deserved his honesty in return.

He cared, just as he'd told her. But he didn't know about love; it wasn't something tangible, wasn't something he could easily grasp. Shadow was unique and different and… special. The way she made him feel was special. She said she loved him.

But, a tiny voice in his head insisted, *plenty of women have claimed to love you.*

Shadow shoved herself up into a sitting position. She brushed her hair out of her eyes. "I need to go home, Brent. I have to check my messages and—"

"You're coming back here tonight, Shadow." He had no intention of letting anyone, especially some loony secret admirer, get near her. She wouldn't be hurt. He'd see to that, one way or another.

"Don't get all heavy-handed and bossy on me, Brent. I said I would spend the night. But I need some clothes and my makeup and a few other things. Tomorrow is a workday, and I'll probably go straight from here."

"All right." Brent lifted them both to their feet. He couldn't keep his eyes, or his hands, off Shadow's naked body, with her standing so sweetly before him. He touched her cheek, her kiss-swollen lips. "Will you try to hire someone tomorrow? I don't want you working alone anymore." She started to draw back, ready to refuse, and he teased, "I did ask nicely that time. No demands at all. You see, I'm trying, even though I personally think I'm much better at issuing orders." He grinned at her. "Ah, the concessions I make for you."

"True." She chuckled, then gave up with a groan. "I'll see if there isn't a worthy applicant in the bunch first thing tomorrow morning. How's that?"

"It's great." Then he added, "For now."

CHAPTER EIGHT

STILL HEARING THE ECHO of the last message to play, Shadow stared at her answering machine. He'd called her again, not once, not twice, but *three times*. And he hadn't been happy. No, he'd been nearly incoherent with jealousy and anger.

She rubbed her arms and looked at Brent.

"This changes everything," Brent said, and his voice was as hard as his expression.

What could she say? "I…I don't know."

Brent nodded, then started for her bedroom.

"Where are you going?"

He didn't look at her. "To pack some of your clothes."

She hustled after him. "I can do that." Though she'd never admit it to Brent, she was relieved she wouldn't be staying home alone tonight. "I'll only need a few things for tomorrow."

Brent ignored her, rummaging through her closet until he found a suitcase, then opening it on her bed.

"Brent, I don't need that case. I'll only…wait a minute! Brent, *stop*." She caught his hand, now in possession of two shirts. "What do you think you're doing?"

"You're not staying here alone."

She didn't want to, but she heard herself say, in a firm voice, "You can't force me to stay at your house."

He leaned down, eyes narrowed, and said through his teeth, "Watch me."

"I don't believe this!" Her nervousness over the calls was forgotten, smothered beneath her need for independence.

He stepped past her. "What's your parents' phone number?"

Shadow watched him suspiciously. She'd seen many moods from him, but this was a new one. "Now, Brent..."

He stalked to her little telephone table by the front door, opened a drawer and riffled through it until he located her personal phone book. Intent on his purpose, he paid no mind to Shadow's escalating temper.

She practically shouted, "I don't have my parents' number written down! Good grief, I know it by heart. It hasn't changed since I was ten years old."

Brent faced her. "Tell it to me."

This was interesting. She folded her arms over her chest, wondering what Brent intended to say to her parents. She'd told them a little about him, but nothing at all about the anonymous calls. Deciding quickly, she recited the number.

He dialed it without hesitation.

"Hello, Mrs. Callahan? This is Brent Bramwell, a friend of Shadow's." He paused, then said, "Oh, she told you about me?" His gaze met Shadow's briefly and she could have sworn that was raw satisfaction dancing in his dark green eyes. "She's fine, ma'am. No, I swear, nothing's wrong with her. That is, nothing you aren't already aware of. Yes, of course I was joking."

Shadow stuck her tongue out at him. He covered the mouthpiece and whispered, "Not yet, honey. How about when we get to my house?"

Her face colored, which only satisfied him more.

Brent listened a few minutes, laughed a few times, then explained about the calls, the flowers, the notes. He was very detailed, Shadow thought, peeved. But he was also calm enough that he wouldn't alarm her mother. He surprised Shadow by telling her mother that he wanted Shadow to stay with him.

"Yes, ma'am, but the thing is, she's concerned she'll shock you. I understand, but she'll be much safer with me until this whole thing can be resolved. I thought you might be able to talk some sense into her."

Brent's gaze filled with triumph and he handed her the phone. His grin was entirely too smug.

Shadow, knowing her mother well, took the phone and said without preamble, "No, Mom, I won't come home. I know, but I'm fine, really. No, it's true. I have this outrageously expensive security system Brent insisted on me buying…." She paused, then said, "Yeah, I suppose he is. I'm not sure about that. He hasn't really said. Yes, I love him."

Shadow could tell by the look on Brent's face that this wasn't the conversation he'd anticipated. Rather than her mother telling her to go with Brent, she was trying to coerce her into coming home. Shadow could have told Brent what the outcome of his call would be.

She rolled her eyes. "All right, Mom, I'll think about it. Give my love to everyone." She laughed. "Right. Goodbye."

Brent scowled at her. "What in hell was that all about?"

"My mother said you sound like a rascal and a thoroughly likable young man. She also said I should try to keep you happy so you'd stick around."

"What did she say about you staying with me?"

"When she accepted that I wouldn't come home, she said that I probably should and to be very careful if I don't."

"Aha! So she agrees with me?"

Shadow shrugged again, barely managing to hold her laughter. "I suppose she did. But, Brent, I'm thirty-one. I don't always do what my parents want me to. I told you before, I've been on my own since I was seventeen."

"Does that mean you will or won't stay with me?" he demanded.

"Tonight I'll stay. Tomorrow I have to be at my own house." His anger and frustration were palpable and Shadow went to him, gently touching his arm. "Brent, can't you understand?"

"That you want to drive me nuts? Oh yeah, I understand that well enough."

"If I come to stay with you, it will mean I let him drive me out of my house. I'd be miserable knowing I'd given up."

"I wouldn't let you be miserable."

He was such an easy man to love, she thought with a small chuckle. "We both have jobs to go to, other commitments." He didn't relent, and she added, "Would you leave your home because of a few phone calls?"

He snorted at that, then turned thoughtful. "All right," he said finally. "But remember, I did give you options."

Shadow was surprised and perversely disappointed by how quickly he gave up. She turned away to finish her packing.

It was already dark outside, even though it wasn't quite seven. Brent stood by her side as she turned on the security system, then walked out to his car. He held her small overnight bag in one hand, her arm with the other. She was silent on the drive to his house, feeling melancholy again, a mood she wasn't familiar with and didn't quite know how to handle.

They entered Brent's house to the sound of a ringing

phone. Brent had headed for the bedroom, so Shadow picked it up. She listened for only a moment, not saying a word after her initial greeting. Brent sauntered back in, and she handed him the phone with a wry smile. "It's your stalker, not mine."

"What?" Brent took the receiver with a curt, "Hello?" Then he groaned. "What do you want, Joan?"

Wanting to give him privacy, Shadow wandered aimlessly through the house. It was beautiful, but not decorated to its full potential. With diamond-paned windows, hardwood floors and a fireplace in nearly every room, the place bordered on historic, but the spacious rooms were largely empty, the walls bare. The few pieces of furniture or rugs were purely functional, not at all decorative. The only completed rooms in the entire massive, five-bedroom house were the family room, the kitchen and Brent's bedroom. These were furnished with heavy mahogany and cherrywood pieces done in bold, basic designs. There wasn't a plant or a picture to be found.

Shadow was looking at a guest bedroom, one close to the hall bath, when Brent found her. She'd been thinking what a wonderful room it would be for a child. Overlooking the backyard, it had a closet big enough to be a play space, filled with plenty of shelves for toys.

She turned to Brent, trying to mask her thoughts. "Did you get everything straightened out with Joan?"

"She wanted me to have dinner with her."

"You told her no?"

"Of course I told her no. I have no interest in seeing her again. I wish to hell she'd leave me alone."

Shadow smiled. "She told me yesterday that you were unfaithful to her during your engagement."

Brent stiffened. "What did you say?"

"Not much. Mostly I just listened. I decided she was lying." Shadow looked down at her hands, clasped in Brent's much larger ones. "She's not a happy woman, Brent."

He rubbed her knuckles and asked, "Why do you say that?"

"Because she doesn't understand what will make her happy. She thinks you and your money will do it for her. She doesn't know she has to make herself happy, not rely on someone else to do it for her."

Brent frowned at her. "What're you trying to tell me in your twisted way, Shadow?"

She asked suddenly, "You haven't done much with this house. Why is that?"

He searched her face. "Your quick turns in conversation make me dizzy. All right. I haven't done much here because I wasn't certain I'd stay, and I haven't had a lot of free time."

"Are you certain now?"

Borrowing her tactics, he didn't answer but asked his own question instead. "What's this all about, honey?"

"My mother asked me if you planned to stay in town or if this was a temporary visit to take care of business. I didn't know the answer to that. It made me realize there's a lot I don't know about you. What your plans are for the future, what you want say…five years from now. If you've set any long-term goals for yourself. I was just curious, I suppose."

Brent chewed on the inside of his cheek, scrutinizing her. "And you decided to ask all these questions here, in this particular bedroom? Or was it because of Joan's call?"

Shadow shook her head.

"I don't understand you, Shadow. Nothing new in that, I suppose. But I've asked you to marry me and that alone should tell you I don't plan to uproot anytime soon. Or even if I had planned to, I wouldn't go unless you could go, too. And as far as my goals for the future, I haven't set any. My business ventures are forever expanding, so I don't have to consciously set goals for them. I simply grow and expand with them."

"And personal goals? Any thoughts on them?"

"Only to the point that I'm thirty-four and therefore at an age where I should be having children of my own, a wife to come home to." He lifted her hand to his chest. "We could have a very nice life together, Shadow."

It wouldn't be enough, she knew, not without his love. But she couldn't tell him that. She'd made too many demands already. "Don't you see? We could have a nice life apart, too. You shouldn't consider marriage just because it'd be convenient right now."

He placed his palm over her flat belly. "And if you're pregnant? That would be a lifetime commitment for both of us."

"You wouldn't have to be married to me to do your duty to the child."

Brent thrust his hands in his pockets and turned away. "It wouldn't be a matter of duty." He whirled back to face her. "Do you think I'd avoid involvement in my child's life?"

Helplessly, she stared at him. "I don't know, that's just it. I mean, there's involved, and then there's *involved*." She smiled, trying to lighten the tension in the room. "This may all be a moot point. The odds of me being pregnant can't be all that great."

"Oh, I don't know. Not to brag, but I'm good at anything I do." He touched her belly again and looked almost wistful. "I'd say it's possible."

"But not probable. Let's wait before we worry that topic into the ground, okay?"

Brent gave long consideration to her suggestion and finally nodded. Shadow had the distinct impression he'd made a strategic—and temporary—retreat. "What would you like to do for dinner? We haven't eaten yet."

"Do you have peanut butter and jelly?"

"Uh, no. I don't think so."

"Then the first order of business is a trip to the grocery. Then—" she yawned dramatically "—I think I'd like to make an early night of it. What do you say?"

"Do you intend to attack me again?"

"I was considering it."

Brent instantly feigned his own yawn, complete with an elaborate stretch. "I suddenly feel faint with exhaustion. An early night it is."

SHE GOT ANOTHER CALL the next day. Shadow's temper was frayed to the limit, her disposition not to be envied, and she hadn't gotten enough sleep the night before. The only bad thing about that was it couldn't be blamed on Brent. They'd made love twice, then he'd fallen asleep, his arms around her, her head on his shoulder. It was the most comfortable position imaginable, yet sleeplessness had kept her up long into the night.

The call was short, something about showing her who was in control. Ha! She already knew—Brent was.

Without trying, he'd managed to control her thoughts, her feelings. Effortlessly, he made her want him, love him... *almost* need him. Life had taught her to need no one but herself.

Her life would be every bit as complete without him.

Who was she kidding? Brent was the part of her she hadn't known was missing, a part that filled her up, made her whole, more content, more fulfilled. She could make it without him—she wasn't dramatic or a fatalist. Life wouldn't end without Brent. But it sure wouldn't be as wonderful, either. Not even close.

Shadow paced, ignoring the pile of papers on her desk that needed her attention, knowing she should be out front helping train the new girl she'd hired just that morning. But she couldn't seem to clear her mind. The papers would wait and Kallie did a commendable job of training. When the phone rang, Shadow stared at it, a malicious smile slowly dawning over her face. She needed an outlet for her temper and her annoying admirer would do just fine.

"Hello?" she fairly sang.

"I wanted to give you fair warning."

Oh, hell. Wrong stalker. "What do you want, Joan?"

"I told you. Just a friendly little warning. Brent will tire of you soon. Then I'll have him back. Why don't you save yourself a little heartache and give up?"

"Well, now," Shadow said, her voice sugary sweet with politeness, "I appreciate your concern for my welfare, indeed I do. But it's unnecessary. Truly. You see, I'm enjoying every little minute I spend with Brent. So no matter how long it lasts, there won't be a single wasted second."

"You little bitch! Can't you see he's only using you?"

"That's okay. I'm using him, too." Shadow could hear Joan gnashing her teeth. It pleased her.

"I'm going to see him this afternoon. He likes to make love in his office, did you know that?"

Her words had been softer, more in control. Shadow grimaced, not liking the mental picture that formed. She said carefully, "I had the impression Brent liked making love just about anywhere. But no, I haven't been to his office."

"Well, I have. I *will* get him back."

Rapidly tiring of the game, Shadow said, "Joan, if you can get him back, then I don't want him anyway. I wish you luck." And she hung up. *Spiteful witch.* She thought about calling Brent and warning him, then decided it might smack of jealousy, so she resumed her pacing instead.

Ten minutes later, she got yet another call and this one was from her number one annoyance. Shadow thought, rather humorlessly, that he must be as bored as she was, but most probably for different reasons. She already missed Brent terribly. This guy was just plain *missing.*

"What do you want now?" she asked.

"Are you going to spend the night with him again?"

She didn't bother asking which "him" he meant. "That's really none of your business and if you don't stop pestering me I'm going to have my calls traced."

He yelled, "You stay away from that businessman and I won't have to call!"

"Everyone seems to want to issue warnings to me today."

He was thrown by her words. "What's that supposed to mean?"

"Never mind. Inside joke. But tell me. I have been wondering and since you seem determined to keep calling, we may as well talk." She felt smug at the thought of his silent confusion. "How did you get Brent's phone number?"

"I saw the two of you together," he accused.

"Where?"

"At the shop, at your house."

His answers were smooth. Too smooth. And suspiciously smug. "So how did you know who he was?"

"I followed him back to his office. Once I knew his name, I looked up his number in the phone book."

Shadow felt a chill, but concealed it behind her cool manner. She was only just realizing that any threat to her extended to Brent as well. Maybe more so. "Why are you doing this? Why me? Was it something I said," she asked carefully, "when you entered the contest?"

He laughed. "I have no idea what you're talking about."

"That doesn't surprise me."

She actually felt his anger as he blustered into the phone. "He doesn't love you, you know. He won't be around forever. You can keep throwing yourself at him, keep chasing him, but it won't do you any good!"

Shadow hung up, his words too closely resembling her own thoughts and Joan's warning. She opened a file drawer and pulled out the phone book. Quickly flipping through the pages, she stopped at the *B*s. Brent's name wasn't listed; he hadn't been in town long enough. How had this nut gotten the number?

Had he, at some point, been close enough to listen to one of their conversations? Shadow envisioned him hiding behind a bush, concealed by the heavy snow and the early winter darkness. She and Brent had had several talks on the walkway, both in front of her house and at the shop. It sent shivers down her spine to think of someone watching and listening so intently.

She couldn't let it affect her like this, making her paranoid. She forced herself to take a deep breath, to calm down. The police had told her that lots of people got strange calls. Usually it turned out to be nothing. She had taken precautions; he couldn't touch her, if that was even his plan.

She put on her coat and walked to the coffee shop. She

was skittish, and as she walked, even in the light of day, she found herself looking all around, being overly cautious. It irritated her.

There were several friends at the coffee shop, different proprietors of the various businesses. The big talk over coffee was how the contest was faring. Shadow hadn't met the two men Brent sent to fill her quota. But the women were very enthusiastic about them. The men were described as successful, handsome and charming. The photographer was more than ready to brag that she had a date lined up with one of them already.

That sounded just a tad unethical to Shadow, but she didn't say so. After all, the shoppers would make the ultimate decision on the winner, not the shop owners.

When Shadow returned to her office, she called her mom. Thanksgiving was just around the corner so she made a last-minute check on what, if anything, she should bring. All that was required was herself. She dragged the conversation out for a good fifteen minutes, trying to distract herself from her worries, but she finally ran out of gossip and was forced to hang up.

She hesitated a few minutes, at loose ends as to what to do next. It was a given that she wouldn't accomplish any work. After a brief struggle with herself, she gave in and called Brent. His secretary, a very pleasant woman, announced he was busy in his office and not to be disturbed.

His office. The question came out without her mind's permission. "Is he with Joan?"

The secretary, Micky, was clearly surprised as she answered. "Yes, he's with Miss Howard. Were they expecting you?"

It took Shadow a moment to reply because she had to

find a way to keep the screech out of her tone. Finally she said, "Nope. They're not expecting me."

"Oh. Well then, can I take a message?"

"Yes. Tell Brent, er, Mr. Bramwell, that I went home for the day."

"Yes, ma'am. And what is your name again?"

Shadow hung up without answering. Brent would know who the message was from. There was no need for her name to be announced to the secretary or possibly in front of Joan.

She didn't want to indulge in wicked imaginings, but her mind refused to listen to her, conjuring visions of Brent and Joan together. Shadow had never been jealous a day in her life. It had always been a foreign emotion to her, something other people suffered through insecurities and indecision. Her attitude had always been that if a man wasn't trustworthy you got rid of him.

Of course, she reminded herself, Brent was trustworthy. It was that she-devil Joan who couldn't be trusted. Brent was probably doing everything possible to put her off. Did he truly loathe Joan as he said, or was it possible she might seduce him?

Thoroughly disgusted with herself, Shadow threw on her coat and went out to the sales floor to announce to Kallie that she was leaving. Kallie looked at her with concern. "Are you all right? You look a little down."

Shadow laughed. "You're shocked by such a notion, Kallie?"

"Well, you're always so chipper. I don't remember ever seeing you looking quite so...glum."

"I think I've just been fed a good dose of reality, that's all. I'm sure I'll recover. But I am tired and I'm not doing a single constructive thing around here, so I might as well get out of your way."

"You be careful going home."

"I will. And you be careful locking up. Make certain you're not alone in the parking lot at night. Now that we have another helper, we should always leave here in twos."

Kallie agreed, then gave Shadow a hug. "Get a good night's sleep and I'll see you in the morning."

Shadow drove home by rote. Even the freezing chill of the air didn't faze her.

The sight of her house did, however. Shadow finally thought of something to do that would take her mind off Brent. She went in, using the remote control device so her alarm wouldn't sound, then turned off the system. She would be running in and out and didn't want to be bothered using the remote each time.

She changed into her oldest jeans and a baggy, well-worn sweatshirt that read Talk Is Cheap (But the Action Will Cost Ya). She spent the next half hour shoveling snow off her porch and walk. It felt good to do physical work instead of sitting in her office; the exercise helped clear her mind. The day was so cold, not a single neighbor ventured outside and no cars drove by.

When she'd finished, she went inside and made herself a sandwich, with a glass of juice and two cookies for lunch. She sat at the table, pensive as she waited for Brent to phone. There was no doubt he would call. It was only a matter of when he finished with Joan.

She cringed at her own mental wording. Downing the last of the juice, she stood to leave the kitchen. She needed a hot shower to warm herself.

Outside, the wind blew, chasing snowflakes past the

windows, rustling the trees, forming drifts around the yard. She heard the occasional creak and snap as the house settled. She realized how alone she was; she'd never felt lonely before, but now, without Brent, she did.

She recalled the security system, which she hadn't turned back on. She barely got it reset when her head started to swim. She stopped, flattening one hand on the wall. Her stomach pitched, churned. She forced herself to breathe slowly, but a heavy lethargy was settling in. It was just like the night she'd spent with Brent. She barely made it to the bathroom on time. Her stomach was completely empty before she could finally leave the toilet.

Wondering if she had the flu, she walked slowly into her bedroom and stripped off her clothes. After pulling on a short, thermal nightgown, she crawled beneath the covers and tried to find a comfortable position. She was about to doze off when the phone began ringing.

She thought, *please, not again.* Groaning, she leaned out of bed and picked up the receiver on the nightstand. Her voice was a hesitant croak. "Hello?"

"Why did you leave the shop without telling me first?" he demanded.

Shadow hung up on him. The last thing she wanted was to have Brent yelling at her.

He called back immediately. She picked up the receiver and he said, his voice low and mean, "I wouldn't suggest you do that again."

Shadow waited. Brent said, now more cautiously, "Shadow?"

"What?"

"Are you all right?"

"Yes. No, actually, I'm sick."

Trying for a more moderate tone, he asked, "Then why didn't you tell my secretary that when you called? You know I don't want you driving home alone."

"You were with Joan. I was having my first major bout of jealousy. I didn't want or need to get your approval to go home. And besides, I just got sick. I wasn't sick when I left."

There was a moment of silence while Brent digested everything she had just said. Without addressing any one issue, he said, "I'll be there in just a minute, honey."

"I might be catching," she said, thinking of the flu. This time he hung up on her. Shadow put her head under the pillow. It seemed like only minutes later that Brent was pounding on the front door.

"Wow. You look like hell. Are you okay?"

She glared at him. "Thanks, Brent. I needed to hear that."

Brent grinned at her disgruntled frown, watching as she walked, hunched over like an old woman, back to bed. He followed behind her. "What's the matter, honey?"

"I got really tired again and then sick to my stomach. Just out of the blue—ugh. I hate throwing up."

"Well, I can understand that." Brent helped her into the bed and under the covers, then he felt her head. "You don't have a fever. Did you eat anything bad?"

She shot him a venomous look through shadowed eyes. "If I knew it was bad, would I have eaten it?"

"Okay." He pursed his mouth to keep from grinning. She was so testy when she didn't feel well. "What *have* you eaten today?"

"Breakfast with you this morning. Then a sandwich and a couple of cookies just a little bit ago. That's all."

"What kind of sandwich?"

"Peanut butter. And no. The peanut butter wasn't bad."

Brent frowned. "I'm going to call the doctor."

"No, Brent, that's silly. I'm fine. I'm already starting to feel better. Not so weak."

Brent stared at her thoughtfully, his mind churning over possibilities. "What did you drink with your lunch?"

"Just some fruit juice."

"Is there any left?"

"In the fridge."

He stood. "I'm going to dump it just in case it's bad. I'll also make you a cup of hot tea. Does that sound good?"

Shadow nodded. "It's odd. But I feel almost hungry again."

"Do you have any canned soup I could warm up for you?"

She curled a fist under her pale cheek, looking beyond pathetic, then mumbled, "I don't want you waiting on me."

Her stubbornness passed all bounds. He said without a hint of a smile, "I'm still annoyed with you, sweetheart. Don't press your luck."

"All right!" she said, flopping onto her back and then groaning from the sudden movement. She put her hands over her eyes. "Make the damned soup. You can feed it to me, too, if you want. After all, I'm completely helpless, right? That is why you're angry? Because I did the unthinkable and came home on my own, actually driving myself! Why, it's unheard of! Scandalous!"

Brent retained his stern expression all through her theatrics. When she quieted, holding her belly and squinting in pain, he asked, "Are you through? Good. Now, I think I'll fix the soup, which you will feed to yourself, then you and I are going to straighten a few things out."

"You're not my boss, Brent Bramwell!" she called after him. "Why do I have to keep reminding you of that?" He didn't answer, and she added very quietly, for her own benefit, "You're not even my husband."

But Brent heard. "I will be," he stated firmly, loud and clear. "I've made up my mind, Shadow. And there's no way you're going to change it now."

CHAPTER NINE

"ARE YOU DONE SULKING?"

Shadow flashed him a narrow-eyed look filled with promised retribution. Brent only raised his left brow, waiting.

She set her soup bowl, now empty, on the nightstand. "I never before sulked in my life. I was never melancholy and I never, positively *never* suffered jealousy. There are definite side effects to loving you, Brent Bramwell. Unpleasant ones."

He grinned at her. "Then we're even. You've made me face up to a few unfamiliar feelings, too. Believe it or not, I've never been so protective, though the women I've known wanted someone to take care of them, to make their lives easier. You, on the other hand, are too open and friendly for your own good. You scare me to death."

"Scare you?" Shadow asked blankly.

"That's right. And fear is another emotion I'm not exactly used to dealing with. And possessiveness and this damned tenderness that nearly chokes me. On top of all that, I'm forever losing control around you, one way or another."

Shadow fiddled with the edge of the blanket, running the silken hem between her fingers. "Are we hopeless, then, do you think? Are you saying it's not worth it?"

Brent leaned forward intently until their noses nearly

touched. "I'm not saying anything of the kind." He kissed the tip of her chin. "You expect me to label what I'm feeling, Shadow. But I've never felt it before, so how can I? I understand that you're impatient. You're filled with energy and excitement. You want to do everything now, right this minute. But I'm not that way. Believe it or not, I'm generally concise and controlled. Everything I do is well thought out and planned. But you have me jumping through hoops, making an ass of myself with great regularity. As far as carefully planning anything, I haven't had a peaceful moment to do that since I met you."

"It hasn't been very conventional, has it?" she asked. "Our time together, I mean. What with the phone calls, and then Joan showing up." She was silent a moment. "Have I really been rushing you so much?"

Brent laughed, chucking her chin. "You rush everything and everybody, honey. It's part of your personality. I've never known anyone whose mind worked so quickly, always changing directions, leaving me and everyone else in your dust."

She laughed. "Stop it, Brent. I'm not that bad."

"You're not bad at all. You're wonderful. And I'm enjoying every minute with you, chaotic as it may be. I want you to remember that, okay?" He rose to stand beside the bed. "Now, are you feeling better?" At her nod, he said, "Good. We have other things to talk about."

"You're back to sounding stern, Brent."

"I'm feeling particularly stern, too. It was foolish of you to leave the shop alone today. And don't think I didn't notice that you shoveled the walk. You left yourself out in the open, vulnerable, and all because you gave in to some completely unfounded and ridiculous notion of jealousy. I told you I didn't care a thing about Joan. I thought you trusted me. I thought you believed me."

Shadow stiffened dangerously. "Are you through?"

"No, I'm not. I feel like turning you over my knee."

"I'd like to see you try it." She looked mutinous, murderous, all one hundred twenty pounds of her. He bit back his pleased smile. God, he enjoyed her gumption.

"You scared me spitless, for no good reason. You acted selfishly, not caring how I might feel when I found out you'd gone home alone, how rejected I might feel."

She snorted at that obvious nonsense. Brent ignored her.

"I understand, what with your history with men, why you want to be independent. I respect that, too, because I know I wouldn't want to be dependent on anyone else. But sweetheart, there's such a thing as being too independent. Since I've decided we will marry—no, don't shake your head, I'm confident I'll be able to wear you down—"

"Ha! Not by acting like an autocratic jerk."

"—I'm going to move in."

Shadow could only stare. *"What?"*

"You heard me. You won't come to my house, so I'm coming to yours. You're putting me through hell with your contrariness, and I can't take it anymore." He stared down at her, not blinking, then said again, "I gave you the option of moving in with me. You turned me down, so I'm moving in with you."

"No."

"Afraid so. If you don't want to sleep with me, I'll camp out on the couch. Or I'll open one of your rooms upstairs. But I'm going to be close so I'll know nothing can happen to you."

"My couch is too short for you and I told you those

rooms upstairs haven't been touched since I bought the place. They're not even furnished."

His expression was wry. "I can afford to buy a damn bed."

"They're cold! You wouldn't be comfortable there."

"I'm sure as hell not comfortable sitting at home and worrying either." He added more softly, "I don't like to worry, Shadow. It's not something I've had much practice with. I don't think I do it particularly well. So I'm moving in."

It took Shadow a minute of silent consideration and then she grinned, totally confounding Brent. But that was okay, he was used to it by now.

"All right. You can stay here."

Brent hadn't realized how tense he'd been until she said that. He relaxed, letting out a held breath. His fists uncurled, opening as he smoothed his palms up and down his thighs. He realized she was watching him with a calculated gleam in her honey-colored eyes, and he nearly grimaced. Was a man ever in such desperate straits? And even more important, would he ever feel like himself again? His old self, the one he knew so well?

With forced aplomb, he managed a cocky grin and said to Shadow, "All right then. I'll go grab a few things and be back in under an hour. If you're up to it, why don't you make a grocery list for me? I want to buy some bottled water, anyway. It could be your cistern is contaminated, or the pipes in a house this old might be causing a water problem. That could be why you've been ill."

Shadow smiled complacently at him and started to leave the bed. Brent stopped her. "I don't like these strange illnesses that keep hitting you. I'll get you a pen and paper and you make the list right here."

"I feel fine now, Brent, you don't have to coddle me."

Exasperated, he growled, "I'll damn well coddle you if it pleases me to do so!"

His outburst brought her a fat smile. He threw up his hands and left the room to locate the paper and pen.

When he returned, Shadow was sitting cross-legged in the center of the bed. She said, "All right. I'll write down a few necessities and you can explain to me what you were doing in your office with Joan."

"Doing? I wasn't doing anything with her. We talked." Brent handed her the pen and paper.

Shadow wrote a few items on the list, then asked, "About what?"

"You're not still jealous, are you? There's really no reason, honey."

"No. I believe you. But I'm still curious. She called me earlier today." Shadow peeked up at him. "She informed me that you like to make love in your office and that she was going to see you. She also made some general insults. Nothing new."

Brent flushed. "I didn't touch her."

"I didn't really think you would."

At least she trusted him that much, Brent thought. "I considered what you told me. About each person finding his own happiness. When Joan tried to resurrect the past, I asked her how much money would make her happy enough to leave me alone."

Shadow gaped. "You didn't!"

"Yes I did. She slapped me, then screeched for a minute or two, looking frankly insulted, and finally demanded I apologize." Brent smiled at Shadow's enthralled interest. "I did. And then we talked, probably for the first time. Before she left, she offered to give me back the bracelet."

Shadow waited, her eyes wide.

"I insisted she keep it. As a sort of farewell gift."

Shadow scampered from the bed and threw her arms around him. "You really are a nice guy, you know that?"

"Then you're not mad anymore?"

Shadow kissed him. "Of course not. I'm glad you were kind to her."

"And you'll quit complaining when I want to coddle you?"

"We'll deal with that on an as-it-comes basis."

Smoothing down her unruly curls, Brent hugged her, his eyes filled with tenderness. "You're incredible." She lowered her gaze, toying with his shirt buttons.

Feelings swamped him—overwhelming, invading feelings—and he shook his head to clear it. "Did your swain call again?"

"That's right! I meant to tell you. He said he got your phone number from the book. But you're not listed."

"If he knew my name, he could have called information."

"I suppose. But he said other things. It almost sounded like he'd overheard us talking." She shivered. "It gives me the creeps to think about him being close enough to listen in on our conversations."

"He won't get close to you again. I promise."

"My hero," she teased. "Brent, it's not your responsibility to make that promise."

"I'm not about to let anyone hurt you, whether you think it's my responsibility or not." The idea of anyone threatening her did more than give him the creeps; it filled him with rage and scared the hell out of him. He had a gut feeling about all this. And until that feeling went away, he planned to stay close to Shadow's side, guarding her whether she thought she needed him or not.

They went over the grocery list together, a domestic chore they both enjoyed. Of course, anything Shadow did she did with laughter and teasing and pleasure. And Shadow was so openly sexual, so honest in her enjoyment of Brent, she didn't think twice about suggesting he add condoms to the bottom of the list.

Relieved that he wouldn't have to sleep on the couch, or renovate her vacant upstairs, Brent promised to pick up an adequate supply.

He left Shadow lying drowsily in her bed, looking so soft and feminine and desirable he wished he'd already gone and was on his way home. He kissed her gently on the forehead, listened to her whispered words of love and left with his mind a jumble of emotions, some so sweet they made his teeth ache, others so all encompassing he found it hard to draw a breath.

"DO YOU HAVE TO WORK late today?"

Brent smiled at Shadow over his morning coffee. "I can get off anytime. Why? You got something special in mind?"

Appearing vaguely shy, Shadow replied, "No. I took the day off. I was just thinking we could watch a movie and maybe pop some corn. I think I could even do dinner if you're interested."

She was nervous, uncertain how they should proceed, Brent realized. It had been a long time since she'd had anyone live, even temporarily, in a house with her. Checking his watch, Brent calculated quickly in his mind, then said, "I can be home by four. Will that do?"

Shadow beamed at him. "That would be perfect. I have laundry and a little cleaning to do before then, anyway."

"Don't overdo it, sweetheart. If you're still not feeling well…"

"Oh, I feel fine now. Just a little tired, is all. But I did hire an extra girl for the shop and she's anxious for the hours. Kallie said she's doing fine, so there's really no reason for me to go in. Besides, the weather looks nasty again. And they're predicting a record low today. I just thought it would be nicer to stay home for a change."

Brent searched her face. "If I didn't have a board meeting, I'd cancel my appointments…."

"Don't be silly. I'm fine. Really."

He could tell she wasn't fine. She was nervous, probably thinking about the phone calls and how close someone had gotten to her. Brent felt the now familiar rage, but squelched it. It wouldn't do to frighten her further.

He finished his coffee, stood to put his cup in the sink, then went to Shadow, pulling her from her seat. "Give me a hug and a kiss that will last me until I get home."

Home. That sounded very nice to Brent. Shadow squeezed him fiercely, almost desperately, then curled his toes with a passion packed, tongue licking kiss. She nearly fried his eyeballs with her enthusiasm. "Be careful, Brent. The roads are icy and too many people drive like idiots in the snow."

"I will. And Shadow?"

"Hmm?"

"It was very nice waking up with you beside me this morning."

"Especially since there weren't any screams?" she teased.

"It would have been nice even with a scream." He sought words to explain to her how much it meant to him, exactly how nice it had been, but came up blank. She gave her love so freely, but it wasn't that easy for him. He wasn't now and never had been a free spirit. His businesses, his life, his background all had required iron control.

He settled on saying simply, "Thank you."

Her smile warmed and her gaze lazily caressed his face. "You're very welcome. It was my pleasure." She touched his jaw. "I like waking with you, too, Brent. You're very handsome with your hair on end and whiskers covering your face. Your eyes are so dark in the morning, very sexy. Bedroom eyes."

Brent groaned. "Keep that up and I'll never get out of here." He kissed her again, quick and hard, then grabbed his coat. "Set the alarm as soon as I'm out the door."

"Quit worrying. I'll be fine."

"We already established my right to worry if I feel like it." He opened the door, then turned to her. "Be good," he said.

Shadow gave an exasperated laugh. Closing the door after him, she said to herself, "I'm not certain you'd enjoy me quite as much, Mr. Bramwell, if I actually behaved myself." She had a lot to do before Brent got home.... Home. The sound of that sent a thrill down her spine. She headed off for the laundry room, whistling happily.

SHE'D BEEN RIGHT to let him move in, Shadow decided a few days later. Once she'd thought about it, it had made sense. If he didn't love her yet, familiarity might take care of that. And in the meantime, she had him all to herself.

They'd settled into a domestic routine. The weather turned abominable, but even that suited Shadow just fine. Outside of work, they spent all their time together and were learning more about each other with every passing day.

They missed Thanksgiving. With temperatures dropping to fifteen below, the windchill was at a dangerous level. Rather than brave the cold evening, they opted for their own private dinner.

There were no more phone calls, and more important, Shadow became increasingly positive she was pregnant.

Brent hadn't asked, so she hadn't yet volunteered the information, preferring to make certain with a medical exam before telling him. But as each day went by, she felt his love grow. No, he didn't voice it, didn't say the words she wanted to hear, but he showed it in a thousand different, more important ways. And that was what mattered, she assured herself. The words would come when he was ready. In the meantime, she'd force herself to be patient, even if it killed her.

She had an appointment for Monday morning with her gynecologist. She wrote the time down on her personal calendar and then stuck it in the drawer of the phone table. It seemed, for once, that things were going right for her.

Annie called and they made plans for lunch and a day of hitting the malls. Shadow wanted to find something special for Brent for Christmas. She didn't know what it would be yet, but she'd come up with something.

She was deep in thought, contemplating shopping and loving Brent, when he came through the front door.

She went into his arms for a warm hug.

There was deep satisfaction in his eyes as he kissed her. Seconds later, he held out a small gift, beautifully wrapped in pink-and-silver foil. "I bought something for you."

Shadow stared at his hand, unblinking. "A Christmas present?"

"No. This is for now, today."

She still didn't take it. "Why?"

Brent barked a short laugh, took her hand and put the gift into it. "Because I wanted to give you something."

Her fingers curled around the small box, her hand shaking

slightly. "You don't have to buy me things, Brent. I'm not Joan."

"I know you're nothing like Joan. You're not like any woman I've ever known." His voice grew soft. "I just saw this and wanted you to have it. Please. Open it."

Shadow carried the tiny package to the sofa and sat down, holding it in both hands. She gave Brent a tentative smile, then pulled loose the ribbon. She had a feeling she knew exactly what was in that small box and it made her insides quiver. She didn't want an extravagant piece of jewelry in place of Brent's love. Gaudy diamonds or flashy chunks of gold meant less than nothing to her. She held her breath and lifted the lid.

Tears immediately sprang to her eyes. The ring was exquisite, simple and elegant and so unlike anything Shadow had ever seen before, she knew it was unique, just as Brent was. "Oh." The word emerged as two syllables, breathless and filled with wonder.

Two slender bands, one silver, one gold, twisted into a lover's knot, tied around a single perfect teardrop diamond. Brent saw the tears gathering in her eyes and asked hesitantly, "Do you like it? I know it's kind of different, but that's what I wanted for you. Something as special and one of a kind as you are."

Shadow held the ring in her fist and covered her face. She felt like a ninny, but tears overflowed her tightly closed eyes.

"You can have a different ring if you like." Brent sounded uncertain and unnerved by her show of emotion. "Hell, you can have anything you want. If you'd like a bigger diamond, a different setting, I'd be glad to take this back…."

He reached for the ring, but she snatched it to her chest. "Don't even think it!" Her bottom lip quivered as she looked at it again. "Oh, Brent. It's so beautiful."

After a silence, he said hesitantly, "You like it?"

"I *love* it." He stared hard at her, an intense expression in his eyes, and she added, "It's the most beautiful thing I've ever seen."

His smile was slow and hot. "To match the most beautiful woman I've ever seen."

"The cold has affected your brain." She continued admiring the ring.

Brent took her hand and slipped the ring from her fingers. "I've asked you before. But you're the most stubborn woman I've ever known, so I'm asking you again. Shadow, will you marry me?"

She touched his face, loving him, and nodded. "Eventually."

"That's…" He stalled, her answer belatedly registering. His shoulders shook with silent laughter. "Always the unexpected, honey?"

"Always the truth."

Brent held her hand and carefully slid the ring over her finger. It was a perfect fit. He said, "I called your mother to ask what size to get."

"Oh, no! I'll never hear the end of it now! She'll be expecting us to get married soon."

Brent grinned wickedly. "I figured as much." He ducked as Shadow playfully swung at his head. "I'll take all the help I can get to convince you." He pulled her head down and whispered against her lips, "I want you."

The sudden lump in her throat wouldn't go away. She buried her face against his neck and held him tight. Would he ever tell her he loved her? Or were the words impossible for him to say?

Her heart ached; the ring felt warm and heavy on her hand. *Patience,* she reminded herself. But it was hard, so damned hard. She understood his reluctance; his only experiences with women had not been conducive to trust or sharing or true love. They were mercenary relationships, superficial and short-term. Brent was used to women who wanted something from him, not himself. It broke Shadow's heart to think of how he must have felt, knowing it was his bank account they found most attractive, not the man he was, not his character. It also left her feeling utterly helpless, because she could never again plan to marry without knowing there was love on both sides. She deserved that much. She wouldn't settle for less.

Shadow leaned forward, kissing him urgently, needing to show him her love, wanting him to see how important he was to her. She kissed his face, his nose, his eyes, his jaw. She heard his chuckle of appreciation. Her hands stroked over him, pushing clothes out of her way to feel his warm flesh, so hard and smooth, so strong.

Between returning her kisses, Brent made the enormous mistake of saying, "I should buy you jewelry more often. I love the way you show appreciation."

Shadow drew back. "Damn you, Brent Bramwell," she whispered, the words hoarse with emotion. She tried hard to tug the ring from her finger, but it was a snug fit and then Brent was there, covering her hands with his own.

"Hey, come on. I was only teasing."

"It's not funny," she tried to say, but the frustration was overwhelming, making it difficult to speak. "It's impossible for you, isn't it?" she finally asked. "You can't accept that I would love you, just *you,* for no other reason than that you're all I've ever wanted. And I'm not talking about money, damn you, so don't raise your eyebrow at me!"

"But that's a big part of me, Shadow. I am a business-man, a successful businessman. And even if I weren't, I come from money. I could have gone my entire life without ever working a job and not wanted for anything."

"You're wrong, Brent." She gave him a sad, deliberately pitying look. "You've been wanting all your life, only you won't admit it. At least I'm honest with myself. You could come back here tomorrow penniless and I wouldn't love you any less. Money never has and never will be one of my priorities."

Brent's laugh, filled with derision and disbelief, sounded forced to her discerning ears. "You would fall in love with a man who had no prospects, no way to support himself?"

"I didn't say that. You're not ignorant. I have no doubt you're more than capable of doing anything you put your mind to. You wouldn't starve or become helpless, waiting for others to do for you. That's not part of who you are, of your character. It's not a matter of finances, either. You're strong and self-confident, independent, intelligent, creative and compassionate—"

"Enough!" He rose to his feet, towering over her. "I'm not some damn paragon of humanity! I'm not perfect."

Shadow eyed him narrowly. "No. No, you're not. You're also insecure and cynical on occasion, and entirely too hung up on maintaining control. It's why you won't admit you love me, I think. If you do that, if you make that final commitment, I'd have a part of you, wouldn't I, Brent? I'd have some of the control. I could possibly use that against you, though exactly how escapes me since I love you and would never be able to bear seeing you hurt."

Brent turned away from her. He stalked the length of the front room a few times, and when he turned back to Shadow, she saw that he was in perfect control again, and she wanted to howl, to scream and rant and sit in the middle of the floor and cry like a baby. She did nothing, simply watching him, waiting.

"Look, sweetheart, this isn't what I intended when I gave you the ring. I thought you'd be happy about it. I want to marry you, I want to have children with you and live together and spend every available moment with you. I don't want to argue with you."

Shadow looked down at her hand. The beautiful ring caught a glimmer of light and reflected it, shining brilliantly. She wanted to take it off, to do the intelligent thing and save herself a lot of heartache. She wanted to hand it back to him and ask him to go.

But she couldn't. She shook her head, feeling more helpless than she could ever remember. She forced a small smile.

"I think I'll take a warm bath and go to bed early. I'm going shopping with a friend tomorrow. I'll be gone most of the day—that's how Annie and I shop. We do breakfast, then hit the stores, we do lunch and then hit the stores. When our legs get tired, we stop to have coffee and a doughnut or something. I haven't even started my Christmas shopping yet."

"Shadow…"

"There's some lunch meat in the fridge if you're hungry. And soup in the cabinet." She tried for another smile, but couldn't quite manage it. "I…" She shook her head, not sure there was anything else to say. She left the room in a hurry, unwilling to make him suffer through her tears. She was a coward and a fraud. She was a hypocrite of the worst sort. And she wanted so badly for Brent to love her she didn't think she could have stood there another single moment looking into his face, so filled as it was with uncertainty and confusion.

The warm bath did little to help her relax. She fought the tears, but they came anyway. She dunked her head under the water and scrubbed with a vengeance.

There were so many decisions to be made. If she was pregnant, what would she do? Could she marry him with the very real possibility that he could never learn to trust her completely, never allow himself to love her as she wanted? Maybe she had been misreading him all along. Maybe this was as much as he had to give. He seemed to care for her, to actually love her, but if the words were never spoken, if he couldn't give voice to them, were they real? Would his love ever be the tangible, solid emotion she wanted?

She laid her cheek against her wet knees, drawn up in the tub. She supposed the bigger question, the only real issue, was could she give up on him? Could she let him go? And that answer was a resounding, emphatic *no*.

She wasn't a quitter. And Brent was far from a hopeless case.

With those thoughts in mind, she went about making herself as attractive as she knew how. She hadn't won Brent over by being herself, spontaneous and lighthearted. *Fun*. She would now try the calculated measures many women employed. She dabbed on perfume, brushed her hair until it shone, then slipped on the tiniest, sheerest teddy she owned.

It was a shimmering shade of creamy beige, nearly the same as her skin, giving her the appearance of nudity, but with decoration. The neckline scooped low, edged in a narrow rim of lace. Shadow surveyed herself in the mirror. She supposed she looked as attractive as possible. That Brent would appreciate the look, she didn't doubt. She slipped on a robe, then padded barefoot out of the bathroom.

BRENT PACED AROUND the kitchen pondering how things got so confused. Life used to be straightforward, easy to understand and easy to bend to his preferences. Until he'd met Shadow.

Damn, but she made him crazy. He'd already given her more of himself than any other woman he'd known. He'd asked her to marry him. But was that enough for her? No, she wanted more. She wanted things he wasn't certain he had to give.

He should just tell her he loved her. He'd told women that before; it was something expected during sex, and when he'd been younger, he'd also been more obliging. The words meant nothing.

But Shadow thought they did. And he believed her, believed that she felt that elusive swell of emotion that enabled her to commit herself completely to him. She felt and saw things other people never experienced, Brent included, which he supposed was one of the qualities he enjoyed most about her.

She was right about the control, too. He'd learned early in life that you had to command your own small portion of the world. Otherwise, people used you. It was human nature.

A dull ache started behind his eyes. He didn't know how to make things right with Shadow. He'd gladly give her anything, but he didn't know how to give her what she wanted. He couldn't lie to her and claim a feeling he wasn't certain of. She deserved better than that.

He leaned on the counter, staring out the kitchen window into the frozen darkness, and then he sensed her. His awareness of her was uncanny—one more thing he couldn't accept. Slowly he turned and there she stood, looking so beautiful she made him hard and hungry and needy.

He couldn't think of a single thing to say, so he merely took in the sight of her, his soul somehow comforted by her presence even though his body went into spasms with her scent, her nearness. And that was another weakness, the way he felt more complete with her, which would indicate he was incomplete without her. *No.*

Her fingers toyed with the ends of the belt to her terry robe. Shoving away from the counter, Brent went to her, his hands hanging at his sides, his eyes watching her intently.

He wanted her. More than that, he craved her. Always. Very softly, he asked, "Ready for bed?"

She nodded.

Brent felt that damn lump stick in his throat again. He reached out to touch an impossibly soft curl above her left ear, twining it around his finger. "Did your bath make you feel better?"

Shadow took another step nearer him and he breathed in her scent, which was strangely different, like flowers, rather than herself. It was enticing and at the same time a bit unexpected. He liked her own scent. He wasn't used to her wearing perfume.

"I'm sorry, honey, for upsetting you. It was never my intent," he murmured. She lowered her head and her hair fell forward, hiding her face. He smoothed it back. She was so soft, so sweet. He raised his other hand, framing her face, his thumbs stroking over her temples. "I can't bear to see you cry, Shadow. I—"

"That was unforgivable," she said quickly, "and so unlike me. I hate tears. But I hate even more showing them to you. I'll try not to let that happen again."

Brent closed his eyes, pulling her close and pressing her cheek to his chest. Damn, she could rip him apart so easily. "Don't, sweetheart. Don't apologize to me and don't ever hide yourself, especially your upset, from me. I only meant I was sorry I caused you to cry, not that you shouldn't cry if you felt like it. Hell, everyone feels like it sometimes. Besides, you were entitled. I've been a jerk. You were right about getting a good night's sleep. You'll feel better in the morning."

Brent was so relieved to be able to sidestep Shadow's earlier accusations about love and commitment, he didn't at first notice her chagrined expression. When he did finally see that she was watching him with a touch of embarrassment and determination, he assumed it was caused by the awkwardness of their first real argument. Not wanting to, but seeing no way around it, he said, "Why don't you go on in to bed now. I'll be there in a bit."

She caught at his hand. "You can tuck me in and give me a good-night kiss, okay?"

Brent felt his heart kick into double time. He looked at Shadow's slender form as she led him toward the bedroom. Her bare toes peeked from beneath the edge of her robe. With each step, her hips swayed. The woman could incite his lust with nothing but a smile, and now her toes were turning him on.

Shadow stopped beside the bed and pulled back the spread. His stomach tightened, his thighs grew tense.

Sometimes the wanting was so bad, so all encompassing, he thought he'd never get close enough to her, be with her enough, hold her enough.

Those times almost made him panic, which made him even more determined to retain control.

He was semihard by the time she finished preparing the bed. But as she turned, unknotting her belt and shrugging out of the robe, he gained full arousal, getting so hard he ached. Whatever she had planned, he was all for it.

"Damn," he whispered, spellbound by the sight of her in the revealing teddy. His gaze ran hungrily over her body, from the tips of her small pink toes to the vulnerable pulse in her exposed throat. He said again, very softly, *"Damn."*

Shadow reached out to unbutton his shirt. In a husky, enticing tone, she said, "If you won't give me your love, Brent, I'll have to take everything else that you've got."

Her fingertips touched his chest, tangled in his hair and then found his nipples. He shifted, but that didn't deter her. Her fingers drifted slowly down his abdomen, and lower still. "Sweetheart," he groaned, "whatever I have is yours."

She reached his belt and deftly unbuckled it. "I like your attitude, indeed I do. Just remember that sentiment," she warned softly, "because I fully intend to have it all."

It wasn't a threat that alarmed him. Not at all. In fact, at the moment…it thrilled the hell out of him.

CHAPTER TEN

BRENT WOKE EARLY the next morning, still slightly confused by the night's events. Shadow had been magnificent, giving and loving and quietly content. It was the quietly content part that alarmed him, because Shadow was not a quiet person. She was always bursting with energy and enthusiasm. Even in her sleep, she was so alive, so vibrant. But last night she'd been content. Damn.

He couldn't say exactly how she was different, only that he'd noticed the difference and didn't like it.

Was he the cause?

She'd taken their lovemaking too seriously. Shadow always found a dozen different reasons to laugh and tease and smile whenever they made love, but last night had been almost grave. And her gravity, having replaced her unique form of fun, had Brent scowling, even though Shadow was cuddled against him, her body soft and warm.

He lay silently in the dark, holding her close, trying to decipher in his mind what had gone wrong and how he could fix it. Shadow was trying to change on him and that thought was enough to give him cramps. Damn it, he wanted her just the way she was.

She wanted his love—she'd said as much in her bold,

blatant way—but did she think changing herself was a means to an end? He wouldn't have it.

Driven by his tumultuous thoughts, Brent glanced at the clock. It was only six o'clock. He slipped into the bathroom to shower. Half an hour later, he was dressed and sipping coffee in the kitchen. He wanted to relax, but couldn't. He was a coward, which was an entirely new concept for him. He couldn't recall ever fearing anybody or anything. But Shadow scared the hell out of him, just as he'd once told her. However, this time his fear was motivated more from the very real possibility of losing her than from her lack of caution.

If he didn't give her the love she wanted, would she leave him? That asinine thought made him laugh with self-mockery. Who was he kidding? Not himself, surely, because he knew that without her, he'd be miserable. Though he'd fought it hard, if he was honest, if he looked inside himself, he'd admit that she had his love. Hell, she'd owned it almost from the first moment he'd seen her and summarily fallen on his ass.

Brent finished his coffee with a gulp. Being a decisive man by nature, he made up his mind in a heartbeat. He'd never quailed from the truth before and damned if he'd start now. He wanted to pull her from her bed, to wake her with kisses and touches and the words she'd almost demanded to hear.

He wanted her laughing again, teasing him even as she drove him over the edge.

But he wasn't a selfish man. He'd kept her up most of the night and she needed her sleep.

Brent decided to leave her a note, to tell her to plan on going out for dinner, someplace nice. Maybe she would wear black for him again. The thought made him chuckle.

He went to the small telephone table to hunt up a pencil and paper. And it was then, rummaging through the drawer, that he found her calendar with the appointment for the gynecologist written in on Monday.

SHADOW WOKE WITH A START when the bedroom door opened. Brent stood in the doorway.

He flipped on the light, temporarily blinding her, and when she managed to open her left eye a crack, she saw he was angry.

"What's the matter?"

"Why didn't you tell me? And don't try to claim this is your regular checkup. You think you're pregnant, don't you?"

Shadow blinked, rubbing her face tiredly. Through her fingers she saw that Brent had her calendar in his right hand. Then she peeked up at his face. *Oh boy.*

"I suppose," she said around a yawn, "it's a possibility, since I didn't start my period on time. I thought I'd have it confirmed before I said anything."

Brent sat on the side of the bed. "You would have told me, one way or the other? You're certain?"

She couldn't lie to Brent, but sometimes innate honesty was a real pain in the butt. "Probably."

He exploded. "What the hell does that mean? Probably? Would you have told me or not if you'd found out you were pregnant?"

Shadow closed her eyes a moment. "I most likely would have told you right away. I'm not really dishonest, and I know you would want to be a part of your baby's life. But I kept thinking… Brent, do you realize how hard it would be on me? Seeing you constantly, having you nearby, if we weren't still intimate, if we weren't a couple?" She looked away, suffused with guilt. "I just don't know if I could bear that."

Brent went very still. His eyes narrowed and a nerve ticked in his jaw. "Were you planning on calling it quits?" he asked in a deadly calm voice. "Is that what this is all about?"

"No." She shook her head adamantly. "I decided last night I couldn't give up on you. But I don't know if I can be what you want, Brent, if I can be someone you can love."

His angry expression crumpled, and his eyes filled with pain. Shadow rushed on. "Love is necessary, Brent. Especially if we're going to raise a baby together. I could maybe get by without ever having you love me. I'm tough, you know," she said, trying for a spot of humor. "But a baby, well, that's different."

He stood and she grabbed his hand. "Please, Brent. Try to understand—"

"Oh, I understand. Perfectly." He walked to the window and stood there looking out. Shadow couldn't see anything of interest beyond a very fat moon hovering low in the darkened sky. Finally he said, "I think it's past time we talked. Seriously."

Scooting up in the bed, Shadow wrapped her arms tight around her bent knees and bit down hard on her bottom lip, refusing to cry again.

Brent turned to her, giving her a small strained smile. "I was going to suggest we go out for dinner tonight. With the weather so disagreeable, we haven't been out much lately. What do you think?"

Shadow stared at the blanket covering her feet. Dinner? He wanted to go for dinner? She looked up at him, drowning in confusion. "But I thought—"

"Shh. We'll talk tonight." He came to her, leaning over the bed and trapping her between his outstretched arms, his hands braced on the headboard. "I think we both need a little time to think, don't you?"

Not really, but she nodded anyway. Brent gave her another small, tight smile, then touched his mouth to hers, so very gently her eyes filled with tears despite her resolve.

"Have fun shopping and remember to—"

"Be careful," she finished for him. "I will." She waited, but he didn't say anything else. He left the room silently and a moment later she heard the front door close.

With a deep sigh, Shadow forced herself from the bed. She was an optimist, she reminded herself. Everything would work out for the best.

But as she dressed and prepared to leave to meet with Annie, her mind drifted back to Brent. He'd been awfully quiet, introspective. She wished she could read his thoughts, know what, exactly, he felt. He had been angry, she wasn't wrong about that. But he'd also looked sad. Right before he left, he'd seemed very determined. She shook her head in wonder.

It was a good thing she'd planned on shopping because she definitely needed a distraction. Her last thought as she walked out the door was that even another disturbance from her so-called admirer would almost be welcome. Anything to keep her mind off Brent and the fiasco she'd made of their relationship.

THERE'S A WISE SAYING that claims you should be careful what you wish for, or you just might get it. Shadow would later wonder if she should have that sentiment embroidered and hung on her wall.

She was already in her car when she realized she'd forgotten her shopping list. Feeling like a dunce, she walked back to the house. But the moment she reached the front door, she felt someone looking at her.

She turned, and came face-to-face with Chad Moreland. He stood uncertainly on the bottom step of the porch.

She stared, a little stunned, a little confused and plenty alarmed.

Red swollen eyes glared at her and he said in a voice hoarse and deep, "I saw you leave," then immediately broke into a fit of coughing. His body was racked with it, the sound pitiful and strained.

Shadow blinked at him, watching as he grabbed the handrail for support. As if in pain, he bent low while more coughs shook his body.

She saw quite a bit in that moment. The handsome man who'd entered her contest no longer existed. This young man looked ravaged. He was dirty, badly in need of a shower, his clothes wrinkled and worn. A scraggly smattering of beard stubble covered his gaunt cheeks and his face was pale, sallow. He was sick, very sick, she realized, and wondered what to do.

When his coughing subsided, he held his chest and stared at her.

"I...I came back for my list." Shadow watched him closely, scared, but even more concerned. "Chad, what's wrong with you? What are you doing here?"

He laughed, the sound raw and ugly. He started up the steps toward her, but stumbled drunkenly. He stopped and held the railing again, scowling at her. "He doesn't deserve you! You're wasting yourself on him and you've made me so angry, Shadow. Very angry."

She suffered a stunned silence.

Chad hitched a dirty finger over his shoulder. "Let's go in the house where it's warm. I want to talk to you."

She shook her head. "I don't think so."

"Don't be afraid," he cajoled, his voice now low and wheezing. "I'd never hurt you. We just need to figure out how to get rid of him."

Her heart shot into her throat and she said without thinking, "You stay away from Brent!"

He scowled darkly, stepped toward her. "You can't want him," he rasped. "You can't—" The words splintered, interrupted by another round of hacking, breath-stealing coughs. He crumpled to his knees, a fist squeezed to his chest.

Shadow made an instinctive move toward him, but halted. What to do? She'd never seen a man so pitifully weak and ill, but he was still dangerous, unpredictable.

He broke into her thoughts, his words now slurred with fatigue. "I put something on your cookies…something to make you pass out so you wouldn't sleep with him. You were so nice to me…."

Sudden anger overshadowed her fear. *"You poisoned my cookies?"*

He smirked. "I was going to come over and take care of you. But he stayed." He maneuvered another step closer. "Why him, Shadow? Why do you want him?"

Chad was a pharmacist, she remembered with dawning horror. He'd used his knowledge of drugs against her. "How did you get to my cookies?" The thought that he might have been in her house made her ill all over again.

"You left the bag in your car. You always park so far out, it was easy to sprinkle something on them. Everyone knows you never lock your car."

He drew himself up, weaving on his feet, and gained yet another step. He was closer now, too close, and she pressed herself backward even as she heard him say, "I didn't want you with him, but he stayed, even though I knew you were sleeping. He stayed and you let him!"

She backed up, explaining stupidly, while stalling for time, "It's this seven-year-itch thing, I think. It's just my time—"

He took the final step, a low growl emerging.

Shadow didn't delude herself into thinking she was a physical match for him, even in his weakened condition. She wondered if she could make it into the house, to the phone. Chad read her intent and lurched forward, wanting to reach her.

But he was too weak. He hit a patch of ice, flailed about, then stumbled off the top step. His legs buckled beneath him and he screamed. As Shadow watched in horror, he tumbled, his body limp, crashing several times into the railing before landing with a sickening thud at the bottom of the porch steps. His head cracked hard against the icy walkway and a small patch of blood appeared.

He moaned softly, galvanizing Shadow into action. Rushing toward him, she cried, "Chad? Are you all right?"

He grabbed her hand, his grip surprisingly strong, his flesh burning with fever. "I'm so damn cold," he whimpered. His eyes rolled into his head and he quieted, his body going still.

BRENT WAS MORE THAN a little distracted when his secretary buzzed him. "Yeah, Micky, what is it?"

"You have a personal call on line two."

Brent tensed, a typical reaction for him. Wherever Shadow was concerned he suffered from extremes, both sexual and emotional. "I'll take it. Thanks, Micky."

Releasing the intercom button, Brent hesitated. He'd been thinking about her all morning, wanting to call her, wishing he'd admitted his love this morning rather than putting it off. He'd been ridiculous and he knew it. Shadow felt hurt over his attitude, thinking him ambivalent to her. It pained him every time he remembered the look on her face, her admission that it would be too much to see him regularly, knowing he didn't love her.

It was past time to set things right with her. He picked up the receiver and settled back in his chair. "Hello, sweetheart. Done with your shopping so soon?"

"Uh, I hope the sweetheart you're referring to is Shadow. But I'm not her. I'm her friend Annie."

Brent went still. "I'm sorry, I just assumed…is anything wrong? Where's Shadow?"

"That's just it. I have no idea. I was afraid something was wrong because she's never stood me up before."

"Stood you up?" He shot forward in his seat again. "What the hell do you mean? Where is she?"

"I already told you, I don't know. She was supposed to meet me at the mall. I waited and waited, but she didn't show and now I'm worried."

"She never called?"

"No. I tried phoning her house, but there was no answer. She gave me your name and number awhile back, so…I tried you." There was a heavy pause, filled with worry. "You really don't know where she is?"

"Go back to your place in case she tries to call you. I'm going home to check there right now."

As if his urgency alarmed her even more, Annie said hurriedly, "Please, let me know if you find her! She told me about that guy who's been calling—"

"Yeah." Brent cursed low, then forced himself to be calm. Trying to convince himself as much as Annie, he said, "I'm sure everything's okay. Don't worry. I'll find her."

He hung up and was out of his seat in the same movement. As he passed his secretary, he said, "If Ms. Callahan calls, let me know immediately. I'll be at home." He started out, then thought to clarify, "Not my house, but—"

"Yes, sir. I know."

"Thanks, Micky."

Brent made it home in record time. His heart pounded heavily, his teeth were clenched in fear. If anything happened to her... He couldn't, wouldn't finish that thought. His palms were sweaty by the time he pulled into the driveway.

He ran up the walkway, then came to a staggering halt. "Oh, God, no." A patch of dark blood made a stark contrast to the white snow at the bottom of the steps. He stared at it, his insides twisting, his heart knocking in his chest. In that moment, he suffered a fear he'd never known before, a blackness that obliterated every other sensation. He couldn't breathe, couldn't think.

It hit him—a desperate hope that she might have merely hurt herself, then gone inside.

Praying, he went up the steps in one jump, jerked the door open and shouted her name. No answer. He went through the house at a dead run, again calling out for her. He stopped, not knowing what to do.

He squeezed his eyes shut, then jerked around when the phone gave a shrill ring. He grabbed it up, his voice gruff with emotion. "Shadow?"

"It's Micky, Mr. Bramwell. I—"

"Where is she, Micky?" The words were choked, raw.

Very gently, Micky said, "She's fine, sir. She just called. She's at Memorial Hospital—"

Brent dropped the phone. Memorial was only a short drive away, but at the moment, it seemed like the span of a continent. All his good intentions, the alarm system, his constant reminders for caution—they hadn't been enough. *He* hadn't done enough.

He drove like a madman, alternating between silent threats and thoughts of retribution, to heartfelt prayers that she'd be all right, that she would eventually forgive him his stupidity.

She was a part of him, the most important part. The part that made him smile and filled him with happiness and security.

He loved her. And there was a very good chance he'd waited too long to tell her.

SHADOW PACED THE HALLWAY, exhausted from all the questions the police had asked her. She wished Brent would come, just to hold her hand if nothing else.

She didn't know if Chad was going to live. He'd seemed so sick, and the doctor had come out to tell her he had a bad case of pneumonia and a concussion. He'd spent so much time outside, spying on her, rather than seeking a doctor when he became ill. He'd gone into a coma shortly after Shadow had gotten him to the hospital, and he hadn't opened his eyes since. His condition was critical. Shadow, unbelievably, felt responsible for him. She couldn't leave without first finding out if he'd be okay.

But she would have appreciated Brent's support. She had, after all, been through a lot. It wasn't every day that you had a near delirious madman bleeding all over your car, reciting in great, babbling detail all the ways he loved you.

The irony of it had nearly choked her. She had an unwelcome and unhealthy declaration from Chad, yet Brent, the man she loved, wouldn't even hint at such words.

Damn, she wished Brent were here now.

As if summoned by her, he burst through the waiting room doors at that precise moment. He looked like a wild man, and Shadow automatically groped behind her for the nearest chair.

Brent saw her, and his expression shattered. His chest heaved and then, with a fast, purposeful stride, he started toward her.

No sooner did he take a step in her direction than two men standing nearby—one an orderly, by the looks of him, the other a guard—tried to stop him. Brent shrugged off their restraining hands, his gaze never leaving Shadow. He was gripped more firmly and promptly shoved against the wall.

Shadow's eyes widened. In a rush, she explained, "He's with me. He...he must have been worried?" It sounded like a question—it *was* a question! Whatever was the matter with him?

Brent reached her, then literally hauled her off her feet and into his arms. "Are you hurt?"

"No," she squeaked, still unsure of his mood.

He reared back, gently shaking her. "You're all right? You swear?"

"I'm fine."

All the rigidity left his body with one deep breath. He hugged her to him, treating her to a bone-crushing embrace, her feet still dangling off the floor. "God, you scared me," he mumbled into her neck, and Shadow could feel him trembling.

She stroked his back. "Brent, I'm fine. Didn't your secretary give you my message?"

He shook his head, unwilling to release her just to explain. He hadn't given Micky the chance to speak, he had been so overwhelmed with terror.

Aware of the curious glances from the other occupants of the waiting room, Shadow whispered, "Brent, put me down now. It's okay."

He lowered her into her seat, but he didn't release her, which meant he ended up kneeling in front of her, his head still buried against her neck.

Shadow became worried. "Brent?"

"I love you, sweetheart. God, I love you so damned much it's killing me."

Stunned, Shadow took a moment to digest that bit of information, and then she grinned an enormous grin. "Well, for heaven's sake, don't die!" she exclaimed, then added more softly, "Just keep on loving me. Always."

Brent squeezed her closer. Shadow had to protest or end up in a faint because she positively couldn't breathe. At her first grunt, Brent loosened his arms, then leaned back, but not too far back. His hands came up to frame her face and he said again, "I love you. If you love me, too, even a little, you won't ever scare me like that again. Promise me."

Her eyes filled with tears and this time she didn't mind in the least. "I promise."

"Good." He stood suddenly, his hands fisted on his hips. "Where the hell is he?"

And Shadow saw the murderous intent in his eyes.

"He has pneumonia, and on top of that, he fell down the steps and gave himself a concussion. Right this minute, he isn't even conscious!"

Brent closed his eyes. "That was his blood, then, that I saw at the bottom of the steps?"

"Yes. You didn't think… Oh, Brent. I'm sorry."

"It doesn't matter now." Then he looked at her in disbelief. "Don't tell me you're feeling sorry for him!"

"In a way I am. He's so pitiful."

Brent clenched his jaw, a telling sign that he wasn't as forgiving.

"He put something on my cookies," she admitted. "That's why I fell asleep so suddenly. He wanted to keep us from making love. He's so sick, Brent. I mean, mentally. He needs help."

"I'll kill the bastard."

A young officer approached, the same one who had asked Shadow dozens of questions earlier. She gave him a wan smile, then introduced him to Brent.

Officer Grange nodded. "The doctor just spoke with me. They have him stabilized, but he hasn't regained consciousness. There's no need for you to stay. We'll need to know where to reach you, however."

Brent gave him his own address. "We'll be getting married, soon. Anytime you need her, try my number."

That got a smile from both Shadow and Officer Grange.

"I'm really sorry for what you've been through," Grange offered. "At least he got caught before either of you were hurt. You shouldn't have any more trouble from him. There are other officers at the house right now, looking over the scene, taking evidence. You can rest easy now."

Brent shook his head. "You must not know Ms. Callahan

very well. You can never rest easy around her. You have to keep on your toes…or she'll stomp all over them."

Shadow punched playfully at Brent's shoulder. Then allowed him, with a small show of resistance, to lead her from the hospital. Despite everything that had happened, she felt good. Very, very good.

THE MORNING SUNSHINE WAS bright as Brent stretched awake. The snow was gone, and the May weather had turned mild. He smoothed his hand over Shadow's hip and rumbled, "G'morning, sweetheart."

"Hmm," she whispered back, wiggling her hips into his lap.

Brent's hand went to her belly and he asked, "Any morning sickness?"

"No. I guess the doctor was right," she said around a yawn and an elaborate stretch. "The second trimester isn't so bad."

"I'm glad the first was a false alarm. Your parents will like it better that the baby's born nine months after the wedding and not a day before."

"Maybe. But they would have been thrilled either way."

"I know. My mom was ecstatic over the idea of a grandchild. She was a little concerned, though, over what you might name the future Bramwell."

Grinning wickedly, Shadow said, "I told her I favored mythology over weather conditions. How do you like Zeus? Or Aphrodite?"

Brent bent to kiss her shoulder. "I love you, Shadow."

"You've gotten so good at saying that."

"Well, you see, this slightly goofy, unbelievably sexy woman I know insisted on showing me how much fun love can be."

"She convinced you, did she?"

"Yes, she surely did. And she'll be stuck with me now. Forever."

"Hey, she sounds like one lucky broad to me."

 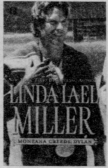 

REQUEST YOUR
FREE BOOKS!

2 FREE NOVELS
FROM THE ROMANCE/SUSPENSE
COLLECTION PLUS 2 FREE GIFTS!

YES! Please send me 2 FREE novels from the Romance/Suspense Collection and my 2 FREE gifts (gifts are worth about $10). After receiving them, if I don't wish to receive any more books, I can return the shipping statement marked "cancel." If I don't cancel, I will receive 4 brand-new novels every month and be billed just $5.49 per book in the U.S. or $5.99 per book in Canada, plus 25¢ shipping and handling per book plus applicable taxes, if any*. That's a savings of at least 20% off the cover price! I understand that accepting the 2 free books and gifts places me under no obligation to buy anything. I can always return a shipment and cancel at any time. Even if I never buy another book from the Reader Service, the two free books and gifts are mine to keep forever.

185 MDN EF5Y   385 MDN EF6C

Name _____ (PLEASE PRINT) _____

Address _____ Apt. # _____

City _____ State/Prov. _____ Zip/Postal Code _____

Signature (if under 18, a parent or guardian must sign)

Mail to **The Reader Service:**
IN U.S.A.: P.O. Box 1867, Buffalo, NY 14240-1867
IN CANADA: P.O. Box 609, Fort Erie, Ontario L2A 5X3

Not valid to current subscribers to the Romance Collection,
the Suspense Collection or the Romance/Suspense Collection.

Want to try two free books from another line?
Call 1-800-873-8635 or visit www.morefreebooks.com.

* Terms and prices subject to change without notice. N.Y. residents add applicable sales tax. Canadian residents will be charged applicable provincial taxes and GST. Offer not valid in Quebec. This offer is limited to one order per household. All orders subject to approval. Credit or debit balances in a customer's account(s) may be offset by any other outstanding balance owed by or to the customer. Please allow 4 to 6 weeks for delivery. Offer available while quantities last.

Your Privacy: Harlequin is committed to protecting your privacy. Our Privacy Policy is available online at www.eHarlequin.com or upon request from the Reader Service. From time to time we make our lists of customers available to reputable third parties who may have a product or service of interest to you. If you would prefer we not share your name and address, please check here. ☐

BOB08R

LORI
FOSTER

77306   FALLEN ANGELS   ___ $7.99 U.S. ___ $9.50 CAN.

(limited quantities available)

TOTAL AMOUNT $ _____
POSTAGE & HANDLING $ _____
($1.00 FOR 1 BOOK, 50¢ for each additional)
APPLICABLE TAXES* $ _____
TOTAL PAYABLE $ _____

(check or money order—please do not send cash)

To order, complete this form and send it, along with a check or money order for the total above, payable to HQN Books, to: **In the U.S.:** 3010 Walden Avenue, P.O. Box 9077, Buffalo, NY 14269-9077; **In Canada:** P.O. Box 636, Fort Erie, Ontario, L2A 5X3.

Name: _____
Address: _____ City: _____
State/Prov.: _____ Zip/Postal Code: _____
Account Number (if applicable): _____
075 CSAS

*New York residents remit applicable sales taxes.
*Canadian residents remit applicable GST and provincial taxes.

HQN™

We *are* romance™

www.HQNBooks.com

PHLF0309BL